*Gre...*

"If you invade my bedroom again, I'm going to take it as an invitation," Julian warned. "I've wanted you from the moment I first set eyes on you, and I know damned well you want me too. Do I make myself clear?"

Anna's mouth dropped open. How dare he speak so to her! "You conceited beast! I don't—want—you, to use your nasty phrase! I came in here to—"

He interrupted her ruthlessly. "You can lie to yourself if you want to, Anna my sweet, but you can't lie to me. You're a flesh-and-blood woman, and you look at me like a woman looks at a man she wants to bed. Hell, you *kiss* me like a woman kisses a man she wants to bed—"

"Stop it!" Anna cried, almost screeching. "Just stop it!"

"Oh, no, my lovely little hypocrite, it's too late for that. You had your chance!" He reached out and dragged her close, then lowered his mouth to hers . . .

# KAREN ROBARDS

"Karen Robards writes spellbinding romance"
*Publishers Weekly*

"Gives the reader incomparable sexual tension"
*Affaire de Coeur*

# KAREN ROBARDS

# Green Eyes

AVON BOOKS ◆ NEW YORK

GREEN EYES is an original publication of Avon Books. This work is a novel. Any similarity to actual persons or events is purely coincidental.

AVON BOOKS
A division of
The Hearst Corporation
1350 Avenue of the Americas
New York, New York 10019

Copyright ©1991 by Karen Robards
Cover art by Fredericka Ribes
Cover author photo by Herman Estevez
Published by arrangement with the author
Library of Congress Catalog Card Number: 90-93191
ISBN: 0-380-75889-X

First Avon Books Printing: January 1991

AVON TRADEMARK REG. U.S. PAT. OFF. AND IN OTHER COUNTRIES, MARCA REGISTRADA, HECHO EN U.S.A.

Printed in the U.S.A.

RA 10 9

To Christopher Scott—
Welcome to the world, April 7, 1990!
And as always,
With love to Doug and Peter.

# I

The choice was a simple one, Anna Traverne reflected dismally: agree to become Graham's mistress, or starve.

If she had only herself to consider, she would choose starvation with scarcely any hesitation, but there was Chelsea, too. In the end Anna knew that mother love would prove stronger than pride, morality, or physical revulsion. She simply could not allow her five-year-old daughter to be thrown with her into a cold and uncaring world when it was within her power to prevent it.

But the idea of lying with her brother-in-law, of suffering his hands on her person and his body invading hers, made her physically sick.

"Dear God, please help me find some way out of this mess." As a clergyman's daughter, she naturally turned to prayer when she was desperate, but Anna uttered this one without much hope. Lately God hadn't seemed particularly interested in listening to so insignificant a being as herself, so the whisper was more an automatic response to her upbringing than a heartfelt plea for divine intervention. She had prayed so much and so hard during the last harrowing hours of her husband's life that she now seemed to be incapable of sincere prayer. She had broken down completely at his funeral. Since then, her emotions had been muted. She had not felt anything—not hatred, or fear, or love, or even grief—very intensely. It was as if a cold gray fog had fallen over her life.

Six months now she had been a widow and the last three of those, at Graham's insistence had been spent in England. From the moment she had first set foot again in Gordon Hall, Graham had been after her. At first he'd been subtle, and she'd hoped she was mistaking the motivation behind his overly enthusiastic kisses and squeezes. After all, she was the new widow of his younger brother, his only sibling. Perhaps lavishing caresses on his brother's relic was how he dealt with his grief. But even as she had tried to convince herself of that, Anna had suspected differently. She'd known Graham too long, and too well, to truly believe it.

Graham had wanted her from the time the three of them were children together. Wanted her, not loved her. Paul had loved her, despite the fact that she was only the daughter of the local vicar, when he and Graham were the sons of the rich and powerful Lord Ridley. And she had loved Paul in return. They were the same age, their birthdays only one month apart, and from childhood he had been her dearest friend. Marriage had only slightly altered their relationship. Theirs had been a happy union, full of mutual affection and respect, and devoid of surprises on either side, so well had they known each other. Anna had fully expected it to endure, and ripen, over the course of their natural lives. Then, at the unbelievably young age of twenty-four, Paul had died. With his death her life, and Chelsea's, had shattered like fine glass.

Unlike the bull-like Graham, Paul had been slender, with a pale complexion and flaxen hair so like Anna's own that strangers had sometimes mistaken them for brother and sister instead of husband and wife. But for all his appearance of fragility, Paul had always seemed perfectly healthy. Although, as Anna's father had often said, appearances could be deceptive. After Paul's death, the doctor had told her he must have always had a weak heart.

If only she had known! If *they* had known! Then they would never have embarked on their wild adventure, would never have thumbed their noses at his family and the world they had known and set off for Ceylon.

They had made a runaway match of it. Their act of defiance had left Paul's autocratic father and brother screaming with outrage, though for very different reasons. After the wedding, old Lord Ridley had objected because Anna, as a mere clergyman's daughter, was not a fit wife for his son. Graham had been angry because even then he had wanted Anna for himself. Oh, not to wed, of course—Graham had too high an opinion of himself for that—but to bed. The very idea had sickened Anna then just as it sickened her now. Paul's father had cast him off, and the newlyweds had found themselves almost completely without funds. Their sole resources had been a small legacy left by Paul's long-deceased mother and a tea plantation on the island of Ceylon that had been his mother's girlhood home.

Anna and Paul had been young and high-spirited, and so in love that they hadn't cared. They would take up tea planting and make their own way. It had seemed a marvelous adventure at first. The very strangeness of her new home had entranced Anna. But the hot, steamy climate of Ceylon had never agreed with Paul. After Chelsea's birth, he had fallen prey to a succession of fevers that had left him thin and paler than ever, and had weakened his already less than robust heart. At least, so had said the doctor, finally summoned against Paul's wishes by Anna when he had been stricken yet again with one of the everlasting tropical illnesses that continually plagued him. That particular fever, generally mild, should not have killed him—but it had.

''Why didn't we come back to England as soon as

we saw the climate didn't agree with him?'' Guilt served no purpose, Anna knew, even as she muttered the agonizing thought aloud. But the knowledge that Paul would still be alive had he never married her and as a consequence been forced to leave his home was always there, lurking on the edge of her consciousness. In a way, she had killed him, she and his unforgiving martinet of a father. . . .

Anna shivered as a waft of cold air unexpectedly reached her, and pulled the shawl that covered her night rail closer about her neck. She was huddled in a big leather wing chair in front of the tiny fire she had built in the little-used library, and until that icy finger had touched her she had been toasty warm. Where could the draft have come from? She had taken good care to close the door from the hall, and the windows of the second-story room were shut tight, their dusty velvet hangings drawn.

"Paul?" Even as she breathed it, his name no louder than a soft exhalation of her breath, she knew the very notion was absurd. But ridiculously, she allowed herself a moment's fantasy that the chilling touch might presage a visit by Paul's ghost. She had felt so terribly alone since his death that she would welcome even his shade. What a relief it would be to lay her burdens on his shoulders, even if for no more than a minute or two! She was so very tired, so close to despair, and there was no one in the world who cared. Her own family was dead, and of Paul's only Graham was left. Lord Ridley had died a scant month before his younger son. As for Graham—Anna thought for what must have been the hundredth time that she would almost have been better off with no one at all to turn to. When he had offered to let her and Chelsea make their home with him, she should have known better than to trust him. But Paul's death had left her and Chelsea destitute; by the terms of Paul's mother's will, even the plantation had reverted to Graham upon his younger brother's death. When Graham had offered them a home, Anna had been grateful, even eager to return to England for Chelsea's sake. Of course, then she had not known the price she would be expected to pay.

Even before she had left with Paul, Graham had clearly noticed that the little girl who had run tame at Gordon Hall had grown into a desirable young woman. In that last year before she became Paul's bride, Graham had tried by fair means and foul to lure her into his bed. Why should she have expected the passing of six years to have changed him? The only difference she found at Gordon Hall upon her return was that old Lord Ridley was dead, which just gave Graham, who was made in the old lord's insufferable image, that much more power.

A minute passed, two, and no shade appeared, as of course Anna had known it would not. Her spine sagged with disappointment, and her head fell back to rest against the smooth leather. She was alone. There was no one to help or advise her, no one to save her from what she already knew was inevitable. Though she might delay it, as she had tonight by hiding, there was no real salvation; sooner or later she would be forced to accede to Graham's demands.

"I can't! I just can't."

Tears puddled in her eyes. Closing them tightly in what she knew would be a futile defense, she pulled her knees up to her chin inside the voluminous white nightdress she wore and wrapped her arms around her legs. Crying would serve no purpose, she scolded herself. Certainly it would not bring back Paul. If tears could accomplish that, he would have been resurrected long since.

What sounded remarkably like a soft footstep behind her chair caused Anna's eyes to open. Paul? The thought popped into her mind again. But no, of course not! A ghost would shimmer and float, not walk, across the creaky plank floor.

If there was a presence in the room with her, and her every instinct told her that there was, it was assuredly not a ghost. What then—or more properly, who?

At the thought of being discovered by Graham, Anna shuddered, and instinctively she made herself as small as she could. It was possible that, in the gloom of the library, with her chair facing the fire while its tall back was presented to the rest of the room, she might contrive to pass unnoticed. Possible, but not likely, at least not if the trespasser were Graham. The only reason for his presence in the library at such an hour would be that he was looking for her. Anna had fled her room as soon as the house had grown quiet for the night to avoid him should he decide to come seeking her. Locked doors were useless in keeping him out, as she had learned to her dismay: Graham possessed a key to her chamber. Indeed, just the night before she had awakened to find him climbing into her bed. Only her strenuous physical objections, and last desperate threat to scream and awaken his wife, had caused him to leave her, finally, relatively untouched.

But he had not left without telling her that she would share his bed—or leave his house forthwith.

Tonight she had feared he meant to put the matter to the test. Although in her heart she knew the conclusion was foregone, she could not bring herself to surrender to the hideous inevitable—yet. Miracles happened every day, as her gentle father had reminded her until the moment of his death. Anna wasn't greedy; all she asked for was a small miracle. Just enough of one to save her from Graham and provide for her and Chelsea. Surely that wasn't too much to ask of a God who had already taken from her almost more than she could bear.

There was another footstep, as quiet as the first. Anna was just registering that it didn't sound like Graham's deliberate tread when, out of the corner of her eye, she glimpsed a man. A tall man in a billowing black cloak who glided past her chair almost as silently as would have the shade he assuredly was not.

Anna froze, her breath suspended as her eyes locked on him. She had never seen the man before in her life!

He was tall, with black hair. The cloak made him seem massive as it rippled behind him, drawn, Anna saw, by the draft from the partly open door that led into the hall. The door that she had taken such care to close earlier. That, then, explained the draft. But nothing could explain the presence of this man. There were no houseguests at Gordon Hall just at present. A house party was planned for this, the Christmas of 1832, a little more than a fortnight away, but none of the guests would arrive for several days yet. And, anyway, this man was certainly not one of Graham's cronies, who tended to be as thick-headed and dandified as he was himself.

Nor, she was quite certain, was he a servant, which left only one breath-stopping possibility: dear Lord in heaven, she was faced with a housebreaker!

Screaming was the most immediate course of action that occurred to her, but it had two drawbacks: first, the criminal was far closer to her than any help she could summon, and would certainly be upon her in an instant if she disclosed her presence, of which he was obviously unaware. Second, a scream would certainly bring Graham along with the rest of the household. Under the circumstances, she would almost rather deal with the housebreaker than with her brother-in-law.

Almost.

Anna only hoped that the housebreaker was not a murderous sort. Huddling in her chair, her eyes never leaving him, she scarcely dared to breathe.

# II

He was lifting books off the shelves that flanked the fireplace, placing them in neat piles on the desk nearby. Clearly he had no inkling that he was being observed. Unmoving, her arms clasped so tightly around her knees that the circulation to her legs was in danger of being cut off, Anna watched as he pressed the bare wood of the wall behind the shelves where the books had been. It took him several tries, but finally there was a thud and then a creak. To Anna's amazement, a small panel slid open where only seconds before had been a wall of seemingly solid walnut planks. Anna's eyes widened. She'd played freely at Gordon Hall for most of her life, and she'd had no inkling that such a hidey-hole existed.

How had the housebreaker known?

He thrust both hands into the hole, and withdrew them holding a small leather case. Although Anna couldn't see his face, his bearing radiated satisfaction. Turning, he set the case on the desk, opened it, and stared down at the contents. There was an air almost of reverence about him as he stood there, head bowed, looking at the case's contents, which were hidden from Anna. Frowning, she tried to guess what the case could contain. Not the Traverne jewels, which were most lately the possessions of Graham's wife, Barbara. They were safely locked away in Barbara's bedroom in the same spot where they had been kept secured for generations.

What then was this? Something small enough to fit into a case no larger than a cigar box, secret enough to be secured in a hidey-hole that she had had no inkling existed, and valuable enough to attract the attention of an obviously well-informed housebreaker. What?

Anna watched, fascination momentarily making her forget about being afraid, as the man lifted a flat velvet envelope from the case, opened the flap top, and peered inside. Whatever he saw must have pleased him, because he was smiling as he set the pouch on the desk, folding back the sides and feeling whatever lay within to lift it in his hand. He seemed almost to gloat as he turned slightly toward the fire to examine his prize more closely, thus affording her the first glimpse of both the object and his face.

Anna's first thought was that he looked like a gypsy. His skin was swarthy, the thick slashes of his eyebrows as inky black as his hair, which was secured by a thin black ribbon at his nape. His features were boldly masculine, looking more as if they'd been hewn from teak with an axe than delicately sculpted from fine marble as Paul's had. He was a big man, massive of shoulder, broad of chest, tall. Although it was too dark in the library to be absolutely sure, she thought he looked almost dangerously handsome in a wild, rough way.

But handsome is as handsome does, as her father the vicar had often said, and this man was a thief. It was more than possible that, if he discovered her, he might do her bodily harm. That thought brought Anna back to a precise awareness of the precariousness of her position. She stayed perfectly still as he lifted his hand so that whatever he held might catch the light from the fire. The faint orange glow revealed that the objects were a brilliant green—and

Anna had to stifle a gasp as she realized just what he held: the Queen's emeralds!

Anna had seen them only once before, as a child. She and Paul had ducked behind the curtains in this same room when his father had entered unexpectedly with a guest. The guest, a stocky bewigged man of middle years, had apparently, from his dress and manner, been some sort of solicitor. The details of their conversation escaped her now, if indeed they had ever registered, but she would never forget the magnificent necklace, bracelet, earrings, and stomacher that the solicitor had held up, one by one, to examine, all the while shaking his head in clear disapproval. The two men had had some sort of disagreement about the gems, but neither she nor Paul had paid much attention. They were too intent on trying not to make a sound that would reveal them to Lord Ridley, who would have certainly caned Paul for spying and sent Anna home along with a stern note to her father demanding that she be punished for her misdeed.

In the years since she'd first gotten a glimpse of the Traverne family's dazzling treasure, Anna had heard the story many times. Paul had gotten it from Graham, and what Paul knew she knew soon afterwards. It seemed that the emeralds were part of a cache that had once belonged to Mary Queen of Scots, who had given them to an admirer to finance an attempt to overthrow her cousin Queen Elizabeth's throne. Mary had lost her head instead, and the jewels had vanished, only to turn up centuries later in the possession of Lord Ridley. Just how he had come by them was not known, but he guarded them zealously. Indeed, until this moment Anna had almost forgotten their very existence. That long afternoon spent hiding behind the curtains with Paul could almost have been a dream.

But clearly the emeralds were no dream. They were as real as she was, and about to be stolen by the thieving rogue from whose hands they now dripped!

In her indignation, some small sound must have escaped Anna. The would-be thief looked up suddenly, and over the gleaming condemnation of the emeralds his eyes locked with hers.

For a hideous moment Anna simply stared into eyes that by firelight seemed as black and fathomless as the darkest midnight; she was too frightened to so much as summon the breath for a scream. Her limbs seemed to be frozen, and her heart stopped as well. Dear God in heaven, what would he do to her?

Though he, too, was perfectly still, he recovered from his shock more quickly than she did. His eyes never left her as he scooped up case, pouch, and emeralds, and thrust them together into some inner compartment of his capacious cloak. His mouth curled into an expression that was half snarl, half sneer, and his eyes glittered like twin pieces of jet as they moved from the small white triangle of her face over her barely clad form and back to her face again.

Though Anna didn't know it, she looked very young and very scared, perched as she was in the enormous chair. Her silver-blond hair, unconfined, tumbled over the lavender shawl and prim white nightdress to end in a riot of waves at her hips. In her pale face her eyes were huge, framed by lush dark brown lashes that enhanced their remarkable color: a green as vivid as the emeralds concealed in his cloak. Her body was even more slender than usual because she'd had little appetite since Paul's loss; except for the maturity of her breasts, which were at that moment hidden by both the shawl and her hair, she could easily have been mistaken for a child.

"Well, if it isn't a Christmas angel. What are you doing belowstairs at this time of night, sweetheart?"

He sounded sane, if a little mocking. Anna felt her

heart start up again. Her eyes never left his face. Her throat was so dry that speech was an effort.

"If you leave now, I won't scream." Her attempt to bluff him would have been more convincing if it hadn't been made in a creaky whisper.

"Generous of you. But I have no intention of leaving until I'm good and ready. And I must warn you: if you were to scream, I'd have to throttle you, and you're much too pretty to meet your end like that."

Despite the matter-of-fact tone, it was a very real threat. Anna looked into those fathomless eyes and realized he was perfectly capable of doing exactly as he said. He would choke the life from her if he had to, probably with about as much compunction as he would swat a fly. In fact, Anna decided as the shock that had held her in thrall began to thaw, he would likely throttle her anyway. After all, was she not the only witness to his crime?

If she had any sense, she would act to save herself at once, while she still could. Once he got his hands on her, she would be helpless. The sheer size of him told her that.

Her hands closed tightly over the arms of the chair. Her knees stiffened, ready to send her catapulting from her seat. She would run for her life, and scream for it too. Her body tensed, her mouth opened—and he reacted before she could so much as move. With a curse he lunged toward her, his hands outstretched to wrap around her neck.

# III

His hands closed on air as Anna sprang upward with the speed and agility of a hunted hare, screaming as she went. To her horror, only the veriest squeak emerged instead of the terrified shriek she'd been counting on. Fright had closed her throat! Squeaking again, frantically, she dodged around the side of the chair, trying her best to force out enough air for a scream.

"Come back here, you little . . ."

Cursing, hissing threats, he grabbed at her again, his arms long enough to reach around the barrier of the chair. Anna ducked, but his fingers closed on the shoulder of her nightgown. She felt the brush of those hard fingers against the soft skin of her neck, and at the last second managed to jerk away. His fingers caught in the neckline of her night rail, her shawl having been lost in her first desperate leap. The material gave with a loud rip. Cool air caressed her skin as she whirled, ducking free of the hot grip of his fingers as they slid across the smoothness of her now-bare shoulder. She tried again to scream. The sound that emerged would have shamed a terrified mouse.

"Keep quiet, you bloody little vixen!" His growl was terrifying, his grabs at her vicious. No gentleman, this! But of course he was not a gentleman. He was a thief, and clearly a violent and dangerous man who was presently bent on doing her bodily harm! If she could not save herself, she would no longer have to worry about Graham, or Chelsea, or anything else. In the morning the servants would find her cooling corpse sprawled on the floor of the library!

Gasping, Anna bobbed up and down like a cork in water behind the first chair's twin, keeping its solidness between herself and the enraged man who snatched at her, hissing curses as she successfully eluded his grasp. Her eyes, which felt as if they were starting from her head with terror, never left his fury-contorted face. Her palms were sweating with fear, making the leather chair back slippery beneath them as she danced around the chair. Her heart was pounding so loudly that she could scarcely hear over it. Though she tried time and again to scream, her throat obstinately refused to emit anything louder than a squeak.

Shutting her mouth, Anna gave up all thought of summoning help. Her only hope of salvation lay in keeping herself out of the thug's reach, and that feat, if it were to be even faintly possible, would require every ounce of concentration she possessed.

They were playing an almost ridiculous game of cat and mouse around the chair. Panting, her heart pounding, Anna feinted this way and that as he grabbed at her. Fleet of foot as she had always been, she dared not try a run to the door. He would almost certainly catch her if she abandoned the protection of the chair.

"Come here, damn you!"

To Anna's horror, he ended the contest by picking up the chair and flinging it aside. Anna had neither the time nor the inclination to marvel at the strength thus revealed. The chair skittered across the floor, crashing into the desk and sending books and various other paraphernalia flying. Anna picked up her skirts and ran.

Instantly he was behind her. She felt rather than saw him, a dark, terrifying presence breathing fire down her neck as she darted toward the half-open door.

"Ah!" It was a sound of satisfaction. He grabbed for her. She twirled desperately to one side, hoping to dodge behind a small table, but his hand caught in the swirling folds of her nightdress and twisted so that she could not escape. The sound of ripping cloth was almost buried under the rasp of her terrified breathing as he reeled her, struggling, in.

"Please don't hurt me!" She panted, wild-eyed, as she slewed around to bat futilely at the hands that dragged her toward him.

"Keep still, then," he growled, yanking her against his wide chest, his arms clamping hers to her sides. "Do you hear me? Keep still!"

Anna was almost beyond listening. The sheer strength of him terrified her. The top of her head barely cleared his shoulder. He dwarfed her in every way. The material of his coat, into which her face was pressed, was abrasive against her skin. She felt as if she were being suffocated; her nose and mouth were crushed against his chest. The layers of his clothing acted like a pillow to impede the flow of air through her flaring nostrils and gasping mouth. The arms holding her against him were iron hard. They were clamped around her rib cage, further impeding her breathing. The heat his body gave off was overpowering; Anna's head whirled, and for a moment she feared she might faint. His left hand rested dangerously close beneath her right breast. It occurred to her suddenly that murder was not all she had to fear. The specter of rape reared its ugly head and had the perverse effect of clearing her mind.

"Let me go!" The words were muffled by his coat,

but the stiffening of her spine and her renewed struggles were unmistakable.

"Keep still, damn it!" This he muttered in a harsh tone in her ear as she kicked and writhed in his hold like a small trapped animal, to no avail. Her slippered feet made bruising contact with his shin. He didn't even appear to notice. It was Anna who winced. His calves were as unyielding as tree trunks, and hurt her toes. Her elbows found his sides as she twisted and squirmed, and at last she had the satisfaction of hearing him grunt. Then he shifted his grip on her so that his fingers brushed the underside of her breast. With only the thin cloth of her nightdress separating her unconfined bosom from his touch, she could feel the shape and heat of his hand nestling under the soft mound.

The sensation was galvanizing. With every ounce of her strength, Anna fought to win free. She succeeded in executing a half-turn in his arms before he recovered enough to once again hold her fast. Cursing, he shifted his grip so that his hand covered her breast completely! She could feel it, hard and hot and unwelcome, burning into her flesh through her nightdress. Her nipple hardened against the crushing heat of his palm.

"Take your hand off me!" she cried, and when he made no move to obey, she went mad, fighting like a wild thing in her effort to escape his touch. He was very still suddenly, but his hold remained unbreakable. The hand that was not crushing her breast moved to cover her mouth, pressing so hard that it forced her lips apart; she could taste the salt of his skin.

"Be quiet!"

His hand tightened over her mouth, hurting her. Hit by a sudden inspiration, Anna clamped her teeth down over the fleshy part of his hand with a viciousness of which she would never have thought herself capable.

"Arghh!"

Yelping, he dropped her, shaking his hand. Anna scrambled away. She got a fleeting look at his face as she flew toward the door. If ever murder was written on a man's countenance it was written at that moment on his.

Then he was after her, his gypsy-dark face made even darker by furious blood.

Panting, terror-stricken, Anna burst through the door into the hall. It was as dark as a cave, the only light coming from the flickering of a candle set high into a sconce at the far end. The family bedrooms were on the floor above; she had only to gain the end of the hall, leap up the stairs, and help would be at hand. At this point even Graham was preferable to the madman behind her.

It was cold in the hall, too, and in her slippers and nightdress that fact ordinarily would have struck Anna at once. But she was too terrified even to register the cold. He was coming after her. . . . She ran, only to hear him running as light and fast as a panther behind her. The race was hopeless, she knew from the start. When his hand tangled in her flowing hair and he stopped her with a yank that brought agonized tears to her eyes, it was almost, in a strange, terrifying way, a relief.

As he dragged her backwards she recovered the full use of her vocal cords at last and let loose with a shrill cry. Immediately his hand clamped over her mouth, cutting the scream off practically at birth. Her heart pounded. Would it be enough?

"You—little—bitch." He sounded grimly furious as, hand still clamped over her mouth, he swung her off her feet and into his arms. "I ought to throttle you for that. Damn it to bloody hell and back. Now what am I to do with you?"

Crushed against his chest, feet dangling uselessly high above the floor, Anna realized that the answer to that was, anything he wanted. Her eyes were huge with fright above that stifling hand as they met his. The scowl he bent on her was terrifying. Those glittering black eyes held out no hope of mercy. For a moment Anna was in imminent fear for her life. Her limbs trembled like a blancmange. Then his eyes raked over her as she lay, small and helpless, in his arms. Miraculously some of the black rage seemed to drain from his face. When he met her wide-eyed gaze once more, he was, she realized thankfully, more resigned than angry.

"Are you always this much trouble, Green Eyes?" he murmured. "Christ, what a coil! Well, never mind. You'll just have to come with me, I suppose. At least you're not the child I first thought you. We might even have some fun."

Then he was striding along the hall toward the stairs that Anna had striven for so frantically, smiling down at her as he went. It was an evil smile, full of mockery and foul intentions. Dear Lord, she was helpless as a babe in the face of his strength.

Where she would have gone up, he descended, seeming to know just what turns to take to reach the front hall. It was a vast room, freshly bedecked with Christmas garlands in honor of the coming festivities, freezing now that the fires were banked for the night and snow lay thick upon the ground outside. Arched passages opened from it in four different directions. Clearly, to have reached this chamber from the library without once taking a wrong turn, he had at some time had occasion to become acquainted with the house.

Who was he? Anna wondered again, her eyes searching that dark face. There was nothing about him that seemed remotely familiar, yet he knew the house. Was he a servant who'd been turned off? Or . . .

Her brain emptied of every rational thought as he stopped walking to stand frowning thoughtfully down at her.

"Make one more sound and I'll knock you uncon-

scious, I swear,'' he told her. From the grimness of
his tone, Anna took him at his word.

She was obediently silent as he set her on her feet
before him. She could feel the iciness of the flag-
stone floor through the thin soles of her slippers.
The room's stone walls added to the chill, and Anna
shivered. With her shawl long gone and her night
rail torn so that it bared one milky shoulder almost
to the point of indecency, she was next door to naked. His eyes moved over her, lingering briefly on
her breasts. An expression that she feared to deci-
pher flickered in his eyes. Anna shrank back, only to
be caught and held by one hard hand on her arm.

''Please . . .'' she said, her voice quavering,
scarcely above a whisper, only to be silenced by a
single hard look.

''Hold, now,'' he said, his tone a warning, and
before she knew what he was about he had untied
the strings of his cloak and swung it from his shoulders to wrap around hers. She blinked at him, startled, as he pulled the velvet-collared wool that was
still warm from his body close around her, then released his grip on her arm to tie the strings into a
neat bow beneath her chin. The garment was large
enough to wrap around twice, and its hem dragged
on the floor by a good foot if not more, but the kindness of the gesture surprised her. Perhaps, then, he
was not an entirely cruel man. . . . The thought gave
her the courage to try once more.

''If you'll let me go, I won't tell anyone I saw you,
I swear.''

''Now that I can't do, Green Eyes. But at least I'll
not let you freeze. 'Tis cold out,'' he said, then
caught hold of her again. Anna expected to be
swung off her feet once more, but instead his eyes
seemed caught by something above them.

'' 'Tis too good a chance to miss,'' he murmured
almost as if in explanation. Even as Anna, uncom-
prehending, followed the path his eyes had taken to
discover high overhead the candle-bedecked kissing

ball already hung by the servants as part of the preparations for Christmas, his head was bending to hers.

Anna gasped as his mouth found her lips.

# IV

His lips were scorching hot, faintly moist, hard. Anna stiffened, her spine going suddenly ramrod straight as they moved softly over her mouth. Her hands came up to push against his shoulders in instinctive, outraged denial, but she might just as well have pushed against one of the stone walls of Gordon Hall for all the effect it had on him.

"Shh, sweetheart. This won't hurt a bit, I swear," he murmured against her lips. Then he was pulling her to him, his hands sliding beneath the cloak to her back to mold the slight curves of her body to his. Anna gasped as one large hand slid up the length of her spine to cradle the back of her skull, imprisoning her head in the position he wished. To her horror his tongue took advantage of the moment to slide inside her mouth.

She tried to protest, but the only sound to emerge was a muffled squawk. She tried to pull away, but he held her in a grip of iron. She tried not to notice the turgid swelling that spoke of the swift rising of his desire pressing against her soft belly, or the rock solidity of the muscular chest against which she ineffectually shoved, or the taste of his mouth, which was some indefinable combination of brandy and cigars and man.

She tried not to feel the warming of her own blood

21

as he took the kiss he wanted with bold impudence, laying claim to her mouth as no one, not even her husband, had ever done.

Paul had kissed her many times, but never had he stroked her tongue with his, drawn it into his mouth, sucked on it. Never had he ravished her lips with seductive little nibbles, rubbing his lips against hers until the sheer friction was enough to make her dizzy. Never had he claimed her mouth with such easy confidence, making her want more, making her want *him*.

When he drew his mouth away to stare down at her for a hot, breathless moment, surprise and puzzlement widening his eyes, Anna was so disoriented that she barely knew where she was. Her hands clung to his shoulders for balance, and she no longer struggled to escape. It was almost as if she were drugged.

"Sweetheart, don't you ever kiss back?" he murmured, his mouth twisting into a crooked half-smile that was almost as dazzling as his kiss. Anna, mesmerized, could not reply. She could only watch with huge, dazed eyes as his smile broadened, and then his head descended once more.

Her last thought, before he took her beyond the realm of consciousness again, was that his eyes were not black at all; they were a deep, velvety blue, as nearly black as a midnight sky.

Then he was kissing her again.

He drew her up on tiptoe, tilting her so that she had no choice but to cling to him, her nails digging into the hard strength of his shoulders, her head resting against the steely bulge of his upper arm. Her eyes closed, her mouth opened without the least thought of resistance as he slanted his lips over hers, his tongue seeking instant entrance. Her body quaked, quivered, as he plundered her mouth with leisurely mastery. She was no innocent miss, not after having been married and having borne a child, but never, ever had she felt anything like this.

Paul's kisses had been comfortable, affectionate, because of course he had respected as well as loved her.

He would never had dreamed of using her, like a common wench, a hussy.

He would never have dreamed that the vicar's gently bred daughter could respond so wantonly to such vulgar ill-usage. Anna would never have believed it herself.

What was wrong with her? Even as his hand slid down her spine to cup and caress her small bottom through the thin gown, Anna began to panic. Her bones were melting, her heart was pounding, her insides were about as solid as quince jelly. And all because this man—this criminal—had dared to force her to accept his kisses, his hands on her person.

She must be depraved.

On the heels of that thought came the realization that the hand that was not squeezing her bottom was sliding along the bared skin of her shoulder, sliding down along the base of her neck, the long fingers seeking—and finding—her naked breast.

Even as the large, hot hand closed over her soft flesh, a shaft of pure fire shot through her clear down to her toes. Her nipple hardened instantly against the scorching caress of his palm—and from somewhere Anna found a strength she had never dreamed she possessed, a tremendous surging strength that enabled her to wrench herself from his arms.

"How dare you! How dare you touch me, you—you *swine!*" she cried, panting, backing away as he made a move as though to come after her. She could tell her face was flushed; she could feel the hectic flags of rosy color that flew in her cheeks. Her hair was tousled, tumbling over the black cloak that she clutched to her as if it could, magically, protect her from him. Her lips were parted as she struggled to control her breathing, and tender and swollen from his kisses. Her eyes, which never left him, were huge with a jumbled mixture of confusion, shame, and fright.

At her words he stood still.

"There's no need to be in such a taking," he said, his voice soothing, those unsettling eyes watchful as they tracked her progress. Like hers, his breathing was faintly uneven. Dark patches of color burned high in his cheekbones, and those midnight-blue eyes had darkened once again to something more nearly resembling jet black. " 'Twas only a kiss, no more."

Anna took another step away from him, coming to an abrupt stop as she backed into one of the long tables that graced either side of the hall. The silver on it rattled, and she put a hand behind her instinctively to keep a tall candlestick from toppling over. Her knuckles brushed the top of a glass display case. Her eyes flickered as she suddenly remembered what it contained: a pair of silver dueling pistols once prized by old Lord Ridley as a gift from his father. Although they would not be loaded, and probably not even functional after all this time, *he* would not know that. If only the case was not locked—it was not. Stealthily she lifted the lid and slipped her hand inside to seek and close over a cool metal handle. Lifting the pistol from its velvet nest, she withdrew her hand, keeping the pistol concealed behind her back. With that, she might, with any luck at all, succeed in holding him at bay. Her eyes never left him. He had made no further move to come after her, but she knew that he did not mean to simply bow and leave. No gentleman, this, she reminded herself, then blushed to the roots of her hair as she remembered how she had responded to this man she had never in her life set eyes on before, this rogue, this nonrespecter of women, this thief!

"I have a gun," she said hoarsely. Withdrawing the weapon from behind her back, she leveled it at him. "If you come one step nearer, I'll shoot."

His eyes widened in surprise, then narrowed. For

one moment they fixed on the pistol, then lifted to
her face. He looked unnervingly cool—but he made
no move to call her bluff, and even lifted a placating
hand. Anna steadied her trembling fingers with
sheer force of will and made herself meet those dark
eyes with a calm that, she hoped, belied her wildly
beating heart.

"Let's not be hasty, now," he said, his gaze sliding to the pistol again, briefly. "I've done you no
harm at all, nor do I mean you any."

Anna snorted, and the pistol wobbled in a way
that would have alarmed her had she been the one
on the business end of it. But he seemed unrattled.

"You will leave—*now.*" Anna tried hard to sound
authoritative, but she feared her voice was not altogether convincing. In any case, he made no move
to obey. Instead, he shook his head regretfully.

"I can't do that, I'm afraid. At least, not without
you." He smiled at her then, a roguish smile that
might, under other circumstances, have charmed her.
"You've no reason to fear me. I'll not hurt you—
nor force you into giving anything you don't wish
to give—but you must see that I cannot leave you
behind." His voice was soothing, his tone eminently
reasonable. Anna blinked at him. If she had not
known better, she would have thought from his tone
that *she* was the one being outrageous, while he tried
to gently cajole her into more acceptable behavior.
He had quickly recovered his composure, if indeed
he had ever lost it, and stood easily erect, watching her—and the pistol—keen-eyed. Without the
cloak, he was still formidable-looking, a tall man
with wide shoulders and an athlete's powerful build.
His coat was black like his cloak and not overly fash-
ionable. His breeches were black too, not as snug as
was the current style but still close-fitting enough to
reveal the powerful muscles of his thighs. His boots
were not Hoby's, but well-scuffed and worn, black
like the rest of his attire. His linen was white, but
faintly crumpled, and his cravat was carelessly tied.

Not a gentleman, she decided again, but frighteningly attractive for all that.

"Just go away! Please!" For all her good intentions, her voice wobbled more alarmingly than the pistol.

He smiled again and shook his head. "I can't do that either, I'm afraid. I've no doubt that as soon as I'm gone you'll run screeching for reinforcements. I don't fancy a bullet in the back—or a noose around my neck. But I'll set you free as soon as I'm safe away, and give you money for your passage back here. You'll come to no harm, I promise you."

"I won't go with you! Have you no eyes in your head? I have a gun!" Anna practically hissed the last words.

His mouth tightened fractionally, and his brows twitched closer together. "I haven't time to stand about arguing with you. There's no help for it; you must come with me. Your only choice is whether you walk out of here with a modicum of dignity or whether I stuff my handkerchief in your mouth, bind your wrists behind your back, and carry you out on my shoulder."

"I'll shoot you if you take a single step toward me. I will, I mean it." Panic edged her voice. He could not really mean to ignore a pistol pointed squarely at his head—could he?

"That pistol looks older than I am—and unless I much mistake the matter it seems to be missing its hammer." He shrugged. "Under the circumstances, I believe I'll just have to chance it. Fire away."

Even as the sense of that sank in, and her eyes dropped in questioning horror to the maligned pistol, he lunged toward her. His movement was so unexpected that Anna squeezed the trigger automatically. The gun went off with a deafening boom. Then he was wresting the pistol from her grasp and flinging it aside. She gasped, struggling, as his hands closed on her arms and yanked her toward him, twisting her at the same time so that she was

falling through space. Her fingers scrambled frantically for something, anything to break her fall.

Anna was too shocked even to scream as she hit
the floor with a jarring force that bruised her hip and
rattled every bone in her body. Already he was
looming over her, making good his threat to stuff
his handkerchief in her mouth. She choked, spluttered, struggled, gagged, but he rammed the dry
linen in and twisted her around, meaning, no doubt,
to bind her hands before scooping her up again. She
was lying on the floor, half on her side and half on
her back, one of his large hands and a knee holding
her down. He was in an awkward position, a kind
of half crouch, his hands busy with the knot of his
cravat. No doubt he meant to use it to tie her hands.
Soon she would be helpless, and he would carry her
away—to do what with her? Murder no longer
seemed such a strong possibility, but ravishment, or
rather his particular brand of seduction, did.

To her eternal shame, the thought of enduring
such, with him, brought with it not fear but a shiv-
ery excitement that heated her blood and quickened
her heart.

"Next time, Green Eyes, don't be so gullible."
The amusement in his voice rankled more than his
words. So his distracting comment about the gun
had been as much a bluff as her holding the gun on
him in the first place, had it? She'd been a fool to
look down. The knowledge that she'd actually had
a loaded, working pistol in her hand and let him
trick her out of using it lit her temper. Not that she
would have actually shot him—at least, not on purpose. Although, had she the thing to do over again,
the grinning creature might very well end up a
headless corpse. . . .

She was at his mercy—again. At the realization
she went cold all over. And then Anna realized
that she held the key to her own salvation in her
hand: the heavy silver candlestick that had stood on

the table beside the display case. She had instinctively grasped it as she felt herself fall.

Her hands were hidden by the cloak. His hold on her was loose, his attention half distracted as he sought to wrench the cravat from around his neck. Anna clutched the candlestick, shut her eyes, and waited.

The game was not quite played out yet.

Then, when he had his cravat free and was lifting her to her feet, she struck. Her hand clutching the candlestick snaked from beneath the cloak with desperate speed. Arcing toward his head, the candlestick was a mere silver blur. His eyes barely registered surprise before weapon and temple connected with a sound that at any other time would have turned Anna's stomach.

Chest heaving, eyes huge, Anna stared into the rogue's widening eyes for a timeless instant as he continued to loom threateningly over her.

Then, with a little grunt, his eyes rolled back in his head and he crumpled soundlessly at her feet.

At last she managed a real, full-bodied scream. As she stared down at his motionless form, the hysteria she'd held at bay for weeks finally claimed her. Earsplitting cries emerged from her mouth of their own volition. Had she wanted to, she could not have stopped.

# V

"For the Lord's sake, Miss Anna, what is it?"

"Miss Anna, Miss Anna, is you killed?"

Anna's screams still echoed off the stone walls when Davis, the grizzled, portly butler who had been with the Traverne family since before Paul's birth, burst into the front hall accompanied by Beedle, the first footman. Both men were less than fully dressed, with Davis's shirt hanging out of his breeches and Beedle barefoot. They were armed, Beedle with an ancient axe that ordinarily hung above the entry to the kitchen (and that probably hadn't been moved for a hundred years) and Davis with a poker. Panting, breathless, they charged through the door only to come to a sudden stop. Their eyes popped as they beheld Anna, both hands pressed to her mouth in an effort to stop the shattering cries that issued from it, her hair wildly disheveled and her night rail clearly visible beneath the too-large cloak that fell from her shoulders. She was leaning over the prostrate form of a very large, unknown man. The heavy silver candlestick that normally stood on the hall table lay on its side at Anna's feet, and a pistol rested on the flagstones some little distance away. Smoke and the acrid scent of gunpowder filled the air.

"Miss Anna, what's happened? Who is that?"

29

Davis had known her from childhood. With the privilege of an old family retainer he hurried across the floor to give her shoulder a good shake. "Miss Anna, hush that noise and tell us: are you hurt?"

The old butler's obvious concern did more than the one-handed shake to silence Anna's hysterical cries. She gulped once, twice, shuddered, and looked down at the man she had felled.

"Oh, Davis, have I killed him?" she asked faintly. The housebreaker lay inert on his back, his face as pale as hers felt. From where she stood, it was impossible to tell if he still breathed. Anna remembered the sound of the blow and felt sick. Abruptly she sank to her knees as her legs refused to support her any longer. Davis hovered over her while Beedle shifted from foot to foot, both men clearly at a loss.

"Miss Anna, did he harm you? Are you shot—or worse?" Davis's voice was low and fierce.

Both servants' eyes were fixed on her person. Anna looked down at where their eyes rested and felt herself blush. A too-thin shoulder and the upper slope of a creamy breast, exposed by the rip in her night rail, were clearly visible beneath the open cloak. Made clumsy by shock, her fingers fumbled to close the sides of the cloak and hold them together, thus restoring her modesty.

"No. No, he didn't hurt me. And nobody was actually shot," she said in a low voice, her eyes moving to the man who lay so frighteningly still less than a foot away. "There was a struggle and the gun went off, but it missed. Then I—hit him. With the candlestick."

"Miss Anna, you never did!" Beedle's voice was full of admiration. Davis shot him a silencing look and bent to rest a cautious hand on the housebreaker's neck, his poker held at the ready.

"He's not dead."

At Davis's pronouncement Anna felt a quiver of relief. He was a thief, and an impudent rogue, and undoubtedly a very bad man, but she wouldn't want his blood on her hands. Not even when she remembered the heart-shaking power of his kiss—or the shocking way he had dared to touch her.

At the memory, her body went first hot, then cold. Her eyes moved warily to the unconscious man on the floor even as her hand lifted of its own volition to scrub across her mouth. She knew it had to be her imagination, but it seemed as if the taste of him lingered still.

"What's 'appened? What's 'appened?" Mrs. Mullins, the stout, white-haired housekeeper, came puffing up through the passage that led to the servants' quarters, bearing a lighted taper that she carefully shielded from the draft. At any other time Anna would have smiled to see her in her night rail with her feet bare and her cap askew. But at the moment she was in no mood for smiling. Her stomach churned, and she felt curiously light-headed. The thought that popped into her mind, refusing to be banished, was, Dear Lord, what have I done?

If she had it to do over again, she would have choked on the end of his cloak before giving way to the screams that had brought the household down upon them—although of course the shot would have brought them running in any case. She could not have let him just carry her off; the idea was unthinkable. But now that he was captured, the housebreaker would likely be hanged. At the thought of that powerful body dangling at the end of a rope, Anna felt a sharp wave of nausea.

True, he was a criminal, but his smile had held a wealth of charm. He had frightened her half to death, but she had suffered no real injury at his hands, and he had even taken care to wrap her in his cloak before, as he had meant to do, carrying her outside. The kisses he had stolen had been shameful, a disgrace, the way he had touched her too disturbing even to think about, but still—she could not wish to see him dead.

At the thought Anna shuddered and dropped her head to her hands.

"Here, ducks, 'tis all right now. Mrs. Mullins is 'ere," the housekeeper crooned, fixing her taper in a holder on the wall and returning to bend over Anna. Clumsily she patted Anna's shoulder. "Whatever's 'appened, 'tis not so bad, you'll see."

"She said he'd not harmed her." This was Davis, sounding disapproving, as he always disapproved of Mrs. Mullins.

"Of course she'd say that, you dunder'ead! Miss Anna's that modest, she is," Mrs. Mullins returned fiercely. At that Anna looked up.

"Truly, I'm all right. He—meant to make me go with him, but I hit him. He never harmed me."

"Thank the Lord!"

While Mrs. Mullins was offering up thanks, the housemaids, Polly, Sadie, and Rose, peeped cautiously around an arch to take in the scene. After a moment, apparently convinced that it was safe enough to do so, they sidled into the front hall. A sheepish-looking Henricks, the second footman, followed close on their heels. All wore night attire, with various bits of daytime clothing hastily thrown on. All looked more curious than inclined to be helpful. Anna was not surprised to see both Mrs. Mullins and Davis, acting in concert for once, scowl at them in a way that boded them no good before their attention returned to Anna and the housebreaker.

"Who is 'e?" Mrs. Mullins spoke for them all as she leaned closer to stare down at the man's bloodless face. His head was turned slightly toward Anna, and she could see the bruise already darkening his temple. Wincing, she tried not to think that she might have done him a permanent injury.

"He's a bloody thief, that's who he is, 'tis clear as the nose on your face! What else would he be doing skulking about the house in the middle of the night? We should be searching him for his booty, not standing around gawking like a bunch of bloody imbeciles!'' Beedle had finally dared to edge closer, but he stood poised as if for attack, axe at the ready.

"Did you see 'im take anythin', Miss Anna?''

Just then the cause of all the commotion groaned and stirred. All of them, Anna included, gasped, their gazes fastening fearfully on the intruder.

"Here, now, don't you be movin', you, or it'll be off with your head!'' Davis shook the poker threateningly, but the housebreaker was already still once more. If the man heard, he gave no indication of it. Anna was conscious of a moment's deep relief that she truly hadn't killed him after all. Then, as Mrs. Mullins repeated her question, Anna slowly shook her head.

Perhaps if they found no evidence of thievery, they wouldn't be able to hang the man after all. She could hurry up to the library, replace the jewels in the hidey-hole, tidy up the mess, and no one would be the wiser as to what he had been about.

Suddenly the jewels inside the cloak she wore seemed to burn. Never before in her life had Anna told such a monstrous, deliberate lie.

But what was a man's life worth, when all was said and done? Surely more than one small lie!

"Somebody go summon the master! You, there, 'Enricks, don't stand about lookin' as stupid as can be! You go!'' Mrs. Mullins gave the order over her shoulder, her tone a decided snap.

"Henricks takes his orders from me,'' Davis reminded the housekeeper glacially. Even in the face of an emergency, the butler was not about to forget his long-standing feud with his rival for power in the household. Mrs. Mullins harrumphed. Davis looked at the footman, who stood hesitating behind the housemaids, with triumph. "Go along with you, Henricks, and fetch his lordship.''

"Yes, Mr. Davis.'' Henricks nodded and departed. The maids, reassured by the housebreaker's continued prostration, formed a small circle around him.

"Miss Anna, did he—scare you?" Polly asked in a thrilled whisper.

Anna, knowing very well what the maid longed to hear, managed to shake her head. She still felt very odd, almost boneless, and she had to clamp her teeth tightly together to keep them from chattering. Even sprawled unconscious on the floor, the intruder looked huge, muscular, and unnervingly tough. Impossible to believe that she had emerged the victor in their battle. Impossible to believe that that firm mouth had taken hers, or that long-fingered hand caressed her breast.

"Oh, well, that's a blessing," said Polly, clearly disappointed. At that moment the intruder stirred again, lifting his head from the floor and shaking it, then getting his arms beneath him as he tried to rise. Anna gasped and scooted back. The maids jumped.

"Oh, no you don't!" shouted Davis, and to the accompaniment of a cacophony of shrieks and shouts, he clouted the man over the head with the poker. The resulting thump made Anna wince. The housebreaker immediately collapsed again.

"We'll have to tie him up," Davis said, looking around him as though hoping a rope would miraculously appear.

"Why don't you just sit on 'im, Mr. Davis? That'd 'old an army down, it would!"

Mrs. Mullins's suggestion, referring as it did to Davis's substantial girth, was maliciously meant, but the other servants seized on it.

"Aye, Mr. Davis, you sit on 'im. We'll all sit on 'im! That'll hold 'im right and tight for the master!"

Anna felt her composure, and with it her sense of humor, start to return as that suggestion was carried out. Davis, poker held stiffly in front of his chest, straddled the housebreaker's back while Beedle sat on his shoulders, brandishing the axe. Polly and Sadie perched on his legs, and Mrs. Mullins, muttering, hovered over all. An elephant would have had a hard time moving under that combined weight.

"Don't you be afeared, Miss Anna, we've got him fast," Beedle assured her, seeing the way her eyes fixed on their prisoner.

"I'm not afraid," Anna answered in a voice that was rapidly growing stronger. Her mind was beginning to function normally as well. In a very few minutes Graham would appear. The confrontation she had been dreading since the previous night was at hand—although perhaps he would be too caught up in the drama to worry about her. In any case, if she were to carry out her plan, she must get up to the library at once. . . .

And then she would sleep the rest of the night with Chelsea. Even if she must give in to Graham eventually, it would not be this night.

"I—I'm going up to bed," Anna said, forcing her still jellylike knees to stiffen so that she could stand.

"But, Miss Anna, won't you be wishful of telling 'is lordship what 'appened? After all, 'twas you who captured 'im!"

"'O' course she wants to go ter bed, ox-brain! Miss Anna's a lady, she is, and she's 'ad quite a shock! She can talk to 'is lordship in the mornin'!"

This exchange between Beedle and Mrs. Mullins left the footman looking mulish. Davis clenched the matter with a silencing glare at his fellow servants.

"You go along now, Miss Anna. I'll tell his lordship what's needful, and then you can tell him the rest in your own good time."

Anna, with a wan smile at the butler and a last, quick glance at the motionless housebreaker, picked up the overlong skirts of the cloak and started to hurry from the room. The best she could do for him now was to replace the emeralds and disclaim all knowledge of what he had been about at Gordon Hall. Could they hang a man merely for breaking into a gentleman's residence? She didn't think so.

But she was too late. Already, approaching rap-

idly along the very passage she meant to take, came
the heavy tread and deep voice that she had learned
to dread. Seconds later her brother-in-law filled the
doorway.

Graham was a large man, tall and stocky in a way
that promised considerable girth later in life. His
once-fair hair had darkened to an indeterminate
shade of brown, and his blunt features would not
have been out of place on a pugilist. The only things
that he and Paul had in common were the same pale
blue eyes that Chelsea had inherited. Dreamy and
thick-lashed on Paul, they were hard and keen in
Graham's face. Where Paul's jaw had been round,
and perhaps softer than a man's should be, Graham's was square and jutted. But the difference in
the brothers was not only physical: Graham possessed not a whit of Paul's sensitivity or kind nature. Graham was about as sensitive and kind as
a hound on the hunt.

"Good God, Anna, what mad start is this?" With
Henricks fluttering in obsequious attendance, Graham strode through the door, still tying the knot of
his dressing gown as he surveyed both her and the
scene. Anna had come to a dead stop just a few feet
from the arched doorway and stood clutching the
housebreaker's cloak closely about her person as she
looked at Graham without replying. How she had
come to despise him—and fear him too! She could
barely be in his company for a matter of minutes
without feeling her skin crawl.

" 'Tis a thief, my lord. Miss Anna's caught 'im!"
Mrs. Mullins's shrill voice drew Graham's attention.

"A thief? Is this true?" Graham caught Anna's
arm in passing and dragged her along with him as
he moved to stand staring down at the housebreaker. Anna resigned herself to the fact that, for
the moment, escape was impossible. With Davis,
Beedle, and the maids still straddling the housebreaker's back, it was difficult to see much of the
man himself. Graham's hand around her arm, even

with the material of the cloak and her nightdress to protect her from his actual touch, was making her feel faintly sick. All she could think of was getting away. . . .

"Anna?" When she said not a word, Graham shook her arm, his eyes narrowing on her face. "What happened?"

After the way he had tried to force himself upon her the previous night, she could not bear to be so near him. She had awakened to find him crawling naked between her sheets, his hand already groping along her thigh. . . .

"Anna?" His hand tightened on her arm, and he bent so close that his breath fanned her cheek. Anna averted her face. For the housebreaker's sake, she could not tell the unvarnished truth. She must prevaricate—but it was hard to lie when she could barely even think!

"I came upon him . . . by accident. He meant to carry me off, and I . . . I tried to shoot him with your papa's dueling pistol, but I missed, and then I hit him with that candlestick." She nodded toward the object in question.

"He tried to carry you off?" Graham's voice was shrill with incredulity. "Who the devil is he? Do you know him? What did he want here?" His rapid-fire questions were accompanied by another shake of the arm.

"Why, I came to call on you, brother," came the reply, in a gravely voice that was familiar to Anna. She started, even as the servants gasped and Graham's head swung sharply around. All eyes fixed on the housebreaker, whose eyes were open. Despite his ignominious position and the great bruise purpling his temple, his gaze was both fearless and mocking.

"You!" Graham sounded as if the work choked him. His face had turned an alarming shade of puce.

"In the flesh. Were you not expecting me? You should have been."

"Summon the magistrate! Quickly!" Graham sounded more agitated than Anna had ever heard him. The servants were looking from one man to the other, their expressions as baffled as Anna felt. They were so bemused, in fact, that not one of them made so much as a move to obey.

"Did you hear me? I said summon the magistrate! Now!" Graham was practically screaming, his fists clenched at his sides, his face purple.

"Yes, your lordship!" Henricks responded to that shouted command with a hasty bow and a flurry of feet. As he ran, hatless and coatless, out the front door into the December night, the housebreaker spoke again, drawing all attention back to himself.

"And here I thought you'd be glad to see me," he said, and laughed softly. "As your last surviving male relative, you know."

Standing beside Graham, Anna could hear the grinding of her brother-in-law's teeth.

"You've overreached yourself this time, you bastard! You'll go to gaol for this! Search him! Let's see what the thieving gypsy bastard tried to steal! Search him, I say!"

"But my lord . . ." Davis tried to protest. Graham, his mouth contorting and his eyes bulging with fury, made an angry gesture.

"I said search him!" he screamed.

"Yes, my lord. Move, you idiot." This last, muttered in an undertone to Beedle and accompanied by a shove on his underling's shoulders, caused the footman to rise hastily to his feet. Davis put down the poker and shifted his position, clumsily patting his hands over as much of the housebreaker's person as he could reach. As Davis scooted backwards, the maids stood up to get out of the way. Graham moved closer, an expression midway between a gloat and a snarl twisting his face as he stared down at the housebreaker—who chose that moment to make his move.

His hand snaked out, and with a quick, powerful

grab he caught one of Graham's ankles, jerking it from beneath him and flipping him backwards as neatly as a card through space. Graham yelped, Anna and the maids screamed, Beedle jumped back and cursed, and the housebreaker let out a mighty roar. Then he shoved himself to his feet, toppling the bellowing David like Humpty Dumpty from the wall.

"Get him! Get him!" Beedle charged, swinging the axe—and the housebreaker, ducking, felled him with a right to the jaw that lifted the footman clear off his feet. The axe went one way, skittering harmlessly along the floor, and Beedle went the other, cannonballing into Anna, who was knocked flat. Beedle fell on top of her, his weight driving the breath from her body with an audible whoosh. She lay there for a moment, stunned, as Beedle, gasping apologies, at last managed to roll off her.

"Catch him, damn it! Don't let him get away!" Graham's shout reverberated through the hall as Anna, winded, lay motionless. When she was once again able to move, the housebreaker had already disappeared out the door. Davis and Graham, the latter waving Beedle's recovered axe and cursing like a stevedore, were after him like baying hounds after a fox.

# VI

Anna, shaken, had just gotten to her feet when Graham came barreling back through the door with Davis trailing unhappily behind him. Graham was scowling ferociously as Davis quietly shut the door. Davis, in response to a discreet look from Beedle, darted a glance at his lordship and shook his head.

"You lot clear out of here," Graham snarled, glaring at the gaping servants as though looking for someone upon whom to vent his wrath. The maids and Beedle, needing no more than the expression on the lord's face to give the command emphasis, immediately melted away. Mrs. Mullins, a hardier type, offered to make tea. She was shooed away with a peremptory movement of Graham's hand, and left looking offended.

Davis, his face wooden, bent to retrieve the pistol and the candlestick from the floor. He replaced the former gently in its case and the latter in its customary position on the table, and looked around to see if he could discover any other offenses against tidiness. There being none, he took himself off, the dignity of his bearing almost making up for the shambles the night's work had made of his appearance.

Quickly recovering her wits, Anna made a move as if to follow him. Not for anything in the world

40

did she wish to be left alone with Graham. But she was too late.

Even as she murmured a hasty good-night, Graham came up behind her and caught her arm.

"I want to know what happened. Everything." There was a harsh edge to his voice that made it totally unlike his normal hearty tone. Caught by his hand on her arm, Anna had no choice but to stop and look up at him.

"I told you. He—I saw him, and he tried to carry me off, and I shot at him. Then I hit him with the candlestick, and he was knocked unconscious. Then Davis and the others came and—you know the rest."

"How did he get in? What did he want?" The question had an urgent undertone that bewildered Anna.

She shook her head. "You heard what he said—that he came to visit you. Graham, who is he? What did he mean by calling you 'brother'?"

Graham's mouth twisted. "He's a low-life bastard who's been trying to pass himself off as my father's by-blow for years. My father never acknowledged him, and I mean to follow that example. His mother was a gypsy whore; his father could have been anybody. He hates us all, every living Traverne. I suppose we must count ourselves lucky that we weren't all murdered in our beds."

The expression on Graham's face was so dark that Anna involuntarily shivered. If the housebreaker hated all Travernes, then it was clear that Graham returned the favor with interest. Hatred shone from his pale blue eyes.

"He was up to no good, you may be sure. It was fortunate that you came across him." Graham's expression changed. His eyes sharpened as they looked down at her. The hold he had on her arm tightened too. "What were you doing from bed at such an hour? I was on my way to visit you."

Anna lifted her chin. Her eyes as they met his were unflinching. She was small-boned and fragile next to his bull-like frame, and his hold on her arm was tight. He could break her in two with a minimum of effort—but still she meant to stand her ground.

"That was why I was from my bed," she said steadily, and for a moment his grip on her arm tightened so cruelly that she winced. Then his hold eased, and he began instead to subtly knead her arm. There was something obscene about the almost gentle caress, and something obscene too in the tiny smile that played across his mouth as he watched her face, feeding on the revulsion she could not quite manage to hide.

"I meant what I said, Anna. I mean to be repaid for my kindness in taking you and your gel in."

"Chelsea is your niece! You have a moral obligation to provide for her!"

Graham snapped the fingers of his free hand. "That's how much your moral obligation means to me. But don't worry, I don't mean to abandon the brat, unless you make it necessary. I just want to be recompensed for her upkeep. Something for something, you know. A business transaction, pure and simple."

His head dipped toward hers. The hand on her arm tightened again, and his eyes were on her mouth. Anna, shuddering, realized that he meant to kiss her. Summoning her last reserves of strength, she managed to jerk her arm free and step back.

"You make me sick!"

Graham's eyes glittered at her. His expression was not pleasant as he surveyed her. "And you make me— But you know what you make me, don't you, my dear sister-in-law? You've always teased me, batting those big eyes at me and then running away like a skittish virgin. But you're no virgin any longer, and the time has come to pay the piper. You'll bed me, my dear, or get the hell out of my house. You and your brat."

"I'll tell Barbara. . . ." She made the threat in sheer desperation. Graham laughed.

"And thus cut your own throat. Barbara doesn't care for having a widowed young sister-in-law in her house constantly taking the shine out of her. She'd welcome the excuse to throw you out on your pretty ear. I don't want you to be under any illusions about that."

Anna stared at him. The smirking smile on his square face made her long to slap him; she had to close her hands into fists to resist the impulse. Reading defeat in her face, Graham smiled wider and reached out as though to catch her arm again. But before he could touch her the front door burst open. Through it hurried Henricks, followed by a short, greatcoated stranger. Both stopped just beyond the doorway as they became aware of Graham's presence.

"I've brought the magistrate, your lordship. And 'twas quite a task getting him to come, I must say. Didn't believe me, he didn't!" Henricks's voice was both triumphant and indignant.

"Your man here tells me you had a break-in, my lord?" With a single annoyed look at Henricks, the magistrate focused on Graham. His voice conveyed polite skepticism.

"I'll be with you in a minute," Graham said shortly, clearly not pleased at the interruption. He turned back to Anna, lowering his voice so that she alone could hear his words.

"I mean to have you, and I won't be put off any longer. When I've dealt with this, I'll be coming along to your room. I expect to find you there, warm and welcoming. You always were a sensible little puss." He smiled at her. Anna, hating him, also hated herself as, in the face of that hot stare, her eyes faltered and dropped.

His hand came to rest briefly against her neck. She jerked away. He scowled.

"You'll lie with me, Anna, one way or another.

You don't have a choice.'' Then his voice rose so that the others could hear. ''Go along up to bed now.''

He turned away from her and moved to join the men. Anna, feeling as if she had just been punched in the stomach, slowly left the hall. Graham meant what he said, she knew he did. He would have her, by force if necessary, or he would toss her and Chelsea out of his house.

It was frigid December, she had exactly five pounds and her clothing to her name, and there was no place for her and her innocent child to go.

She shivered as if from a chill and drew the enveloping cloak more closely around her neck. Something hard bumped against her thigh, and she was reminded of the emeralds concealed in the folds. She must return them to the library. . . .

And then a thought so evil that it must have been prompted by the devil popped full-grown into her brain.

Concealed on her person was a fortune in emeralds that no one short of heaven knew she had.

The housebreaker had stolen them. When they were missed, he would be blamed. If she kept her mouth shut, no one would ever connect her with them at all.

And he was gone, escaped, certainly never to be seen around Gordon Hall again. He would suffer no punishment for her misdeed.

Stealing was wrong. But so was succumbing to Graham. Of the two evils, stealing was probably the lesser. And certainly it was the more bearable.

The miracle she had prayed for earlier had just been delivered into her hands.

# VII

Julian Chase rode through the icy night like a
centaur. Bent low over Samson's neck, his knees
gripping the stallion's heaving black sides, he might
have been a part of the horse. He'd learned to ride
before he could walk, as most gypsy children did,
and this wasn't the first time the instinctual communion between man and beast would stand him in
good stead. Already the hallooing pursuit set on him
by his beloved half brother was fading into the distance. In another few miles he would be free and
clear.

Damn, his head hurt! Throbbed so much that he
could barely focus his eyes, let alone think! What
the hell had the little besom hit him with? Impossible to imagine that a chit that small and fragile-
looking could inflict such a blow.

Who the devil was she, anyway? Not Graham's
wife, he knew. He'd seen Lady Ridley twice in London and once during a scouting expedition to Gordon Hall. She was a handsome enough woman, tall
and full-bosomed, with a loud voice and an obviously high opinion of herself. But she wasn't a patch
on the angel turned hellcat who'd clouted him on
the head.

Masses of blond hair, green-as-grass eyes. For
some reason that combination stirred a vague mem-

ory. But of what, or whom, he couldn't have said.
Besides, his head hurt too much to make the effort
to sort it out.

A six-foot-high stone wall, nearly hidden by a
copse of trees, loomed up out of the darkness. Julian
scarcely saw it before Samson was up and over,
landing lightly with hardly a slackening in his pace.
At the barely felt impact a sharp pain shot through
Julian's head. He reined Samson in, blinking in an
effort to drive away the pain as he slowed the animal's headlong pace. For a moment he swayed in
the saddle, on the verge of losing consciousness, before the iron control that had played a large part in
keeping him in one piece for the thirty-five years
he'd been alive asserted itself. He would not pass
out. To pass out would almost certainly result in a
fall from the saddle, and then he would very likely
be taken by Graham's men. Might as well shoot
himself in the head here and now as let himself be
captured by men loyal to his brother.

Samson bunny-hopped over a fallen log that lay
in his path, and another blinding pain pierced Julian's head. Good God, had the thrice-damned chit
actually managed to crack his skull?

But then, Julian supposed he was lucky to have
escaped with no more hurt than that. If his brother
had succeeded in holding him, he would be in worse
straits indeed. Graham had hated him ever since he
had first been made aware of his half brother's existence, half a lifetime ago when Julian was sixteen
and Graham was twelve.

With the cockiness of youth, Julian had traveled
down to Gordon Hall to confront his supposed father about the truth surrounding the circumstances
of his birth. His granny had always told him that
he, Julian, was the lord's rightful heir, as her daughter Nina had been the earl's legal wife and not his
mistress at all. In Julian's only other encounter with
his father, Lord Ridley had had all the advantages.
But then Julian had been a frightened eight-year-old,

painfully eager for his father's love. At sixteen, he considered himself a man grown, toughened by years of living by his wits and fists in London's meanest slums and well able to take care of himself.

If the memory weren't so painful still, he might smile at the recollection of his sixteen-year-old rashness. Instead of being greeted with the common civility his father would have accorded even a chance-met stranger, Julian had, after being admitted no farther than the front hall by the servants, been ordered by his icy-voiced father to take his person from the premises and never return. When Julian had attempted to argue, the old lord had had him bodily thrown out. The mother and father of a fight had ensued. By its conclusion, fully half a dozen fellows wielding stout sticks had joined together to beat Julian to a bloody pulp. Finally the servants, at Lord Ridley's direction, had thrown the barely conscious Julian into the road, where they had let him lie.

And then a pudgy youth had run up to him and spit full in his battered face, hissing "Gypsy bastard" with hatred glittering in his pale blue eyes. That youth had been Graham, and Graham hated him still. Julian suspected that he feared him, too. If, as Julian suspected, Graham had somehow gotten wind of the notion that Julian might, just might, be the legitimate offspring of the old earl instead of a by-blow, then seeing his brother shot or hanged for thieving would simultaneously soothe Graham's anxiety and fill him with glee.

No doubt he'd been a fool to put himself within Graham's reach. But the emeralds were his, and he wanted them. And wanted, too, the mysterious "proof" they were said to contain.

His granny had always insisted that her girl Nina would never have lain with a man outside of marriage. Of course, mothers being what they were, Julian had taken that pronouncement with a grain of salt. But soon after the old earl's death, he'd received an anonymous note that had read simply: "The proof is in the emeralds."

From whom it had come, or exactly what it meant, he had no idea. But he knew about the emeralds. He'd been raised on the story, heard it nearly every day of his life until his granny's death when he was eight.

The emeralds had belonged to the Rachminovs, a sprawling gypsy clan whose chieftain had been Julian's grandfather. No one knew precisely how such an itinerant tribe had come to possess such a treasure, but Julian, knowing his relatives, had his suspicions. When Nina, his mother, had run away with her noble lover, she'd taken the emeralds with her as, presumably, her dowry. Months later Nina had returned, heavy with child. The emeralds had not returned with her, and Nina had died giving Julian life.

His granny always insisted that Lord Ridley, having gotten what he wanted from the gypsy girl, had cast off Julian's mother because he was ashamed of her low birth. But he'd kept the gems. After his granny's death Julian had learned that something of the sort was indeed the case.

An uncle had taken him to Gordon Hall. He'd been a tall, sturdy boy of eight with a shock of black hair and a sullen air that had proved most successful at disguising the mingled fear and longing that overwhelmed him at the idea of confronting the nobleman who was supposed to be his father. The uncle had tried to barter Julian and a sheaf of papers that supposedly proved the nobleman's paternity for the emeralds. The earl had agreed, extracting the emeralds from the same hidey-hole in the library from which Julian had retrieved them just a short while earlier. The exchange completed, the uncle has hastened away with the emeralds. Julian had been left at the mercy of his father.

The old man had regarded him as if he were a garden slug, rung a bell, and ordered him removed to the stables until ''something'' could be arranged. Six days later one of the grooms had taken him to London, where the "something" had turned out to be a stint as a cabin boy in the Royal Navy. That hellish voyage, complete with almost daily floggings and never-ending, violent seasickness, had lasted years. The ten-year-old Julian who had returned to England had been a far different boy from the green lad who had left.

Looking back, Julian thought that it was a near miracle he had survived. The other cabin boy on his ship, the *Sweet Anne*, had not. Perhaps it had been assumed that he himself would not survive. Julian heard long afterwards that his uncle had been found murdered not far from Gordon Hall on the very day he had left with the emeralds. The emeralds had not been on his body when it was discovered.

Somehow the gems had found their way back to Gordon Hall. While the evidence might not be enough to convict Lord Ridley in a court of law, it was enough to convict him in Julian's mind; the earl had engineered the murder of Julian's uncle, and quite possibly schemed to rid himself of the problem of Julian as well.

But here he was, some twenty-five years later, hale and hearty (except for his damaged head) while his doting father rotted in his grave. There was some justice in the world, after all.

He would not be satisfied until he had the emeralds that by rights should have been his anyway and seen for himself what proof they did or did not contain. If he had not been such a nodcock as to let the green-eyed little vixen's delicate appearance prompt him to a quite ridiculous chivalry, he'd have the emeralds at that very moment. But he'd wrapped her in his cloak to protect her from the cold, and now he was paying the price for his quixotic act: the emeralds, his emeralds, had been left behind at Gordon Hall. Graham was no doubt crowing over his brother's failure, and would certainly keep the gems closely guarded for some time to come.

But Julian meant to have them, by whatever means it took.

Tonight's debacle might slow him down, but it wouldn't stop him. Nothing short of his own death could do that.

# VIII

Two months later, Anna stood on the deck of the
*India Princess*, watching as the islands of Adam's
Bridge, an archipelago stretching from the south-
eastern coast of India to Ceylon, slid past one by one
off the port bow. Taking a deep breath, she drank
in the heady smell of the tropics. A scent like no
other, it was rich and thick, composed of exotic
flowers and spices and rotting vegetation. That, and
the ever present heat, assured her as nothing else
could have done that she was truly on her way home
again.

Funny that she, an Englishwoman by birth and
breeding, should consider a small emerald island in
a sapphire sea her home. The happiest days of her
life had been spent in its exotic environs, and her
daughter had been born there. And Paul had died
there, of course. His grave on a small knoll just beyond the Big House at Srinagar seemed to call to
her.

"Mama, will Papa be there?"

The tiny voice recalled her attention to Chelsea,
who stood beside her at the rail, her hand tightly
enfolded in Anna's. Looking down at her small
daughter, her flaxen hair braided into a single thick
plait down her back and her soft blue eyes wide and
serious as they looked up at her mother, Anna felt

51

her heart swell with fierce maternal devotion. How she loved this child! She had done the right thing, she knew, to return Chelsea to the only true home she had ever known. Even if she'd had to put her immortal soul in jeopardy to accomplish it.

"Papa's in heaven, darling. You know that." Anna tried hard to keep her voice matter-of-fact. She and Chelsea were close, but Paul had adored his silver-haired little daughter, and Chelsea in turn had thought the sun rose and set on her Papa. The hardest thing of all about Paul's death—and there had been so many hard things—had been explaining to Chelsea that her beloved Papa had gone away and was never coming back. Since that time, Chelsea had changed from a giggling, romping little girl to the preternaturally serious child she was now. She seldom smiled, and Anna had not heard her laugh since they had lowered Paul's body into the ground.

"What about Kirti?"

That question was easier to answer. Kirti had been Chelsea's ayah since the child's birth. Parting from Kirti had been a wrench for both Chelsea and Anna, but Graham had simply not included enough money for the elderly Tamil woman's passage when he had sent for Anna and Chelsea to come to Gordon Hall. Not that Anna would have been entirely easy in her mind about taking Kirti with them even if there had been available funds. Kirti was as much a part of Ceylon as the rough stone Buddha of Anuradhapu-ura—like the Buddha, which had been there for hundreds of years, it was impossible to imagine Kirti existing anyplace else. When the time had come for Chelsea to leave, Kirti had flung the end of her sari over her head and parted from her charge with loud wails of grief. Anna had no doubt that Kirti would welcome their return as a blessing from above.

"Kirti may not be at the Big House, but once she knows you're home she'll come running."

"I've missed Kirti."

"I know. I have too."

"Will—"

"All right, missy, enough of badgering your poor mum with questions. Tell me something, young lady, did you wash your face like you was told?"

The fierce voice belonged to Ruby Fisher, a handsome, buxom woman of middle years whom Anna had turned to for help when she had fled Gordon Hall the morning after the housebreaker's advent. Ruby was a former London prostitute who had had the good fortune to wed one of her clients, a tenant farmer who had been a member of Anna's father's parish. John Fisher had been a godly man as well as a hard worker, and he had resolutely brought his wife to church every Sunday. Ruby, with her penchant for garish dresses and occasional booming vulgarities, had scandalized the congregation. The vicar had stood her friend when his parishioners would have ostracized the sinner brought to live in their midst, and Ruby had never forgotten it. Fiercely loyal to those who had shown her kindness, because few people ever had, she had ever afterwards had a special fondness for the vicar—and for Anna.

Ruby's attempts to pass on nuggets of worldly wisdom to his "poor motherless chick" had at times horrified and at times amused the good reverend, but it had forged a link of friendship between Anna and Ruby that never had been entirely broken. Even after Anna had wed Paul and gone to live in Ceylon, they had stayed in touch by regular, if infrequent, correspondence. Ruby was the only person Anna knew who would not be horrified by her theft of the emeralds. Indeed, Ruby was the only person Anna knew who might be able to tell her how to convert them into what she needed most: cold, hard cash. If Ruby, then several years widowed, had not been living on a minuscule income in a tiny rented room in an unsavory section of London when Anna had discovered Graham's foul intentions, Anna would have run to her long since. But such an environment would have been unsuitable in the extreme for Chelsea, and Ruby's income, which barely fed one, could not have been stretched to feed three.

Anna, a tired and hungry Chelsea in tow and the emeralds stitched securely into the hem of her cloak, had arrived on Ruby's doorstep unannounced after a harrowing two-day journey by public stage and then a hackney. After her initial surprise Ruby had greeted the pair of them with open arms. Too tired to be shy, as she usually was with strangers, Chelsea had allowed Ruby to tuck her into bed while Anna sipped a restorative cup of tea. Then, when the child was settled, Ruby sat down and listened while Anna spilled the whole of what had happened into Ruby's fascinated ear. Ruby, chuckling over the note Anna had left behind in which she had told Graham that she would sooner starve with her child in a gutter than give in to him, was not shocked by the theft; she applauded it. She was also comfortingly practical. It had taken her less than a day to dispose of the bracelet—the whole set, unique as it was, could not be sold together for fear of attracting unwanted attention, she said—through "a gent" she "knew," and she had returned with more money than Anna had dreamed the trinket could be worth. When Anna would have given her a share, Ruby had indignantly declined. What she wanted, she said, was to accompany Anna and Chelsea back to Ceylon. After all, what was there for her in England, now that her John was dead? And who would look after Anna and her daughter, babes in the woods that they were, as they traveled to that heathenish place?

Over the course of the journey, Anna had thanked her lucky stars a dozen times for Ruby's presence. The other woman's fierce manner and blunt talk accomplished miracles when it came to dealing with shipping clerks and overly free-mannered sailors, and Chelsea had grown to like her very much. Anna herself was heartened by Ruby's presence. It was a relief to have another adult to share the inevitable problems that accompanied such an undertaking as the removal of three females to such a faraway place as Ceylon.

As Anna's father had often said, the Lord moved in mysterious ways. Who would have guessed that a henna-haired former *fille de joie* would one day prove a godsend to the vicar's gently bred daughter?

"Poor little mite." Ruby's voice was low as she watched Chelsea, who had confessed all with a single guilty look and run off to wash her face. Anna smiled at Ruby. If her crimson silk dress was a trifle garish, especially when contrasted with the improbable orange of her hair, what did it matter when weighted against the priceless gift of her friendship?

"She minds you better than she minds me."

"Because I don't coddle her. You're too soft, Anna, and not only with Chelsea. With everyone. Like your da before you." Ruby stopped to fan her moisture-beaded face with a lovely scrimshaw fan, which had been presented to her with a flourish and a fusillade of compliments by one of the sailors some two weeks before. Exactly what Ruby had done to deserve it Anna wasn't sure, and feared to inquire. Ruby had always liked, and had a way with, men. Further than that Anna refused to allow herself to speculate.

"Gawd, it's hot!" Ruby leaned against the rail, plying the fan vigorously enough so that Anna, too, felt the breeze. Ruby was right: it was hot, despite the easterly wind that sent the ship scooting through the waves. Moisture dampened her own forehead and beaded on her upper lip. Her long-sleeved black mourning gown clung unpleasantly to her body. But except for Ruby's fan there was no relief to be had: below deck was even hotter than above. During her years in Ceylon Anna had thought her body had grown accustomed to the relentless heat, but perhaps it would take a while to acclimatize herself again after the chill of England.

"It'll be better in the summer. The monsoons cool things off."

"I hope so. A body could melt in this." Ruby turned, sighing, to stare at the cloudless horizon. "Cap'n Rob says we should make port before nightfall tomorrow."

"Cap'n Rob"—a very distinguished gray-haired gentleman—was another of Ruby's numerous admirers. Whether or not their acquaintance went beyond the bounds of mere flirtation, Anna did not allow herself to consider. But everyone else on board called the autocratic ship's captain Captain Marshall.

"How wonderful. I can't wait to get off this ship. It feels as if we've been traveling for months."

"Time would have passed a lot quicker if you'd looked back at some of those brawny gents who've been looking at you."

A sidelong glance accompanied this trenchant observation. Anna sighed. They'd had this discussion at least a dozen times, but Ruby obstinately refused to let it drop.

"I'm a widow, remember?" Anna said. "I've been married, had a child. I'm not interested in looking back at men."

Ruby's nose twitched disapprovingly. "It's unnatural, a pretty young thing like you not being interested in men."

"Paul's not even been in his grave a year!"

"They say if you fall off a horse, the best thing to do is get right back on."

"Marriage is not a horse!"

"Who's talking marriage? I'm talking about letting yourself enjoy life a little. Have a little fun. And men are the best way I know to have fun."

"You're shameless, Ruby." A smile flickered on Anna's mouth.

Ruby shook her head. "Not shameless. Honest. Come now, confess: you can't tell me that not one of these gents makes you wonder what it would be like to have him put his arms around you, kiss you. . . ."

"Ruby!" Despite Anna's half-scandalized protest, Ruby's words summoned up an all-too-vivid, unwelcome image that had been plaguing her dreams for weeks: the swooping of the housebreaker's darkly handsome head, the claiming of her lips with his, his hands on her breast and hips. . . . With an almost physical effort she shook the pesky memory off. "I'll say it again: I am not, for the time being at least, one bit interested in men!"

Ruby opened her mouth to reply, only to be interrupted by the reappearance of a small figure walking sedately toward them.

"I washed my face."

Chelsea was back, her face scrubbed and glowing. Anna, thankful to be saved further discussion of the subject of men, smiled down at her. So did Ruby.

"You certainly did a good job." Anna ran a finger down her small daughter's cool cheek. Her hand rested briefly on the silken head. "Your nose is turning pink. You need your hat."

"Oh, Mama, I forgot!" Chelsea's obvious distress over so small a transgression made Anna wince inwardly. Although she'd always been a good, obedient child, since Paul's death she seemed terrified of displeasing her mother in any way. It worried Anna, but she didn't know quite what to do about it.

"It doesn't matter, chicken. We'll simply go along to the cabin and get it."

"How about if you and me go on up to the quarterdeck and see what Cap'n Rob's doing?" Ruby intervened, seeing the pain behind Anna's careful smile. "They've got a canopy rigged up there so you won't need to bother with a hat. Who knows, he might even let you steer the ship. Would you like that?"

"Do you think he really would?" Chelsea's eyes

widened at the distraction. Anna smiled gratefully at Ruby over her daughter's head.

"There's only one way to find out." Ruby, winking at Anna, took Chelsea's small hand in hers and started off with her along the deck. "Mind you don't run us aground, now."

"How could I? There's no land for ever so far." Chelsea disappeared with Ruby in the direction of the quarterdeck.

As Captain Marshall had foretold, the *India Princess* dropped anchor at Colombo, Ceylon's major trading center, before sunset the next day. Theirs was just one of many ships of varying sizes and descriptions that were disgorging passengers or taking on tea or cinnamon, the island's two major cash crops. The entire expanse of the rickety wooden pier teemed with activity. Small boys darted everywhere, begging from the new arrivals and stealing what they could not beg. Coolies in their funny hats trotted hither and yon, bearing all manner of burdens on their backs. White-veiled women in their shapeless robes glided amongst the rough-voiced merchants and sailors who sometimes turned to stare, to the loudly expressed annoyance of the ladies' attending servants. Lower-caste women, their silky black hair unveiled, were the recipients of more than stares. Saffron-robed monks made their stately way through the massive confusion. Despite the setting sun, the heat was palpable. The ritual chanting of the Buddhists floated across the water to the ship along with the spicy smell of the incense that was indigenous to the island. Taking a deep breath of the pungent air, Anna realized for the first time that she was really, truly home.

After eight weeks spent in the close confines of the ship, she was anxious to get ashore. The forty-some-odd other passengers were equally restive, but Captain Marshall was adamant. They would not dock until high tide the next morning. Therefore

Anna and her fellow travelers had to spend one last night on the ship, looking longingly across the short expanse of the bay that separated them from the domed mosques and dagobas that dominated Colombo's skyline.

As she stood at the rail watching night descend over the city, a stabbing memory of the first time she had stood on a ship's deck overlooking Colombo came back to her. Paul had been with her then. They'd been wed only a couple of months, and his arm had been around her waist as they had stared, both entranced, at the exotic scene spread before them. Anna had been a little scared at the prospect of the strange new life that awaited them, and Paul, though he pretended to courage, had been apprehensive, too. And rightly so, as it turned out. Paul had never left Ceylon; if, on that bright September night so many years ago they had known of the tragedy that awaited them, they would have caught the next ship back to England. But, of course, they hadn't known.

Regrets served no purpose, Anna reminded herself sharply. Now it was up to her to put the pieces of her life and Chelsea's back together again.

Her chin raised defiantly, Anna turned her back on the memories and the skyline and went below.

# IX

Julian, on the other hand, spent most of the selfsame two months positively awash with regrets. No sooner had he made it safely back to his posh London town house than he'd found himself under arrest. Thinking that he was in the clear once he'd gotten beyond the reach of Graham and his henchmen, he'd taken no particular precautions to insure his safety once he reached town. After all, with the emeralds left behind at Gordon Hall, Graham was sure to be having a high old time of it crowing at Julian's failure. Without the loss of the emeralds to goad him, he would be loath to take the extreme step of bringing the authorities into what had all the earmarks of blowing up into a sensational family scandal. Or so Julian had thought. Unfortunately, in that, as in so many other things in his life, he'd been wrong.

But hindsight was always keener. He'd had no inkling of danger as he'd walked up his front steps and put his hand on the knob. Then all hell had broken loose behind him.

"That's 'im!"

"You're under arrest!"

"Watch out, 'e's said to be armed!"

"Don't ye move now, ye miscreant, or we'll be blowin' out yer brains!"

Julian had whirled at the first shout. By the last one, he was standing still as a rock, his hands lifting, palms outward, into the air. The quartet of men who had sprung like rabbits from the bushes across the street might be buffoonish, but they were also heavily armed.

"There must be some mistake," Julian began, heart sinking as he recognized his assailants as Bow Street runners. From the way they were clutching their weapons as they closed on him, it wouldn't take much more than an unexpected sneeze on his part to start them shooting.

One of the quartet snorted as they came up the steps with more caution than his unthreatening demeanor demanded.

"Aye, guv, o' course there is. Don't you be doin' nothin' stupid, now. 'Twould be a shame to get your 'andsome 'ead shot off, now wouldn't it?"

They reached him then, laid hands on him, dragged his arms behind his back. Julian didn't even try to fight. Clearly it would be futile, and just as futile to run. They had him, good and proper, curse them to hell and back. His confidence in Graham's reluctance to bring outsiders into their private quarrel had apparently been seriously misplaced.

"May I ask what you're arresting me for?" Although he was sure he already knew the answer, Julian asked anyway, wincing as they clamped cold shackles tightly around his wrists.

"Search 'im, Mick." The man who spoke was apparently the leader of the group. Another man, Mick presumably, ran his hands along Julian's body, while the first man, standing back, answered his question with a sneer. "That's right, guv, play innocent. They all do, every last one. We're arrestin' you for the theft of a certain set of emeralds, rightly the property of one Lord Ridley. I don't suppose you know nothin' about them?"

"They're not stolen," Julian protested in surprise. The only response was another snort. He frowned as the man searching him straightened with a negative shake of his head.

Good God, what was this? Graham's hatred and fury must have finally turned his brain if he had called in Bow Street on a trumped-up charge. Julian's eyes narrowed as he pondered the ramifications. Would Graham really go so far as to accuse him of stealing the emeralds when they were, in fact, once again securely in Graham's possession?

If so, Graham was more Machiavellian than Julian had dreamed.

Although if Graham had the least inkling that the proof of Julian's identity, which Julian had spent most of his life seeking, was somehow linked to the emeralds, he would personally smash the stones to dust despite their value to keep them out of his despised half brother's hands. Graham would stop at nothing to keep the name, title, and fortune that legitimacy would transfer to Julian. Nothing, Julian reminded himself grimly as he found himself being driven off to Newgate Prison, up to and including murder. His murder.

By the time Anna set eyes on Colombo, Julian had been reduced to a state as nearly inhuman as that of the other denizens of Newgate. The howls that reverberated constantly through the dank cells could as easily have come from his throat as from any of the other poor souls trapped there. He was dressed in rags, so filthy that he stank, and hungry enough to contemplate eating one of the dozens of rats with which the place was infested. If he wasn't thirsty, it was only because water trickled down the walls at a steady pace. At first he had shuddered to put his tongue to the filthy stone, but by the time a week had passed he felt no reluctance at all. He had made up his mind that whatever it took to survive, he would do.

At first he'd been convinced that Graham had the emeralds safe and had seized on his attempted appropriation of them as the means to remove Julian from his path. But he had been speedily disabused of that notion. Some three days after he had arrived, a guard had appeared at the cell door and called his name. Still an innocent to the ways of Newgate, Julian had eagerly answered the summons. Perhaps they had discovered that it was all a hideous mistake and meant to let him go. . . .

So much for innocence. He had been escorted to a tiny inner chamber where even the door was made of stone, chained face to the wall, and stripped to the waist by the simple method of having his shirt half ripped from his back.

About the time it dawned on him that they had no intention of letting him go, a voice that sent chills down his spine spoke behind him.

"So, gypsy bastard, you're finally getting the comeuppance you deserve."

Graham. Julian identified the speaker even before he slewed his head around and found him with one eye.

"Hello, brother." Despite his sinking premonition of trouble to come, his voice was mocking. Bravado was the only defense he had left.

"Don't call me that."

Graham made an abrupt gesture to someone—Julian assumed it was one of the guards, although they were out of his line of vision. A faint whistling noise warned him of what was to come; he'd heard that noise often enough on the *Sweet Anne*. The cat. He cringed before the leather bit into his back.

Even as the burning pain shot along his shoulders and sliced his flesh, he refused to cry out. Graham had always hated him; Julian would not give him the satisfaction of despising him, too.

If it killed him, he would not show weakness before the little brother who had set himself up as his mortal enemy.

"I want the emeralds back. Where are they?" There was a gloating edge to Graham's voice. How he must enjoy having the upper hand in this encounter! The last time they had met, Julian had been twenty-four and Graham twenty. They'd crossed paths in the dead of a winter's night in one of London's more notorious gaming hells. Graham had been slumming, looking for excitement with a group of the young lordlings who were his friends, and he'd found it. Julian had been running the hell and had spotted his brother at the table of a dealer who took particular delight in the fleecing of flats. It had given Julian a peculiarly painful pleasure to watch Graham lose on the turn of a single card a sum that would have kept Julian in comfort for a year. It had given him even more pleasure when Graham, in his cups and not liking to lose, had sprung roaring from his chair and flipped the table on its side.

The toughs that kept order on the premises had been on Graham instantly. Julian had let them land a few punishing blows before signaling them to stop.

"Let him go," he'd ordered quietly.

Graham's eyes had swung around to him and narrowed in recognition as the men had stepped back. His blunt-featured face, already flushed with drink, had reddened still more.

"I should have guessed I'd run into you at a place like this." Loathing had mixed with scorn in Graham's voice.

Julian laughed, although there was no mirth to the sound. "You have it wrong, brother. I should have expected to see you here. Only fools with more money than sense patronize this place."

"Are you calling me a fool, gypsy bastard?" Enraged, Graham had swung at him, and Julian had taken great satisfaction from knocking his brother down before ordering his men to throw the fool out.

Now, in Newgate, the tables were turned with a vengeance.

"I'm going to ask you one more time: where are the emeralds?"

"I haven't the least idea," Julian said truthfully.

The beating that followed was severe. Subsequent

beatings were worse. Graham was convinced that
Julian had stolen the emeralds and had managed to
hide them somewhere before being caught. He
wanted the emeralds back almost as much as he
wanted Julian dead.

Which was why Julian volunteered nothing during the frequent beatings he endured. His silence
had bought him, he guessed, perhaps an extra
month of life as Graham tried to torture the whereabouts of the gems from him. Now his time was just
about to run out. On the morrow he was to hang.

All because of a deceptively angelic-looking chit
who, he'd finally deduced, had quite obviously succeeded in stealing what he had not. How he'd like
to get his hands around her slender white neck and
squeeze!

She'd put him in quite a predicament. As he'd
thought the matter over—and he had precious little
else to do but think—it had become clear to him that,
if he didn't have the emeralds, and Graham didn't,
the little hellcat must. He was still teased by the feeling that he had seen her before, and had spent much
time running through his mental list of childish
pickpockets and thieves who'd been running loose
in London's streets as he, perhaps a decade older,
had been striving toward a more legitimate life. But
he had come up with nothing and had finally concluded that, if he had known her before, it wasn't
as a pint-sized thief.

Although a thief she certainly was. She'd been
wearing his cloak, after all, and the emeralds had
been in the pocket. In a way, Julian almost had to
admire the clearheadedness that had allowed her to
come up with so ingenious a scheme. Only a very
clever little puss would realize that, by merely keeping her mouth shut, she could sneak away with a
fortune in emeralds while the foiled would-be thief
took the blame!

But telling Graham the truth would accomplish
nothing except his own demise. Julian had no doubt

that Graham, once he was convinced that Julian could not restore the emeralds to him, would see to it that his hated half brother met a quick end. With Julian in the bowels of Newgate, such an arrangement would be laughably easy. In Newgate, money talked far louder than guilt or innocence. It could buy a man an easier life—or a speedy death.

Julian suspected that Graham had already greased a few palms to get him a sentence of hanging instead of transportation, which was more usual for the crime of theft. But the sentence had backfired, in a way. It was to be carried out before Julian had revealed what he supposedly knew about the emeralds' whereabouts. Graham must be gnashing his teeth about that, although Julian guessed that the prospect of his being removed permanently from the world was some consolation to Graham. In any case, so far as Julian knew, Graham had not bothered to bribe anyone to keep him alive.

At least the thieving little vixen hadn't returned the gems to Graham. With any luck, the stones, along with whatever proof they offered, would be safe from Graham's machinations until Julian figured out a way to retrieve them.

Which, of course, was easier said than done. His situation was looking increasingly dire. He had only some six or seven hours of life left in which to elude the hangman. The proof against him, even in the absence of the emeralds, was overwhelming. The trial had been speedy, the verdict swift and harsh. At dawn he was to be hanged in Newgate's small inner courtyard; they were not even going to drag him off to Tyburn and thus offer him one final chance to escape.

Probing his psyche, Julian decided that his uppermost emotion was anger. Furious anger, which was at least an antidote to fear.

Anger because he, Julian Chase, had endured the ignominy of being arrested, the pain and humiliation of torture, and finally the dread of hanging, for a theft he had been unsuccessful in committing.

While that green-eyed little fraud of a witch had endured nothing—and gotten clean away with a fortune in emeralds with no one but himself the wiser.

A pretty trick. He had to give her that.

He'd like to give her something else, too, if he ever got the chance. Like the sole of his boot planted hard against her fancy-nancy backside.

The rattle of keys warned him that a guard was coming. Julian just had time to arrange his face into a hard, blank mask when the lock clicked and the cell door was thrust open. Immediately the dozen or so poor souls with which the cell was filled crowded away from the opening toward the rear, obscuring the corner where he sat.

This was the cell where the condemned awaited execution, and the visit of a guard at such an unusual hour brought primal terror. More than one of their number had been taken in just such a way, without warning, never to return. To hang? Who knew? Maybe to be tortured to death. Maybe . . . but speculating was worse than useless.

Julian could smell the fear of his cellmates even above the stench of their excrement, which lay in an open pile in another corner as no other facilities had been provided to deal with it. With the coming of the guard, the fear-smell intensified nauseatingly.

"Chase!"

Good God, surely they weren't going to torture him on his last night on earth? But of course they were. They wouldn't get another chance to wring his supposed knowledge from him.

Corpses keep their secrets.

"Chase! Get yer bloody arse out 'ere!"

The guard was a fine Cockney lad named Shivers, all six and a half feet and three hundred pounds of him. Julian was willing to bet that for sheer meanness, he hadn't an equal even here, on Murderers' Row.

"You gonna make me come in an' get ya, Chase?" Shivers's voice took on a taunt. Wincing inwardly while still careful to keep his face blank, Julian rose to his feet. His cellmates, relieved that the call was not for them, had already cleared a path to his corner. As he stretched to his full height—still some inches short of Shivers's—he hurt in places he hadn't known he possessed.

None of the dread he felt showed on his face.

"We both know you know better than that, don't we, Shivers?" The insolence would cost him, Julian knew, but his pride was about all he had left. He wouldn't let that be stripped from him along with everything else.

"Get out 'ere, ya bloody bugger! An' it's Mister Shivers to the likes of you!"

His movements severely hampered by the chain linking his ankles, Julian was not quite able to achieve the careless saunter for which he strove. Still, the leisureliness of his gait earned him a clout on the head from the stout staff Shivers carried.

Julian's ears rang, but he didn't even wince. By this time, he thought sourly, he'd grown almost accustomed to skull-splitting blows on the head.

"You deserve 'angin', you do, and drawin' and quarterin', too! I jest wish . . . ah, weel. Some things a body's got to do to live." With this obscure speech, Shivers relocked the cell door and turned to prod Julian along the narrow corridor. From either side came the catcalls and jeers of desperate men. None wasted a word of sympathy on Julian. Instead of promoting camaraderie among the prisoners, the brutality of life in Newgate turned them into little better than beasts. If they couldn't reach the guards, they were more than willing to attack each other, physically or verbally.

Wherever they were going, it was someplace Julian had never been. The hellhole where they usually tormented him was in the opposite direction.

Surely they had not decided to go ahead and hang him tonight. . . .

Fear made his mouth go dry, but he allowed no sign of it to show in his face or bearing.

Shivers taunted him, and Julian responded in kind, earning another clout on the ear as he shuffled ahead of the guard. Once, he stumbled on the uneven stone floor, only to be jerked to his feet by a hand in his collar. The ragged cloth ripped in half down the back. Shivers laughed. Julian felt an almost irresistible urge to turn and wrap the chain linking his wrists around the guard's stocky neck.

Only the knowledge that, in his present condition at least, he was no match for Shivers stopped him.

This might be his last night of life, but while life remained to him it was sweet. To grapple with the burly guard would be nothing short of suicidal.

Shivers nudged him to the left, down a passage so dark that Julian could barely see where to put his feet. The hideous possibility that Shivers meant to murder him himself, for his own amusement, occurred to him.

Why else would they be moving down this little-used passage? Julian tensed all over, ignoring the shooting pains that wracked his muscles. At any minute he expected Shivers to put a stranglehold on his neck.

At the end of the passage was a small wooden door.

"Turn around," Shivers ordered. Julian, stiff with suspicion, turned.

Shivers knelt and in one quick movement unlocked the leg irons. Julian's heartbeat quickened. Was he to be hanged, or . . .

Then the guard removed the irons altogether and stood up to repeat the operation on the chain linking Julian's wrists.

"What . . . ?" Julian began warily as his hands were freed. His eyes never leaving Shivers, he began to rub his raw wrists.

"Keep yer bloody mouth shut. You done been bought and paid for," Shivers answered with an unpleasant curl of his lip. "Pity, too. Yours is one 'anging I woulda enjoyed."

Then, before Julian could do more than blink, Shivers unlocked the door and pushed it open.

Beyond the door, which Julian saw to his amazement was set into Newgate's formidable outer wall, lay a stinking gutter, a deserted alley—and freedom. Stars glinted in the black velvet of the sky; a chilling wind—never mind that it bore the noxious odors of slum London with it—ruffled his hair like a doxy's carcass. Almost involuntarily he looked back down the passage through which he had come. The slight upward slant of the last few yards and his memory of the darkness and dankness of the rest brought with it realization: he had just traversed one of the secret underground tunnels with which Newgate was supposed to be rife.

"Get the 'ell out o' my sight," Shivers snarled, and pushed Julian out. Before he could so much as recover his balance, the door slammed shut behind him.

" 'E gave us some bloody good advice, guv'nor. 'Ere, wrap this cloak around you and let's be away."

"Jim!" Julian whirled to see the wiry form of his groom cum valet cum henchman and friend step from one of the deep pockets of gloom at the base of the wall.

"None other." Jim threw the cloak around Julian's shoulders and secured it as though the bigger man was naught but a babe. Then he took Julian's arm, tugging him along the alley toward the only slightly less menacing-looking street that lay beyond. From the occasional glances Jim cast over his shoulder, Julian deduced that he was anxious to get the looming walls of Newgate safely behind them. Despite the surprising lack of strength in his legs, Julian stepped up his pace. He'd breathe easier, too, when they were well and truly away.

"How the hell did you manage that?" As they approached the end of the alley, Julian looked down at Jim in amazement. It was becoming increasingly clear that somehow Jim had performed the impossible: he had secured Julian's release!

"It cost us plenty, don't think it didn't. In fact, that bloke 'ad almost the last coin we 'ad in the world between us. 'E was dead set on seein' you 'ang, but 'e was a greedy bastard. What finally saved you was you weren't worth nothin' to 'im dead."

"Shivers may have been greedy, but I can't believe he'd be stupid enough to put himself in jeopardy for a few pounds. They'll miss me when they come to hang me in the morning. They're bound to suspect he had a hand in my disappearance. Not that I'll mourn his passing, but they're liable to hang him in my stead."

Jim cast Julian a sideways look as he hustled his master around the corner onto the shadowy cross street. A spluttering street lamp glowed faintly about a block farther along. All else was in deep shadow. Jim hurried him toward the lamp, ignoring the skulking figures that slunk out of their way as they passed as completely as he ignored the furtive eyes watching their progress from recessed doorways.

"Prison's rotted your brain, Julie my lad. I tell you, it's all fixed. Come the dawn, they'll be 'angin' somebody. It don't matter to them or to us who."

Julian saw it all then. Jim had bribed Shivers to let him go and hang someone else in his stead! Neat, very neat.

"Poor soul," he said of his replacement, and meant it.

"Aye, but better 'im than you, right?"

Julian barely saw the closed, darkened carriage that waited at the curb before Jim was opening the door and thrusting him inside. After climbing in behind him, Jim banged on the roof. The carriage immediately lurched into motion.

Resting back in the far corner of the seat, Julian regarded his henchman with some fascination.

"You amaze me. Half an hour ago I wouldn't have bet a groat on my chances of seeing another nightfall."

Jim grunted and settled onto the seat beside him. Julian said nothing more for a few minutes, savoring the idea that he was really, truly free. Without an abiding fear for his life to dull lesser aggravations, he was becoming slowly aware of a variety of ills. His ribs, where they had been nearly stove in with a cudgel by Shivers and his cohorts, ached abominably. His wrists and ankles, rubbed raw by the shackles, stung. His head pounded, his empty stomach growled, his parched throat burned. But he was alive—and free!

"It'll be good to get home." Julian allowed his head to drop back against the seat. Christ, he was tired! In the aftermath of this nightmare, he firmly expected to sleep for a week.

Jim snorted. The carriage was dark inside, but by the light of a street lamp they rattled past Julian was able to see Jim's expression. The thin, weathered Cockney face was twisted into a rueful grimace.

"What is it?" Julian asked with resignation. He'd seen that expression on Jim's face before.

"Well, you see, the thing of it is I 'ad to sell the 'ouse. I 'ad to sell everythin' the both of us owned, and it still weren't 'ardly enough. 'Ad to bargain 'ard with that bloody guard, I did."

"Samson?" Julian asked faintly.

Jim snorted again. " 'Ell, I never even got a chance to sell 'im. They took 'im off somewheres when they took you."

"Is anything left?"

Jim shook his head. "Not much more than'll pay for a night or two's lodging and a few decent suppers."

Julian was silent for a moment, absorbing the enormity of the loss. Not that he had been a wealthy man, but he'd earned enough from his business enterprises—some of which were legitimate and some of which weren't—to allow him to live very comfortably indeed.

As a green lad, he'd managed to accumulate a tidy nest egg by a series of increasingly risky robberies, which Jim had assured him would one day get him hanged. But Julian, no fool even then, had known enough to realize when to quit. He'd taken the proceeds from his thieving and bought a gambling hell, and with the profits of that hell he'd purchased another. Making money wasn't hard, once he'd gotten together his stake. In fact, he had discovered that he had a knack for it. Now he'd have to start over again. But at least he was alive, and that was enough for the time being.

"You could have let them hang me, and then the lot would have been yours."

Jim regarded him sharply. "Aye, and you could 'ave let me bleed to death in that gutter all them years ago, but you didn't. Just a couple of bleedin' 'earts, we are."

This reminder won a grin, though faint and rueful, from Julian. He'd met Jim a year or so after he'd escaped from the Royal Navy. Knowing that without his granny he had no place in the gypsy tribe that had always considered him an outsider because of his mixed blood, he'd made his way to London from Portsmouth, where he had jumped ship. One of his shipmates had been full of tales of London's glories, and Julian had decided that it sounded like the kind of place where a clever lad could make his own luck. In fact he had barely succeeded in keeping starvation at bay, and that in ways that he shuddered to remember. After turning his hand to everything from pickpocketing to begging, he fell in with a gang of older boys whose lay was robbing drunks. Jim had been lying in a London gutter, a great deal more than three sheets to windward, when the gang had fallen upon him, intent on lifting his purse. Drunk or no, Jim had put up a hell of a fight, which had ended when one of the lads sank a knife in his gut. Blood had spurted everywhere, Jim had fallen gasping to the street, and the rest of the lads had run for it. But Julian, victimized by another of those quixotic gestures that he had to constantly guard against, had stayed to help the flailing, swearing victim. They'd been together, one way or another, pretty much ever since.

"I'm grateful, you know."

"And so you should be. I 'ave to tell you, it was awful temptin'. Only I figured, ornery as you are, you'd probably 'aunt me. I ain't got no use for 'aunts."

Julian didn't even bother to reply to that. The truth was, he and Jim were the only family either of them had. Julian would have done as much for Jim had the situation been reversed.

"I suppose Amabel will put us up for a while." Amabel, a pretty little black-haired armful, had been Julian's *chere amie* for the six months before he was arrested. In point of fact, the house where she lived had once belonged to Julian, but she'd started crying one night, worried about her future when he would tire of her, she said, and he'd ended up signing the house over to her. Another of those quixotic gestures, he supposed, but not one that he particularly regretted.

Jim shook his head. "Ahh . . . she's took up with some other gent. Sold the 'ouse and gone off to the Continent with 'im. Didn't think to see you again, if you take my meaning."

"Money-grubbing wench," Julian said without heat. Oh, well, he'd been getting tired of Amabel anyway, though the loss of the house rankled. "What we'll do is hole up at an inn for the night and tomorrow travel down to Gordon Hall. That green-eyed little vixen'll get the surprise of her life. I'll have those emeralds out of her if I have to wring her neck."

Via a smuggled-out message—it'd cost a packet, too—Julian had managed to convey his suspicions as to what had happened to the emeralds to Jim. Jim had been charged with keeping an eye on the little witch to make sure she didn't dispose of the gems— or make a run for it. Although with Julian in gaol it had been doubtful that she would see the need. If she was smart, she'd stay put until the heat was off, then dispose of the stones at her leisure. And Julian had the idea that she was very, very smart.

"Uh, Julie."

There was something in Jim's tone that caused Julian to glance sharply at him. "What now?"

Jim, looking unhappy, fished inside the front of his shirt. After a moment he extracted something that he passed to Julian. Accepting it, Julian didn't even need to look at the hard, cool object stretched across his palm before he knew what it was: the bracelet that belonged to the emeralds.

"How did you come by this?" Julian's voice was tight.

"Well, see, she was gone by the time I got down to Gordon 'All. It was right after you tole me, but she'd 'ad a week or so, you know, and she was gone. I put out the word on 'er and the emeralds, in case she tried to sell 'em. A friend 'o mine sent word that a few days back 'e 'ad bought somethin' I might be interested in, and when I got there it was that there bracelet. 'E'd bought it from a gentry-mort, 'e said. An' I bought it from 'im."

"A lady? Pretty chit with silver-blond hair and big green eyes?"

"Actually, 'ow 'e described 'er was a red'eaded whore."

"A redheaded whore?" Julian was incredulous. By no stretch of the imagination could the chit he'd suspected be described in such terms.

"That's what Spider said. But then 'e tole me the name of the gent what sent 'er to 'im, and I checked with 'im. Seems the red'ead 'ad another gentry-mort stayin' with 'er. This one was a real looker, with real fair hair and green eyes, just like you said. And there was a little lass, too.''

"And so where is my lady Green Eyes now?'' Intent on his prey, Julian pounced on the part of the information that interested him and disregarded the rest.

"Uh . . .'' Jim rubbed his finger down the center of his nose, a habit of his when he was distressed. "You ain't gonna like this part of it.''

"So tell me.''

"Seems like the whore and the chit and the little lass sold that bracelet to get some money. The next day they was on a ship. To Ceylon.''

"Ceylon!'' For a moment Julian felt as if he'd been kicked in the stomach.

"Told you you wasn't gonna like it.''

"What about the emeralds? Did she sell the rest of them before she left?''

Jim shook his head. "I couldn't find 'ide nor 'air of the rest. And if I couldn't find 'em, they ain't in London.''

"Damn it to bloody hell!'' Julian slammed his fist into the side of the carriage. It hurt, which didn't make him feel any better. For a long moment he sat there, nursing his bruised hand and thinking furiously.

"You gotta put it outta your mind, Julie. We need to lay low for a while, get outta London. You're supposed to be bloody dead, remember? We got enough to catch a packet to France—''

"France, hell! We're going after those emeralds.''

Jim groaned and shook his head. "I just knew you was gonna say that. Can't you let those bloody things go? They've caused you nothin' but trouble already.''

Julian flicked him a look. "You don't have to come with me.''

Jim snorted. "If you go, I go. But we ain't got enough money."

Julian smiled grimly. "We'll sell the bracelet. That should bring more than enough to get us to Ceylon."

# X

Srinagar . . . verdant land. Never had the name seemed so appropriate as when Anna set eyes on the estate again after an absence of three quarters of a year. Despite the humidity, which made the air almost too thick to breathe, she jumped to her feet and removed her hat to improve the view as the ox cart in which they were riding rocked into sight of the Big House.

"Missy sit. Missy fall," the coolie driving them scolded, but Anna paid him no heed. Ruby, with an impatient "Tch-tch," pulled her down again, but Anna's eyes never left the house.

It was a large house by English standards, made to look even larger by the verandas that surrounded it on all sides. The dazzling white walls were set off by cool green shutters. When Anna and Paul had been in residence, green-striped awnings had shaded many of the windows. The awnings were missing now, and the once well-kept lawn had degenerated into a waist-high tangle of weeds. The estate had been on the market since Graham had acquired it. Anna, fearful that Graham might learn the identity of Srinagar's purchaser, had let Ruby, using her maiden name and money from the sale of the rest of the emeralds, buy the property from the broker. Ruby had then, in a private transaction that Graham could not possibly get wind of, turned the property over to Anna. The funds that were left over from the purchase would be enough to get Srinagar back on its feet again, as well as provide a small nest egg for herself and Chelsea.

"Mama, isn't anyone here?" Chelsea asked in a small voice, her hand creeping into Anna's. Anna cast a quick look down at her daughter and gave her hand a reassuring squeeze.

"How could anyone be here, since they didn't know we were coming?" Anna asked reasonably. "We'll get all the servants back soon enough, don't worry."

Chelsea said nothing more, but continued to look wide-eyed at the house. The ox cart jerked to a halt before the front door.

"Come on, chicken, we're home." Anna's tone was bracing as she jumped to the ground. After the nearly day-long journey from Colombo, it felt good to stretch her legs. When Chelsea continued to stare at the house without moving, Anna reached up to lift the child out of the cart and set her down.

"It'll be cooler inside."

Ruby made a face at Anna behind Chelsea's back. "Place is spooky," she muttered. Anna threw her a quelling look and tried not to notice how tightly Chelsea clung to her mother's hand as they entered the house.

As Anna had predicted, it was much cooler there. The long windows were built into recesses, which made the interior surprisingly dark. Dust lay inches thick over everything, and the insidious rot that was so much an enemy of all things remotely perishable in Ceylon had gotten a good start on overtaking the house and furnishings. Curtains and carpets stank of mold, and great greenish-gray mildew stains had formed in the corners of the rooms near the ceilings. To make matters worse, an army of spiders the size of Anna's fist had colonized the bedrooms. Ruby took one look and was all for heading back to Cap'n Rob and his ship, and thence to England. Anna had her work cut out for her to persuade Ruby that all these deficiencies could, in relatively short order, be corrected. Chelsea stayed close by her mother's skirts. Anna was perturbed by the child's wide-eyed silence, but she told herself that it was only natural that Chelsea be subdued under the circumstances. Once the Big House was in order and Chelsea was used to being home, the child would gradually revert to the ebullient little girl whose laughter had once echoed off these walls.

It took much effort, but over the course of the next few weeks matters at Srinagar improved out of all recognition. The morning after their arrival, Kirti appeared out of nowhere, sensing in the uncanny fashion of the Tamils that her English family was back. Kirti and Chelsea greeted each other with loud cries. Tears rolled down Kirti's plump brown cheeks as she cuddled her beloved nursling.

"Missy, missy, oh my little missy!" Kirti, her arms tight around Chelsea, rolled tear-wet eyes up to Anna. "Bless you, memsahib, for bringing her back."

"Kirti, I've missed you!" Chelsea hugged the old ayah as if she would never let her go. Anna felt her own eyes grow moist as she watched the pair. In that moment, Anna realized just how very bereft Chelsea had been. Their removal to England had coincided with the loss of everything, except for her mother, the child had loved: Papa, ayah, home. Anna was suddenly desperately glad that she was able to give back to Chelsea a little of what she had lost. All at once the theft of the emeralds did not seem nearly so reprehensible. Wasn't there a saying about the end justifying the means? Chelsea had needed to come home.

With Kirti to take charge of Chelsea, Anna was

left free to attack the worst of the neglect, with Ruby's help. Great winged insects were swept from the house along with dust and stray leaves; bedding and window hangings were aired or replaced; floors and walls and windows were scrubbed. In the mysterious way that news always managed to spread about the island—Anna had never been sure whether it was clairvoyance or something more nearly resembling jungle drums—the rest of the household staff began to drift back by ones and twos.

A week after their arrival, Raja Singha, the imperturbable magician whom Paul had always referred to with enormous understatement as their houseboy, appeared on his elephant with all his worldly goods strapped behind him. Anna had rarely been so glad to see anyone in her life. Raja Singha was the Ceylonese equivalent of an English major domo, with a touch of black magic thrown in. As if it were the most natural thing in the world for him to appear out of nowhere, he responded to Anna's joyous greeting with nothing more than a solemn nod. He then proceeded to transfer his belongings back into the mud-and-thatch hut beyond the garden that had been his home from the time Paul and Anna had first arrived in Ceylon. Within an hour of his arrival he had taken over the running of the house. In his own silent and inscrutable way Raja Singha drove the rest of the staff without mercy. As a result, the work was completed in half the time Anna had guessed it might take. It was certainly pleasant, she reflected, to be able to crawl into bed at night without having to worry about what kind of creature one's toes might encounter between the sheets.

Sleeping alone in the bedroom she and Paul had shared proved impossible. At night Anna would fall into bed, exhausted, only to lie awake while images of Paul flickered through her mind. Although she hated to admit it even to herself, a smidgen of guilt might have been part of the reason she was so afflicted. Because sometimes, in the dead of night, Paul's dear face and form grew blurry to her mind's eye. Instead she saw a darkly handsome visage with wicked midnight-blue eyes; felt the strength of a tall, muscular, overwhelmingly masculine body clamped to hers; experienced again the devastation of a bold stranger's kiss and touch. Then, to her secret mortification, her body would burn for more of the same. She would toss and turn, fighting the shameful feelings that grew stronger as time passed, refusing to allow herself to dream of a dark, impudent stranger who had dared to treat her as a woman, not a lady.

On more than one occasion, she rose from her bed before dawn and visited the solitary grave on the knoll behind the house, where she would keep a lonely vigil until the sun began to creep over the horizon. Then, like a thief in the night, she would creep back into the house.

Still the image of the housebreaker refused to be erased. At night his shade came to torment her at least as often as Paul's, pushing aside her gentle husband's smiling face with the memory of how his mouth had claimed hers, of how her flesh had grown hot under his hands. Where Paul's ghost racked her heart, the housebreaker's racked her body. Tormented and ashamed, Anna could find no surcease from the longings that plagued her. Quite disregarding her mind, her healthy young woman's flesh hungered. Try as she might, she could not drive from her dreams the way the housebreaker had made her feel. That she could fantasize so about another man, and not just any man but a stranger, a criminal, with Paul not yet a year in his grave, appalled her.

Sick with guilt, she took what steps she could to alleviate her nightly suffering. To that end she moved into one of the other bedrooms, a large sunny room overlooking the rear instead of the front lawn.

The bed was small and narrow, almost austere, designed for one, not two. The nursery was just along the hall. Anna took comfort from the knowledge that Chelsea was nearby. In this new setting, free of memories of the days and nights she had shared with her husband, Paul's shade haunted her less. But with Paul's lessening grip on her dreams, the housebreaker gained strength. He came to her almost nightly, kissing her as he had kissed her that night at Gordon Hall, his hand hard on her breast. And so, ashamed, she writhed and burned.

With Raja Singha to see to the house, Anna's only remaining worry was to find someone to oversee the growing of the tea. More from necessity than choice, Paul had always performed that function himself. His efforts had sometimes been less than successful, although Anna felt disloyal even admitting such a thing to herself. Still, Paul had been a gentleman, not a planter. When they'd arrived in Ceylon, she an eighteen-year-old bride and he scarcely older, he'd known next to nothing about the cultivation of tea plants. Over the years he'd read a great deal and learned a little, although from one cause or another Srinagar had never turned a steady profit. But now that, thanks to the emeralds, she could afford to do so, Anna was determined to hire the best overseer she could find. She meant to make a success of Srinagar this time.

To that end, about a month after their arrival, Anna sent a note to Major Dumesne asking him to please call at Srinagar as soon as possible. The Major and his wife, Margaret, were not only the undisputed social leaders of the English colony in Ceylon. Their plantation, Ramaya, was also the most prosperous on the island.

The Major came two days later. Raja Singha installed him in the front parlor, then came to find Anna. She was in the garden with Chelsea and Kirti, using pruning shears to vigorously attack the ubiquitous vines that had all but taken over her vegeta-

ble garden. Keeping good English vegetables alive
and well in the heat and humidity of Ceylon required constant hard work. Between vines and rot,
the battle was never ending.

"Memsahib, Major Dumesne has called."

Anna looked around at that. Raja Singha, in the
sarong and turban that, along with a long, collarless
shirt, made up his customary dress, stood waiting
for her impassively just beyond the garden gate. As
usual he was expressionless, but something in his
stance told her that he was perturbed.

"Is anything the matter, Raja Singha?" she asked,
feeling faintly worried. Raja Singha was not one to
allow trifles to disturb him.

He shook his head in the abrupt negative that was
so characteristic of him. But he still stood waiting for
her instead of taking himself off, so Anna divined
that he wanted her to hurry. Pulling off her garden-
ing gloves and hat, with a promise to Chelsea that
she would be back as soon as she could to play hide-
and-seek, she went inside. Raja Singha followed her.

Anna stopped only to wash her hands at the
washstand near the back door—a task with which
Raja Singha was clearly impatient—then continued
to the front parlor. Although it had been in dreadful
shape just a month before, it now looked much as it
had before Paul's death. The walls had been
scrubbed and whitewashed, the furniture and floor
polished, and the upholstery beaten to within an
inch of its life. In fact, the tall-ceilinged parlor looked
quite nice, Anna thought, entering with Raja Singha
hovering behind her. Like her bedchamber, it had
white muslin hangings that could be adjusted to
block the worst of the afternoon sun. A portrait of
Paul's mother hung in the place of honor, its soft
blues and rose picking up the colors in the carpet
and upholstery. A mahogany bookshelf filled with
Paul's beloved books took up most of the space
along one wall, and small mahogany tables glowed
with the rich patina produced by much elbow grease.

Perched on a corner of the rose brocade sofa was Ruby, resplendent in one of the bright silk dresses that not even the heat could dissuade her from wearing. Clearly Ruby had already taken the entertainment of the Major upon herself. She was leaning forward tantalizingly, offering the Major, who was smiling broadly, what Anna feared was an overabundant view of her décolletage as she handed him a cup of tea. At once Anna understood the reason for Raja Singha's agitation. The Ceylonese were a puritanical lot, and Ruby was outside their ken.

"Thank you, Raja Singha, I'll ring if I need you," Anna said quietly to her shadow. With a bow Raja Singha took himself off. At that moment Major Dumesne and Ruby became aware of Anna's presence. Major Dumesne stood up, looking a little flustered at having been caught so obviously enjoying the view. Ruby grinned unrepentantly at Anna.

"Mrs. Traverne, we're so pleased that you were able to return to us. Life had grown very dull around here without the sunshine of your presence."

"Thank you, Major." As he approached her, Anna held out her hand which he shook and then carried briefly to his lips. Really, despite his clear appreciation for Ruby, the Major was a very nice man. Anna had grown fond of him and his wife, and they had helped her immeasurably in the dreadful days after Paul's death, when she had been nearly demented with despair. "Chelsea and I are very glad to be back. I see you've met Mrs. Fisher, who was kind enough to accompany us on our journey."

"Ah—yes. How delightful that you have brought with you a rose to add to our lovely garden of English blossoms."

"A rose . . . now that's what I call a pretty compliment. You certainly have a way with words, Major," Ruby said, beaming at the Major as, following Anna's lead, he resumed his seat.

The Major laughed, then glanced rather guiltily at

Anna. She couldn't decide if the guilt was because he had laughed in her presence—her widow's weeds might make him feel that his merriment was somehow inappropriate—or because he was enjoying Ruby too much for a man with such a nice wife.

"And how is dear Margaret?" The inquiry was not meant to be pointed, although the Major's smile vanished with it. The look he gave Anna was grave.

"I'm afraid I have sad news. Margaret passed way some six months ago. As with your husband it was a fever—in three days she was gone."

"Oh, no! Oh, Major, I am so sorry! She was such a wonderful woman—I was so fond of her. How awful for you! Such a tragedy!"

Major Dumesne nodded. For a few moments he looked far older than his forty-some-odd years as lines of sorrow deepened in his face. "It has been hard on the children, of course. Gideon and Simon are at school in England, so they at least are removed from their sorrow. But Laura—she misses her mother very much. I would appreciate it if you would bring Chelsea to see her. Perhaps, given the similarity of their losses, they can console each other."

Laura was the Dumesnes' seven-year-old daughter. She and Chelsea had been fast friends since they could toddle.

"Of course I will. And you must bring her to see us. We'd be glad to have her any time. And you too, of course. I know how dreadful it is to lose one's spouse."

"That's kind of you. Perhaps, like our children, we can console each other." He smiled at Anna, and some of the lines in his face eased. "And now, let us speak of other things. I didn't mean to put such a damper on good company."

Anna regarded him with compassion. He and his wife had had a good marriage, and their three children had adored their mother. Life was horrible sometimes, she reflected. Horribly unfair.

"Would you want another cuppa, Major?"
Ruby's voice was soft with sympathy, although
Anna recognized the glint in her eye as purely feminine interest in an attractive man. And the Major
was attractive, Anna realized. With his graying fair
hair and erect military posture, he was quite
distinguished-looking. From long experience she
knew that Ruby was nothing if not an opportunist.
And with the news that the Major was a new wid-
ower, she had clearly spied a golden opportunity. It
was written all over her face.

"Thank you, I believe I will have another." The
Major accepted a refill from Ruby, smiled at her
warmly, then turned to Anna. "Was there a particular reason you wished me to call, Mrs. Traverne?"

"Oh yes, of course."

Anna outlined her problem as succinctly as she
could. Major Dumesne frowned.

"I'll tell you frankly, men such as you need do
not grow thick on the ground," the Major said
thoughtfully. "However, I'll ask around. I've heard
a rumor that the Carnegans may be going home
soon—they've been here close to seven years, you
know, and Mrs. Carnegan's health has never been
very robust. If it's true, their overseer, Hillmore, is
a sound man. He should do for you."

"That would be lovely. Thank you."

"Until you find someone, I'll be happy to come
around to keep an eye on things for you. Give your
men some idea of how to go on."

"Would you? That's very kind of you. I would
appreciate that very much."

The Major shook his head, set the cup back on the
tray, and stood up. "It's the least I can do for a
friend. And perhaps you and Chelsea will call on
Laura."

"Of course we will, just as soon as we may. Thank
you, Major."

"You're very welcome, Mrs. Traverne. And now

I must get on. It was a pleasure making your acquaintance, Mrs. Fisher.''

"Not at all." Ruby twinkled, standing. Along with
Anna she walked the Major to the door. Though it
probably wasn't obvious to one who didn't know
her well, the expression on her face was purely
predatory.

After the Major's visit, Anna began to get out
more. It began with the call to Laura Dumesne that
she had promised the Major. Laura, a sturdy, brown-
haired child who looked absurdly like her father, was
upset because her ayah was urging her to accept an
invitation to Rosellen Childers's tenth birthday
party. Laura, sniffling, insisted she did not want to
go. Anna, with her painfully acquired knowledge of
the intricacies of grief, suspected that the prospect
of enjoying herself so soon after her mother's death
was filling Laura with guilt, and guilt was the reason
for the child's refusal. But by representing how kind
it would be of Laura to accompany Chelsea on her
first such outing since her father's death, Anna
talked Laura into going, thus earning Major Dumesne's undying gratitude. One of the conditions of
the excursion was that Anna ride with the girls and
their ayahs in the carriage as they were taken to the
Childerses' from Srinagar, where Laura would have
spent the night, and then fetched back home. Of
course Mary Childers, hearing that Anna was in the
carriage, had invited her in, making much of a friend
whom she had not seen in nearly a year. Other ladies, old friends of Anna's, were present as well,
and Anna passed a pleasant afternoon renewing ac-
quaintances. By the time the children's party was
concluded, Anna had a dozen invitations pressed
upon her.

"Paul's been dead nearly a year. You can't bury
yourself with him," Mary Childers advised her
bluntly when Anna pointed out that she was still in
mourning for her husband. Although Anna refused
to leave off her blacks, she did agree to attend a few

of the smaller supper parties. And she found that
company did tend to help her forget her grief.

As her social life picked up, Anna found herself
growing happier. It was not that she was forgetting
Paul—she would never forget him. It was just that
she was slowly becoming accustomed to his absence. Chelsea was adjusting, too, although she was
still far from the happy little girl she had been before
her father's death.

One steamy afternoon some two months after
their arrival, Anna decided to tackle the accumula-
tion of junk in the attic. It was a mistake, she acknowledged as she sank back on her heels, wiping
perspiration from her brow with a grimy hand. Although summer, with its cooling winds, was almost
upon them, up under the eaves the air was so hot
and thick as to be almost visible. She'd sorted
through only two trunks of old papers, and already
she was feeling as though she needed to lie down.

"Memsahib, a gentleman has called."

Raja Singha, who always moved as silently as a
ghost, stood at the top of the attic stairs, watching
her impassively. Anna started a little at the sound
of his voice, looked around, and then smiled.

"Major Dumesne?" The Major—whom she now
called Charles—had become a frequent caller. Under
the pretext of overseeing the cultivation of her fields,
he took dinner with them two or three nights a
week. Anna welcomed his visits. He had become a
good friend, and, although he had never said anything, his actions gave her the impression that one
day he might like to be a great deal more. But there
was no urgency to his courting, if courting it was,
and Anna was content to let things develop as they
might.

"No, memsahib. Another gentleman. He did not
give his name."

"Oh?" Anna considered, then realized that her
caller was likely the overseer—Hillmore, she thought
his name was—that Charles had told her about. The

Carnegans were leaving within the next two weeks,
and Charles had mentioned that their overseer
would be coming over to talk to her before they left.

"I'll be right down," she promised, and with a
bow Raja Singha left.

Anna stopped by her room for the few minutes
needed to wash her face and hands and pull the
kerchief from her hair. She tidied the blond mass,
repinning it so that it formed a cool roll at her neck,
but didn't take the time to change her dress. If the
man was the Carnegans' overseer, she didn't wish
to keep him waiting any longer than she must. Srinagar needed him.

When she walked into the front parlor, she was
smiling. A tall man with very broad shoulders and
straight, coarse hair the color of a raven's wing stood
with his back to her, looking out the window. He
was poorly dressed in rusty black breeches and a
bottle-green frock coat, both of which had clearly
seen better days. His black boots were dusty,
scuffed, and run down at the heels.

Anna blinked, coming to a halt just inside the door
as she surveyed her guest from the top of his black
head to his feet. Apparently the Carnegans had not
paid the man very well, certainly not the simply
enormous amount that Charles had informed her
was necessary to secure the services of a first-class
overseer. Or perhaps the man simply did not believe
in spending his blunt on clothes.

In any case, she was not hiring him for his sarto-
rial elegance. She wanted the best man for Srinagar,
and Charles had assured her that Hillmore was that.

"Mr. Hillmore?" she inquired, having regained
her poise enough to advance with a smile. "I'm Mrs.
Traverne. It's good of you to call."

The man turned to face her. Anna's breath caught
on a shocked gasp. She stopped dead, and her
hands flew to press against her mouth. Her eyes
went huge.

"Mrs. Traverne, is it?" he asked almost affably,

but she could have sworn the glint in his midnight-blue eyes was menacing. "And here I've been thinking of you all this time as my lady Green Eyes. Dare I hope that you remember me?"

# XI

✿✿✿✿✿✿✿✿✿✿✿✿✿✿✿✿

"Dear God!" She stared at him as if at an apparition. It could not be—but it was: the housebreaker. There was no mistake.

"I see that you do." There was grim satisfaction in his voice at her apparent horror. Anna could do nothing but stare as he folded his arms across his chest and cocked his head at her.

"Tell me something," he continued conversationally. "Exactly how are we related? If you really are Mrs. Traverne, that is."

"Of course I am Mrs. Traverne." Anna still felt as if she were suffocating, but she had recovered enough presence of mind to drop her hands from her mouth and straighten her spine. He was not a ghost, not an image out of her fevered dreams, but the man himself, which was even more dreadful than the possibility that she had lost her mind. "What do you want? What are you doing here?"

He smiled, a mocking smile that bared dazzling white teeth, but didn't answer her question directly. Instead, he said, "If you are indeed Mrs. Traverne, then you must be the widow of my youngest half brother. I should have guessed it during our first meeting, I suppose, but my thoughts were otherwise occupied at the time. Pray accept my condolences on your loss. Julian Chase, at your service."

92

He made a sketchy bow, his hand pressed soulfully to his heart. Anna got the feeling that she was being toyed with, rather as a cat might a mouse before pouncing, but she was too unnerved by his appearance to feel even the first spark of anger.

"What do you want?" she asked again. Her voice sounded hollow to her own ears.

His purposefully charming smile did nothing to soften the hard glint in his eyes. "I think we both know the answer to that. I've come for my emeralds."

"I don't know what you're talking about."

His mouth twisted. "Come now, Green Eyes, that card won't play. Surely you don't suppose I'd have traveled all the way from England on the off chance that you might have the gems? No. I know bloody well you have them, and I want them. You might say I insist on having them."

He moved toward her then, with the quick, fluid grace Anna remembered so well. She barely had time to register his intent before he was upon her, his hands curling around her upper arms. Anna squeaked with fright as he pulled her onto her toes and loomed over her threateningly.

"Don't play games with me," he warned her, his face so close she could see the tiny lines fanning around his eyes. "I don't like being thrown into Newgate and nearly hanged for a crime I did not, in fact, commit. I don't like traveling to a hellhole halfway around the world to retrieve what properly belongs to me. And I hate women who lie. Any one of those things is enough to make me angry. All of them together—well, let's just say I'm not in the best of tempers at this moment. I want those emeralds, and if you have the sense that I perhaps mistakenly credit you with, you'll give them to me, now. Otherwise . . ."

He let the threat trail off, but the tightening of his hands on her arms and the baring of his teeth in that travesty of a grin were quite enough. Anna, practically dangling from his hands, looked into those penetrating eyes and knew that lying was useless. The truth was going to make him furious enough.

"Please let me go."

Her voice was low. An appearance of calm was what she strove for, but she doubted she was achieving her aim. His hands burned her flesh even through the wrist-length taffeta sleeves of her mourning dress. In deference to the heat, her dress was thin, and she wore only a single petticoat beneath it. Through it she could feel the powerful muscles of his thighs brushing hers, and the sensation made her shiver. He was holding her close, too close, so close she had to tilt her head back to meet his eyes. It didn't help that the hard mouth presently scowling at her was the same mouth that had kissed her so many times in her dreams, or that her imagination had relived almost nightly the way his hand had cupped her breast that never-to-be-forgotten night at Gordon Hall. The memory of the fantasies she had had of him made her cheeks pinken and caused her to hastily drop her eyes.

"When you agree to return my emeralds."

"I don't have the emeralds."

He gave her a little shake. "Don't lie to me."

"It's true. I don't. I—sold them." She dared another look up at him. He met her eyes with a hard, ugly expression in his own.

"You sold the bracelet, true. But not the rest. That bird won't fly."

"I did. I did! I had to have the money. For Srinagar."

His eyes narrowed. "You little liar. If you'd sold the rest I'd have heard. I made inquiries all over London."

His fingers were digging into the soft flesh of her upper arms. On tiptoe as she was, the top of her head barely reached his chin. Although he was clean shaven, she could see the shadow of stubble there. With her head thrown back, her neck was starting to ache, but that was the least of her problems. Anna suddenly realized that, if he chose to harm her, she would be powerless to stop him. Julian Chase was easily twice her size, his shoulders wide enough to block her view of the rest of the room behind him. His jaw was rigid with barely controlled temper, his mouth thin with it. Those blue-black eyes glittered as they impaled hers. He looked capable of any degree of violence. The romanticized image of the dream lover who'd so shamefully haunted her nights shattered there and then. This man was hard, and cold, and dangerous.

"I sold them in Colombo." It was a desperate admission, and it had the effect for which she had both hoped and feared. It looked as though he was starting to consider the possibility that she just might be telling the truth.

"What?" He stiffened, his eyes boring into hers.

"It's the truth, I swear. At the market. I—needed the money."

"You sold the emeralds?" His voice was awful.

"Y—yes."

"You little bitch," he said, and practically threw her away from him. Anna stumbled backwards, and regained her balance by catching hold of a chair back. Casting a surreptitious look toward the partially open door beyond him, she rubbed her arms where his fingers had gripped her. Surely someone would appear at any moment to come to her aid. Or she could run. . . .

He seemed to be thinking furiously. Suddenly he glared at her. "You sold them, you say. How much did you get for them?"

"Uh . . ."

"How much?"

Anna named a sum that made his eyebrows twitch together.

"Who bought them?"

"It was at a stall in the market. A man—he dealt

in jewels. I could probably find him again—if he's
still there.''

''You'd better pray he is.'' With that growling
pronouncement he clearly accepted the possibility
that she was telling the truth. He took a step toward
her, stopped, and thrust his hands into the pockets
of his coat.

''Pack a bag. We're going to Colombo.''

''What?'' Anna's eyes widened.

''You heard me. Get moving.''

''But—I can't leave. There's Chelsea. . . .''

''Who the devil is Chelsea?''

''My daughter. She's five. And—''

''If you can't leave her, bring her.''

''No!''

His eyes sharpened on her. ''Don't tell me no
again. It may have escaped your notice, but you are
not exactly in a position to dictate terms. You are a
thief, my dear, and in England they hang thieves.
When last I set eyes on my very vindictive brother
Graham, he was foaming at the mouth over the loss
of those emeralds. You can be very sure that he
would love to find out what really happened to
them.''

That silenced Anna. Looking satisfied with the effect of his threat, he jerked his head toward the door.

''So go get your things together, your daughter,
whatever. I want to be on the road within an
hour. Oh, and bring the money. If we can find the
vendor who bought the emeralds from you—and
you'd better pray we do—I don't suppose he'll give
them back just on the strength of your sweet smile.''

There was a moment's silence. Anna stood as if
frozen to the spot, her hands clutching the chair
back, his eyes narrowed at her.

''I said get moving.''

''I don't have it.''

''What did you say?''

''I don't have the money. I spent it.'' Her confes-
sion had a desperate edge. As she had expected, the

effect as it sank in was dramatic. His jaw clenched, his mouth tightened, his eyes blazed. His pockets bulged as he clenched his fists. Then his hands were out of his pockets, and he was coming toward her, reaching for her. Anna squeaked as he dragged her from behind the chair.

"Say that one more time." His voice was ominous. His hands were gripping her upper arms again, and again Anna found herself on tiptoe. Her eyes were huge with fright as they stared into his furious face.

"I spent the money."

"You sold the emeralds and spent the money. Spent a small fortune in a matter of some two months. Do you take me for a flat?" He was practically hissing the words into her face. "There's no bloody way in hell you could have spent that much money in so short a time. Lady, you're insulting my intelligence."

"I bought Srinagar—this place. And—I had to spend most of what was left to get it back on its feet. It had been deserted for nearly a year. Vines had all but strangled the plants we had—I had to buy new seedlings and clear whole fields. Then there was the irrigation system. . . ."

His mouth curved into a snarl. He yanked her up against him, holding her imprisoned by his hands on her arms, lifting her so that her body was pressed intimately against the hard length of his.

"You stole my bloody emeralds, sold them, and spent the money on this damned white elephant of a place. Lady, if that's true, then the place is mine. And—"

"They weren't your emeralds."

Where Anna got the courage to protest she never knew. He looked like a man bent on murder, her murder. His hands were tight on her arms, his body overpoweringly strong as he loomed over her. His eyes blazed into hers. His breath was hot on her face.

He continued as if she hadn't spoken. "And you're mine. You owe me, and I'm going to take what you owe me out of your soft white hide."

"You . . ."

Before Anna could protest further, he had yanked her even tighter against him and his head had descended to trap her mouth. At the feel of those hard, hot lips against hers, Anna made a mewling sound of outrage and tried to jerk free. He released her arms to wrap his hands around her back, clamping her to him. She could feel every hard millimeter of his body as it burned into her skin. When she wouldn't open her mouth for him, one hand moved up her back to grasp the neat coil at the back of her head. He imbedded his fingers in her hair, pulling the tender roots so that she cried out. Triumphant, he thrust his tongue inside her mouth, pillaging the soft interior, his fingers holding her skull so that she couldn't break away.

His kiss was meant as punishment, and punish her it did. Because despite the violence of it, despite her shameful despair that her body could betray her so, her breasts swelled against his chest, and that terrifying quickening that she remembered from before quaked to life deep inside her belly. Her woman's body responded to the sheer male force of his. Her lips trembled beneath his, and her hand, which had been shoving futilely at his shoulders, went still.

"You want this, don't you? So do I."

Before Anna could quite register the sense of what he whispered against her mouth, he was pushing her back against the wall, kissing her again, while his hands reached down to gather her skirt in bunches and pull it up around her waist.

Not until she felt him pressing against her, his knees wedging between hers and the hard bulge of his manhood nudging hotly against the juncture of her thighs with only his breeches to separate her flesh from his, did she realize what he meant.

"No!" She shoved at his jaw, managing to free

her mouth from the devastating heat of his kiss, and tried to struggle free. But he had her backed up against the wall, and the sheer weight of his body held her in place. To Anna's horror she discovered that, with her skirt bunched up and her thighs spread, she was helpless to prevent him from thrusting himself against her naked flesh. The hard, hot friction against that most intimate part of her made her lips part and her knees go weak. The softness of her inner thighs was abraided by the scratchiness of his wool breeches, his buttons dug into her stomach, and the wall behind her hurt her spine. But what she felt was not discomfort, not fear or panic or even outrage, but a sharp, hot longing that filled her with shame.

"Stop! How dare you? Let me go!"

"Don't worry, I'll not think any the less of you when we've finished."

That snide whisper against her ear as his mouth slid along her cheek and down her throat made Anna catch her breath. What he was doing to her was only what he had done to her countless nights in her dreams, and her body quaked in hungry remembrance. But this—this was reality, and this man was not her dream lover but a dangerous stranger. They were in the front parlor at Srinagar, it was broad daylight with the door to the hall half open, and Ruby, Raja Singha, or even Chelsea could happen upon them at any moment. And he was treating her like a whore!

"Let me go!" Her voice gained strength even as his mouth slid down the front of her bodice to find her breast. She gasped, quivering, as the moist heat of his mouth burned through the thin layers of cloth to her nipple, scorching her flesh. The tiny bud hardened painfully. Anna's back arched in instinctive response—and then she felt his hands between her legs, touching her *there.*

"You're every bit as hot as I thought you'd be." It was a husky murmur.

"Get your hands off me!"

He paid her no heed. His fingers stroked her dampening flesh, leaving fire in their wake as they gently explored clefts and crevices, while she stood frozen with a dreadful mixture of humiliation and desire. Then, to her horror, she felt him fumbling with the buttons to his breeches. . . .

One part of her, the shameful, animal part, quivered and quaked and ached for him, whispering for her to acquiesce, to permit him to finish this wickedness that he had begun. Her mouth went dry and her heart pounded deafeningly. The raging fire that he had kindled inside her with his first kisses had lain not quite dormant, smoldering for months, and had needed only his touch to stoke it to white heat. Now she needed him, wanted him, to put out the conflagration. Dear Lord, her body hungered for him!

But the other part of her, the decent part, the part that had been born and bred a lady, knew sheer horror at her own depravity. That part reached out blindly, groping for the nearest solid object. It was a vase set into a niche in the wall. Anna's fingers closed around it. She raised it high, closed her eyes, and brought it crashing down on the side of his black head.

# XII

It was a crude method of securing deliverance, but it worked. He staggered a pace or so backwards, his hand going to his head. Then he straightened slowly, awfully, to his full height. Those midnight-blue eyes blinked at her with pained disbelief. Anna saw to her horror that she had cut him. A trickle of blood ran from a gash in his temple. Pulling his hand away from his head, he saw the blood on his fingers and swore furiously. Then he looked at her again. His eyes blazed murder.

"What the bloody hell did you hit me for?"

"I'm sorry."

Anna had not moved from the spot against the wall where he had held her. As he had stumbled away from her her skirt had fallen into some semblance of decency, and she stood now with both hands pressed against it as if to hold it down. She felt as though she might faint. Her legs trembled with the aftermath of what had happened.

His expression turned ugly.

"You little hypocrite, quit looking at me like that! You're no bloody virgin. You wanted it. Don't try to tell me you didn't. You wanted it that night at Gordon Hall, and you wanted it just now. You wanted it so bad that you were wet—"

"Stop it!"

Anna shuddered with shame and clapped her hands to her ears to ward off his jeering words. His lip curled at her, and then he reached into his coat to withdraw a handkerchief, which he pressed to the gash in his temple. After a moment or so, during which he glared at her balefully, a muscle twitched in the corner of his mouth.

"Stop cowering. I'm not going to touch you." The words were curt.

Pride stung, Anna dropped her hands and straightened her spine. Her chin lifted, and she regarded him steadily. If her cheeks burned with humiliation, well, she couldn't help that.

"Would you please just leave," she said steadily.

He laughed. The sound was crude, brutal. His eyes as they swept her were hostile.

"You must not have been listening to what I said earlier. Until I get those emeralds back, this hellhole of a place is mine. Understand?"

"You can't just come in here and—"

"Oh, can't I?" he interrupted. "Why not? What are you going to do to stop me? Report me to the authorities? Did no one ever warn you what happens to pretty young ladies in glass houses? Go on, Mrs. Traverne, throw your bricks at me and see how long it takes for you to find yourself in gaol for theft."

"This is our home! You can't—"

"I can do any bloody thing I want, under the circumstances. You, my dear, are a thief, and I know it. If you don't want me to tell what I know, then you're going to have to go along with whatever I decide to do. And from where I'm standing, the best course of action is to sell this place, take the money, and buy back the emeralds. Do you have any better suggestions?"

"You'll never be able to sell it. It was on the market for almost a year before I bought it. It—"

"But you've made tremendous improvements since then," he jibed, and turned toward the door.

As she stared at that broad, retreating back in growing horror, something he had said earlier suddenly
clicked into place in her mind.

"Stop!"

He did, turning back to look at her with raised
brows.

"Well?"

"How did you get out of Newgate? You said they
hang thieves in England."

His eyes narrowed at her. "None of your bloody
business."

Anna met those hard eyes with a courage born of
desperation. "While we're threatening each other, I
wonder how you would like it if the authorities in
England found out where you are? I have a notion
that they might be very interested indeed."

His eyes narrowed until they were no more than
glittering slits. "If you had a brain in that very pretty
head, you wouldn't threaten me. The way I feel right
now, it wouldn't take much to induce me to wring
your neck."

Then he turned on his heel and strode from the
room.

# XIII

Frightened, furious, Anna saw nothing for it but to trail him. His walk had an annoying swagger, and there was an irritating cockiness to the tilt of his black head that made her long to hit him again. How dare he walk into her home and behave as he had? Just who did he think he was? Then the answer popped into her head, frightening her anew: the one person on earth besides Ruby who knew that she had stolen the emeralds. He held her freedom, security, indeed her whole way of life in his hands. The thought of what would become of Chelsea, to say nothing of herself, if she were sent to gaol made her feel ill.

The path that ran from the road to curve in front of the house had recently been weeded and strewn with a thick layer of ground shells. The lawn that sloped away from the house was just scythed and lushly green. To the east and west, acres of white-blossomed tea plants flourished under the care of turbaned islanders produced without seeming effort by Raja Singha. The sweet smell of the blossoms was cloying in the steaming heat of the afternoon. Farther in the distance was the dense blue-green barrier of the jungle, looking deceptively cool. Beyond the jungle rose the towering mountain known as Adam's Peak, because it was to that mountain that

Adam supposedly had fled when cast out of the Garden of Eden. In the large bo tree at the corner of the yard a pair of leaf-monkeys played and chattered. A male peacock spread his tail and strutted for the benefit of his admiring flock of peahens along the edge of the lawn.

Anna had eyes for none of this. Her attention was all for Julian Chase. What did he mean to do?

Two broken-down horses stood at the bend of the drive, cropping halfheartedly at her grass. Julian Chase strode up to them and spoke quietly to the wizened man who held the reins. The second man's eyes narrowed as they spied the gash on his cohort's temple and the bloodstained handkerchief in his hand. Following the other man's gaze, Julian grimaced and thrust the handkerchief into his pocket. The second man said something, his expression sour. His clothes were even more ragged than the housebreaker's. As Anna watched with horror he actually spat upon her lawn.

Julian started untying the bundles fastened behind the saddle of one of the horses, dropping them one by one to the ground. Dear God, did that mean that he actually meant to stay at Srinagar? Surely her threat would make him think twice about that.

Just then she heard the scrunching sound of carriage wheels approaching. Anna caught her breath. There was no mistaking the dignified black of Charles's carriage or the upright bearing of its driver! Oh, dear Lord, however was she going to explain her unlikely visitors? What could she say?

Her heart rat-a-tatting against her chest, she waved a hand at Charles, then hurried over to Julian and his even more disreputable companion.

"Visitors?" her nemesis asked with an irritating lift of his brows.

The other man spat again, barely missing the toe of her shoe. Anna cringed.

"It's a neighbor—Major Dumesne. He's the one

who's been overseeing the fields—oh, for goodness' sake, please won't you just go?''

Her disjointed speech was interrupted by the arrival of Charles's carriage, directly opposite where she was standing and not three feet away. Anna turned toward him with a false smile of greeting. A panicked flush was washing over her in waves.

''Afternoon, Anna,'' Charles called jovially, stepping down and securing his horse's reins to the iron hitching post at the foot of the steps. Another man climbed down on the opposite side, but Anna barely noticed him. She was too busy trying to think of what to say.

''Hello, Charles,'' she croaked, looking desperately for the tall, broad form of Julian Chase behind her in hopes that he might simply have disappeared. But of course he hadn't, and was in fact unloading the last of the bundles from his horse. He flashed Anna a sideways look that she could have sworn was full of malicious amusement, then shook his head at her. From that she deduced that he had no intention of leaving. Flushing even more deeply, she turned back to Charles.

''You have visitors, I see.'' There was mild surprise in Charles's voice as he stepped toward her. ''How nice for you.''

''Yes,'' Anna managed to say, her eyes rolling to Julian Chase for a pregnant second. How on earth could she explain him? Charles caught the outflung hand that he must have thought she was extending to him and carried it to his lips.

At that Julian dropped the last of the bundles to the ground and turned to Charles, unsmiling. Charles, taking in the height and breadth of him, as well as the grim look in his eyes, released Anna's hand, looking surprised.

''Who . . . ?'' he began.

''Julian Chase,'' Julian said, introducing himself curtly. ''And you are . . .''

''Charles Dumesne,'' Charles answered, examining the other man with a degree of caution. " 'Tisn't often we get visitors—from England, is it?'' Julian gave a nod of confirmation. ''Are you planning a long stay?''

Anna, listening, felt sick to her stomach. Who knew what the devil might take it into his head to reply?

''The lady is my sister-in-law,'' Julian answered before she could hurry into speech. ''I'll be here as long as it takes to help her put her affairs in order.''

His sister-in-law! Anna's eyes widened at the untruth. Then she remembered what Graham had told her about this man's parentage. If Julian Chase's claim was valid, then he was her brother-in-law in truth!

''Very kind,'' Charles said, sounding surprised. ''Her brother-in-law, you say? Chase? I thought the family name was Traverne.''

Julian looked dangerously impatient at what he clearly considered an impudent question. Before he could say anything too rude, Anna broke in, desperate to avert any unpleasantness.

''It is, of course. Ju-Julian is really my—my half brother-in-law.'' Although the explanation was far from complete, and clearly did not satisfy Charles, he had the good manners to let the matter drop.

''Oh. Well, nice for you to have family here to look out for you. You know I never was easy about you staying here without a man in the house. That Hindu of yours—Raja something, isn't that his name?—is all very well, but still . . .''

''Raja Singha takes very good care of us,'' Anna replied stiffly.

''I'm sure he does, I'm sure he does. Still—well, that's neither here nor there now that your brother-in-law's come. I have to tell you, sir, that we dearly love your sister here in these parts. She's a ray of sunshine for us all.''

''I'm sure she is. She's a regular little ray of sunshine for me, too.'' Anna hoped she was the only one to detect the dryness in Julian's voice.

"Charles, I see you've brought a visitor of your own." Desperate to change the subject, she grasped at the first straw that came to hand. Charles looked surprised for a moment, then slapped his thigh.

"So I have! Hillmore, come meet Mrs. Traverne. And her brother-in-law, Mr. Chase."

Hillmore stepped forward, shook hands with Julian, and nodded to Anna. "Pleased to make your acquaintance, Mrs. Traverne. Mr. Chase."

"Mrs. Traverne has been in dire need of an overseer, Hillmore, as I've told you. She wants to make Srinagar the best producing tea plantation on Ceylon."

"I'd be real interested in helping you, ma'am. With the Carnegans moving home, I could use the job."

"It's yours, Mr. Hillmore, if you want it. Major Dumesne has praised you so highly to me that there's really no need for us to go through the usual formalities."

"Thank you, ma'am." Hillmore hesitated. He was a small man, wiry, fit, and brown as a berry. His pale gray eyes were faintly uncertain as they shifted to the tall, black-haired man who stood so easily at Anna's side. "Mr. Chase?"

Anna felt a sudden flare of fury so hot that she was surprised steam didn't come out of her ears. Srinagar was no concern of Julian Chase's! Despite his threats, it was hers—*hers!* But there was nothing she could do but stand there, falsely smiling, as her "brother-in-law" shrugged.

"As to permanent employment, we'll have to see. There's a question in my mind as to whether this kind of life is suitable for a woman alone, and I have business interests of my own in England. I can't stay here indefinitely. I may advise my sister to sell out and move back home."

"You know I don't want to do that," Anna protested, forcing a stiff smile at the man she was rapidly coming to hate more than any other creature on earth.

"I know you don't *want* to, but nevertheless it may come to that. But we'll see, my dear, we'll see."

Then, adding insult to injury, the blackguard wrapped a hard, muscled arm around her shoulders and gave her a brotherly squeeze!

# XIV

Minutes later, the party dispersed. As Charles took Hillmore off to look over the fields, the odious Julian volunteered casually to go along. After all, he said blandly, if he was to help his dear sister make a decision about the plantation, he should know whereof he spoke, and now was as good a time as any to begin to learn. Of course what he really wanted was to get some idea of the extent and value of the estate, and he would doubtless pump the other men to that end. There was nothing Anna could do for the moment to prevent him. Silently fuming, she was forced to smilingly wave the gentlemen on their way. Julian's disgusting friend, with another shower of spittle for her lawn and not so much as a word for her, took himself and the horses around the back of the house, presumably in search of the stable. Anna, feeling as though she might have strong hysterics at any moment, pressed a hand to her churning stomach. Then she hurried back into the house.

Ruby was already coming down the stairs. She was dressed in emerald silk, the gown far too elegant for a simple afternoon at home. But, of course, Ruby would have seen Charles's carriage and changed her dress accordingly.

"Where's Charles?" Ruby asked, halting on the bottom stair and looking around in some surprise.

"He's gone to take the new overseer to look at the fields. Oh, Ruby, the most dreadful thing has happened! Come into the parlor, quickly, before they get back!"

Ruby, agog, followed Anna only to stop short on the parlor threshold, surveying the shattered remains of what had been a prized vase.

"What 'appened to that?" she asked. Anna, unable to control a blush, shook her head. "I—uh—dropped it," she muttered, not meeting Ruby's eyes.

The older woman's eyebrows lifted, but when she would have questioned Anna further, Anna stopped her with a shushing gesture. For the first time in ages, she slid the pocket doors shut so that they might be private. Then, almost whispering, words spilling over themselves in her hurry to get them out, she told Ruby the horrible calamity that had befallen them all. The only thing she left out was Julian Chase's unforgivable assault on her person. That, and her degrading response, she could not bear to think about.

By the time Anna had finished talking, Ruby had sunk down upon the sofa, her forehead resting in her hands. Her eyes were wide.

"And so you chucked the vase at 'im. I didn't know you 'ad it in you, love."

Anna, scarlet, muttered something incomprehensible. But Ruby's thoughts had gone off on a tangent of their own.

"We'll just 'ave to get Raja Singha to shoot 'im," Ruby said.

"What?" Anna stared at her friend, unable to believe her ears.

"You 'eard me. If you've got any better ideas, you let me know."

"But that's murder!"

"So? What 'e's tryin' to do is as bad."

"I don't care. I can't just have him killed!" Although the idea was tempting, Anna thought.

"Then you'll just 'ave to make up your mind to do whatever 'e wants for the rest of your life. You'll never be rid of 'im, and never be rid of the fear that 'e'll be telling what 'e knows."

Anna paled as she considered that. Put so bluntly, the situation was even worse than she had thought.

"But maybe he'll realize that selling Srinagar isn't as easy as it sounds. There's not a big market for tea estates, as he's sure to find out. Maybe—maybe he'll just give up and go away."

"And maybe pigs can fly," Ruby said gloomily. "I still think the simplest solution would be to 'ave 'im shot."

"And what about his friend?"

" 'Im, too."

"No!" Anna put temptation firmly behind her. "Ruby, don't you dare even put such an idea in Raja Singha's head. That would be murder. I know I've done thieving, and that's a sin. But murder . . . ! Even if he does deserve it, we can't do that."

"You're too soft. I've said it before." Ruby shook her head.

"I don't care! Murder is where I draw the line! Ruby, you listen to me: this man—Julian Chase, his name is—is going to be introduced around as my brother-in-law. Until we can think of some non-violent way to get rid of him, you're to act as if he really is my brother-in-law, even in the house. If Raja Singha were to get any notion as to what the real situation is, he probably would do something like slip poison in the blackguard's tea! To say nothing of the scandal if anyone else found out that he's no relation of mine at all, never mind the rest!"

"Poison," Ruby said thoughtfully. "Now that's an idea."

"Ruby!"

"Oh, all right. For now. But what about Chelsea?"

"Oh, dear Lord, I hadn't thought that far." Anna closed her eyes for a minute, then opened them again. "I suppose we'll just have to tell her that he really is her uncle. I hate to do that, but I don't see what else to do."

"That's not what I meant. I meant she's 'appier, lately. Are you going to let 'im overset 'er again with this talk of selling?"

Anna sucked in her breath. "No. No, I can't do that. But . . ."

"We're going to 'ave to come up with a solution," Ruby warned starkly. "So you'd best be making up your mind to that." She stood up, shaking out her skirt. "I suppose there's no 'elp for them stayin' the night. I'd best go see to gettin' rooms ready. In the east wing, mind."

The east wing was a long, one-story wooden addition that some misguided previous owner had tacked on behind the neat rectangle of the original structure. Originally it had been intended as servants' quarters, but her own servants, except for Kirti, who slept in the room next to Chelsea's, preferred the airy mud-thatch huts beyond the garden. The wood siding had begun to rot long since, as wood inevitably did in the heat and damp of the island climate. The floors—also of wood, on a wooden foundation—had warped; in places ripples undulated across the floor like waves in the sea, making walking treacherous for the unwary. The furniture, cast off from the rest of the house, was in uniformly bad shape. The mattresses and upholstery had over the years acquired a musty smell that no amount of beating or airing could eradicate. All in all, Anna decided, a fitting lodging for this unwelcome guest and his companion. A reluctant smile curved Anna's mouth.

"Ruby, what would I do without you?" she asked affectionately.

"Now that's something I 'ope we'll never 'ave to find out," Ruby replied, and with a militant swing to her skirt she took herself from the room.

# XV

It was late that afternoon by the time the men returned from the fields. The necessary preparations had been made to the east wing, and Chelsea, to Anna's amazement, was positively excited about the prospect of an unknown uncle—not Uncle Graham, whom she feared, but a new uncle—come to stay with them. Raja Singha, imperturbable as usual, seemed to accept the advent of a previously unheard of relative without question, although with Raja Singha one could never be sure. Whatever he suspected or didn't suspect, his face gave nothing away.

Exhausted by the emotional strains of the day, Anna was too on edge to partake of afternoon tea. Finally, at Ruby's urging, she sank into a corner of the sofa and forced herself to swallow a few sips of the heartening brew. The pieces of the vase she had broken over Julian Chase's head had disappeared, and she could only suppose that Raja Singha, with his usual efficiency, had seen to the cleaning up. For a moment she wondered what the servant had thought, but she had too much else to worry about to dwell long on that. At the sound of booted feet tramping across the front veranda, her heart lurched. She had just lifted her cup to her mouth, and her hand shook as she registered the

men's return. Half the contents of her cup sloshed
out, spilling onto her lap.

Anna jumped to her feet with an annoyed excla-
mation, swiping with a napkin at the hot liquid,
which was spreading painfully through her skirt and
petticoat.

"Did you hurt yourself?" Julian Chase's all-too-
familiar voice inquired with false sympathy. To her
mingled fury and dismay Anna found the napkin
taken from her hand and her skirt being thoroughly
wiped. Under her dress she wore only a single petticoat, and both layers of cloth were wet. She could
feel his hand boldly stroking her thighs under the
guise of mopping up the mess. Anna, gritting her
teeth, unable to stop from blushing scarlet at the
hideous memories this action evoked, stepped
quickly away from his touch. When he grinned at
her, maliciously, she rewarded him with a glinting
look of dislike and, for the sake of their guests, a
forced smile.

"I'm fine," she said, just managing to keep her
tone marginally pleasant as she smiled at the rest of
the company in turn and shook out her skirt. "Just
a little damp. Charles, Mr. Hillmore, would you care
for some tea?"

"Thank you, I believe I would. Hillmore?"

"It's very kind of you, Mrs. Traverne. Yes, of
course."

"J-Julian?" As much as it went against her incli-
nations to speak to him at all, much less with such
loathsome familiarity, she did not dare leave the
smirking rogue out. If she did not wish to arouse
suspicion amongst her friends and neighbors until
she could manage to rid herself of him, she would
have to treat the viper with all the consideration she
would show to a near relative.

"Thank you, Anna. My, what a charming hostess
you've grown into. When I remember what a shy
little thing you were when you married Paul, I marvel."

Anna, under the guise of another false smile, sent him a look that should have killed him. His bold blue-black eyes laughed at her. Charles, glancing from one to the other, shook his head.

"It's difficult to imagine Anna being shy," he said, frowning slightly.

"Oh, she was, take my word for it. Why, at her wedding she couldn't bring herself to say so much as a single word to me."

"Julian, you're embarrassing me," Anna said through clenched teeth. "And we've left Ruby to her own devices for quite long enough. You do remember Ruby Fisher, don't you? Or has your dreadful memory betrayed you again?"

"Touché." Julian acknowledged the hit with a whisper meant for her ears alone, then turned his impenetrable gaze on Ruby. "Of course I remember you. How do you do?"

Ruby, her eyes plainly admiring as they ran over him from head to toe, merely nodded in reply. Anna felt her stomach tense again. All she needed was for Ruby to develop a yen for her unwelcome guest! Really, when problems came they came in spades!

With a gesture indicating that the gentlemen should be seated, Anna settled back on the sofa and proceeded with remarkably steady hands to pour out.

"And how did you find things, Mr. Hillmore?" she asked the overseer as she passed him his cup.

"In decent shape. Of course, considering that Major Dumesne has been keeping an eye on things for you, that's not surprising. But I do have a suggestion, which I've also presented to Mr. Chase. If you are serious about making Srinagar one of the best tea producers on the island, I would start now nurturing some really fine plants, plants capable of producing orange pekoe. I'd clear about a quarter of your fields for this, and in about three years you'll have the finest crop anywhere. After that crop is mature, we can gradually repeat the process until Srinagar produces nothing but orange pekoe. By then you'll be known as having the best tea and within reason should be able to name your own price. Of course, should you decide to sell . . ." His voice trailed off.

Anna cast a quick, venomous glance at Julian Chase. He returned her look blandly.

"I have no plans to sell," she said. "That idea is solely my brother-in-law's."

"Well, it's only natural that he should want to do what he feels is best for you," Charles said diplomatically. "Although we hope you won't be leaving us, of course."

"It's something Anna and I will have to thrash out. In the meantime, Hillmore, you may consider the position yours." Julian spoke with as much authority as if he had a right to make decisions for Srinagar. Anna regarded him with barely veiled fury. He met her eyes with a mocking smile and took a sip of tea. For a big man, he handled the delicate china cup with surprising grace, she had to admit. In fact, he seemed quite at home settled in one of the dainty French chairs that flanked the sofa. The cut she had opened up on his temple had stopped bleeding long since, of course, but still just looking at it pleased her. If she had to do it over again, she would have hit him twice as hard!

Charles finished his tea and stood up. "Thank you for the tea, but I must get home. Laura grows absurdly anxious if I am away after dark."

Anna put down her cup and stood up as well. "I quite understand, of course. Poor child. She must fear losing you, too."

"Yes." He sighed and turned to the rest of the company, all of whom had risen to their feet.

"It's been a pleasure making your acquaintance, Mr. Chase. We've all worried about Anna, but now of course with you to protect and guide her we may put our minds at rest. The entire community will rejoice in your arrival."

"How fortunate Anna is to have such concerned friends," Julian murmured, shaking the hand Charles extended to him. Anna hoped she was the only one to catch the satirical note underlying his words.

"Yes. Well, Hillmore, shall we be off?"

"Certainly, Major. I shall return and settle in within the fortnight, Mr. Chase, if that is satisfactory with you."

"Quite satisfactory," Julian answered, while Anna, ignored, fumed.

Smiling until her cheeks ached with the effort, Anna escorted her guests to the door. With much waving, she saw them off, continuing to smile until the carriage rocked down the drive. Then she turned wrathfully to the man beside her.

"I would like a word with you, if you please," she said stiffly, mindful that she could not quarrel with him in the hall. Too many ears to hear, too many eyes to see. It was a Sinhalese proverb, and for the first time Anna truly realized what it meant.

"Certainly, my dear sister-in-law. As many words as you like. But first, I need to wash up. Perhaps you could have someone show me to my room?" His eyes swept her face, then down her body before returning to meet her eyes.

"Or you could take me there yourself. Then we could . . . talk . . . in complete privacy. I quite see that that element was somewhat lacking earlier." There was no mistaking the lewd meaning beneath his words.

Anna's cheeks reddened painfully. Her teeth snapped together, and her eyes darted fearfully hither and yon to see if his words had been overheard. Fortunately, no one else stood near enough to hear.

"You are despicable," she whispered through her teeth.

"No, just caigy," he answered with a wicked glint.

Anna gasped. *Caigy* was a gutter word, but she knew from Ruby what it meant: concupiscent, turgid, hungry for sex.

"And so, my dear, are you," he continued, leaning forward confidentially.

Anna stepped back as if the heat from his body burned her. Her eyes, huge and horrified, flew to his. It was all she could do not to clap her hands to her burning cheeks.

His blue-black gaze glittered down at her as he clearly enjoyed her discomfiture. But there was something there—something hot in the backs of his eyes—that told her there was more to his words than a desire to humiliate her: he meant what he'd said.

"Memsahib?" Raja Singha, as always, seemed to materialize out of nowhere.

"This is my—my brother-in-law, of whom I told you. He—please show him to the rooms that have been prepared."

Raja Singha inclined his head. "If you will follow me, sahib."

As solemn-faced as though his obscene comments had not just seconds ago seared Anna's ears, Julian did as Raja Singha asked. But before he disappeared around the corner that led to the rear galleries, he flashed Anna a single laughing look over his shoulder.

Then it hit her: the impudent swine had been making sport of her all along!

Anna gnashed her teeth in impotent rage.

# XVI

"Cor, that is one fine-lookin' man!"

"He's rude, crude, and arrogant, and that's just for starters!" Anna, still glaring down the hall, turned her snapping eyes on Ruby, who stood just a few paces away. Ruby blinked at Anna's vehemence, and she gave an apologetic shrug. But her eyes, looking in the direction in which Julian Chase had disappeared, remained suspiciously bright.

"Oh, I'm sorry, Anna, I'm sure. I know what a weasel 'e is, but that doesn't mean my eyes can't see. Just lookin' at 'im makes my mouth water."

"Ruby!" Taking a quick look around to check for possible eavesdroppers—fortunately, except for herself and Ruby, the hall was deserted—Anna hustled the other woman back inside the parlor before continuing. "How can you even think like that?" she hissed.

"Don't tell me you didn't notice!"

"I didn't!"

"You must be blind, then! So tall, and all those muscles, and those eyes. . . ." Ruby shivered theatrically. "I'll just bet 'e's got black 'air all over 'is chest. Lots of black 'air. Oh, I could just eat 'im up, I could!"

"Ruby!" Anna practically yelped the rebuke. Unable to stop it, her mind conjured up the pictures

121

that Ruby invoked, and she felt her cheeks flush bright scarlet again.

"Oh, stop sounding so 'orrified! We're both grown women, ain't we? When a gent like that comes within a female's ken, she'd 'ave to be dead not to notice. Or so dried up that she's the next thing to it," Ruby added after a second's pause, with a meaningful glance at Anna.

"I am not all dried up," Anna retorted, stung. "I just don't go around slavering over everything in breeches. You're incorrigible, Ruby!"

"I am not," Ruby said with dignity. "Whatever that means, I am not. You can't tell me you didn't wonder, just once when you first saw 'im—before you knew what a weasel 'e was, of course—what 'e'd be like between the sheets?"

"No, of course I didn't!" Despite her best efforts, Anna was willing to bet that she was redder than Ruby's hair. Lying did not come easily to her, but there was absolutely no way she was going to reveal the devastating effect that Julian Chase had on her, to say nothing of what had passed between them at Gordon Hall—and here in the parlor earlier. Those shameful moments were dark secrets she would carry to her grave.

"Then you might as well be dead," Ruby said flatly, and shook her head at Anna in disapproval.

"Memsahib."

Anna whirled around, feeling idiotically guilty, as Raja Singha spoke behind her.

"Yes?"

"The sahib—he wishes you to come to him. Most urgently, he says. He is in the east wing, memsahib."

"Thank you, Raja Singha."

Raja Singha bowed and took himself off.

"I'll come with you," Ruby said enthusiastically.

"Just a couple of hours ago you were all for having him shot," Anna reminded her tartly.

"That was before I saw 'im. Now I think 'aving a

man around might be kind of interesting. I wonder
'ow old 'e is—not that it matters. Old enough to
know what 'e's doing, I guess, and young enough
to do it."

"Ruby!"

"Oh, quit squawkin' at me and let's go see what
'e wants."

They hadn't made it more than halfway down the
corridor when Chelsea screamed. The shrill cry echoed off the walls, and was closely followed by a
pistol shot.

For a moment both women froze. Then, ears ring-
ing, hearts pounding, they exchanged a single glance
and began to run.

Anna, slimmer and fleeter of foot, was the first to
burst into the long corridor off of which all the east
wing's chambers opened to one side. The second
door was standing wide, and through it came the
sound of a child sobbing, accompanied by an earsplitting litany of curses. Dear God, if that despicable man had harmed her child . . .

Anna burst into the bedchamber of the suite that
Ruby had allotted to Julian Chase. She saw at a
glance that it was Julian who held the still-smoking
firearm while his henchman cursed and pounded the
bed with a stout stick. A cloud of dust rose from the
bed to sparkle in the sunlight that slanted through
the long windows, and the smell of gunpowder
smoldered on the air. At first she didn't see Chelsea.
Then Julian moved behind the bed and dropped to
one knee before a tiny form huddled in the corner.
Chelsea! The child was curled into a ball, weeping
into her skirt. Even as Anna watched, stunned for
that single instant into immobility, Julian reached out
and laid a gentle hand on the little girl's bent head.

"Chelsea!" Anna gasped and flew around the end
of the bed to gather Chelsea into her arms. "Shh,
chicken, it's all right, Mama's here."

The child's small arms fastened frantically around
Anna's neck while she buried her face in her moth-

er's shoulder. As she lifted Chelsea, Anna could feel
the child trembling, and she turned furious eyes on
Julian Chase.

"What in the name of God did you do to her?"
Anna demanded fiercely, her arms tight around her
daughter. His eyes narrowed at the accusation, and
he too got to his feet. The very height and breadth
of him in such close quarters should have been disconcerting, but Anna was too ardent in defense of
her daughter to be intimidated. She faced him like
a bristling bantam hen, ready to fight.

"Jim, leave off. It's either dead or gone by now."
This aside was addressed by Julian to his cohort before he shifted his eyes back to Anna. They glinted
unpleasantly.

"And just what do you imagine I did to her,
pray?"

Jim obediently ceased both cursing and pounding
the mattress. Instead he looked accusingly from
Anna to Ruby, who had hurried to Anna's side and
was attempting, by means of pats and whispers, to
console the little girl.

"Mama, it almost got me!" Chelsea's voice, muffled by Anna's shoulder, was scarcely audible.

"What did, chicken?"

"There was a snake—a cobra, I believe. It didn't
touch her." Julian's voice was even enough, although that glint still lurked in his eyes. He ges-
tured toward one of the room's twin windows.

"And a damned great rat!" Jim interjected,
shuddering.

"A rat?" Ruby gasped, while Anna's gaze moved
in the direction Julian had indicated. On the floor
just inside the nearer of the windows lay the curving
black body of a cobra. It was headless. Remembering the shot she had heard, and the smoking pistol
that Julian had been holding when she had burst
into the room—he had since thrust it into his waist-
band—it was clear how the snake had met its demise. The curious thing was how the creature had

gotten in in the first place. The windows were closed, and it was mind-boggling to imagine the snake slithering into the room from somewhere else in the house. Besides, cobras eschewed people most of the time and generally stayed well away from the house.

"I was scared, Mama," Chelsea whimpered.

"It's all right, chicken," Anna soothed, smoothing her daughter's silky hair. She turned back to Julian. "I suppose I have to thank you," she said reluctantly.

His eyes took on a sardonic gleam as they met hers. He opened his mouth to say something in reply, but before he could speak Jim let out a hoarse shriek. Anna jumped, and Chelsea clutched her mother, her legs wrapping around Anna's waist as she tightened her stranglehold on Anna's neck.

"There 'tis!" Jim yelled as a slender brown creature darted from under the bed toward the door. Snatching up his stick, Jim bounded over the bed in pursuit, while Julian reached for his pistol.

"No, sahib!" came a sharp voice from just beyond the door. Raja Singha appeared, and to everyone but Anna's amazement the creature swarmed up his sarong to disappear beneath the tails of his shirt. Moments later a twitching black nose followed by two black eyes peeped out of Raja Singha's shirt collar. Then the creature, which looked rather like a cross between a rat and a snake, slithered out to crouch on the servant's shoulder.

"What the hell . . . ?" Julian, hand still resting on his pistol, stared.

"It's Moti," Anna explained, feeling the beginnings of a reluctant smile twitch at the corners of her mouth. Really, to see two grown men so nervous of a small, furry creature . . . ! It was a little thing, of course, but it made Julian Chase seem vulnerable, and thus more human.

"And just what," inquired Julian with an edge to his voice, "is Moti?"

"Moti is a mongoose, sahib," Raja Singha explained with unassailable dignity. "He is in the house to kill snakes. Doubtless he would have dispatched the one that threatened the little missy if the sahib had not intervened."

"Good God," said Ruby faintly. "I had no idea."

Jim and Julian looked as taken aback as Ruby sounded. With a sheepish look Jim lowered his stick, while Julian allowed the hand that had been fingering his pistol to drop.

"I will take him away and feed him, if you have no need of me, memsahib. Undoubtedly he has been badly frightened."

At Anna's nod of dismissal Raja Singha disappeared with Moti still riding on his shoulder.

"You never told me there was a rat in the 'ouse, much less snakes!" Ruby said accusingly before anyone else could speak.

"Moti is a mongoose, not a rat, and as for snakes, there usually aren't any because he keeps them away. They know he is in the house and don't come in."

"Then why," asked Julian with pointed logic, "was that snake in the room that bloody servant said you had prepared for me?"

Anna returned him cold look for cold look. It was clear that he was almost, but not quite, ready to accuse her of orchestrating the cobra's presence.

"I have no idea," she said.

"Do you mean that rat—" Ruby began.

"Mongoose," Anna corrected.

"Mongoose, then. Do you mean that the creature's been 'ere in this 'ouse ever since we arrived?"

Anna shook her head. "Moti belongs to Raja Singha, just as does Vishnu the elephant. They come when he comes and go when he goes."

Ruby gave a shiver. " 'Eathenish bloody island."

"You said a mouthful there, sister," Jim muttered, and he shuddered. Julian's mouth twisted, and he turned to walk over to where the dead snake lay. A moment later he had opened the window, which pushed outward onto the garden.

"Give me your stick, Jim," Julian directed.

"What for?" Jim still clutched the stout walking stick as though to ward off all comers.

"Just give it to me."

Jim, clearly reluctant, moved to hand the stick to Julian. Julian used it to pick up the body of the cobra and toss it gingerly out the window.

"I ain't sleepin' in this room," Jim said firmly when the remains of the head had gone the way of the body.

"Now there," Julian said, shutting the window and turning back to the room, "we are in total agreement. We'll find our own accommodations, if you don't mind."

Whether Anna minded or not was clearly immaterial. Almost before he had finished speaking, Julian had brushed by her on his way out the door. Jim, with a yelp, was right behind him.

"You ain't leavin' me, guv!"

Anna, both surprised and affronted, was left with nothing to do but hurry in their wake with Chelsea in her arms and Ruby at her heels.

# XVII

"Where do you sleep, my dear sister?" Julian asked over his shoulder, a pronounced sneer on the last word. He had found the main staircase and was taking the steps two at a time. "Somewhere a little more clean, I fancy."

"Where I sleep is no concern of yours—and just where do you think you're going, anyway? This part of the house is private—for the family!"

"I am family, remember?"

He gained the upper landing and hesitated briefly. The staircase was located in the center of the house. A long hallway stetched away to both his left and right. Just as Anna reached the landing, he chose the left side and was off again, throwing open doors as he went.

"No, you mustn't . . ." Anna's protest was in vain as he reached the large room she had once shared with Paul. She winced to see him push open the door just as he had the doors to the small sitting room and the sewing room he had just passed. For a moment he stood in the threshold, surveying the room. Behind him, Anna was prevented from seeing anything by the width of his shoulders. But she could have recited the details of that particular chamber with her eyes shut: four floor-to-ceiling windows overlooking the sumptuous garden at the front of the house, an Aubusson carpet in soft rose that she and Paul had brought from England, the tall mahogany wardrobe, the huge four-poster bed. The softly whitewashed walls glowed in the sunlight, pristine except for a single spot of mildew that had begun to form in one corner of the ceiling. Someone, Raja Singha probably, had seen that the room was set in proper order and kept that way.

"Who sleeps here?" Julian demanded sharply, looking around at Anna, who with the rest of the entourage had come to a helpless stop in the hallway.

"I—no one, n-now," she stammered. He nodded once in satisfaction.

"Then this should do very nicely. Jim, go get our things, and see if there isn't another room along here that you'd like for your own use."

"No, you can't," Anna said faintly, feeling her stomach clench. The idea of him occupying this room that she had shared with Paul, where she had lived with him and loved him and where he had died, made her physically ill. Already he had stamped the room with his despicable presence on those long nights when she had lain sleepless, mourning her husband while Julian Chase's bold image had so shamefully invaded her dreams. He could not take over this place where Paul's memory was strongest in reality, too.

Disregarding Anna's protest, Julian strolled from window to window as he admired the view.

"This is a damned sight more pleasant than the lodgings you intended us to have." He glanced over his shoulder at Anna, who had followed him inside the room, his eyes glinting a warning. "Your nose is out of joint, I know, so I'm willing to overlook the snake and the moldy rooms, but I warn you: no more tricks. If you try anything else, you'll force me to respond in a way that I guarantee you won't like."

"Tricks!" Anna gasped, indignation partially masking the pain she felt on having him intrude into this room. With a murmur of reassurance, she de-

tached Chelsea's arms from around her neck and set
the little girl on the bed. Coming up behind where
he was daring to open the doors to the wardrobe
without so much as a by-your-leave, she hissed:
"You, sir, apparently have a mistaken notion about
how things work here: I am the mistress of Srinagar,
and you are a far-from-welcome guest! Don't touch
that! Put it down!"

"That" was a hairbrush, part of a silver dressing
set that Paul had given her for their first anniversary, which Julian idly lifted from the small dressing
table set between two windows. The sight of the
dainty item in his large hand pained Anna almost
unbearably. He had no right in this room, no right
to touch her things, no right to superimpose himself
on her memories of Paul! But the hateful beast des-
ecrating her dressing table paid no attention to her
words, continuing to finger her brush and comb and
mirror and crystal scent bottle, turning them over to
read the initials engraved on the back.

Her initials, entwined with Paul's, inside a flower-
strewn heart.

"I said put that down!" Anna cried, and when he
still paid no attention, looking at himself in the elegant mirror with a smirking smile meant to taunt
her, she lost control completely and flew at him,
snatching the mirror from his hands.

In her haste she misjudged her grip. The mirror
fell to the floor, shattering. Anna stared down at the
broken glass in numb horror as her hands slowly
rose to her cheeks. Tears rose unbidden to burn behind her eyes, and she drew in a deep, shuddering
breath.

"Here, now," he said, sounding surprised, as two
great tears spilled down her cheeks.

"I hate and despise you," she whispered. Turning her back on him and the shattered mirror, she
went to stand before the window, looking blindly
out over the garden below. Not for anything in the
world would she have Chelsea see her cry.

Julian, coming up behind her, saw her shoulders shake and suddenly felt like the greatest beast in nature. The silken mass of her hair, which she wore twisted into a thick knot at the nape of her neck, glinted with silver and gold threads that gleamed in the late-afternoon sunlight streaming in around her. Her back looked very narrow and fragile in its prim black dress, her waist impossibly tiny. It came to him then how small she was, and how very young. His image of her as a bold adventuress cracked and shattered like that mirror. Watching her as she valiantly fought back tears, he felt once again that nagging sense of familiarity. Like a buzzing insect, the feeling teased him until he swatted it away in annoyance. The maddening chit was crying. There was no time for an exhaustive search of his past.

"Here, now," he said again, feeling helpless in the face of her tears. Clumsily, his hands moved to rest on her shoulders. He would have turned her into his chest for comfort, but she stiffened, shaking him off. Julian, lips tightening, allowed his hands to drop. Her averted face gave him an excellent view of her delicate profile: mouth clamped shut; lashes like fans across her pale cheeks doing nothing to stop the seeping tears; straight little nose reddened from weeping—she was lovely. Then she drew in a deep breath and opened those huge green eyes. The sheer beauty of them, wide and slightly unfocused and awash with tears, struck him like a blow. For a long moment he stared, and as he stared he grew wary: eyes like those could haunt a man for the rest of his life.

"Mama!" The little girl had approached on silent feet to tug anxiously at her mother's skirt. "Mama, are you crying?"

"No, chicken," Anna answered, her hands moving quickly to dash the tears from her eyes before they could give the lie to her words. "Of course not."

"Yes, you are too. Why did you hurt my mama?"

The child turned a mutinous little face up to glare accusingly at him. With her silvery fair hair and tiny frame, she looked ridiculously like her mother. The only difference was in the eyes: the child's were a soft sky blue. Despite her fierce defense of her mother, her lower lip trembled. Julian had never been one to go into raptures over children, but he was absurdly touched.

"I didn't hurt your mother," he explained gently, hunkering down so that he and the child were on eye level. "Something made her sad, and she started to cry."

"Oh." The little girl pondered, the wrath fading from her face. Then she nodded. "I beg your pardon, then. It must have been because she doesn't like to be in this room. My papa died in here, you know."

"Chelsea!" Anna swooped down to kneel at the child's side. Her arms came protectively around the little girl, and she glared at Julian over her daughter's head. Julian ignored her, directing his attention instead to the sweet little face regarding him so solemnly.

"I didn't know that," he said. "I'm very sorry about your papa."

"Thank you. My mama and I are sorry, too." She looked him over, her eyes very clear and direct as she examined each feature, then finally she nodded once, as if pronouncing herself satisfied. "Are you my uncle?"

For a moment Julian was startled. He had never thought of himself as anyone's uncle before. Then he said, "I suppose I must be."

"Uncle—what?"

"Julian," he answered, and smiled. "And you're Chelsea?"

She nodded. Julian held out his hand to her. "How do you do then, Chelsea," he said as she gravely shook his hand.

"Do you know my Uncle Graham? He's mean,"
Chelsea said with a confidential air.

"Chelsea!" Anna tried to pick up her daughter,
but the child squirmed and protested. Scowling at
Julian, Anna let her be, although she hovered just
behind her chick. For a moment only Julian lifted
his eyes to meet that hostile green gaze, then he
switched his attention back to the child.

"I've met him, and you're right: he is mean."

"Mama was afraid of him. When we stayed with
him at Gordon Hall, sometimes at night she would
come and hide in my room. I was afraid of him, too.
But I won't be afraid of you, I think."

"Thank you." His answer was grave, while he
tucked away her revelations to consider at his leisure. The picture he was gleaning of Anna was very
different from the one he'd painted in his mind during those weeks in Newgate and on the ship. Then
Chelsea smiled at him, and he was distracted. The
smile lit up her whole face. He saw very clearly that
one day she would be a heartbreaker like her
mother. A heartbreaker—he didn't like the thought
of that. He frowned, and abruptly stood. Chelsea
peered up at him, her smile fading into an uncertain
expression. Julian, with a supreme effort, managed
to grin down at her. Reassured, she looked less worried.

"Let's go find Kirti, shall we?" Anna asked as at
last she succeeded in picking up her daughter. "She
must be wondering where you've got to. Did you
run off from her again?"

Chelsea hung her head, answer enough.

"You mustn't do that," Anna told her sternly, her
hand stroking along her daughter's spine, deflecting
the severity of the words. "And you know it. If
you'd stayed with Kirti, you wouldn't have run into
the snake, would you?"

"I'm sorry, Mama. But I got hungry, and she went
to fix me a pudding. She was gone a long time."

"I see. And I suppose you were supposed to wait in the nursery?"

"Yes, Mama."

"Well, the next time Kirti tells you to wait for her, you wait, understand? Come on, let's go see if we can find her. She's probably back in the nursery with your pudding, looking under your bed and in your wardrobe and all around, wondering where you could have got to."

This made Chelsea's lips turn up into a tentative smile. Anna smiled back and, with a single cold look at Julian, headed for the door.

Jim hovered there, having apparently just reentered from the hall. As Anna approached him he bobbed his head and stood aside. Ruby was glaring at him, and it was apparent the two had exchanged their own hostilities while Anna had been otherwise engaged.

"I've found some other rooms further along that'll suit instead of this one. If 'tis no problem for you, missus, they'll do us just fine." The new respect in Jim's attitude surprised Anna. She regarded him warily.

"Those rooms will be fine," she said.

"You're not another uncle, are you?" Chelsea piped up.

"No, missy, I ain't. Name's Jim," he replied.

"Thank goodness. One uncle at a time is quite enough to be going with, don't you think?" Chelsea asked, causing Julian, behind them, to choke on a laugh he dared not utter, for fear of hurting the child's feelings.

Anna, back stiffening, moved on through the door. Over her shoulder the child looked back at her new relative.

"I like you, Uncle Julian," she said. "And my mama does too. Don't you, Mama?"

Anna, murmuring something unintelligible, fled.

# XVIII

It was well past midnight when the scream shattered the silence. Anna sat bolt upright in bed, needing no more than a few blinking seconds to realize what was happening. As that first shattering shriek was followed by another and another in a seemingly never-ending wave, she leaped from her bed, grabbed her wrapper from where it lay across the foot of the mattress, and flew from the room, fumbling to drag the wrapper on over her nightdress as she ran.

Chelsea was having another nightmare.

They'd come frequently right after Paul had died, frightening Anna with their intensity. At Gordon Hall they'd come less often, and since their return to Srinagar Chelsea had had none at all. Anna had hoped that they were a thing of the past as her daughter adjusted to her father's loss.

Clearly her hope had been premature.

The door to Chelsea's room was open. Kirti was already there, hovering over the child, her face anguished. An oil lamp sputtered and hissed on a table near the bed, casting an uncertain circle of illumination. By its light, Anna took in the all-too-familiar sight: Chelsea was sitting bolt upright, her arms straight down at her sides with her fists clenched and pushing against the mattress, her eyes huge and her mouth stretched wide with the screams that pealed forth.

Anna knew from grim experience that, although the child's eyes were open, she saw nothing beyond the nightmare in which she was trapped. There was no reaching her in this state; the nightmare must be allowed to run its course. Then Chelsea, exhausted, would fall back into a heavy sleep. In the morning she would have no recollection of the events of the night.

"Memsahib, it comes again!" Kirti's voice was strained.

"It's all right, Kirti. I'll deal with it," Anna said in a quiet voice, and moved to sit on the edge of the bed beside her daughter. Even as Anna reached out to smooth back the tangled skeins of the child's hair, the screams began to lessen in intensity.

"Shh, chicken. Mama's here," Anna murmured. To her surprise, Chelsea's eyes focused. She was suddenly clearly aware of Anna's presence. "I had a bad dream," she said.

"I know, darling. Do you want to talk about it?"

Chelsea buried her head in the hollow between Anna's neck and shoulder. "It was Raja Singha—he was standing over me. He was *looking* at me, Mama!"

Anna could feel her daughter trembling. "That doesn't sound so very dreadful." Her voice was deliberately light.

"It was. It was! He looked so—mean. As if he hated me." Chelsea lifted her head from Anna's shoulder and looked beseechingly at her mother. "And he said, 'Soon, little missy.'"

The quavering voice touched Anna to the heart. She gathered her daughter closer, pulled her head down to pillow on her shoulder again, and began to rock her back and forth.

"It was only a bad dream," she said soothingly. "It's all right. Go back to sleep."

"Why does Raja Singha hate me?" Chelsea was

already relaxing against Anna. Anna's arms tightened around her daughter.

"He doesn't hate you, Chelsea. He's very fond of you. Bad dreams aren't real."

"This one *seemed* real."

"They always do. Shh, now. Close your eyes." Anna brushed a kiss against Chelsea's temple.

"Sing to me, Mama. Like you used to." The little girl's voice was drowsy, her body heavy and trusting. Remembering how she used to sing Chelsea to sleep before Paul's death, Anna felt her heart clench. She hadn't done so in all the months since—how could she have let her own grief so blind her to her daughter's needs? With a catch in her throat, Anna began to hum the long-familiar strains of a lullaby. Then the words came back to her, and she sang them softly, rocking Chelsea back and forth all the while. In a short time Chelsea's even breathing told Anna that she was asleep. Carefully she eased the child down onto her pillow. Chelsea sighed and turned onto her side. Her lashes fluttered once, twice, then closed again. Instants later it was clear she was deep asleep.

"What the hell . . . ?" The deep voice behind her caused Anna to jump. Julian Chase, clad only in a pair of breeches that had, from the evidence of partially fastened buttons, been hastily pulled on, stood with one arm raised, leaning against the doorjamb as he surveyed the room. Anna got a blinding impression of bronzed muscles and black hair before she dragged her eyes away. Standing, her movements deliberately unhurried, she pulled the bed coverings over her sleeping child, then straightened.

"You'll stay with her, Kirti?" she asked the old ayah quietly.

"Of a certainty, memsahib."

Anna started to move away, then hesitated. "Kirti, no one's been in here, have they? Not Raja Singha?" The question was so ridiculous that Anna felt foolish asking it, but Chelsea had seemed so convinced.

Perhaps Raja Singha had popped in just to check on the child. Although, to Anna's knowledge, he had never done such a thing before.

"No, memsahib. No one." Kirti glanced away. When she looked back, there was a faint shadow in her almond-shaped eyes. Was it fear?

"Is anything the matter?" Anna asked sharply. The troubling expression vanished.

"What could be the matter, memsahib? You need not worry over the little missy. I will stay with her. She will not be alone."

Anna's vague suspicions were banished. She knew that Kirti loved Chelsea as her own child. The situation was exactly what it seemed. Chelsea had simply suffered another of her recurring bad dreams. In fact, it was probably a good sign that the child had awakened and been able to recall this one. Surely it meant the nightmares were losing some of their power.

"Watch over her, Kirti," Anna said softly. Dismissing the idea that Chelsea's dream had any basis in reality, she turned back toward the doorway—and Julian Chase.

"I'm sorry you were awakened," she said stiffly, doing her best to ignore his half-naked state as Julian stood aside to let her pass. "Chelsea had a nightmare."

"Good God." He took one final look at the tiny child now sleeping peacefully in her bed as Anna pulled the door shut behind her. "It sounded like someone was being murdered. Does she have them often?"

"From time to time. Since Paul died. Chelsea was very attached to her papa."

"Poor little mite." He was frowning, his brows drawn together over eyes that looked black in the shadowed hall. Only the light that spilled through the open door of the green room, which he had claimed for his own use, and the tiny fairy light at one end of the hall saved the hall from the tomblike darkness of the rest of the house.

"Yes." Anna was all too conscious of how very alone they were in the night. He was so close she could feel the heat of his body, smell his indefinable scent. As Ruby had predicted, his chest was covered with a thick mat of black hair. Above it his shoulders were broad and heavy with muscle. His upper arms bulged in clear evidence of the strength she had only been able to guess at before. His abdomen above the barely fastened breeches looked hard as a board.

In a flash Anna remembered the unspeakable things he had done to her—had it been that very afternoon?—and the wantonness of her own response. Just thinking of how he had made her feel caused her throat to go dry. Her lips parted to suck in air, her eyes traveled once more of their own volition over that mesmerizing bare chest, and it entered her mind to wonder breathlessly if he was still—how had he put it?—"caigy."

Dear Lord forgive her, *she* was!

At the realization her heart pounded, and her breath caught in her throat. She could not, would not let him sense how subject she was to the base hungers of her own body. He would take instant advantage if he knew. Already he was watching her like a beast eyeing prey. . . .

"I used to have nightmares myself," he said.

"You?" She blinked at him, so surprised that she momentarily forgot all about his disturbing state of undress.

Julian nodded. "I was a child once, you know."

"That's difficult to believe." Despite her discomfort in his presence, Anna had to smile at her mental image of Julian as a little boy. "What were they about?"

"The nightmares?" He shrugged. Anna got the impression that he was being deliberately casual about something that had once bothered him a great deal. "About being in the Royal Navy, mostly."

*"Were* you in the navy?'' she asked, suddenly fascinated.

He nodded, then grinned. "Though not by choice, you may be sure."

"Tell me about it. How old were you?"

Julian leaned a shoulder against the wall and folded his arms over his chest. "Eight when I went in. Ten when I ran away from it. In between, I was at sea for two hellish years."

"Were you impressed?" Stories of boys stolen away from their homes and forced to serve in the Royal Navy were common in England.

Julian shook his head. "Not exactly. My loving father simply handed me over."

Anna's eyes widened. "Your father—you don't mean Lord Ridley?"

"The very same. The grandmother who had raised me died, and my uncle—my mother's brother—took me to Gordon Hall. The gypsies—my mother's family were gypsies—had no use for me. They despised me because I had Anglo blood. And, of course, there were the emeralds. My uncle knew my father had them, so he thought to trade me for a fortune in jewels. The emeralds once belonged to my mother's family, you see; my father originally acquired them through her. Unfortunately for my uncle, he had no notion of just how ruthless my father could be. The old man pretended to agree, accepted me, handed over the emeralds—and then the next day my uncle's body was discovered not far from Gordon Hall. The emeralds, as we both know, somehow made their way back into the old man's possession. As for me, his unwanted embarrassment of a son—he hadn't known I existed until I showed up at Gordon Hall—I had nearly a week to imagine that I'd found a home. Then, without any warning, his lordship had me carted off to London where I—poor trusting child—was escorted aboard a ship. The servant who'd brought me to London disappeared. Then I discovered that I'd been bound over to serve as cabin boy on a Royal Navy vessel. There were two cabin boys when we left London. The other didn't live through the voyage.''

He stopped then, took in Anna's wide-eyed gaze, and grinned suddenly. "Oh, don't look so horrified. Despite a few less-than-pleasant experiences, I survived, and very handily, too.''

"But you had nightmares,'' Anna said softly.

He studied her for a moment in silence, his eyes inscrutable as they moved over her face. "Are you by any chance feeling sorry for me?'' he asked, amusement lacing his voice. "That's rather like the lamb pitying the wolf, isn't it?''

He caught her hand and carried it to his mouth before Anna knew what he was about. As he pressed his warm lips against her knuckles, Anna suddenly, vividly, became aware of how vulnerable she was. Just out of bed, she was clad only in her thin nightgown and wrapper, while Julian was positively indecent. And his mouth on her hand was sending shivers clear down to her toes.

"Frightened, little lamb?'' he asked, turning her hand over so that he could press his mouth to her palm.

For a moment longer Anna stood transfixed by the dizzying effect of his mouth. Then, recovering herself, she clenched her hand into a fist and jerked it from his hold.

He watched her mockingly, but made no further attempt to touch her.

"Good night,'' she managed to say with a modicum of dignity. But when she would have moved toward her own room, his hand came out to close around her elbow, stopping her.

"Anna. . . .''

Even that innocuous touch unsettled her. It was all she could do not to jerk her arm away.

"What is it?'' she asked breathlessly, refusing to lift her gaze higher than his black-bristled chin as she battled her shameless inner demons. Even through the layers of her wrapper and nightdress his hand seemed to burn her arm.

"In case you're worried, I wanted to set your mind at ease: I've decided against selling Srinagar."

Her gaze flew to his, her eyes widening with surprise.

"Why?" she asked.

He looked suddenly uncomfortable. The hand on her arm tightened before being removed.

"I'd not turn you and your daughter out of your home," he said, and there was a gruff undertone to the words. "You need have no fear about that."

"What about the emeralds?" It sounded too good to be true, and she was wary.

He grimaced. "I'll find some other way to get them back. And when I do, I'll leave, and you may have this benighted place to yourself."

She was silent, searching his face as she weighed his words. He looked both very handsome and overwhelmingly masculine standing over her with his head slightly bent to make his words more accessible to someone with her lack of inches. The distant light behind him cast blue-black glints in the rough disorder of his hair. His eyes gleamed at her, his skin glowed tautly bronze.

To her dismay, Anna found herself almost liking him. The sensation frightened her, and she vowed to fight it for all she was worth.

"Then I certainly hope you recover the emeralds with all speed," she said curtly, and, turning her back on him, she walked with regal dignity along the hall to her room.

With every step she took she could feel his gaze boring into her back.

# XIX

Over the next few weeks Srinagar was positively inundated with callers. Clearly Charles, or possibly Hillmore, had spread the word that Anna's brother-in-law had arrived from England. Hungry for news from home, whole families came to visit. Anna entertained them, smiling falsely while she claimed Julian as a near relation, which she supposed, if the story of his birth was true, in a convoluted way he was. It was almost impossible to imagine that he could be Paul's half brother. From his height to his coloring to his blatant masculinity, Julian was as different from Paul as it was possible to be.

The morning after Chelsea's nightmare, he had questioned her closely about her disposal of the emeralds. Anna had told him what she remembered of the vendor and his location, relieved that he didn't repeat his original demand that she accompany him to identify the purchaser. Later that day Julian had left, only to return a few days later, empty-handed. The vendor had evidently pulled up stakes and moved on.

After that he and Jim were gone much of the time, traveling to various cities both separately and together in search of the emeralds. Anna got the feeling that it was not their monetary value that

interested him, but she had made up her mind not
to question him, indeed not to allow herself to think
of him as other than a not-very-welcome house-
guest.

He had revealed a little of his past to her the night
of Chelsea's nightmare, and she had found herself
first pitying and then liking him. To learn more
about him might soften her toward him even more,
and that could be dangerous to her peace of mind.
Already she had to remind herself that he was no
gentleman, but a rogue and a thief and very likely a
womanizer as well. If her wayward body sometimes
had other notions about him, why, she ignored its
contrary urgings. She was a widow, a mother, and
a lady born and bred. She would not allow herself
to pant after Julian Chase!

Sometimes, when Julian was not off on what Anna
secretly had come to think of as his quest, he would
join her and her callers in the parlor for afternoon
tea. In his absence, of course, she was obliged to
answer questions concerning him, which could occasionally get tricky as there was little she actually
knew about him. At least, very little she could admit
to. But when he was home, the situation was, if anything, worse.

Antoinette Noack, the land-rich widow of a cinnamon nabob, was perched beside her on the sofa
one afternoon about a fortnight after Julian's appearance, taking ladylike sips of tea while she
pumped her hostess for information about the new
arrival. Across the room sat Helen Chasen with her
eighteen-year-old daughter Eleanor. Eleanor was
conversing with Charles, while Helen looked on be-
nignly. With her nut-brown curls and wide brown
eyes, Eleanor was lovely. She was also, as an only
child whose father owned a vast cinnamon plantation, extremely eligible. But suitable men were rather
thin on the ground in Ceylon. Like Mrs. Noack,
Eleanor and her mother had hastened to Srinagar to

look over Anna's brother-in-law as soon as they heard about his arrival.

It was all Anna could do not to groan as Mrs. Noack asked yet another question about Julian.

"Your dear brother is so charming—how is it that he isn't married? Or, oh dear, perhaps I've been insensitive and he's widowed, or . . ."

Anna, who'd been enduring similar intrusive inquiries for almost a quarter of an hour, swallowed the sudden urge to invent for Julian a wife and five kiddies at home in England. "My brother-in-law has had too much success with females to choose one in particular with whom to spend his life, I believe. I hesitate to say it of such a near relation, but I fear he is something of a rake." She took a sip of tea, hoping that, in her own small way, she might have thrust a spoke in Julian's wheel. No such luck, of course. Mrs. Noack's gray eyes positively sparkled at the thought.

"A rake? Surely not! Rather an extremely charming gentleman."

"How kind you are to see it that way." Anna's response verged on dryness.

"He's not much like your late husband, is he? Oh, forgive me if the topic causes you pain, but after all you've been widowed nearly a year and so surely are well on the road to recovery. Mr. Chase is some years the elder of the two, is he not? How is it that he is not Lord Ridley?"

Mrs. Noack leaned forward, greedy in her quest for information, so that the froth of lace outlining her bosom was in dire danger of being dipped in her cup of steaming tea. Her café-au-lait silk gown was far too elaborate for a mere neighborly call, but, as Anna understood perfectly well, the dress was intended as bait. And Julian was the fish it was intended to lure. Anna took a sip of her own tea, feeling mildly desperate. Her ability to prevaricate was not such that she could sustain such a conversation for long. But there was nothing for it but to answer as best she could.

"He is Paul's half brother, and the title descended through their father," she parried, hoping to imply without actually saying so that Julian was a product of an earlier marriage on the part of Paul's mother. However much she currently disliked him, it wouldn't do to pin the label of bastard on Julian. Besides, the resulting gossip would reflect badly, not just on Julian but on herself and Chelsea as well. After all, was he not living in their house as one of the family?

"How old is Mr. Chase?"

The direct question caught Anna off guard. It came as something of a shock to her to realize that she didn't know.

"Ah—he's—um—you know, it's very silly of me, but I have the most dreadful time keeping my own age straight, much less anyone else's. Julian must be—um . . ."

"I'm thirty-five," a deep voice supplied from behind her. Thankful to be rescued, Anna turned to find Julian, still in his dusty travel clothes with his hat in his hand, coming around the end of the sofa. He smiled charmingly at Mrs. Noack, who simpered and held out a hand to him.

"Mrs. Noack, this is Julian Chase. Julian, Antoinette Noack."

Julian shook hands briefly, then acknowledged the other introductions with a word and a charming smile. Finally he turned back to Anna. "That you don't know my age wounds me. Next you'll be telling me that you don't remember my birth date."

Anna smiled sourly at this sally. "Won't you sit down and join us?" If her voice lacked enthusiasm, it was, she told herself, because his clothes were filthy and she didn't like him much anyway. It certainly was not because Antoinette and Eleanor were eyeing him with as much delight as two mice might a piece of cheese.

"Thank you, I will. That is, if you ladies don't object to me in all my dirt?" A lifted eyebrow accompanied this query. Anna's silence was overridden by enthusiastic disclaimers from the others. With a single sidelong look at Anna—he was laughing at her, she was willing to swear—he pulled a chair up beside the sofa and proceeded to charm the ladies effortlessly. Anna was not sure precisely how it came about, but soon Eleanor had claimed Anna's own place on the sofa. Anna had only stood for a moment to offer more tea to Helen and Charles.

"Your brother-in-law will soon find himself legshackled if he doesn't watch out," Charles said jovially as Anna refilled his cup. Helen tapped him smartly on the arm.

"You gentlemen think that we females have nothing on our minds but marriage," she reproved him as Anna refilled her cup, too, before bowing to the inevitable and taking Eleanor's vacated seat. Then Helen turned to Anna. "Tell me, how is it that Mr. Chase is not a Traverne? I know he is Paul's brother, but I don't understand the precise nature of the relationship."

Anna felt her heart sink. She was going to have to lie; there was no help for it. And lying was something she absolutely hated to do. . . .

"Anna, will you be a sweetheart and refill my cup? Forgive me for interrupting your conversation, but my throat is positively parched." Across the room Julian lifted his cup.

"Of course." Anna got to her feet with rather more alacrity than the request called for. She was so thankful to be rescued that she could not refrain from smiling at him as she poured his tea. He grinned back at her, his eyes midnight blue and devilish. For a moment it was as if they shared a delicious secret. Then Antoinette said something to Julian, and the spell was broken. But, like his confidences the night of Chelsea's nightmare, that mo-

ment of communion touched a chord in Anna. For
that brief time it was almost as if they were friends.

Her friendly feelings for Julian dissipated rapidly
over the course of the next two weeks. The stream
of callers was never ending. Most annoying of all
were Eleanor Chasen and Antoinette Noack, who,
hot on the trail of an eligible male, called almost
every day. What really irked Anna was that Julian
was making not the slightest effort to discourage the
attentions of either of the ladies. In fact, he seemed
to enjoy watching them make fools of themselves
over him.

One afternoon, after a particularly blatant display,
the annoyance finally got the best of her.

"You're hanging out for a rich wife!" she accused
after Antoinette had taken her long-overdue leave.

"Am I?"

Julian was in the hall, having just seen the comely
caller into her carriage, when Anna, seething over
the treacly exchange she had just been forced to witness, confronted him. The look he gave her was inscrutable. Indeed, lately Anna had found *him*
inscrutable, polite but distant. The rogue who had
admitted to being caigy and accused her of the same
had vanished, to be replaced by a cool, if civil,
stranger.

Anna, as distrustful of him in this mood as she
had been when he hadn't troubled to keep his hands
off her, tried to convince herself that his changed
attitude was a gift from the gods and she should be
thankful for it. At least she was no longer in danger
of being bowled over by his charm. But her annoyance at his obvious enjoyment of Srinagar's single
lady callers was such that she could no longer keep
her tongue between her teeth.

Just why his behavior should disgruntle her so was
something she preferred not to face. She told herself
that it was only because he, whom she knew for a
thief and a fraud, was taking blatant advantage of

guests under her roof. Any other motive for her anger she flatly refused to consider.

"You should be ashamed of yourself! At least Mrs. Noack is a reasonable age, but Eleanor Chasen is only eighteen years old!"

In the face of this attack Julian's eyebrows rose, his expression unreadable as he studied Anna's indignant face. His voice had a light tone that merely fed the fire of Anna's anger.

"But Miss Chasen is very lovely, you must agree. With that curly hair and those almond eyes, to say nothing of her shape, she doesn't need to be wealthy to have a man pay attention to her. As for the fair Antoinette, far be it from me to cast aspersions on a lady's character. I will only say, and I am being so frank because you're a widow yourself, that the lady is definitely ripe for the plucking."

Anna's eyes widened at this unlooked-for frankness. Then her mouth clamped tightly shut, and she glared at him.

"There's no need to be vulgar." There was enough dignity in her voice to depress the most pretentious. Unfortunately, it seemed to be wasted on him. Those blue-black eyes smiled at her, and then his mouth followed suit. The cad wasn't even bothering to suppress his amusement!

"I'm not being vulgar, I'm being honest. The lady needs a man, and unlike some she's not ashamed to admit it. Most women who've been married and widowed, being of flesh and blood themselves, prefer a flesh-and-blood man to memories. A memory is not a satisfying thing to take to bed, as, after a year without sex, I'm sure you've discovered."

Anna's mouth fell open. "How dare you speak so to me!" she cried.

"Offended by a little plain speaking, are you?" he asked dulcetly. "Then next time perhaps you should think twice before you question my motives. Whatever my plans are, they're certainly no concern of yours—my dear little sister."

"I am not your sister," Anna said through her teeth. "Nor your sister-in-law. Even if you are Paul's half brother—which I beg leave to tell you that I strongly doubt—I refuse to acknowledge a connection with such a dyed-in-the-wool scoundrel!"

"Do you indeed, milady Green Eyes?" he returned mildly. But the despised name reminded Anna of her own misdeeds, and she felt immediately self-conscious. He took in her discomfiture with every evidence of enjoyment, then suddenly smiled down at her.

For all her dudgeon, Anna was not impervious to the sheer charm of that smile. The midnight-blue eyes held a disarming sparkle, as if inviting her to join in the joke, and his mouth twisted into a crooked grin. They were so close that he seemed to loom over her. Her neck hurt from looking up at him. His gypsy black hair was disordered, his skin swarthier than ever since its exposure to the Sinhalese sun, and his dress—shirtsleeves and breeches, without so much as a cravat—was so careless as to invite reproach. But despite all these defects, there was no denying that he was a magnetically handsome man. As soon as it appeared, Anna resolutely banished the thought, but it lodged somewhere in the back of her mind like a particularly tenacious burr.

"Why don't you relax that ramrod-stiff spine and enjoy life a little?" he asked unexpectedly, reaching around her to trail his fingers along the bone he maligned. Drawing in a quick, startled breath, Anna stepped out of reach. He made no move to come after her, but stood with hands on hips, regarding her with his head cocked to one side.

"While we're exchanging these personal observations, don't you think it's about time you threw out those hideous crow's dresses. I, for one, am sick of looking at them, and it can't do your little girl any good to be constantly reminded that her papa's dead. For God's sake put on something pretty and get on with your life.''

"My husband has been dead less than a year!"

"He's dead. You're not," Julian replied, the smile quite vanished from his face. "Hell, why didn't you just jump in the grave with him and be done with it? Actually, if you think about it, the real thing might have been preferable to the living death you've imposed on yourself all these months."

"You don't know anything about it!" Anna cried, stung. "I loved Paul—"

"Thank God I don't," he interrupted ruthlessly. "I wouldn't want to know anything about the kind of love that condemns a pretty young woman to a life as cold and barren as her husband's grave!"

Before Anna could begin to fashion a reply, he brushed past her without so much as a word of excuse or apology and headed toward the stairs.

Turning without volition, she watched him go. His hair needed trimming, she noticed absently, but his shoulders in the thin white shirt were breathtakingly wide, his hips in their black breeches narrow in comparison, his legs long and powerful, and his bottom—Anna blushed to notice such a thing—as he took the stairs two at a time was taut and muscular.

All in all, a heart-stoppingly attractive man, if a female cared for sheer raw masculinity. Fortunately, Anna didn't. She much preferred a sensitive, courtly gentleman such as Paul had been.

She did. She really did!

And no matter what Julian said, she had no intention of leaving off her mourning clothes. If Julian Chase thought she looked like a crow in the high-necked, long-sleeved dresses, then that was to the good! She didn't want him to think her pretty! She didn't want him to think about her at all.

But, a little voice whispered in her mind, was it possible that the unrelieved black really might be a constant reminder to Chelsea?

Anna shook off the possibility. She was doing the

proper—nay, the heartfelt—thing, in mourning her husband, and in mourning she would remain!

Julian Chase be hanged!

Still, for no reason other than a sudden curiosity to discover where he was going, she trailed him to the back of the house, when, some time later, she heard him walking down the hall. Stopping just inside the rear gallery, she watched him stride along the path to the fenced garden, where Chelsea greeted him with whoops of joy. Kirti, who had been tossing a ball for the child to catch, was immediately supplanted as playmate by "Uncle Julie." From Kirti's indulgent expression and Chelsea's lack of inhibition in the presence of her uncle, Anna was left to conclude that this was a familiar occurrence.

"The little one is fond of the sahib." The voice, coming out of nowhere when Anna had thought herself alone, made her jump. She looked around to discover Raja Singha behind her, thoughtfully watching the trio in the garden.

"Yes," Anna managed to say, feeling absurdly disconcerted. Raja Singha always gave the impression that he knew far more than he was supposed to. It was foolish, Anna knew, but she almost felt that he could read her mind. And just when it had been occupied with thoughts that she herself would rather not acknowledge!

"It is good for her to have a man in the Big House again." Raja Singha's eyes slid from the laughing trio to Anna.

"Yes," Anna agreed, and unbidden came the thought that the same might be said for herself. However angry Julian Chase made her, she had to admit that since he had arrived on her doorstep she had started feeling alive again.

Before she could ponder that any further, Chelsea spied her mother on the gallery.

"Mama, come and play!" she called.

"Oh, no, I . . ." Anna began, flustered at the mere idea.

"Please!" Chelsea beseeched, while Julian, the ball held negligently in his hands, grinned at her.

He thought she would refuse to play because he was there! Chin up, Anna marched down the steps and into the garden, where Chelsea greeted her with a squeal and an excited hug.

"Now we can play keep away from Mama, Uncle Julie." Chelsea danced off. Julian, laughing, obediently tossed the ball to the child.

"You're supposed to try to catch it," Chelsea reproved her mother, who'd done nothing but watch as the ball dropped into the little girl's hands.

"Sorry," Anna apologized, and after that made an effort to enter the spirit of the game.

A quarter of an hour later, laughing and winded, she collapsed in the shade of a spreading bo tree.

"Mama, don't stop!" Chelsea protested, tugging at her mother's hand in a vain attempt to get her back on her feet.

"Chicken, I need a rest," Anna said, and flopped backward so that she was lying flat to illustrate her exhaustion.

"Let your mama be." Kirti, who had watched the antics with an indulgent smile, touched Chelsea on the shoulder. "She is tired. You and I, we will make a flower chain for her. You must find the nicest blossoms, and I will help you weave it."

"Would you like that, Mama?"

Anna nodded and sat up. Chelsea darted away, Kirti following at a more sedate pace. Julian, who'd been retrieving the ball, which had ended their game by getting lost in a particularly dense section of undergrowth, came to drop down beside Anna.

"I'm glad to know you're not a coward." He was sitting cross-legged, leaning toward her with a slanting smile. His eyes were dark blue in the brightness of the afternoon. He looked very handsome and surprisingly young with his hair tousled and his shirt-sleeves rolled up to reveal bronzed and brawny forearms.

"I'm not afraid of you, *Uncle Julie.*" She made a mocking point of using Chelsea's incongruously feminine pet name for him.

He grinned, acknowledging a hit. "No, you're not, are you? You never have been. You look like you're made of spun sugar, but you've got unexpected bottom. I like that in a female."

Anna eyed him. "I'd be flattered, if I didn't suspect there was an insult in there somewhere."

He laughed. "It's a compliment, I promise." Just as Anna had earlier, he stretched out on his back, his hands linked under his head. For a moment he stared pensively up into the interlacing branches above them. Then his eyes slid back to Anna.

"Tell me something: how did you come to be married to Paul?"

Anna was surprised by the question. "We'd known each other all our lives. It seemed natural to marry."

"Weren't you rather young at the time?"

"We were eighteen. My father had just died, and the vicarage was to go to his successor. And Paul's father had decided to send him away on a Grand Tour. Paul didn't want to go."

"So he married you instead." There was a touch of dryness to Julian's voice that immediately put Anna on the defensive.

"We were very happy!"

"I'm sure you were."

Nettled, she sought to turn the tables on him. "Since we're exchanging life histories, perhaps you'd like to continue where you left off the other night. After you ran away from the navy."

"What I did next would shock you." He rolled onto his side, lifting himself up on an elbow.

"Tell me anyway."

"All right." Idly he picked a blade of grass and chewed on the end. "I was raised a gypsy, you know. My grandmother brought me up. She was a grand old woman, very protective of me. She swore to her dying day that my mother would not have lain with a man out of wedlock, which meant that my parents must have been married for me to have been conceived. Mistaken or not, as a boy I accepted her word for it. I thought that those of the tribe who called me 'Anglo bastard' meant the bastard part only in the most general terms. The gypsies despise children of mixed blood just as much as the Anglos do, and I was always being taunted about my parentage. Granny told me to be proud, that I was noble and the ones who tormented me no better than dogs. I had no idea that I was really illegitimate. You can imagine my shock when my uncle took me to Gordon Hall and I found out that, not only did my father not have any idea that I even existed, but that my mother had been his mistress, not his wife. He had a wife, and a legitimate son on whom he doted, and it was clear that he wanted only to be rid of me.''

"He was a terrible old man!" Anna said.

"He was, wasn't he?" Julian smiled at her. "Anyway, after my granny died, there was no place for me with the Rachminovs. And no place for me with my father and his family. So when I escaped the clutches of the navy, I made my way to London. Much to my dismay, I discovered that I fared almost as badly there as I had in the service of His Majesty. Except that I was free."

Glancing at her, he seemed to hesitate.

"Go on," Anna encouraged, fascinated.

He chewed on his blade of grass. "I was clever and quick with my hands, and, the most essential point of all, starving: I became a thief. At first I stole food, and then I picked pockets. I even tried my hand at rolling drunks, which, by the way, is how I met Jim. But I'd seen too much violence in the navy to have the stomach for that lay, so I switched to breaking into rich men's houses."

His eyes flickered to Anna's face, and he seemed to be trying to judge just how shocked she was. After a moment he continued. ''By day I worked as footman for a certain countess whose name I won't mention. At night I robbed her friends. Eventually the countess and I parted company, and I invested the money I had accumulated in a gambling hell. It did well, and I ended up owning half a dozen.'' He smiled wryly. ''Then my father died, I tried to retrieve the emeralds that my mother had supposedly taken from her family to serve as her dowry, and the rest you know. Sheer folly.''

There was a great deal he was leaving out, she knew. Although he had glossed over it, the pain he had felt at his father's rejection had been evident. Just as she had the night when he had first revealed some small bit of his past to her, Anna felt a flash of sorrow for the young boy he had been. It must have hurt dreadfully to feel that he had no place in the world, and no one who wanted him.

''There you go, feeling sorry for me again.'' Julian sat up and flicked her nose with the blade of grass. ''You've a soft heart, Green Eyes. It's liable to get you into trouble.''

''It must have been hard, to see Graham and Paul—your brothers—growing up with things you never had.'' Such as their father's love, Anna thought, although she didn't say it.

''Believe me, it quite broke my heart. Would you like to kiss me to make it all better?'' His tone was flippant, perhaps to conceal the fact that she had touched on a very real truth.

Then he leaned forward, eyes closed and lips puckered as if for a kiss. He looked so ridiculous that Anna had to laugh. She pulled a handful of grass and threw it at him, then jumped to her feet before he could retaliate.

''What, no kiss?'' he mourned, rising easily to stand beside her. He looked down at her, his expression teasing, but whatever he might have meant to say or do was lost as Chelsea ran up to them waving her wreath of flowers.

"For you, Mama."

"Thank you, chicken." Anna accepted the gift and placed it on her head. Chelsea giggled and caught her mother's hand. After that, all chance for any further private discourse with Julian was lost.

# XX

Several weeks previously Hillmore had taken up residence in the overseer's cottage, which had needed much restoration as it had been empty for years. At first he had met with Anna daily to discuss his plans for Srinagar and his progress in dealing with the myriad problems that arose as the remaking of the plantation got under way. But after a fortnight passed in which he failed to call on her even once, Anna finally was driven to send for him. He appeared in the dining room, hat in hand, after the family had finished eating. Julian, who hated the curry that was almost always the main portion of the evening meal, had already excused himself. Jim never took his meals with them, preferring to eat alone in his room, and Chelsea and Kirti had eaten earlier in the nursery, so only Anna and Ruby, who lingered chatting over a cup of tea, were present when Raja Singha ushered Hillmore in. He stood just inside the doorway, looking faintly uneasy, while Raja Singha announced his presence. Then, as Raja Singha disappeared, duty done, he stepped forward.

"Good evening, Mrs. Traverne. Mrs. Fisher."

"Good evening, Mr. Hillmore. Won't you join us in a cup of tea?" Anna smiled at the overseer, who looked only slightly less uncomfortable than before as he shook his head.

"Thank you, ma'am, but no."

The reason for his unease was simple, Anna knew: Ceylon was a class-conscious society. The Hindus, the Muslims, the Tamils, even the Veddahs, all had their own rules about caste, which were strictly adhered to. The English community, while not as rigid as the natives, nevertheless drew invisible lines among such of their countrymen as overseers, governesses, tutors, and the gentry. Hillmore might take a cup of tea in the parlor on the occasion of his first visit to Srinagar, but to sit down at table with the lady of the house was too familiar. Anna, understanding, stood up.

"Excuse me, Ruby."

"Don't mind me. I'll just finish off my tea, then go along upstairs. That weasel Jim bet me a monkey 'e could beat me at whist." Ruby smiled wickedly. "I mean to take 'im up on it. A little extra blunt never comes amiss, after all."

"Don't fleece him too badly," Anna teased, trying to ignore the little voice that whispered that Ruby, like Chelsea, whom Julian had apparently completely enslaved, was going over to the enemy. And this despite all Ruby's protestations of dislike for the intruders in their midst! She and Jim bickered like children, but Anna had noticed that she spent more than a few of her evenings playing with Julian's henchman at games of chance. Actually, to be fair, Anna supposed Jim and Ruby had a great deal in common, seeing that they were both Cockney born and bred, and wise in the ways of London's streets in a fashion that Anna could only guess at. Of course it was natural that Ruby, who was in the awkward position of being a step above servant class but not quite one of them either in the eyes of the local gentry, should be lonely sometimes. Still, Ruby was her only ally, and it was galling to watch her being won over by a handsome face and charming smile on one hand, and a deft hand for cards on the other.

There was no time for further reflection on the subject. Anna dismissed the disgruntling thought, then led the way to the parlor with Hillmore following.

"Will you have a chair, Mr. Hillmore?"

Raja Singha, efficient as always, had already lit the lamps. Gesturing to a chair, Anna made her way to the sofa and sat down. Hillmore sat, too, and looked at her inquiringly.

"You wanted to see me, Mrs. Traverne?"

Anna smiled, hoping to put the man at his ease. Clearly he'd been remiss in not having briefed her of late, but if he'd been working so hard that he hadn't felt he could spare half an hour at the end of the day for a chat with his employer, then far be it from her to berate him. She wanted a hardworking overseer, and she had hoped and expected that one day he would get to the point where he was running the show without discussing any but the most major decisions with her. Only she had not expected that day to come quite so quickly.

"I just wondered how things are going, Mr. Hillmore."

He looked relieved. "Very well, ma'am. I'm having the acreage cleared that we spoke about, and I've ordered the orange pekoe plants—"

"Just a minute, Mr. Hillmore." Anna's voice was suddenly sharp. "The last time we spoke I thought we agreed to think about that for a while before we took any action. I hope you haven't gone ahead without my approval."

Hillmore frowned. "As to that, Mrs. Traverne, Mr. Chase gave his approval. I—it didn't occur to me that the two of you might not be in accord."

This disclosure left Anna speechless for a brace of seconds.

"Have you been reporting to Mr. Chase this past fortnight?" she asked, careful not to let her indignation show. After all, it was not the overseer's fault that the arrogant, impossible intruder had usurped her authority. But that Julian Chase should dare interfere— Anna felt her indignation boil over into good, old-fashioned wrath. Srinagar was *not* his!

"Yes, ma'am. When he's been available, of course." Hillmore sounded unhappy. "He—I—he said I shouldn't be bothering you with problems with the estate, that while he was here he meant to take as many burdens as he could off your shoulders."

"Oh, did he?" Despite Anna's best efforts, there was an acidic edge to her words. Before the constraints she was placing on her temper could give way, she got to her feet. Hillmore rose too, turning his hat in his hands.

"I'm sorry, Mrs. Traverne, if I've done wrong, but I thought—"

"That's quite all right, Mr. Hillmore. There has been a misunderstanding about exactly who is in charge here at Srinagar, but it is in no way your fault. And of course my—brother-in-law—meant only to spare me. Nevertheless in future I would like to be kept informed. Shall we agree to meet two evenings a week, in the office? Will that be satisfactory with you?"

"Yes, ma'am. And like I said, I'm sorry for the problem."

Anna smiled. She was getting good at smiling when she absolutely, positively didn't feel like it.

"Don't give it another thought, Mr. Hillmore. As you've already started clearing the fields for the orange pekoe, of course you must proceed. But we'll discuss it more—next Tuesday, shall we say? At seven, in the office."

"Yes, ma'am."

Hillmore, realizing that he was being dismissed, looked relieved. Anna called Raja Singha to see him out.

When the overseer was gone, the anger she had been holding at bay erupted.

"I'll kill him!" she muttered under her breath.

Raja Singha, passing, paused. "Memsahib?"

"Nothing, Raja Singha," Anna assured him hastily, and was relieved when he seemed to accept that and went on about his duties. Really, although she knew he was totally loyal to herself and Chelsea, at times Raja Singha could be almost spooky.

But that was neither here nor there. Anna straightened her spine, lifted her chin, and went in search of Julian Chase.

# XXI

The door to his bedchamber was closed. Anna tapped smartly on the heavy teak panel. No answer. She knocked again, louder. Still no answer. So she did something that ordinarily she would not have considered: she opened the door and stuck her head in.

The room was empty. The oil lamps were lit, reflecting in cozy pools off the freshly whitewashed walls. The green silk curtains were drawn, shutting out the night. The half-tester bed with its elaborate hangings in the same shade of green as the curtains was turned down, ready for its occupant-to-be. Of course, the maids would have done that, and closed the curtains, as they did for each resident of the house every night. Of Julian there was no sign.

The room was orderly, with only a pair of dusty boots left beside the bed to mar its neatness. The doors of the huge mahogany wardrobe were firmly shut. The shaving stand was wiped clear of any soap residue, and the giltwood chair in the corner was free of discarded clothes. Grudgingly Anna had to admit that she couldn't fault Julian on his personal habits. From the appearance of his room he was as fastidious as she was, which she would not have expected.

Her nostrils caught a faint whiff of something: cigar smoke? She sniffed, then sniffed again.

"Is anyone in here?" she called, taking a step inside. Her eyes told her that the answer was no, but she thought she could almost feel his presence.

Still, when he answered she jumped.

"Anna? Is that you?"

The muffled reply came from another room. Of course, the dressing room. Although she hadn't noticed it before, as it was partially hidden behind the wardrobe, the door was slightly ajar. Good! She wanted to say her piece while she was still angry.

Anna closed the bedroom door behind her with a snap and marched across the room, her posture militant, to fling the door of the dressing room back on its hinges.

She froze, mouth falling open, eyes widening with shock.

Julian Chase stood before her, as naked as the day he was born, clearly on the verge of stepping into a steaming bath!

"Dear God!" Anna squeaked, as the full enormity of what she was seeing struck her, and screwed shut her eyes. "How dare you tell me to come in? You—"

"I didn't," Julian interrupted placidly. There was a splash followed by the sound of water sloshing. Clearly he had lowered himself into the tub.

"You most certainly did! You said . . ." Anna's voice trailed off as she recalled exactly what he had said. To give the devil his due, he had not precisely told her to come in. On the other hand, he certainly had not told her not to!

"I said, 'Is that you?' "

Just because he was right did not make Anna feel any more charitable toward him.

"Any gentleman—"

"Ahh, but I'm not a gentleman. I thought we had agreed on that."

Anna ignored him. ". . . would have given warning that he was not decent. You—"

"But then, I hardly expected you to come barging into my dressing room, did I? And for God's sake, either open your eyes or go away. You look idiotic standing there like that. You're no green girl. You surely saw your husband naked, and basically we're all alike. Just small variations of size and shape, you know."

Unbidden came the thought that, in the case of Paul and this man, the differences were large, not small. Then Anna felt herself flushing at her own wayward thoughts. Julian was physically a far bigger man than Paul had been. Of course his . . . But she refused to carry the comparison to its obvious conclusion. Even to think about a man's appendage was shaming. While as for dwelling on its size . . . !

"Now why are you blushing?" He sounded as if he were hugely enjoying her discomfiture. Anna realized she was being laughed at, and the knowledge gave her the courage to open her eyes.

As she gave him a wary glance, she saw that his vital parts were modestly obscured by the water. If she tried very hard, of course, she might be able to see his—his limbs through the translucent surface, but she had no intention of trying. Anyway, suds would soon provide more coverage; he was working a cake of soap between his hands, raising a thick white froth of foamy lather.

"You mean you're not going to run away? My dear sister-in-law, you shock me." The look he gave her was mocking. The blue-black eyes laughed at her, although his mouth never smiled. The muscles on his arms rippled as he worked the soap; Anna was momentarily distracted by how very large and corded those muscles were. Although his lower arms were in the water from elbow to wrist, his upper arms bulged with every movement of his hands. Her eyes slid up to his shoulders, which appeared so wide when he was dressed. Naked, they were even wider, thick and solid-looking above a broad chest that was, as Anna had noted on the night of Chelsea's nightmare, covered with a thick wedge of black hair.

Anna was conscious of a sudden, almost overwhelming urge to touch that wet pelt, to see whether it felt coarse or silky against her fingertips, to discover for herself whether it could possibly be as springy as it looked.

When she realized what was happening to her, and that she was staring as if mesmerized at his bare chest, she jerked her eyes away. Her cheeks flushed hotly, and she realized that they must be bright scarlet.

If he had not smiled then, a nasty, knowing smile, she would have fled.

"Look all you want," he said, completing her mortification. "I don't mind."

Her cheeks felt as if they were on fire. It was all she could do not to clap her hands over them. He lounged back in the tub, idly rubbing the bar of soap over his chest, and grinned at her.

"You could join me, if you like," he suggested softly, his eyes never leaving her. "There's plenty of room."

Whether it branded her as a coward or not Anna didn't care. She knew suddenly that she had to get away, that very instant. The allure of the naked man in the tub was so strong that she felt it like a physical ache inside her.

Surely she was not tempted to do as he invited and join him? The very thought was horrifying.

But it was also, a tiny voice inside her whispered, the most disturbingly erotic notion she'd ever had in her life.

"I have something important to discuss with you. When you're finished here, please come down to the office. We can talk there." She started to turn on her heel.

"When I finish here I'm going to bed," he said, stopping her. She glanced back over her shoulder at him, then wished she hadn't. He was soaping one hard-muscled leg; his knee and part of a powerful, hair-roughened thigh were clearly visible above the water.

"It's very important," she managed to say firmly, tearing her eyes away from what he was doing with an effort. Really, what was wrong with her? Paul had been modest, but she had seen him in his bath. Never, ever, had the sight made her throat go dry, or her heart speed up, or her mind reel with lascivious pictures of forbidden pleasures. But then, of course, Paul had been her husband and a gentleman. And Julian Chase was certainly neither!

"If it's truly important you can wait for me in my bedroom. Otherwise, it'll have to keep till morning."

He sounded unconcerned. Anna bit her lip, careful to keep her eyes averted from any part of him below his black-stubbled chin, and decided.

"I'll wait then. But please hurry. And . . ." How to phrase a request that he be decently covered when he emerged? She couldn't think of a dignified way to put it.

"And?"

"Never mind," Anna said crossly, giving up. "Just hurry."

She turned her back on him and walked into the bedroom, where she perched on the very edge of the giltwood chair and tried not to picture what he must be doing in the dressing room.

When he emerged, some ten minutes later, Anna was relieved to see that he had at least had the decency to don a dressing gown. More elegant than the clothes he wore by day, it was of dark brown silk corded in gold. It covered him almost to his ankles. Of course, a large vee of black-haired chest was left on view, as were his ankles and bare feet, but still, considering, Anna felt fortunate. She had been half afraid that he would walk in here as bare as a babe.

"Now what was so important that it couldn't wait until morning?" He carried a lit cigar, which he stuck in his mouth. Anna realized that one like it had been tamped out on a dish beside the bath, although the situation had so befuddled her that she had barely noticed. Funny, she had never seen him smoke before. Perhaps it was something he did only at night.

Recalled to her grievance, she sat a little straighter on the chair.

"You told Mr. Hillmore to go ahead with his plans to plant orange pekoe without getting approval from me." Her voice quavered with indignation.

His brows lifted. "So I did."

Anna was nonplussed. Whatever response she had expected to her accusation, it had not been a cool "So I did"!

"Srinagar belongs to me," she said at last, getting her bearings again. "I give the orders here. As a matter of fact, I think it is probably a mistake to clear so much land. True, in three years or so we'll realize a little extra profit, but in the meantime—"

"In the meantime the plants that are there are too overgrown to produce more than the bare minimum of tea. The fields are basically idle anyway, so it makes sense to convert them to something that will eventually pay."

Again he took her by surprise. "You don't know anything about tea!"

He puffed on his cigar, then pulled it from his mouth. "Now there's where you're wrong. I didn't know much about tea cultivation when I came, but I'm a quick study, and I've made it my business to learn. From what I've learned from Hillmore, and your dear friend Dumesne, and the books in your library, I fancy I have at least as good an understanding of what Srinagar needs as you do.''

''You . . .''

''And as for Srinagar being yours, I would remind you that my hide paid for the place. I know I told you that I would leave when I recover the emeralds, and I will. So all you have to do is bide your time until then, and you can do whatever the hell you want. But in the meantime, I'm going to do what I think best. If you don't like it, I'm sorry.'' He crossed to the corner where she sat, stopping just short of where she perched on the giltwood chair, and stubbed out his cigar on the porcelain dish on the drum table.

''And now that you've said your piece, I think it only fair that I have a chance to say mine.''

At the grim tone to his voice, Anna looked up at him, eyes widening.

''If you invade my bedroom again, I'm going to take it as an invitation. I've wanted you from the moment I first set eyes on you in Gordon Hall, and I know damned well you want me too. So I suggest, unless it's your intention to end up in my bed, you get the hell out of here and stay out. Do I make myself clear?''

As she listened to this brutal speech, Anna's mouth dropped open. As he finished, she shut it with a snap. How dare he speak so to her! She surged to her feet. Her movement brought her just inches from where he stood facing her, but she was too angry to notice, or care.

''You conceited beast! I don't—want—you, to use your nasty phrase! I came in here to—''

He interrupted her ruthlessly. ''You can lie to yourself if you want to, Anna my sweet, but you can't lie to me. You're a flesh-and-blood woman, with good hot red blood, and you're in such an itch to be mounted that you can hardly keep your hands off me. You look at me like a woman looks at a man she wants to bed. Hell, you kiss me like a woman kisses a man she wants to bed. Your breasts swell in my hands and your—''

''Stop it!'' Anna cried, almost screeching. ''Just stop it!''

''Oh, no, my lovely little hypocrite, it's too late for that. You had your chance!''

With that he reached out and caught her upper arms. Despite her furious struggles, he dragged her close, until her breasts were crushed against his chest. Then, even as Anna looked up, hurling insults at him like stones, he lowered his mouth to hers.

He kissed her and she was lost. Her head swam under the rough tutelage of that hard mouth, and her knees went suddenly weak. Her hands, which had been beating at his chest, went still and then curled around the cool silk of the lapels of his dressing gown. Beneath the coolness of the cloth her fingers brushed the hair-softened heat of his chest.

Her lips quivered and parted; her tongue answered the fierce demand of his. He no longer had to hold her against him; she pressed close and closer yet, her breasts seeking the hardness of his chest to ease the ache that pierced their softness. Her hands slid up to close behind his neck.

''Now,'' he muttered with fierce satisfaction into her mouth, even as his hands sought the first of the bottons at the back of her dress. ''Now tell me that you don't want me.''

The words hit Anna like a bucket of cold water. What was she doing. . . . How could she let him . . . Had she no pride at all? With a furious hiss she tore her mouth from beneath his and jerked herself out of his arms.

Then, without a word, she dealt him a slap that rocked his head.

For a moment he stood there simply looking at her while the imprint of her hand on his cheek slowly filled with dark red blood. Then he raised his hand to the hurt, and his eyes went as black as jet.

"If you know what's good for you, you'll get the hell out of my sight," he said.

Anna drew in a deep, shaken breath, took one final look at those blazing black eyes, then turned on her heel and fled.

# XXII

The monsoon started, a little later than usual, some four days afterward on the second of August. Anna lay in bed listening to the wind blowing and shivered. So had the wind sounded at precisely this time last year.

At this same time she had been sitting beside Paul's bed, his still-warm hand in hers, his dying breath in her ears, listening to the rushing of the wind.

It had sounded just as it did now. Only the last time it had come, it had taken Paul's soul away with it.

Anna couldn't bear the sound.

She got up from bed and crossed to the window, pulling aside the flimsy muslin curtain. It was well past midnight, and she had been in bed for hours. But she had not been able to sleep, and now she knew that she would not. Not this night.

It was one year ago to the day that Paul had died.

Shadows shrouded the garden, dancing eerily in the pale moonlight as branches and clouds were blown about by the wind. The wind's whistling took on an eery, keening note, as if it, too, mourned.

Beyond the garden, the small fenced-in enclosure at the top of the knoll was thick with shadows. Anna

172

thought she could just make out Paul's tombstone, shimmering white through the darkness. Calling to her.

For a while her loss had been so painful that it was like a blade twisting constantly in her heart. Then, slowly, so slowly that she scarcely realized it at the time, she had started to recover. A whole day would go by, and she wouldn't think of Paul. At night she was able to sleep, untroubled by dream-time visits from his shade. She'd started to feel again, sharply: anger, fear, joy. And passion. Passion the like of which she had never experienced. A passion so strong and intense that it frightened her even to admit it. Even as her heart had grieved, her body had awakened. Perhaps the new vitality of her senses had worked some magic on the ache in her heart.

It was because of Julian, of course. Guiltily, Anna finally admitted to herself what she'd been afraid to face before: he was absolutely right when he accused her of wanting him. Dear Lord, how she wanted him! She wanted to kiss that hard mouth, to touch him all over, to have him touch her.

She wanted to sleep with him, God forgive her.

Anna closed her eyes, clenching her fists as she tried to will the thought away. But it refused to be banished. Suddenly she felt sick to her stomach. On this, the one-year anniversary of her husband's death, it was depraved that she could stare through the darkness at his grave and think indecent thoughts of another man.

Anna reached for her wrapper across the foot of the bed. She tied the garment's belt tightly around her waist, then slid her feet into her slippers.

She needed to be close to Paul. She needed to talk to him, as she had talked to him in the weeks just after he had died. She needed to know that, after all, the love they had shared from childhood had not died with him. Just because her body quivered with hunger for another man in a purely physical attraction did not mean Paul no longer held premier place in her heart.

What kind of fickle, feckless creature would that make her, if she could so soon replace in her affections the kind, gentle man who had been her dearest friend for most of her life?

Anna left her bedroom and moved soundlessly down the stairs and along the corridor toward the rear of the house. From somewhere behind her she heard a scuttling movement. Glancing over her shoulder, momentarily afraid, she was reassured by two small bright eyes gleaming at her from near floor level. Moti. Of course he had the run of the house at night. Reassured, Anna continued on her way, lifting the leather latch that secured the back door and letting herself out of the house.

The tendrils of hair around her face, which had worked free of their nightly confinement, were whipped upward by the wind. She had plaited the long mass for sleeping, as she always did, and it hung in a single braid down her back to her waist. The wind caught at the skirts of her simple white nightgown and wrapper, swirling them around her legs. Above her head branches blew and creaked. Leaves rustled all around her, or maybe the sounds were caused by small things wandering through the night. Anna neither knew nor cared. She felt removed from herself, caught up in a dream, almost as if she were one with the shadows and the wind and the creatures of the night as she climbed the hill behind the house.

The iron spikes of the fence surrounding the small graveyard were cold against her hand. Anna felt for rather than saw the latch. Lifting it, swinging open the gate, she let herself into the tiny cemetery.

There, in the very center, was Paul's grave.

The vines and creeping vegetation that threatened

to take over every other bit of arable land were kept at bay here, on Anna's orders. Good English grass had been planted and was kept neatly scythed. The marker was of the local moonstone, carved simply with Paul's name and the dates of his birth and death. At one end of the small plot a temple tree grew, its tiny white blossoms perfuming the air.

The moon peeping through the scudding clouds picked up the crystals in the moonstone, causing the headstone to seem to glow. Anna stood looking at it, her hands clasped in front of her, her head bowed.

As a girl she had loved him so much. He had been the embodiment of her every childhood dream. The handsome son of the local lord, as far above her touch as if he were a prince of the blood, and also her dearest friend. They had played together, had lessons together, and learned about loving together. Finally, they had run off together, married, come to this strange land and begotten Chelsea. And then he had died.

Now she had no more of him than this shimmering stone atop a plot of earth, and fading memories.

Surely a man as fine and good as Paul deserved more of a memorial than that.

Anna tried to conjure up his face, but his features kept getting confused with Chelsea's in her mind. His face would not become clear. The admission brought tears to her eyes, scalding tears that spilled over her lids to run unchecked down her face.

How could she have forgotten already?

Falling to her knees beside the grave, she dropped her head in her hands and cried.

It began to rain. At first the drops were hesitant, slow fat drops that plopped when they landed. Then they increased in number and intensity until the rain was pouring down with as much force as her tears.

The wind whistled, the rain fell, and Anna wept on, oblivious.

Until a voice cut through the darkness with the angry ferocity of a sharpened knife.

"Just what the bloody hell do you think you're doing?"

# XXIII

Anna looked up to find Julian looming beside her, looking bigger and more powerful than ever with the night turning him into an enormous shape shrouded in shadows. Hastily she averted her face, swiping at her cheeks with her hands, desperate that he not know she had been crying as if all the oceans of tears in the world were hers to command. But he ignored her bid for privacy, if he even saw it, leaning over her and catching her chin with his hand, tilting her face up to his.

His eyes glittered down at her, black as jet in the darkness. He looked angry—no, furious. The rain washed her face. Her eyes closed against it—and him.

"You bloody little fool," he snarled. "You'll catch your death."

Then, before she could gather her facilities enough to enable her to reply, he scooped her up in his arms, his movements rough, and bore her out of the graveyard. Anna turned her face into the damp cloth of his shirt, breathing in the smell of him, burrowing against the solid warmth of his shoulder.

He was so blessedly alive. She was so horribly, guiltily, glad of that.

The thought brought more tears with it.

As he felt fresh sobs shake her, Julian cursed vi-

ciously under his breath. Then, so abruptly that it
shocked her, the arm beneath her knees dropped.
Anna found herself on her feet, her breasts pressed
against his chest as his other arm wrapped around
her back. She looked up at him, surprised, only to
find that his head was descending. Before she could
so much as register his intent, his mouth found hers,
claimed it. He kissed her with savage hunger that
left no room for gentleness, kissed her with a fierceness that rocked her to her toes and made her insides quake.

That kiss reduced her to mindlessness. Anna felt
her wits and her will melt away, leaving her helpless
to deny him or herself.

Julian gathered her close, pulling her up on tiptoe
so that she was aware of the whole muscled length
of him with every millimeter of her skin. Anna quivered in his hold, then gave in to what every instinct
she possessed screamed for her to do and slid her
arms around his neck. He pressed her head against
his shoulder, his mouth ruthlessly forcing apart her
lips, and she did not resist. Did not want to resist.

With a tiny whimper she surrendered utterly, her
hands curling into the broad damp shoulders, her
mouth opening for his plundering.

And plunder he did. His tongue was a bold in-
vader, claiming everything in its path. He stroked
her tongue and the roof of her mouth and her teeth,
demanding an equal response from her. Anna gave
it to him, quivering and quaking as she returned
passion for passion, kissing him back with all the
pent-up longing she had tried in vain to suppress.

Never in her life had she felt anything like the
burning desire that was turning her into flame in his
arms. Never in her life had she wanted anything as,
in that moment, she wanted him.

They stood like that for countless moments, kissing in the night-dark, rain-washed garden with the
wind blowing her hair and her skirts and both their
garments getting soaked to the skin.

Then he seemed to come to some awareness of their surroundings. He muttered something and gathered her up in his arms again.

Heart pounding, arms curled around his neck, Anna lay quiescent in his arms as he carried her across the gallery and into the house.

Neither of them spoke as he bore her along the hall, and this time Anna wasn't even aware of the gleaming watchfulness of Moti's eyes. Her own heart pounded like a kettledrum as she listened, head nestled against his chest, to the rapid thudding of his. Dizzy with passion, she drank in the strength of his arms as he carried her up the stairs with obvious ease, reveling in the solid breadth of his chest, the warmth of him, the smell of him.

There, in the silent darkness of the sleeping house, she somehow lost the person she knew herself to be. She wasn't Anna anymore, but only a woman, and he wasn't Julian, but only a man.

The woman in her, hungry, needy, cried out to the man in him.

Her arms tightened around his neck as he bore her along the upstairs hallway and then, easing open the door, carried her into her room.

# XXIV

"You're not going to send me away." It was a rough whisper, part order, part question.

Her face buried in his shoulder, Anna shook her head. She felt rather than saw the harsh indrawing of his breath. The door clicked shut behind him, and then he was standing her on her own two feet with rather more gentleness than he had shown so far.

"Let's get these wet things off you."

The curtain that she had drawn away from the window earlier permitted the smallest glimmer of pale gray light to invade the darkness. By it, she was able to watch him as he undressed her. He was very big, very dark, very intent as his long fingers dealt clumsily with her bows and buttons. His head was bowed to her so that she could just make out the beads of water glinting on his black hair. His lashes veiled his eyes, but his mouth was hard and straight, not smiling but rather almost grim. Sliding the wrapper from her shoulders, he chanced to glance up and meet her eyes. Still he didn't smile, just watched her, those gypsy-dark eyes glittering.

Still watching her, he reached out and closed a hand around one small, taut breast. The single layer of damp cloth that still covered her was no protection from the fierce heat of his touch.

Anna gasped as a pleasure so exquisite that it was

almost an ache quaked through her. Her head fell back on her neck, and her eyes closed. She trembled, but she didn't back away. Instead one small hand lifted to close over the large, masculine one that was holding her breast.

It was Julian who broke the spell, muttering something hard and fast under his breath as he pulled her into his arms again. He kissed her, endlessly, passionately, and she rose up on her tiptoes and locked her arms around his neck and kissed him back. When his mouth slid down to her ear and then her neck, he, like she, was trembling. Anna could feel the shudders racking the arms that held her, and trembled more in reply.

"Christ," he breathed, and put her away from him. When she reached for him, he shook his head and set himself to undoing the dozens of tiny buttons that closed her gown from neck to waist. His fingers shook so that each button took him several tries. Finally Anna brushed his hands away.

"Let me," she whispered, more wanton than she had ever dreamed she could be. Still she could not quite bring herself to look up at him as she unfastened her gown. When at last it was done she chanced a glance, feeling both bold and incredibly shy. He was watching her with a dark, hooded expression that she couldn't read. The only thing that told her he was as hungry as she was the obsidian gleam of his eyes.

"Take it off," he directed her, his voice hoarse and low. Anna saw the glitter in his eyes intensify as he waited for her to do his bidding. She felt her mouth go dry. Slowly, feeling both sinful and deliciously free, she shrugged the gown from her shoulders, deliberately delaying its fall to expose first small, pink-tipped breasts, then the slenderness of her waist, the gentle flare of her hips, the ash-brown triangle of hair at the apex of her thighs, the creamy length of her legs. When, finally, she let the gown drop to puddle at her feet, his eyes were aflame, and a tiny muscle twitched noticeably at the corner of his mouth.

"You're the most beautiful thing I've ever seen in my life," he said, his hands lifting as though to draw her to him. Anna stepped quickly out of reach, shaking her head.

"You're wet, too," she reminded him in a throaty whisper. For a moment he merely looked at her, his eyes hungry on her flesh, but then his lips curved upwards in the smallest of wicked smiles.

# XXV

"Shall I strip for you, sweetheart?" The question was almost teasing despite its husky undertone. Unable to trust herself to speak, Anna nodded.

Then she watched, barely breathing, as he proceeded to do as she asked.

First he took off his boots. He sat on the end of her bed to pull them off, dropping them side by side on the floor. Then he stood up, unbuttoning his cuffs. That done, he started at the throat of his collarless shirt, undoing the buttons one by one. Anna felt her heart speed up as the broad, black-pelted chest that had seared itself on her mind was slowly revealed. When he pulled the tails of his shirt from his breeches and shrugged out of it, her eyes ran greedily over him. His shoulders were huge, wide and powerful, his arms corded with muscle. His chest was wide, tapering into a narrow waist and hips. Above his breeches were the beginnings of a muscle-ridged abdomen, the round shadow of his belly button. That thick triangle of black hair that she longed to touch arrowed past it to disappear inside his breeches.

His hands were already busy with the buttons of his pants. Anna followed their progress, feeling her heart pound harder with each new bit of flesh he revealed. Until finally the buttons were all undone, and he was sliding his breeches down his legs and stepping out of them, leaving him gloriously naked.

Anna looked at him and forgot to breathe. The thought that came to her then was, simply, that this was a man. She had never seen anything so magnificent in all her life.

Her eyes dropped down his body, rose again. He was hard with wanting her, and huge with it. Anna felt an answering ache deep within her belly. Quivering, she raised her eyes to his face.

"Come here," he said then, and held out his arms to her. Anna drew a deep, shaking breath, and walked into them.

This time, when they closed around her, she had the sensation that he would never let her go. With no barriers left between them, she could feel the abrasion of his body hair against her breasts and thighs. She could feel the heat of his skin, seeming to burn hers everywhere they touched, and the even greater heat and silkiness of that hungry part of him, pressed against her belly.

She wrapped her arms around him, burying her face in the hollow between his neck and shoulder, inhaling deeply of the musky scent of him. His hand came up to find her chin, lift it.

"I've wanted you," he said, and the tip of his thumb stroked the soft line of her mouth. Anna's lips parted helplessly. He smiled at her then, a sweet and tender smile that made her blood heat, and bent his head to her mouth.

Anna strained against him as he kissed her, holding him tightly, kissing him back. She felt his hands slide over the bare skin of her back, and closed her eyes at the sheer wonder of it. He stroked the indentation of her waist, the roundness of her bottom, the gentle curve of her thighs, with slow, sure strokes. By the time he gripped her bottom, cradling a silky half-moon in each hand, to pull her more fully against him, Anna was shaking as with an ague.

"Have you wanted me?" he whispered, sliding his mouth across her cheek to her ear, where he pulled the lobe into his mouth and nibbled it. Anna arched her neck to give him greater access, feeling her bones turn to water. Had she wanted him?

"Yes." Like the rest of her, her voice was shaking. "Oh, yes."

It was such an exquisite relief to admit the truth, to give in to her craving for him, not to fight her own feelings anymore. Had she wanted him? In that moment, Anna thought she would have walked over hot coals barefoot to get to him.

"Lovely, lovely Anna." With one hard arm under her thighs and the other supporting her back, he lifted her off her feet and carried her the few steps to the bed. The covers were pulled back from where she had left it earlier; the pillow still bore the indentation of her head. Gently he laid her down on the cool sheet, then stretched out beside her and turned on one side, one hand propping up his head. His body was very dark against the white sheets; his eyes were blacker than the blackest midnight. With his foot he pushed to the floor the bedclothes that she'd earlier left all of a heap. She lay where he had placed her, naked, exposed, quivering. His eyes roamed over her, touched her breasts and belly and thighs. Then they lifted to meet hers. Dark fires blazed in them as they moved from her eyes to her mouth, drinking in each feature. One long-fingered hand reached out, so slowly, to smooth the tendrils of hair from her face.

Anna watched him, her eyes huge and vulnerable, her hunger for him plain in her face. He was being so gentle, so careful, but suddenly she wanted him to be neither. Her blood had heated to the point where it ran through her veins like raging lava, and she thought that if he didn't put a speedy end to her torment she would be incinerated by her own desire.

"Your eyes glow like a cat's in the dark," he muttered, one finger moving to stroke the soft skin just beside them. Anna moistened her lips, which had suddenly gone dry. Then she caught his hand and carried it to her mouth. Softly, delicately, she pressed her mouth to his palm, her tongue coming out to touch his skin, reveling in the faint taste of salt.

His eyes flickered, narrowed, and his hand moved so that it cupped the side of her face, turning it toward him. Anna rubbed her cheek against that hard palm, closing her eyes, feeling her body simmer and burn until she could bear it no longer. Her eyes fluttered open to find that he was still watching her, a curiously guarded expression on his face. Almost as if he were afraid. . . .

But she could wait no longer. Reaching up, she slid her hands over his shoulders, behind his head, pulling his mouth down to hers. Maddeningly, he still held back, his mouth poised just millimeters from her lips.

His eyes searched hers, asking a question that she didn't see.

"Kiss me," she whispered, ready to beg, ready to do whatever it took to soothe the hunger that clamored inside her. "Please, Julian."

He caught his breath, the sound almost a hiss, and the fire in his eyes flamed suddenly out of control. He bent his head to her mouth.

His kiss was gentle at first, soft and slow, parting her lips so that his tongue could slide inside, nibbling at her mouth. It was Anna who pressed her hand against the back of that black head, tilting her face up to deepen the kiss, her lips and tongue responding ardently to the tenderness of his. His hand found her breast, closed over it. The heat of his palm seared her nipple. Anna gasped, arching her back, wordlessly begging for more. Julian lifted his head and looked down at her. His face was hard with passion, his eyes hot with it. But there was something more than passion there too. And again Anna refused to see.

"Don't stop," she whispered, her hands making begging little forays along his shoulders and the back of his neck. "Please don't stop."

"Christ," Julian said, the word part prayer and part curse. Then he rolled on top of her, pressing her back into the mattress, his hands suddenly everywhere as his mouth staked bold possession. Anna trembled and quaked and clung to him, her nails digging into his shoulders as he kissed her with a fierce need that told her that the time for gentleness was over. One hand found her breast, her nipple, kneaded, squeezed. Anna cried out. His legs shifted, but before he could part her thighs with his knees Anna had already spread her legs, arching her back, offering herself to him.

"Sweet Anna," he whispered against her mouth, and then something else. But already she was kissing him again, clinging to him, wrapping her legs around his waist like the wanton she had never been, and the muttered words went unheard.

His breathing rasped raggedly in her ear; his arms molded her to him. His hand slid between their bodies, between her legs, found the soft hot wetness of her, and stroked her there . . . where he had touched her, to her shame, before. But this time she felt no shame, felt instead a need and a hunger and a heat that made what he was doing seem as necessary to her survival as air. With experienced sureness, his fingers located a place that Anna had never dreamed existed, a tiny reservoir of feeling that exploded when he touched it. She cried out, gasping and trembling with the sheer wonder of it, as with no more than that gentle massage he introduced her to an ecstasy that she had never even imagined it was possible to feel.

Then, even as her body shuddered with its own pleasure, he thrust inside her. He went deep, so deep that at first she was unprepared for the sheer enormity of him and thought that he must hurt her, that the pleasure he had given her must surely be a prelude to pain. But there was no pain, only more pleasure, pleasure so intense that she convulsed again with it. Panting, she clung to him, her nails digging deep into his back and her legs tight around his waist as he taught her exactly how much she had yet to learn about lovemaking. His thrusts were deep and hard, driving into her with almost desperate strength—and she loved them. Her body was by now a thing utterly separate from her mind. It writhed beneath him, a wild thing, and wanton. From her throat came curious mewling sounds that were muffled by the curve of his neck, where she pressed her face. He was hot and wet with sweat, as urgent a primal force as the wind as he claimed her and made her his own. Anna, mindless, matched his desperation. Until at last, with a muffled shout, he found his own release and in doing so again gave her hers.

# XXVI

When Anna surfaced, from somewhere far, far away, she found that Julian was lying on his back with her head nestled cozily against his chest. His arm circled her, held her to him. His other arm was beneath his head. One of her hands rested in the tangle of hair on his chest. He was very warm to the touch, slightly damp, reassuringly solid. And unashamedly, beautifully naked. Her eyes ran along his body with proprietary interest. Hard of muscle, long of limb, bronzed skin roughened by a quantity of dark hair, he was the very essence of man. Her dream lover come to life, in spades. Even sprawling, his body sated, sweat drying on his skin, he was a feast for her eyes. Anna took a deep breath and let it out in what sounded very much like a sign of contentment. Then she looked up to find that he was watching her. One corner of his mouth was turned up in a crooked smile.

"I've been wanting to do that since the first time I set eyes on you," he told her.

Anna fluttered her lashes at him. She felt absurdly lighthearted, girlish, almost flirtatious. The chest that she had been longing to touch waited beneath her hand. Moving her fingers sensuously through the thick nest of hair, she decided that *crisp* was the best word to describe it.

"Have you?" she murmured distractedly.

"Umm-hmm." He caught her hand, stilled it, carried it to his mouth, where he sucked the end of each oval-tipped finger in turn.

"Mm-hm. You looked like a little girl, with your silver braid and ruffled nightgown, all curled up in that chair. Your eyes were huge, and as green as the emeralds in my hand, and your back was as straight as if you had swallowed a poker. Then you jumped up, and I saw"—his hand strayed to cup and jiggle her breast, as if to illustrate exactly what had made him see—"that you weren't a child after all. And I wanted you."

"You frightened me," Anna murmured, watching his hand on her breast through lashes that veiled her eyes. "I thought for sure that you were bent on murder—or rape."

He grinned then, even as his hand stroked along the valley that separated one breast from the other. Attaining his new goal, he ran his palm idly over her nipple, causing it to harden and swell.

"You defended your honor very capably, I must say. If perhaps a trifle excessively. Did you really have to hit me so hard?"

"I'm sorry about that. But I couldn't think of any other way to make you stop."

"You might have tried a simple no."

"You didn't seem to be taking no for an answer."

"Maybe I wasn't," he conceded, cupping her breast with his hand as if to test it for size. Anna, distracted, began to lose the thread of the conversation. "I knew that sooner or later you'd end up in my bed. You might say it was preordained. Destiny."

"As a point of fact," Anna murmured, giving in to the temptation to trace a circle around a pink-brown male nipple, "you're in *my* bed."

"Don't quibble." Her braid hung over her shoulder. He found the ribbon that secured it and tugged it free, running his fingers through her hair until it spilled over her breasts like golden silk. "You have beautiful hair."

"Ummm." Her nail ran over the top of his nipple, making him twitch away. His body tantalized her; she wanted to stroke him all over, to learn the feel of his skin and muscle and hair.

"Want me to show you what to do with that?"

"What?"

"A nipple. Any nipple. Mine. Yours."

He was shifting as he spoke. Before the words were all the way out of his mouth Anna found herself on her back with Julian looming over her, a lop-sided smile playing on his mouth even as he lowered his head.

"This," he said, touching her nipple with his tongue, "is the proper way to treat a nipple."

"Is it?" Anna felt her breath catch as his tongue flicked over her breast.

"Mmm-hmm." Then, with no warning at all, he drew her nipple all the way into his mouth, nibbling it with his teeth, sucking on it. Anna felt a shaft of pure fire shoot from her breast clear down to her toes, and gasped.

"See?" It was a muttered aside, accompanied by a sideways flicker of his eyes to assess her reaction.

"I see." Her response was husky as he continued his breathtaking ministrations. The sight of his black head nestled so intimately against her breast made her heart speed up. Her hand came up to stroke the rough strands of his hair, pressing his face more closely against her.

"You smell good. Like roses." His mouth moved on to the other nipple, which he accorded the same lavish attention. Anna, who had thought she was sated, found that her body was waking up again. Delicious quivers ran over her skin, and the secret place where he'd given her such pleasure before began to throb.

"It's my toilet water." It was a distracted whisper. All Anna's attention was focused on the pink-tipped creaminess of her small breast as it was drawn up into the hard masculinity of his mouth. Watching, she felt a rush of heat.

"What?" Clearly he was as distracted as she.

"My toilet water. It smells of roses."

"Oh."

His mouth left her breast to slide down her body, tracing a scalding path between her ribs and over her belly until he came to her belly button. There he paused, his tongue coming out to explore the small hollow until Anna pushed his head away.

"That tickles," she protested faintly, because indeed it felt very odd, not quite a tickle but a sensation she could not quite describe.

"Let me show you something else that tickles," he murmured, his mouth sliding lower still and his hands moving to part her legs.

"No!" Anna gasped, shocked back to awareness as she realized exactly what he meant to do. Surely gentlemen did not ordinarily do such things? With a *lady*? Such an act was quite beyond her experience, although over the course of the last hour she had come to realize that her experience was sadly limited. But she could not like this. . . . Julian still seemed determined to proceed, however, so to prevent him she quickly rolled onto her stomach.

"All right," he answered obligingly, as he took in her very real shock. Anna relaxed. For a moment she'd been afraid that he would proceed regardless. Then, just as she felt safe, his mouth crawled hot and wet over the soft roundness of her bottom.

"Oh!"

"Shhh. Lie still. This is fun, too."

He was kissing her bottom, running his lips and tongue over the tender curves, nibbling, sucking, exploring all the hills and valleys.

"Oh!" Anna cried again, helplessly, as fresh waves of desire broke over her. He pressed her down into the cocoanut-husk mattress, his mouth moving up her spine. Her hair was flowing down her back now. Pushing the silken mass aside, he caressed her neck with his mouth.

"I love the way you taste," he whispered into her ear. Anna, powerless to so much as speak in the face of her own growing need, shivered.

His tongue slid along her spine, found the cleft between her buttocks and stroked her there. Anna's eyes fluttered shut, and she moaned.

"You've got a beautiful ass," he said, softly biting each trembling cheek. Then she felt his body against her, felt him part her legs so that that part of him that was swollen with need could find its pleasure. He thrust into her from the rear, and because it was so new to her, so unexpected and probably forbidden and certainly nothing like anything she had ever expected a man to do to her, waves of pleasure rocked her almost instantly. His arms came around her, one hand fondling her breasts while the other found the nest of hair between her thighs. He stroked her there again, on the secret place that had exploded for him before. Anna cried out, writhing beneath him, her breath rasping in her throat as he took her to heaven and back.

"Christ, I've wanted you," he rasped against her neck. Then he thrust into her hard one last time and held himself inside her while he groaned and found his release.

# XXVII

In the aftermath, Anna quickly fell fathoms deep asleep. She was exhausted, sated, and ridiculously content as she snuggled close to Julian's hard body. As she drifted into the mists of sleep, it occurred to her that she could not remember having felt so happy for a long, long time. But of course she was happy. Why shouldn't she be? She was the luckiest woman alive. She had a nice home, a wonderful child, a man who had just made the most exquisite love to her. What was there for her to be unhappy about?

If some niggling memory tried to remind her that she had, just hours before, been very unhappy indeed, Anna ignored it.

She was dreaming, but the dream was of ordinary things. Chelsea was playing in the garden with her ball, and Anna was watching her, smiling. The sky was blue as only the sky over Ceylon could be, with soft white clouds drifting on the breath of a gentle breeze. The day was warm, but not too hot, not one of those steamy days that was a staple of island weather. In the distance, the mountains loomed cool and blue. Birds sang, flowers bloomed, monkeys chattered in the trees.

"Anna!" a voice called.

She turned her head, searching.

194

"Where are you?" she responded. She heard him again, fainter this time as he called to her. Frowning, she moved in the direction from which his voice seemed to come.

She saw him then, at the top of the knoll where the tiny graveyard waited. He was standing there, his blond hair blowing in the wind, his slender body awash in sunshine. As he saw her coming toward him, a faint smile curved his mouth. He lifted a hand as if in farewell, then turned and walked swiftly away.

"Wait!" Anna cried, running after him. But however fast she ran, he drew further and further away.

At last, when he was no more than a shimmering image in the distance, she stopped. Her heart swelled, throbbed, as she watched him vanish from sight.

Her hands rose to press against her mouth. He had left her, with a smile and a wave, to continue his journey alone. And so, she realized clearly, must she.

Her heart ached with loss. Her eyes filled with tears as she stared at the place where he had been, but was no longer.

"Oh, Paul," she said.

# XXVIII

Julian lay on his back, his eyes half closed, savoring the feel of the naked woman curled against his side. Her head lay on his shoulder. Her glorious hair spilled across his chest. He stroked those tumbled tresses, marveling that, after all they'd been through that night, her hair still felt like silk. Her naked breasts pressed into his side. Sated now, they were soft and beguiling, small innocent mounds tipped with rosebud nipples that could have belonged to a young girl.

In the past, he'd liked his women fully grown and fully developed. But in this slip of a girl he'd found woman enough to take his breath.

He'd wanted to make love to her the first time he'd set eyes on her. Her slender blond beauty combined with those breathtaking green eyes would alone have been enough to intrigue him. Add to that a nature that was as blazingly passionate as her exterior was coolly innocent, and enough gumption to knock him cold and then make off with the emeralds, and the lady was dazzling. She appealed to him in ways that no other woman, however witty or voluptuous, ever had.

He even liked the fierceness, so at odds with her fragile appearance, with which she protected her daughter. A fine mother, she was. She'd been a fine,

loyal wife too, which he supposed was also to be
chalked up to her credit. Although every time he
pictured her wed to his late, unlamented half brother
he wanted to grit his teeth.

Everything he'd ever striven for, his brothers had
managed to get without even trying. Including, in
Paul's case, Anna.

He'd never actually met the younger of the Traverne brothers. He'd only seen Paul from a distance,
once or maybe twice at Gordon Hall and several
times when Paul and Graham had been brought up
to London on some whim of their father's. It had
been after he'd attempted to force his father to at
least acknowledge his existence, so he'd been about
seventeen. Paul would have been at least six, but
he'd looked like a mere infant to Julian. Guarded by
a nanny-dragon, Lord Ridley's two wanted sons
spent most afternoons of their visit to town in the
park, and Julian felt himself drawn irresistibly to
their vicinity. He had never identified himself, never
made any attempt to approach them, but only
watched.

They were dressed like little princes, in velvet and
lace, with pristine white stockings that made him
green with envy even when they dirtied them playing. Each of them had hoops, which they would roll
with a stick along the paths, and small wooden
boats, which they sailed on the pond. Julian, whose
only toys had been crude ones that he or his granny
had found or fashioned, had coveted those toys with
a fierceness that, given his age, had embarrassed
him. Years later, he had the maturity to wonder if
what he had longed for was not so much the toys
but all that they represented.

Those clean, well-dressed, and well-fed boys were
his brothers, born of the same father. The father
who appeared to dote on the younger pair, while
scorning the elder so much that he refused even to
acknowledge his paternity.

To Julian, who still had moments when he remembered his granny's words, when he believed himself legitimate and the two favored sons the bastards, his father's rejection was a bitter pill to swallow. He fantasized about going to Gordon Hall again with proof that he was the real heir. They would fall on his neck then, and he would cast them out. Or maybe he'd be generous and let them stay.

The choice would be his.

The hardness of his own life compared with the softness of theirs had rankled him well into manhood. The world had been handed to them as their birthright, while everything he'd ever acquired he'd had to scrabble and fight for and wrest from the hands of an uncaring fate.

Including the chit whose sleeping breath now whispered over his heart.

It galled him that one of his fortune-blessed half brothers had had her first. Had loved her, wed her, fathered a child on her, and even in death retained her affections.

She was the first woman since the green days of his boyhood that he'd had to work to win. From the time he'd been taken on as footman by a lecherous countess bent on seduction, to his acquisition of the lovely but ultimately fickle Amabel, he'd found himself in the enviable position of the wooed rather than the wooer. They had all wanted to take him to bed, but only the whores and the barmaids and the serving girls had wanted to wed him. Ladies—like the countess, who had laughed in his face when he, in his youthful innocence and infatuation, had believed that sex equaled love and love equaled marriage and had thus proposed—would have none of him as a husband. With his half-gypsy heritage, he was beneath their touch.

Without conceit, he knew that there was something about him that appealed to women. There were handsomer men, certainly richer and more powerful ones, but not many who were more successful in bedding the ladies. After the countess, he had never again cared if he'd won or lost at the game of love, which he supposed added a certain fillip to his appeal.

But with Anna, he discovered to his growing dismay, he did care. Too damned much. He'd thought that, once he coaxed her into bed, the battle would be won. To his somewhat horrified amazement, he discovered that such was not the case: he could only claim victory if he could also claim her heart.

When, drawn from his bed by some instinct he could not name even now, he'd looked out his bedroom window to find Anna abroad at well past midnight, he hadn't been able to believe his eyes. Down in the wind-tossed darkness of the garden he'd seen a figure, all in white, gliding across the ground without seeming to touch it. At first he'd thought he was seeing a ghost. A shiver had run down his spine.

Then the moon had come out from behind a cloud and its light had touched her hair, making it glow an unearthly silver. He'd been reassured to discover that the spectre was not, after all, a ghost: nobody but Anna had hair like that.

Scowling, wondering what the hell she could possibly be thinking to roam the grounds in the wee hours of the morning, he'd dressed and gone after her. It had started to rain before he'd found her, and he'd been about to give up under the misguided notion that she must have come to her senses and decided to return to the house when he had seen her, crouched on the ground by her husband's grave. Just kneeling there, in the pouring rain.

Fury such as he'd rarely known had sent him storming after her. When he'd tilted her head back and seen her tears falling faster than the rain, he'd wanted to strangle her. Anger had fueled him as he'd lifted her into his arms and carried her back to the house. Anger had fueled that first fierce kiss.

Then, suddenly, he hadn't been angry anymore. He'd known, from the first touch of his lips to hers, what he wanted. She'd been as eager as he, clinging to him, begging him with every movement of her body to make her his.

At last.

He'd waited so long that he craved her like an addict craved opium. He hadn't been able to get enough of the sight of her, the feel of her, the taste of her. Those soft moans that had marked her pleasure had driven him mad. He'd wanted her endlessly, and even now, after the two exhaustive sessions they had shared, he still wasn't sated. Would never, he feared, be sated.

If he'd known what he was risking, he would have stayed safely in England. Not even the recovery of the emeralds was worth this torment.

For almost the first time in his adult life, Julian acknowledged to himself that he was frightened.

He had committed the unthinkable and fallen in love with his golden half brother's still-grieving widow.

And now he was horribly, hideously afraid that she might not love him back. At least not in the way he wanted her to love him.

His eyes slid down to the lovely little face that snuggled so cozily against his chest. She was smiling in her sleep, and Julian knew a faint heartening of his spirit. She was no lightskirt who would bed a man just because the notion took her.

But she had bedded him, and hotly, too. When those breath-stopping green eyes fluttered awake, he would put the matter to the test. He would ask her point-blank if she loved him. And if she said yes, he would take his courage in his hands and ask her to marry him. He wanted Anna in many ways, but most of all for his wife.

In her sleep Anna sighed and muttered, shifting as if she were on the verge of coming awake. Julian reached down to smooth the hair from her brow. Anticipation was making him nervous.

Her brow puckered, and she shifted again, restlessly. Willing to wait no longer, Julian bent his head, pressing his lips to her temple. He'd kiss her awake. . . .

Then she sighed something that made the blood turn cold in his veins.

His teeth clenched as, in her sleep, she called him by his despised half brother's name.

# XXIX

Julian got out of bed, not really caring if he woke Anna or not, and reached for his breeches. He stepped into them, yanked them up, did up the buttons, found his shirt, and shrugged into it. When he started to fasten it, he discovered that he had it on wrongside out. Not that he cared. Leaving it unfastened, he grabbed his boots and headed toward the door.

Behind him, Anna still slept. Julian slanted one quick, furious look back at her, sleeping with one hand pillowing her cheek and looking for all the world like the angel she wasn't, and cursed under his breath.

He had to get out of there before he wrapped his hands around her soft little neck.

He shut the door not at all gently and, stomped along the hall to his own room. He didn't dare let himself think too much.

He hadn't hurt over a woman since the countess and he didn't mean to start over a silver-haired chit of a girl who was, once a man got her where he wanted her, not one bit better than she should be.

The door to his room was closed, but a light glimmered beneath it, although no light had been lit when he left. Julian all but kicked it open, too savagely angry to be cautious.

Jim leaped up from the chair where he'd been lounging, started to say something, took one look at Julian, and shut his mouth. His eyes widened as he absorbed the evidence of the wrongside-out unbuttoned shirt, the partially undone breeches, the bare feet and carried boots. And the utterly ferocious scowl.

"Ah, hell, Julie, you done done it now," Jim muttered in disgust, and spat toward the spittoon Julian had acquired for his friend's use.

"You got something else to say?" Julian asked, his eyes challenging, his voice dangerous. He felt ripe for a fight.

"Yeah." Jim eyed him again and shook his head. But even as Julian felt his temper find a welcome focus, Jim spoke about something else altogether.

"If you can get your mind out of the bedroom for a minute, I think I've found your bloody emeralds."

"Where?" Julian's response was sharp. It was a relief to have something to focus on other than his own bruised and battered heart.

"Anyour—Anour—ah, some bloody 'eathenish town. A fat Khansamah's bought 'em for one of his wives. It's gonna take some doin' to get 'em back, though. Especially seein' as we've got no money to bargain with."

"Hell, we'll steal 'em back." Sitting down in the chair Jim had vacated, Julian started to pull on his boots.

"But these ladies are kept in purdah. Like an 'arem. Ain't no men allowed to even see 'em but their relatives. And the jewels are in there with 'em."

"We'll figure something out."

Jim watched glumly as Julian dressed. "I was thinkin' about waitin' till morning to set out. Seems the sensible thing."

"I want to go tonight."

Jim sighed. "I figured that's what you were thinkin'. The bug's bit ya bad, ain't it?"

Julian looked up from tucking his now rightside-out shirt into his breeches. "What bug are you talking about?" he demanded, scowling fiercely.

Jim shook his head and turned to take aim at the spittoon again. "You're in love, Julie lad, and there's no earthly use your flyin' off the 'andle at me and denyin' it. I've been there meself a time or two, and you've got my sympathy. And that's all on the subject I'm going to say."

"Good," Julian said through his teeth. "Because if you say another word I'm liable to pitch you head-first through the nearest window. Get what you need together and let's get the bloody hell out of this house."

Anna awoke with a beatific smile. She felt wonderful, absolutely wonderful! Stretching, she arched her back, throwing her arms up over her head as she luxuriated against the cool, smooth sheets. She hadn't felt so good in months. No, make that years.

Bright sunlight spilled through the single open curtain, attesting to a day outside that exactly matched her mood. What time was it? It felt as if she had slept for hours. She'd never felt so rested—or so energetic. She wanted to bound from bed and embrace the day.

It struck her suddenly that beneath the bed coverings she was naked.

For a moment she was dumbstruck. Then, like a dam bursting, explicit memories of the night before flooded through her.

Julian. Her head turned, seeking him, but of course he wasn't there. With her mind she was pleased that he'd had the decency to vacate her chamber before anyone found them together. But her heart—ah, her heart. Did she wish he hadn't gone?

At the thought of coming face-to-face with him, after all they'd done together, her cheeks went hot.

What did one say to a man after spending a night of illicit passion with him?

Maybe it was best to say nothing at all.

However, knowing Julian, she doubted he would permit her to get away with that. As soon as he set eyes on her again he would probably sweep her off her feet and carry her back to bed, to repeat the whole delicious performance once more.

Anna started to grin foolishly.

Last night she had behaved like a hussy, acting the wanton with a man who possessed neither her hand nor, officially, her heart—yet she couldn't regret it.

He had stripped her notions of right and wrong, of proper behavior and gentility, from her along with her clothes—and she had revelled in the doing.

A dull pang of guilt smote her as she realized that the lovemaking she had shared with Paul had been a poor thing compared with the glorious passion that had exploded to life when she lay with Julian.

She had loved Paul, of course. One corner of her heart would always be reserved especially for him. But the awful weight of her grief had suddenly, almost magically lifted overnight, leaving the rest of her heart free again, to be bestowed where she chose.

On Julian? At the thought of loving and being loved by Julian her heart speeded up.

The prospect was exciting, dangerous, and breathtakingly alluring.

Did he love her? Oh, she hoped so. How she hoped so!

Did she love him? If she didn't, then she teetered dangerously on the brink of it. It would take only a word, a smile, a gesture, to make her fall fathoms deep.

Her foolish grin widened. If anyone should see her, she thought, they would think her the veriest fool, lying alone in bed grinning from ear to ear at nothing at all. But she couldn't seem to stop. Didn't want to stop.

Happiness was a recent stranger to her, but its return felt glorious. Like the sun bursting through the clouds after a storm, it shone just that much more brightly for having been absent.

Kicking the covers aside, Anna bounced out of bed and made haste to get ready to meet the day.

Some quarter of an hour later, in a dress of smoky lavender half-mourning that did wonderful things for her eyes, she left her bedchamber and headed downstairs. Her heart was beating foolishly, and a little smile played on her mouth. Her eyes were sparkling, and her step was light. In anticipation of encountering Julian at any moment, her cheeks were already warmly pink.

How would he look at her? What would he say?

He wasn't in the house. Anna searched through all the likely rooms and even looked in the garden to be certain, then sighed. Of course he wasn't about. It was nearer noon than daybreak, and he would be overseeing the field clearings that he had approved over her objections.

She must be in love. The idea of his overriding her wishes, which had rankled just the day before, didn't even annoy her this morning. If he wanted her fields cleared, why, it was perfectly all right with her.

From the garden she could hear Chelsea laughing as she played with Kirti. A delicious smell floated in from the outside cookhouse, where bread for the week was being baked. A boy worked the punjab fan in the parlor, circulating a breeze that made the whole house deliciously cool.

Had there ever been such a perfect day?

Raja Singha approached from the rear of the house with his customary stately tread. From his turban to his sandals, he looked the picture of unassailable dignity. Anna was suddenly struck with an urge to hug him, but managed to fight it back.

"Have you seen Mr. Chase?" she asked as he drew near.

"I believe the sahib and his friend have gone on a journey, memsahib."

Anna frowned. "A journey? Where?"

"As to that, I could not say. But Jama in the stables tells me the horses are gone, and some of the sahib's clothes are missing."

"Oh." Anna pondered for a moment. "Did he—ah—leave a message?"

"No message, memsahib. Not with me."

"I see." Anna said, as the special brightness began to seep from the day.

# XXX

$F$ive days later, Julian slipped out a rear window of a sprawling white-tiled residence on the outskirts of Anuradhapura. It was in the small hours between midnight and dawn, and over everything lay the hush of a city at rest. Inside the house, the only sound was the sighing of many sleepers. The Khan-samah had fifteen wives, and they all dreamed on pallets within.

"Did you get 'em?" Jim, waiting inside the walled garden, hurried forward as soon as Julian's leg appeared over the sill.

"Shhh." Julian jumped lightly to the ground, motioning Jim away from the house. "I got 'em."

"You did? You did!" Jim stopped dead, his face transformed by a wide grin. "By God, Julie, you're a wonder! You weren't in there half an hour, and all we knew was that the emeralds were in the women's room!"

"Would you come on? I don't know about you, but I don't fancy being chased down the street by a sword-wielding Hindu and his servants."

Thus recalled to a sense of place, Jim followed Julian over the garden wall. Not until they were well away from the city could Julian be persuaded to stop.

"Would you look at the bloody things?" Jim said

at last in exasperation when they reined in their horses and dismounted for a brief rest.

Dawn was breaking as Julian opened the pouch and spilled the gems into his hand. They were all there, except for the bracelet. A creeping tendril of light touched the gems, making them glow brilliantly green. Julian ran them between his fingers, feeling the stones and their gold setting carefully.

"Nothin'?" Jim asked.

Julian shook his head. Putting the emeralds in his pocket, he turned his attention to the pouch. He hefted it; it felt empty. It would help if he knew what kind of proof he was looking for.

Then his questing fingers encountered a stiffness in an inside seam.

"Do you have a knife?" he asked hoarsely.

Wordlessly Jim extracted a knife from a bundle tied behind his saddle and handed it to Julian.

Feeling preternaturally calm, Julian slit the seam, then ran his fingers along the opening. When he withdrew them, a small, much-folded scrap of paper lay in his hand.

"What is it?" Jim demanded.

Julian was beyond speech. Forcing his hands steady by sheer force of will, he unfolded the paper.

There, written in a spidery hand for all the world to see, were the words he'd been waiting all his life to read.

"Lord Ridley was my father," he said slowly, looking up from the paper at last to focus on the impatient Jim. "And my granny was right: my parents were married."

Jim let out a whoop and clapped Julian on the back. Julian said little as he restored the emeralds and the marriage lines to the pouch, then remounted and rode on toward Srinagar.

The fantasy he had cherished all his life had come true. He was Lord Ridley, rightful owner of Gordon Hall and all that went with it. He was a rich man, a nobleman.

Why didn't he feel overjoyed?

Anna. If he returned to Srinagar and announced his new status, and then she accepted his marriage proposal, he would never know if she loved him for himself. Lord Ridley was a very different prospect from Julian Chase, half-breed gypsy. She'd be a fool not to take him.

So along with the title, and the riches, and the legitimacy he had always craved, he could have Anna too. He would, in effect, be claiming everything that had ever belonged to his brothers. He would have triumphed over them at last.

But he didn't want Anna to be what amounted to a spoil of war. He wanted her to love him.

Riding toward Srinagar with the newly risen sun painting the road before him a shimmering gold, Julian vowed to do his utmost to make sure she did.

# XXXI

He was gone for a week. During that time, Anna's hurt turned to anger, and finally to all-out rage. How dare he disappear without so much as a word after what they had shared? Did it mean so little to him?

That was the thought that stabbed at her. If he could leave her so casually, after a night such as they had spent, then it could mean only one thing: however much their lovemaking had meant to her, it had been no more than one in many such nights to him.

In his mind, his lovers were probably as interchangeable as his linen.

Gritting her teeth at her own stupidity—had she really thought to give Julian Chase the lion's share of her heart, while relegating dear, loyal Paul to a small corner?—Anna threw the lavender dress on the floor of her wardrobe and went back to the long-sleeved, high-necked crow's dresses of full mourning. Indeed, she felt guilty at the idea that she had been ready to don brighter colors, to step forward into a new life. Paul had been a man in a million, a far better man than she deserved, yet she had been ready to relegate his memory to the past in favor of a bold, unprincipled rogue whose sole redeeming

211

characteristic was that he knew how to please a woman in bed.

What kind of female was she, to let such a thing sway her so? The vicar's daughter, for all her genteel upbringing, was at heart certainly no lady!

"Are you sickening for something?" Ruby asked, surprised when Anna snapped at her for the umpteenth time during the course of the week.

Guiltily Anna realized that she had been behaving with poor humor toward everyone in the household. Certainly Ruby's insistence on admiring aloud every halfway eligible man she knew was annoying, but always before Anna had managed to take it in stride. The difference was that, just at the moment, she couldn't bear to hear anyone sing any man's—and particularly Julian Chase's—praises. Even hearing the blackguard's name made her want to scream.

"I must be," she answered Ruby with real contrition. "Forgive me, please. I promise I'll do the same for you someday when you get out of sorts."

Ruby eyed her shrewdly. "You wouldn't be missing a certain black-haired gent, now, would you?"

Anna stiffened, stretching herself to her full height, which was something less than considerable.

"No, I would not," she responded icily. Leaving Ruby to hide a knowing smile, she stalked out to join Chelsea and Kirti in the garden. What she needed was a little fresh air.

Charles called twice during the week, and on both occasions Anna greeted him more warmly than had lately been her wont. She was chagrined to admit that her recently sundered infatuation for Julian had blinded her to this man's very real worth. Charles was solid, steady, and if he wasn't particularly exciting that was all to the good. Anna had had enough masculine-generated excitement lately to last the rest of her life.

On his second visit, he took her for a ride in his buggy. The swift rush of air past her face and the briskly changing scenery lifted her spirits. The sky overhead was a dazzling shade of blue laced with fluffy ribbons of white clouds, Charles's horse was fresh and swift, and birds and monkeys chattered gaily in the trees.

So what if her unprincipled cad of a brother-in-law had been gone from Srinagar for longer than he ever had been before? She didn't need him. She didn't want him. She would be positively glad to learn that he was never coming back.

"There, now, you've got some color back in your cheeks. You've been looking so pale these last few days that I've been worried about you."

Anna smiled at Charles. Really, with his upright military bearing and even features, he was a handsome man. How had she let Julian's devilish attraction blind her to one whose charm might not be as flashy but was certainly far more sincere?

"You shouldn't worry about me. But it is kind of you to be concerned."

He looked at her then, swiftly, his hazel eyes narrowed. "It's very easy to be kind to you."

"You're a nice man, Charles."

"I'm glad you think so. But I don't know about 'nice.' Sounds rather boring."

Anna shook her head. "Not boring. Safe."

"Do you want to be safe, Anna?" The question was a throwaway, almost too casual. Anna deliberately let the nuances pass her by.

"I suppose everyone wants to be safe," she replied lightly.

"Anna." To her surprise and dismay he reined in his horse. When the buggy had rocked to a stop he turned to her. "I had not meant to speak of this for a while yet, but it's been a year now that you've been alone, and I—I'm lonely too. Chelsea needs a father, and my children need a mother. And you need to be taken care of. You're very young and would no doubt like other children—"

"Charles—" Anna tried to interrupt, only to be stopped herself by an upheld hand.

He smiled a little crookedly at her. "Let me speak my piece or I'll never get it said. I suppose I'm doing this badly. What I'm getting at, of course, if that I'd be more than honored if you would consider marrying me."

"Oh, Charles." There was an ache in her voice. Wouldn't life be simple if she could love this good man? If she could give her life and Chelsea's into his hands in the sure knowledge that they both would be cared for and cherished? But she knew even as she wished things were otherwise that she must refuse. She liked Charles, respected him, enjoyed his company. But she did not love him. Not in the sweet, gentle fashion in which she had cared for Paul, or with the explosive passion that she tried her best not to feel for Julian. Whoever said half a loaf was better than none was wrong, at least when it came to men. If she could not have the man she wanted, then she was better off with no man at all.

He sighed. "I see you mean to refuse me. Well, I expected it. It's too soon, I know. But perhaps in time . . . ?"

He looked so hopeful that Anna had not the heart to deny him.

"Perhaps," she said gently.

"I'll say no more, then. For now."

Charles, gentleman that he was, smiled gamely at her, lifted his hands, and clucked to the horse. And true to his word, he said no more on the subject for the remainder of the ride, but was instead as pleasant and undemanding a companion as he had been before.

When they arrived back at the Big House, Charles accompanied Anna inside as a matter of course. Without having to be asked, Raja Singha materialized with a tray of tea, which Charles was pleased to take with Anna in the parlor. They chatted desultorily about commonplaces. Anna was grateful to discover that Charles apparently did not mean to let his unanswered proposal stand in the way of their normal easy friendship. They finished at last, and Charles stood up to take his leave. Smiling at some quip he'd made, Anna rose, too, to see him to the door. The movement brought her so close to him that her skirt brushed the shiny calves of his boots. Looking down at the delicate black silk of her gown where it billowed against the smooth leather, Charles appeared suddenly shaken. He drew in a breath, turned toward her, and took her hands in both of his.

"Anna . . ."

Caught by surprise, she could only look up at him. Charles hesitated, his eyes searching hers as if for some sign. His hands held hers tightly, his thumbs running lightly over the soft skin on the backs of her hands. His eyes were some inches above hers, although he had not Julian's overpowering height. His brown hair had just begun to recede at the temples, which gave him a distinguished look. All in all, he was a man whom most women would be proud to call their own. Maybe, in time, she . . .

Without another word he bent and swiftly kissed her mouth. It was a soft kiss, and quick, not a bit demanding. Not like . . . But Anna flatly refused to allow herself to make the comparison. Charles's kiss was perfectly pleasant, like the man himself. A gentleman's kiss, to a lady he respected.

It was the kind of kiss every decent woman should want.

And if she found herself secretly preferring a far different sort, well then, the fault was in her, not him, and she must work to eradicate it.

"I hope you don't mind," Charles said, smiling down at her, "but . . ."

Whatever else he said Anna missed. She had just become aware that they were no longer alone. Lounging in the doorway, eyes slightly narrowed as he watched the affecting scene being played out before him, stood Julian.

He was back!

Her traitorous heart leaped at the sight of him, dusty and disheveled and looking out of sorts as he was, all the while her ears refused to hear Charles's softly cajoling words.

"We're not alone," she managed to say clearly. Charles looked surprised, then, as he glanced around and spied Julian, annoyed and self-conscious in rapid succession.

"Major." Julian straightened from the door, nodding curtly. There was an expression on his face that told Anna, at least, that he was not best pleased at what he had seen.

"I suppose this looks most peculiar," Charles began, with an air of making explanations to one who had a right to demand them. Anna, now that the initial euphoria of seeing Julian again had been replaced by a towering blast of rage at him, scowled at Charles and pulled her hands from his. Julian, of all people, had no right to play propriety!

"Indeed." Julian's response was cool, but there was an expression in his eyes that made Charles color up.

"See here, there's no question of anything wrong. I've asked your sister-in-law to marry me."

"He has no right to any explanation. He's not my keeper," Anna snapped, her words for Charles while her glare was focused on Julian.

"As your nearest male relation—" Charles started.

"Pshaw!" Anna refuted rudely, her fists clenching at her sides.

"Anna's right, of course. She need make no explanations to me." Julian's brusque reply was directed over Anna's head to Charles. "Excuse me."

Without another word he turned and quitted the room. Anna was left seething to listen to his booted feet retreating along the hallway toward the rear of the house. Where was he going? Not that she cared, except that she was itching to tell him to his head all the highly unflattering thoughts she'd been harboring about him over the past seven days.

How dare he bed her, then disappear without a word, as casually as if she'd been the merest lightskirt? How dare he!

"I fear your brother-in-law has legitimate cause for complaint. I should not have kissed you." Charles sounded so humorously contrite that Anna forced herself to drag her attention back to him.

"Whether you kiss me or not has nothing to do with him." For all her care to keep her tone even, an acidic note crept through.

"Nevertheless . . ." Charles sighed and regarded Anna with a touch of humor. "As a would-be Romeo I come off somewhat badly, don't I? Well, maybe on another occasion I'll contrive to do better. In my own defense I must say that I haven't had a lot of practice recently."

"I think you make a wonderful Romeo, Charles," Anna defended, her heart touched by his rueful words. " 'Tis I who am a most unsatisfactory Juliet."

"We must both contrive to do better then."

Jollying her in this way, he managed, as Anna saw him out to his carriage, to lighten the uneasy atmosphere left in Julian's wake. At least until the buggy bowled along the drive and out of sight.

Then Anna turned and, in high dudgeon, went in search of Julian.

# XXXII

He was not in the garden. Anna waved to Chelsea and Kirti, and forced herself to smile, but she did not stop. The next most likely place was the stable. If he was not there, then she would find herself temporarily at a loss. The notion did not please her.

It was late afternoon, and the stable was mostly empty. All the horses and donkeys were being worked except Sister, a hardy island pony who had sprained a hock a few days previously. Sister nickered softly at Anna's entry, and Hugo, the resident goat, bleated. Anna patted Sister's velvety nose, rewarded Hugo's attempt to eat the hem of her skirt with a shove, and looked around for Julian.

"Memsahib?" It was Jama, the stable boy, who glided out of the shadows where, as was evident from the pitchfork in his hand, he had clearly been mucking out a stall.

"Have you seen Mr. Chase?"

" 'E's done took 'imself for a walk. Said 'e misliked the air up in the 'ouse.'' Jim's voice was unmistakable. Whirling, Anna discovered him behind her. He looked her over with disapproval, then turned his head to spit in the straw.

It was all Anna could do not to shudder with distaste.

"Which path did he take?"

Jim eyed her sourly. "I figure 'e wants to be let alone. When 'e gets a certain look in 'is eye, most people are smart enough to leave 'im be."

"Do you know where he went or don't you?" Anna asked impatiently.

Jim shrugged. "Mebbe."

Anna's temper began to sizzle with fresh heat, but she did not want to vent her anger on Jim when its real target was Julian. Accordingly, she bit her tongue and turned her eyes to Jama.

"Did you see which way the sahib went?"

"Toward the waterfall, I think, memsahib."

"Thank you." Anna allowed a small degree of triumph to color her voice as she turned back to walk past Jim without another word.

To her annoyance he fell into step beside her.

"Did you want something?" she asked haughtily.

Jim grimaced. "What I wants and what I gets ain't too often the same thing. What I wants is to be sittin' down to a meal. What I gets is to make sure you don't get your damn-fool self 'urt walkin' through this 'ere jungle by your lonesome. There's been some talk about some strange goings-on around here lately."

"That's ridiculous." Anna walked faster. "I don't need your escort, thank you. I have been along this path many times."

"Don't matter. Julie'd be wroth with me, did I let you come to 'arm." Jim swung along at her side, a wiry little man not many inches taller than Anna herself. Like Julian when he had entered the house, he bore the marks of recent travel. His white shirt was wrinkled and grimy, and his breeches and boots were splotched with mud. He seemed to list slightly to one side, as if either his legs or shoulders were not quite even.

"I don't mean to be rude, but I'd prefer that you didn't come with me. What I have to say to Julian is private." Anna stepped into the cool green darkness of the jungle as she spoke. She moved swiftly along the path, more swiftly than she would ordinarily have done had she not been so bent on losing her escort. She knew to watch for snakes and such that took refuge from the heat of the day under the cool leaves on the jungle floor.

"I s'pose it is," Jim said nonchalantly, and kept pace behind her with seeming ease.

Anna's lips tightened, and she cast him a narrow-eyed look over her shoulder. Surely he could not know what had occurred between herself and Julian. How could he? With all his many and varied faults, Julian did not strike her as the kind of man to brag of his conquests. On the other hand . . .

"Don't get your wind up," Jim advised her, apparently reading her growing annoyance in the stiffening set of her back. "When I see you safely to Julie, I'll leave the two of you be. I reckon 'e's just a might wroth with you, too."

Anna took a deep breath as alarm mingled with her anger. If Julian had told this little gnome anything of what had passed between them . . .

"I don't know all the particulars, mind, but I do know Julie. Were I you, missus, I'd steer clear of 'im until 'e works whatever ails 'im out of 'is system. 'As a nasty temper, 'as Julie, when 'e's pushed 'ard enough."

"Thank you for the advice," Anna said through her teeth. She yanked her skirts a little higher to keep them out of the damp mulch that lay inches thick on the forest floor, set her jaw, and stalked forward.

"I've known 'im since 'e was a lad of twelve or thereabouts, and I can tell you, boy or man, 'e's a good un. Don't come any better than Julie. 'E don't deserve a fancy petticoat playin' fast and loose with 'im."

As the meaning of this cant speech sank in, Anna stiffened in outrage. Turning, she stopped dead in front of Jim, her eyes sparkling with outrage.

"If you are referring to me as a fancy petticoat, and implying that I have in some way wronged your—Julie, then I take leave to tell you that you have gone beyond the bounds of what is pleasing by a considerable degree!"

"Good God, she can't even speak the King's good English so's a body can understand it. Like I tole Julie, the 'eat must've turned 'is brain."

Livid, Anna whirled back around and marched on down the path.

"But there's no accounting for tastes, after all," Jim said philosophically to her back. Anna would have turned and annihilated him there and then had she not heard the muted roar of the waterfall just ahead.

Rather than expend her fury on the minor irritant, she would save it for the primary object of her wrath!

Pushing through the veil of flowering vines that blocked the end of the path, she stepped into a verdant clearing. At its center was a small, clear pool that ran downhill by way of a narrow creek. The pool was fed by a cascade of water that fell noisily over a twenty-foot-high wall of rocks that nature had over the course of thousands of years carved from the mountainside. Overhead, exotic birds fluttered in the thick canopy of interlaced branches that kept the sun from reaching the clearing. The few rays that filtered down provided a soft, diffused light that gave the setting an otherworldly aspect. Large, flat-topped rocks fringed part of the pool. Leafy kudzu vines covered the other banks with lush greenery. The scent of mangoes and frangipani made the air as fragrant as fine perfume. A small orange-faced monkey, which had been sitting on a rock regarding its reflection in the pool with fascination, scampered off at Anna's advent. To her disappointment, it seemed to be the only living creature on the ground. Julian was nowhere in sight. Annoyed, she realized that he must not have taken the path to the waterfall after all. If he had, and had already turned back toward the house, they would have passed him en route.

Drat the man! Disappearing was getting to be a habit with him. Where could he be?

Just then a seallike black head broke the surface of the water. For a moment Anna was startled. Then she realized that the head, and the broad bare shoulders that rose after it, belonged to Julian. He must know how to swim!

Impressed despite herself with that accomplishment, which was rare in an Englishman, she nevertheless fixed her quarry with angry eyes. It was clear that he had not yet discovered her presence. Over the rushing of the waterfall it would be impossible to hear her footsteps as she made her way purposefully along the water's edge. Behind her, Jim melted into the jungle without so much as a word. So focused was Anna on Julian that she was scarcely aware of his going.

Still plainly unaware of her presence, Julian swam across the pool with long, clean strokes. He was bare from the waist up, and it occurred to her that he might be equally bare below it. But if he was, the water protected his modesty well enough. And if he should choose to come out of the pool—well, that was fine, too. She was too angry to care.

He reached the far end of the pool, dived under the surface of the cascading waterfall, and after a few moments surfaced again, heading back in the direction he had come.

Then he saw her.

Anna knew the exact moment from the instant contraction of his brows and the brief hesitation in his steady stroke. Then, to her annoyance, he continued to swim, ignoring her as if she was no more than another of the poolside trees. Since she could not swim so much as a stroke, entering the pool to confront him there was not an option. She had no

choice but to stand at the side of the pool, arms
crossed over her breasts and toe tapping, until he
chose to stop and acknowledge her presence.

He swam for at least another quarter of an hour,
ignoring her all the while.

Finally he quit and stood up in the center of the
pool. The water came to just below his chin. As he
walked toward the bank—the one directly opposite
from where Anna was sitting—she was afforded an
excellent view of emerging broad shoulders, a wide
back that tapered to a narrow waist, muscular buttocks, powerful thighs that rippled when he moved,
strong calves, and, finally, long, lean bare feet.
When he splashed out of the shallows, still ignoring
her, Anna's temper snapped. She would have
screamed at him if she'd thought he could hear her
over the gurgling water. But as he probably could
not—or would at least pretend not to—she stalked,
fists clenched, around the perimeter of the pool until
she reached the hollow between two rock forma-
tions where he stood. He was toweling himself dry,
and he barely glanced up as she stopped just a foot
short of him.

"Where have you been?" she demanded, her
voice gritty. Despite her fury, one part of her mind
admired the sheer muscled magnificence of his naked body while the other sternly cautioned her not
to notice.

"I don't see that my whereabouts is any of your
concern." Still he barely glanced at her. He was bent
over, rubbing the towel along his legs. Anna scowled
at the top of that wet black head. Now that his lust
for her had been satisfied, he was acting as if she
were barely alive!

"Not my concern?" she repeated, voice rising.
"Listen, you blackguard, Srinagar is not a hotel
where you can come and go at will without a word
to anybody!"

"Since when have I been required to report my

comings and goings to you?'' he asked insolently.
He straightened, looking directly at her at last.

Anna spluttered. ''I want you out of my house.
Permanently. Today!'' It was the culmination of all
the furious things she wanted to say.

For a moment he said nothing as he finished drying himself. Then, instead of wrapping the towel
strategically around his waist as any decent man
would, he draped it over his shoulder. So casual
was his attitude that it was an insult in itself. Anna
kept her eyes on his face and resolutely refused to
notice anything else. His nakedness was neither
embarrassing nor enticing. It had no effect on her
whatsoever, and so she meant it to be if it killed
her!

''Just in time for the wedding, I take it.''

''What wedding?'' Anna was momentarily all at
sea.

''Forgotten already? Poor Charles!''

''Oh, that. I—I've refused him. For now. Not that
it's any of *your* concern.'' Anna's voice rose. ''Anyway, that's beside the point. I want you out of my
house!''

''Then it seems you're destined to want what you
can't have. Must be your lot in life.''

''And what does that mean?''

''It means I'm not going anywhere until I'm good
and ready. And if you don't like it, then so be it.''

Anna blinked. He was as angry as she. It was clear
in the darkening of his eyes to near black and the
hardening of his voice. But for the life of her she
couldn't figure out what he had to be angry about.
She was the one who had been callously used and
discarded, not him!

''Tell me,'' Julian continued with false cordiality,
''does Dumesne realize you're not interested in him
at all, but in finding a man to replace Paul?''

Anna stared at him. ''What are you talking
about?''

"You and Dumesne certainly looked cozy. Have you bedded him yet?"

"That's a foul thing to say!"

"I'm feeling foul. So foul that I suggest you leave me the hell alone."

He turned his back and reached for his breeches. Anna, incensed, tapped him sharply on his arm.

"Don't you turn your back on me! I have a few things to say to you!"

"Do you now?" He faced her, slowly, a peculiarly satisfied expression on his face. "Well, you can't say you weren't warned."

With that he reached out, caught her shoulders, and yanked her against him. There was no longer any ignoring the fact that he was naked—and fully aroused. She could feel the unmentionable part of him stabbing at her belly through her dress and petticoat. His body was still slightly damp, she discovered as she pushed furiously against his chest with both hands, and warm and hairy—and as unyielding as the stone wall behind them.

"Let me go! Take your hands off me! Do you hear me?"

"Oh, I hear you all right," he said, his tone ugly. His mouth sneered. His hands on her shoulders tightened, then shifted. All at once, Anna felt herself being scooped off her feet.

"Don't you dare! Put me down! Put me down!"

He was carrying her, both her wrists imprisoned in one of his hands, ignoring her furious kicking and squirming as if she were no more than a spitting kitten he could control with ease.

"I said *put me down!*" Anna practically shrieked the command, her eyes blazing as they raked his dark face. Those obsidian eyes glittered with what she could have sworn was satisfaction, and his mouth curled into a mocking parody of a smile.

"Your wish, of course, is my command," he murmured.

Then, without so much as a word of warning,

Anna found herself tossed from his arms to go sailing through the air. She barely had time to close her eyes before she hit the pool with a tremendous splash.

# XXXIII

She sank like a stone. The water closed, cool and wet and all-enveloping, over her head as she hurtled straight to the bottom. Still in a semisitting position, she felt her posterior touch first, then she was clawing for the surface, fighting, flailing in an effort to rejoin the world of light and air. But the pool was too deep; she couldn't touch the bottom and reach the surface at the same time. Bouncing, trying not to panic, she bobbed up and managed to get her face out of the water and gulp some air before she sank again.

It occurred to her, as she found the bottom with her toes and again thrust upwards toward the light, that she could drown. Surely Julian would not leave her. . . .

But he could swim. Had the swine stalked off before realizing that she could not?

Fear exploded like a bomb in Anna's brain just as she felt something grab one of her flailing hands and haul her toward the surface. Her head broke the water, her shoulders too. Julian was lifting her into his arms, his face both pale and grim. Nothing and nobody had ever looked more wonderful to Anna in her life. Choking and spluttering, gasping for air, she locked her arms around his neck as if she meant never to let him go. He waded from the pool with her in his arms as she wheezed and trembled and clung to him. Once they had attained the safety of the bank, he still held her, his body warm and hard against the shivering chill of hers.

Anna was sopping wet, her hair straggling in dripping rat's tails around her face and down her back, her gown pouring water. Even her shoes were soaked. She was trembling in the aftermath of fear, and for a few minutes it felt wonderful to be held in his arms. Then she remembered how she had come to be in the pool in the first place.

"You—swine," she hissed on her first steady breath. She pulled back to glare at him, sweeping the soaking strands of hair from her face with one hand.

"I'm sorry," he said tightly.

"Sorry! I could have drowned!" It should have been difficult to quarrel with a man who was both naked and holding her cradled in his arms, but Anna was too angry to care.

"I didn't realize you wouldn't be able to touch bottom."

"You don't realize all kinds of things! You're an unprincipled blackguard, a womanizing cad, an untrustworthy, shameless—"

"Whoa!" he said, and to Anna's fury she saw that her insults had brought a faint smile to his mouth. "That's—"

Red rage burst inside her. Before she even realized that she meant to do it she had doubled up her first and punched him right in the eye.

He yelped, jumped back, and dropped her. Anna landed painfully on her hip on the slippery carpet of vines and scrambled to her feet with scarcely a wince. Her sole desire was to kill him with her bare hands. The hurt and humiliation she had suffered over the past week combined with her recent fright to make her so angry that she seemed to view the world—and him—through a red fog. He had clapped a hand to his eye and was regarding her with such astonishment that it would have been comical had she been in a mood to laugh. But she was not. She wanted to scratch and bite and claw and punch. . . . With a wordless cry she flew at him, fingers curved into claws.

"Anna! Stop!" He retreated before her onslaught, his hands outthrust to hold her off. To her absolute fury she saw that he was beginning to smile again. Soaked or not, her feet were clad in sturdy leather shoes, and he was as bare as the day he was born. Drawing back her foot, she kicked him as hard as she could in the shin. He yelped, hopping on one leg, and made the ultimate mistake of bending down to massage the aching shin.

Her next blow caught him squarely on the temple.

"Enough!" he roared, straightening, and grabbed her upper arms to give her a rough shake. "Stop, you little hellcat, or I'll turn you over my knee and beat the temper out of you!"

"Just you try it!" Anna dared, panting, and aimed another kick at his shin.

He dodged it. His hands tightened on her arms as he held her carefully at arm's length, and for a moment the same fury that blazed in Anna was reflected back at her from his eyes. But even as she glared at him, chin outthrust and head thrown back so that her hopelessly loosened hair streamed down her back, his eyes softened. Anna saw that sudden glint of blue where only black had been before, and felt an unexpected clenching in the pit of her stomach.

"Oh, Anna," he said in an odd voice. Then those eyes went black again, and his hands moved up to close over the neck of her gown. Before she had the least inkling what he meant to do he gave a tremendous yank, and her gown split to the waist with a loud rip.

Anna gasped, screeched a protest, and tried to jerk away. He would not let her go, but continued to rip at her gown despite her struggles.

"Have you gone mad? Stop it! What are you doing? Julian!"

"I'm sick of your bloody black dresses," he growled, giving the gown a final mighty yank that rent it clear to the hem.

"Stop it!" she screeched again even as he jerked the dress clean off her. Futilely she tried to catch the soaked panels of shredded black silk as he snatched them away from her. He eluded her clutching fingers with a grim smile. Wadding the ruined cloth in both hands, he strode for the pool. He stopped only to scoop up a rock, which he placed in the center of the parcel. Then he heaved the bundle into the middle of the pool. Speechless, Anna could only watch what had once been her dress disappear beneath the surface.

Only then did he turn back to her. His eyes moved over her with fierce satisfaction.

"That's better," he said.

Anna gasped. "Better?" Her voice rose shrilly as she looked down at herself. Clad in a muslin chemise that left most of her décolletage and the entirety of her arms bare and clung to her bosom with immodest tenacity, a single petticoat, garters, stockings and shoes, every single item of which was dripping wet and clinging, she was positively indecent. Certainly she could not return to the house in such a state!

"Better?" she wailed. "How dare you do that? What am I going to do now?"

He was approaching her, a determined expression on his face. Something about the gleam in those blue-black eyes made Anna take several hasty steps backward.

"Make love with me," he said, and reached for her.

"What? No!" She yelped as his hands closed over her upper arms. "Let go of me, you . . ."

"You know you want to. And I want to. I mean

to love you till you can't think of anything else. Or anybody else. Just you—and me. . . ."

He dragged her close and bent his head to find her mouth despite her struggles. Anna tried to resist the hot allure, but in the end she could not. All her instincts shouted a warning, reminding her to consider how he had used and left her before, but her body wasn't listening. It responded to the hard demand of his with a single-minded surge of longing that washed away every obstacle in its path. Like an addict in desperate need of opium, she was helpless in the face of her craving. Her arms went around his neck, her fingers curled in the coarse strands of hair at the back of his head. She let him draw her up on tiptoe, pressed her body against his, and clung.

His hand was on her breast even before his tongue entered her mouth. Swirling away on a whirlwind of desire, Anna felt her breast swell against the abrasive heat of his palm. Her nipple hardened, thrusting upward, begging for his touch. He obliged, running his thumb over the aching nub, his other hand supporting her back as he lowered her to the ground.

His mouth never left hers. His tongue explored the eager wetness of her mouth, greedy in its demands. Anna, trembling and nearly mindless with passion, answered as best she could, shyly venturing to enter the hot cave of his mouth with her tongue, exploring there, licking his lips as he licked hers. So enraptured was she with this game that she scarcely felt the coolness of the vines beneath her back, or the hardness of the ground beneath that. The roar of the waterfall, the chattering of the birds, the rustling of small creatures in the undergrowth nearby might have been a heavenly chorus for all she heard of them.

She was deaf, dumb, and blind to everything but Julian and the way he was making her feel.

His hands were trembling as he yanked the straps of her chemise down to bare her breasts. For just a

moment he lifted himself away from her, staring at
the bounty he had uncovered. The fire in those eyes
as they feasted on her breasts made Anna whimper
with wanting. Instinctively she arched her back in a
gesture of offering as old as woman. Then she cried
out as he bent his head to take an aching nipple into
his mouth.

The straps of her chemise were tight just above
her elbows, binding her arms to her sides. He suck-
led first one breast than the other as she struggled
to free herself from the constrictions of the under-
garment so that she could touch him as she was
longing to do. But her arms would not come free;
she could only lie there, squirming, as he tormented
her breasts with teeth and lips and tongue, setting
her body afire.

Then his hands were at her waist, untying the
tapes of her petticoat with fingers that fumbled.
When at last the knot came free, he lifted himself off
her just long enough to yank the skirt away from
her, tossing it aside to land crumpled at the base of
a bush. He was kneeling beside her, and for a long
moment he stayed that way, looking down at her.
His eyes touched on the drying strands of her silvery hair, spread in a tangled fan shape that framed
her body against the background of deep green
vines. His eyes moved over her face with its passion-
drugged eyes and parted lips that were rosy and
swollen from his kisses. His eyes slid down to her
small naked breasts with the tiny nipples that were
distended now and the color of strawberries. His
eyes drank in the soft creaminess of her skin, then
registered the chemise, which still imprisoned her
arms and was twisted around her waist, leaving her
lower body as bare as her breasts. He made no move
to free her from this remaining garment, or even to
release her arms. Instead his eyes flared, darkened,
then wandered farther, lingering over the gentle
curve of her hips, the hollow of her belly button, the
ash-brown tangle of curls between her thighs. Fi-

nally his gaze moved down her slender thighs, pale above the black cotton stockings that ended in ribbon garters inches above her knees.

And then, at last, he touched her. His hand gently traced the line where her legs pressed together, running between her thighs from her knees to the nest of curls. Anna caught her breath at being so caressed. Her eyes, languorous and heavy-lidded, watched the progression of that long-fingered, swarthy-skinned hand against her white skin. When it reached its goal, her lids fluttered down, then up again, and she quivered visibly.

"Let me in," he whispered, his fingers delving between her legs. His eyes never left her face, watching her helpless reaction to his touch with a hard satisfaction that mixed oddly with the dark fire of his hunger for her. "Open your legs for me, Anna."

The words were shocking, her response more shocking yet. She drew in a harsh little breath, held it—and timidly parted her legs.

As if to reward her, he gently stroked the sensitive insides of her thighs.

Anna moaned.

It occurred to Julian then that maybe, just maybe, he might get her to fall in love with him yet. Her helpless reaction to his touch could be turned to his advantage. He would win her heart through his mastery of her body, by bedding her until she couldn't think of anything—or anybody—else.

For a moment longer he allowed himself the luxury of looking at her. Almost naked, she was spread before him like a feast. Her lips were parted, hungry for his kisses, her back arched, offering him her swollen breasts, her legs spread in shameless invitation. She wanted him—him—and the evidence before his eyes was intoxicating.

He slid inside her carefully, held himself there,

waited. Sure enough she began to writhe, then buck up against him as if she couldn't stand the delicious torture any longer. Julian held off as long as he could, until sweat beaded his upper lip and his arms trembled. Then he plunged into her fiercely, once, twice, three times to the accompaniment of her frantic cries before he exploded with an intensity that left him shaking.

Afterwards he lay atop her, cradling her in his arms. He did not quite dare look into her face. He'd been angry over seeing her with Dumesne, and he'd behaved badly. But he'd made amends at the end— he hoped. Still, it was possible that, once she got over the shattering effects of their lovemaking, she'd be furious with him all over again.

When what he badly wanted to see in her face was love.

The maddening little witch spoke not a word.

Finally Julian rolled off her and sat up.

At last she opened her eyes to smile dreamily at him. Julian watched her, almost holding his breath. Then, as her eyes focused, the dreamy look vanished. She scowled at him and sprang to her feet.

"Oh, no!" she said. "You'll not do that to me twice! You fickle swine, how dare you make love to me, vanish for a week without a word, then come back as unpleasant as can be and make love to me again! I'll not stand for it!"

Julian got to his feet, sighing. "Just where do you imagine I was?"

"I don't care!" She found her petticoat and pulled it on. She snatched up her stockings and her shoes. "Just look what you did!"

She shook the garment at him.

"I'll make it up to you," he promised.

"I don't want you to make it up to me! I don't want you to come near me ever again," she hissed. Grabbing her remaining pieces of clothing, she darted away down the path.

Julian was left to stare thoughtfully after her. It might, he decided after a few minutes, be best to let her have a few days to cool off before he began his campaign to win her heart in earnest.

# XXXIV

Five days later, Anna was perched sidesaddle on the back of Baliclava, a tan donkey with a moth-eaten hide, which had the lone virtue of being the only ridable animal left in the stable. She was headed resolutely down the mountain toward the section of land that Hillmore, during their meeting the night before, had told her was targeted for clearing that afternoon. On her head was tied a huge, faded blue sunbonnet with a flapping brim. Her feet and ankles were protected by stout boots, her hands by leather gloves. These additions to her mourning costume looked ridiculous, she knew, but she was too angry to care. She meant to see what was going on in the fields for herself, however much Julian might dislike her interference. Indeed, she hoped he did dislike it! Because she disliked everything about him, from his dark, arrogant handsomeness to the way he turned up his nose at curry for dinner!

Since their shattering encounter by the stream, she had been deliberately cool to him. She was not a wanton, to be used and discarded at will! Julian spent most of his time riding about the estate with Hillmore, directing the clearing of the most promising fields for the planting of orange pekoe. When Anna informed him that she preferred to try Hillmore's experiment on a far smaller scale than the two men envisioned, Julian replied that he had given Hillmore the go-ahead and meant to see the scheme carried out whether Anna liked it or not.

She didn't like it, but there didn't seem to be much she could do about it. Hillmore, while humoring her as the titular mistress of the plantation, more and more openly took his orders from Julian. Her efforts to order Julian off the place had proved futile. Arguing with him had proved worse than futile, with Anna ending up screeching furious insults at him as he mocked her or, equally maddening, just walked away. The fields would be cleared, and orange pekoe would be planted, and if she didn't like it then that was too bad—this was Julian's attitude to her objections. Anna, furious, became all too aware that she was helpless to stop him from doing anything he wished and had decided reluctantly that she must use reason rather than harsh words to get across her very real objections to the plan. But first she had to know whereof she spoke. If she found, as Julian insisted, that the tea plants being destroyed were practically worthless anyway, then she might, just might, be left with nothing to say. But she did not think that fully half of her fields could be to all practical purposes nonproducing.

"Be careful, Baliclava," Anna said, as the donkey picked his way over some exposed roots.

The path through the rain forest was relatively clear. As part of the modernization of the plantation, a new series of tanks, or water reservoirs, was being built. Elephants had dragged fallen trees along this route just a few days before to be used to dam natural depressions in the ground near the fields to be cleared. The depressions would fill up with rain during the half of the year that was wet, and then, when the dry season came, would be drained of water as needed to soak the parched fields. This system of irrigation was common all over Ceylon, but on Srinagar there had never been enough money to do the thing properly. Now, of course, there was.

Leaf monkeys chattered in the trees overhead,
causing Anna to look up. With their red faces and
rough brown coats, they were comical-looking, and
their antics were usually enough to draw a laugh
from even the glummest observer. But today, even
as Anna smiled at their games, she saw something
that made her shiver: a venomous golden tree snake
slithered along a branch, its slender body gleaming
through the half-gloom of the forest. Cringing
slightly, Anna leaned forward in the saddle and
urged her plodding mount into a trot. She had always had a horror of having a snake drop from a
tree onto her. It occurred to her, annoyingly, that
perhaps Julian's objections to her galivanting (as he
put it) about the jungle alone were at least partially
justified. In England, a lady was always accompanied on her jaunts out of a respect for propriety. In
Ceylon, such companionship was more of a safety
precaution. The natives were gentle, harmless people as a rule, and Anna felt far safer with her fellow
humans on Ceylon than she did in England. But ac-
cidents happened so often in Ceylon that they were
regarded almost as routine. A tree branch fell, im-
paling a man to the ground and leaving his wife a
widow; a wolf snake struck and parents lost a child;
a sinkhole opened up unexpectedly and whole families disappeared.

Anna shivered, glancing up again. The tree snake
was left behind, but the creeping sense of dread remained. She'd actually thought about asking Ruby
to accompany her (despite the fact that she hated to
give Julian the satisfaction of seeming to bow to his
wishes), but Ruby was not exactly enamored of the
local fauna. Spiders made her scream, and she lived
in fear that Moti the mongoose would find its way
into her bed some night.

That left Raja Singha, the three housemaids, Oya
the cook, Chelsea, and Kirti as prospective companions for this ride through the jungle, none of whom
were available at the time. So Anna had come alone.

Which, if Julian and his disgusting henchman had not filled her ears with warnings about possible dangers, would have bothered her not at all.

Blast the man!

"Slow down, drat it!" she said, but the donkey paid her no heed.

Still bouncing inelegantly as Baliclava, having quickened his pace, refused to slow it again, Anna burst out of the forest into the first field. She sawed at the reins, trying to slow the beast to a walk, but without much hope of success. The donkey's mouth was as tough as leather. Fortunately, a trumpeting elephant nearby distracted him, making him look around and bray an answer. Taking advantage of his lack of concentration, Anna was able to pull him down to a walk and take her first good look in months at the plants that had fueled so much controversy.

Laboriously cleared years ago by the process of chena-farming, or burning down existing vegetation to plant crops, the jungle that had once flourished undisturbed all over the island had been turned into acre upon acre of verdant land for the cultivation of tea, cinnamon, and rice. As she passed what remained of that particular field's once orderly rows, Anna was chagrined to find that the tea plants she had been championing so passionately had grown to, in some instances, as much as thirty feet tall. The stalks were thick as tree branches, and looked to be as tough. She could see the all-important flushes, or new shoots, only at the very top of each plant. As much as she hated to admit it, it looked very much as though Julian and Hillmore were right—about this field, at least. Still, she couldn't believe that half the plantation was in such bad shape. Why, such neglect must date back to Paul's stewardship!

Elephants and oxen labored side by side with turbaned islanders some two hundred yards away, clearing a firebreak between the tea plants and the forest. As she emerged at the end of one row, Anna saw a telltale plume of smoke at the far side of the field; apparently the burn-off had just begun.

Clucking to Baliclava, she turned him away from where the islanders labored. Her first view of the tea plants had not been promising; she wanted to examine them more closely before they were burned.

The possibility of the fire spreading out of control never even occurred to Anna; fields were cleared all the time by burning, and no one was ever hurt. Besides, the small plume of smoke had been at the opposite end of the field, some ten acres away. She would have plenty of time to judge the condition of the plants and get out of the way before the fire was remotely in her vicinity.

Thus, as she rode slowly along the rows of plants, it came as a surprise to her that the smell of burning was so strong. The acrid odor was enough to make her eyes sting, and she wondered at it briefly. But there was a wind, after all; it was monsoon season. That must explain it, of course. The smell had been carried farther than usual by the wind.

It was only when wisps of smoke began to curl through the rows that Anna began to suspect that something was horribly wrong.

The fire was much closer than it should have been.

The knowledge hit her suddenly, making her go cold. Baliclava, apparently coming to the same conclusion, tossed his head and brayed. Rubbing her stinging eyes, trying not to panic as more smoke with its attendant stench of burning poured in her direction, Anna tried to see exactly where the fire was.

The plants were too tall to permit her to discern much except her immediate surroundings. All she could see on all four sides were stout stalks of tea and smoke—and a strangely costumed man. Anna's eyes widened. She blinked, and he was gone. Had she imagined him, or . . .

Baliclava brayed again, then began to dance on his four tiny hooves as lizards by the dozen appeared, swarming toward him from the depths of the field. They seemed to come from every direction, and mixed with their number were fast-slithering snakes and leaping Indian hares. In a matter of seconds the earth was covered with an undulating carpet of living creatures, all trying to escape the fire. Baliclava panicked and pawed the earth, shrilly braying for help.

Anna screamed and kicked the donkey into motion, heading him back in the direction from whence they had come. She bent low over his neck, trying not to breathe the hot, thick air that was increasingly laden with smoke and sparks. Then she heard it, and it seemed to come from all around her: the ominous crackling of the approaching fire.

Above and dangerously near, the thick foliage of a tea plant ignited with a roar. It flamed like a torch, dropping sparks in a rainlike shower. One hit Baliclava's rump. The donkey screamed, whirled, and galloped in the opposite direction, nearly unseating Anna and causing her to lose her reins. She clung to the saddle with both hands, terror alone giving her the strength to hold on. If she fell, the fire would surely consume her. Baliclava was the only chance she had.

The donkey plunged headlong through tea plants that were as closely entwined as jungle. Branches struck Anna's face, stinging her. Only the protection of her clothing kept her skin from being burned. Then a spark hit her bonnet, causing it to smolder. Frantically she beat at her head with one hand, putting out the small flame. Only then did it occur to her that the falling sparks might set her clothing afire, and a fresh spurt of terror hit her. It seemed likely that she would be incinerated in her own field!

"Dear God, please help me!"

Another spark hit Baliclava. The donkey reared, bucked, and tore over the ground in a maddened plunge for safety. Anna, nearly blinded by the smoke, gave up all attempts to guide the animal.

Wrapping her arms around his neck, she buried her face in his stubby mane and clung.

The crackling was louder, louder, building into a roar. The heat was so intense that Anna felt her skin blister. Smoke made breathing almost impossible, and if it had not been for the brim of her sunbonnet forming a tent against the side of Baliclava's neck, Anna was sure she would have suffocated.

It occurred to her, unbelievably, that she was going to die. Paul's face swam before her eyes: had he been this frightened when he'd realized his time was upon him?

Chelsea; she couldn't leave Chelsea.

And Julian. . . .

Baliclava's shuddering scream snapped her head up. The smoke was blinding, but not so blinding that Anna couldn't see the wall of fire roaring toward them. Gasping in terror, she choked on the smoke. Coughing, glancing frantically behind her, she tried to turn the donkey, who seemed determined to throw himself on his own funeral pyre. Then her steaming eyes widened with horror, and she gave up the attempt. Behind her roared another wall of fire, far taller and faster than the first.

They were trapped!

Anna screamed, despairing, and buried her face in Baliclava's neck again as the donkey obstinately raced toward the smaller of the two walls of fire. She was going to die, here, today, in just a few minutes. Please God, she didn't want to die! Not yet, oh, not yet!

Beneath her, she felt Baliclava's muscles bunch, and her arms tightened instinctively around his neck. Then, with a powerful thrust of his hindquarters, the animal leaped like a jackrabbit right into the middle of the raging inferno.

# XXXV

❦❦❦❦❦❦❦❦❦❦❦❦❦❦❦

"Anna! Anna! My God, Anna!"

Miraculously, Baliclava was through the fire, racing as if maddened across the already blackened portion of the field. Workers, elephants, and oxen scattered as the donkey, braying as if he were possessed by banshees, flew past them. Anna clung to his neck, her arms locked into position. She was only dimly aware that somehow, by some miracle, they had survived.

"Anna!"

The smell of burning was strong again, acrid as it singed her nostrils. Baliclava galloped frantically toward the forest, bucking as he went. Anna felt her grip being dislodged and screamed as she slipped sideways and crashed to the ground.

She lay where she had fallen amongst the prickly, blackened stubble of the burned-off plants as the donkey raced off without her. She was dazed, not quite sure what was real and what was not.

Voices shouted, someone yelled her name, and the ground vibrated beneath her ear as dozens of feet ran toward her.

Julian reached her first. Funny, she was almost glad to see him—until he dropped to his knees beside her, uttering a hoarse cry, and began to pound her legs and hips with his hands.

"Stop!" she tried to cry, rolling over to escape him, but the protest emerged as a croak. There was the sound of ripping cloth, and she realized to her horror that he was tearing the clothes from her body.

"No! Stop!" she cried again, trying to fight him off with arms that were unexpectedly weak. He was stripping her, rending her dress, right in the midst of an open field with Hillmore and a crowd of turbaned islanders gathered around staring!

"Your clothes are on fire, you bloody little idiot!" Julian yelled at her as she struggled. Even as the sense of that sunk in, and she ceased to fight, he had her dress off her, then her bonnet as well. She was left with only her thin white chemise and a single petticoat to cover her nakedness. Weak as she was, she managed to cross her arms over her bosom in an effort to preserve what she could of her modesty from the staring throng of men.

Julian scowled fiercely at her. Anna's eyes flickered beneath the sheer savagery of his gaze. His face was a carved teak mask of anger, its harsh lines forbidding. His eyes blazed at her as hotly as the fire she had just escaped. His cheeks and forehead were streaked with soot—Anna guessed from her charred dress, or perhaps the ground. His black eyebrows met in a single straight line over his nose, and his lips were clamped tight. As his gaze ran over her, then flicked back up to her face, it was pure onyx, alive with some unidentifiable emotion. Raw fury, Anna thought, and something more.

"Get back." He turned his head to snarl at the gaping workers. "Get away from her. Hillmore, bring me something to wrap her in. A blanket, anything."

The islanders, lowering their heads, retreated a few paces. Hillmore left at a run. There had been something in Julian's voice that cracked like a whip, and none dared to risk his wrath by not doing his bidding posthaste.

"Do you hurt anywhere?" Julian turned back to

her and waited until she shook her head. Then his eyes moved over her again, more carefully this time, examining her from head to toe. His hands, surprisingly gentle, smoothed the hair from her face. Between her wild ride and his ungentle method of removing her bonnet, the sunlit mass had fallen from its neat knot and tangled wildly all around her face and shoulders and down her back. His hand ran over the tumbled strands, and some emotion that Anna was afraid to define made his eyes flare. When he pulled his fingers away she saw that several silvery strands clung to them; apparently the hair around her face had been singed. Carefully, as if the detached strands might still have the power to hurt her, he untangled the gossamer tendrils from his fingers and laid them aside. Next he touched her cheek with an exploratory finger, winced, then pulled the tail of his shirt free of his breeches to dab at her face. When he pulled the once-white linen away, Anna saw that it was smeared with soot and blood—her blood. Remembering the branches stinging against her cheeks, she realized that her face must have been badly scratched. Strangely, the scratches didn't hurt. Nothing seemed to hurt. She felt as if she were floating. . . .

"What the hell were you doing in that field anyway?" he demanded, sounding as if the words were forced from somewhere deep inside him. His hands caught hers, lifting them from their protective posture over her breasts with a gentleness that belied his tone. Holding them loosely in his, he examined first the backs and then the palms. Looking into that harsh, begrimed face, Anna felt an amazing sense of peace. Whatever his faults, and they were many and varied, there was no one on earth to whom she would rather entrust her well-being than her impossible brother-in-law. He would take care of her whether she wanted him to or not, and at the moment she wanted him to. Even thinking clearly was difficult. It seemed to require all her energy just to catch her breath.

"Don't you have enough sense at least to let someone know you're there? It's a bloody miracle you weren't killed! You knew we were burning that field! Why the hell did you go in there? Don't you have a brain in your head?"

His fierceness barely penetrated. Her dreamy answering smile must have alarmed him, because his face tautened and his mouth turned down sharply at one corner. Anxiety mingled with anger in his face as he stopped speaking, then looked up suddenly as Hillmore approached. Anna knew instinctively that the white heat of his fury stemmed from fear, pure and simple. Despite everything, he had been frightened for her. The knowledge warmed her.

"Here," he said roughly. But his hands were gentle as he wrapped her in the blanket Hillmore handed him. The wool was scratchy and smelled of the outdoors, but Anna was thankful for its warmth. She was suddenly freezing cold despite the steamy afternoon heat.

Clamping her teeth together, she fought not to give in to the shivers that threatened to consume her. But long tremors raked her body despite her best efforts. Julian, seeing them, said a word that under ordinary circumstances would have reddened her ears. Anna scarcely registered it. She was caught somewhere between awareness and lack of it as he gathered her into his arms and stood up, lifting her as if she weighed no more than Chelsea. Anna didn't even have the strength to help him by putting her arms around his neck. She lay against him, snuggled into the cocooning blanket and his hard arms, and felt, curiously, as if she had come home at last. Her head drooped against his chest, where she could hear the strong, reassuring beat of his heart beneath her ear.

She felt protected, even cherished. Ephemeral as

she knew his tenderness was, she soaked up the sensation greedily. In that moment, all she cared about was that it was Julian who was holding her, protecting her, taking care of her.

He was carrying her toward some destination that Anna had no inclination to worry about. Without the slightest hesitation she trusted him to know and do what was best for her. On that realization she sighed and let her eyes flutter shut. Drowsily, she was aware that Julian and Hillmore were carrying on a low-voiced conversation. But their words barely registered until finally Julian, clearly angry, spoke with such an edge to his voice that it cut through the mist.

"Damn it, I want to know who the hell set that backfire. It wasn't supposed to be set unless the original fire got out of control and couldn't be stopped any other way. Find out who did it and get rid of them, do you hear me?"

"Yes, sir, Mr. Chase," Hillmore said, his tone respectful. Anna opened her eyes in time to see the sun-dried overseer lifting his hand in an obvious salute. Julian, accepting the gesture as no more than his due, dismissed Hillmore with a curt nod.

Anna realized something then, even as Julian, with a brief word to her, set her in the saddle of his horse and climbed up behind her.

There was no longer any doubt in the mind of Hillmore, or probably any other of the servants except Kirti and Raja Singha, as to who was in charge of the plantation: the de facto master at Srinagar was now Julian Chase.

And Anna, to her befuddlement, found that she was curiously content to have it so.

# XXXVI

Julian held her carefully in front of him all the way back to the house. One of his hands held the reins, and his other arm kept Anna from sliding from the saddle. She was finding it increasingly difficult to catch her breath, and kept lapsing in and out of awareness. If he hadn't held her upright, she would have slithered from the saddle like a cooked noodle.

Long before the house came into view, Julian was cursing viciously under his breath.

Anna was barely conscious when they reached the house. She was vaguely aware that the horse had stopped, and that Julian, kicking his feet free from the stirrups, somehow managed to maneuver both of them to the ground. Then she was lifted into his arms again.

"What has happened to the memsahib?"

"Anna!"

Raja Singha and Ruby met them in the front hall. Ruby exclaimed in horror over Anna's condition, while Raja Singha was characteristically silent. Julian tersely filled them in on what had occurred even as he was taking the stairs two at a time, Anna cradled against his chest. At the end of the upstairs hall Kirti popped out of the nursery, wide-eyed and curious at all the commotion. Julian shook his head to tell her to keep Chelsea away, and Kirti disappeared into the nursery again.

Anna was glad. She didn't want her daughter to be frightened when there was no need.

"Send for a doctor," Julian ordered grimly as he lowered Anna to her bed. The sheets felt icily cold against her skin as she was slipped between them. She shuddered. As if that one shudder had broken through the dam of her control, her entire body began to tremble. Long spasms racked her, and her teeth chattered.

"Get some clean blankets. Wrap her up."

Ruby ran to fetch the blankets, but it was Julian who pulled back the bedclothes to bundle her in them, then sat on the edge of the mattress holding her on his lap, his arms wrapped around her, as Ruby gently sponged her face. The blood and soot on the cloth made Anna wince. Julian's arms tightened.

"They're just small scratches. Don't worry, they won't leave a scar." That harsh voice, speaking with absolute certainty close to her ear, reassured Anna. She allowed herself to relax against him, enjoying the luxury of being cradled as if she were entirely precious to him.

It felt good to imagine that he cared for her.

Her eyes opened, then closed, then opened again, fixing on Julian's grim face before moving on to Ruby and Raja Singha and the maids beyond them. Ruby looked frightened, but Raja Singha was as impassive as ever. What, she wondered groggily, would it take to make the servant show emotion? Was he even capable of feeling it? The maids bustled about bringing fresh water and cloths with which Ruby gently sponged Anna's face, neck, and hands.

"What were you about, to let 'er get 'urt like this?" Ruby burst out fiercely to Julian as she discarded yet another bloody, blackened cloth for a fresh one. "You should've 'ad a care. . . ."

Anna opened her eyes and saw Julian's jaw

tighten. Before he could say anything in his own defense, Anna summoned the last of her reserves of strength to break in.

"It wasn't his fault. I shouldn't have been in the field without letting someone know I was there. Anyway, I'm all right," she said firmly.

Then she fainted.

Made continually drowsy by the doctor's potion, Anna was aware of little for the next twenty-four hours. She came briefly awake at the sound of Chelsea's frightened voice piping "Mama!" by the bed. Rousing herself enough to smile at her daughter, she managed to mumble that she wasn't sick, only very, very sleepy, and would be all right on the morrow. Then Julian entered, and Chelsea greeted him with a convulsive hug that showed Anna how high a place in her daughter's affections her newfound uncle claimed. If she had been in full possession of her senses, the knowledge would have dismayed Anna, but under the circumstances she found the odd pair's obvious fondness for each other comforting. Knowing that Chelsea had someone other than a servant, someone whom she considered both friend and relative, to turn to in her fright made all the difference in the world to Anna's peace of mind.

Which certainly, when she mistily thought about it, was another surprising example of how thoroughly she had come to rely on a man who was no more than tenuously related to them; who was a thief and a rogue and a conscienceless libertine; who had, moreover, blackmailed his way into her life. Anna was still pondering the ramifications when she fell asleep.

The English community thereabouts with tight-knit, and word of Anna's accident soon spread far and wide. There was a constant stream of callers to inquire about the state of her health. Her lungs soon felt recovered, although Dr. Tandy disputed this, but the scratches on her face remained as visible remind-

ers of her ordeal. It was nearly a week before she
felt presentable enough to receive a few select visitors in her bedchamber. Charles was the first, and
he hastened to her bedside as if she were on the
brink of death.

"I'm fine, Charles, truly," Anna insisted for what
seemed the dozenth time. "Or at least, I will be fine.
The doctor insists I stay in bed to give my lungs a
rest, but only for another few days. And the
scratches look much worse than they are, truly."

She was propped up in bed on a mound of pillows, a frilly bedjacket concealing her nightdress.
Her hair was freshly brushed and styled so that it
was drawn back from her forehead with a ribbon to
cascade over her shoulders in a mass of silvery
waves. Except for the scratches, which were fading
from red to soft pink, she looked fetching. At least
Charles evidently thought so. He sat by the bed in
a straight-backed chair he had drawn up and refused to dispossess himself of her hand.

"When I heard you'd been in an accident, it
frightened me to death," he said, his eyes warm on
her face. "I wish you'd give me the right to take
care of you. You need a man, Anna, and it's time
you started letting the past go and looking to the
future. I . . ."

Something caused her to glance toward the open
door to her bedroom. The sight that met her eyes
made her completely miss Charles's next words. Julian, clad in his usual work uniform of black breeches,
boots, and collarless white shirt, stood glaring at
them. Silhouetted, his broad-shouldered, lean-
hipped frame seeming more powerful than ever in
comparison with the slender Charles, he looked
thoroughly menacing. From the scowl on his face
Julian was clearly displeased with her visitor. But
scowl or no, he was handsome enough to stop
Anna's breath.

When he saw her gaze on him he nodded, the
gesture curt, and stepped into the room.

"Hello, Dumesne," he said, unsmiling, as Charles turned to greet him. Anna managed to unobtrusively tug her hand free, but the displeasure on Julian's face scarcely eased. Still, he politely if unenthusiastically shook Charles's hand as the latter rose and extended it to him, and exchanged the pleasantries with him that were required by common civility.

"What are you doing here in the middle of the day?" Anna asked Julian. Since her accident, she'd seen him mostly in the evenings or early mornings, when he would stop by her bedroom to check her progress and give her an account of the improvements he'd made to Srinagar that day.

"I brought you something," he answered briefly, and for the first time she became aware of the large, string-tied box tucked beneath his arm.

"Why, thank you." Her surprise showed in her voice. Julian threw her a quick, glinting look before laying the box across the foot of her bed.

Then he turned his hard eyes on Charles.

"I'm sure Anna is very pleased to see you, but the doctor tells us she needs to rest."

"I'm just going," Charles assured him, although Anna protested that he didn't have to leave just then.

Julian overrode her words with no more than a lift of his eyebrows, then said to Charles, "If you're leaving in the next few minutes, I'll wait for you. We've just gotten in a shipment of tea plants that you might like to see."

"I'd like that. Thank you."

"I'll see you downstairs, then. Anna."

With another of those unsmiling looks for her, he took himself off. Charles, left alone with her for what could only be a precious few minutes, smiled ruefully.

"Protective sort of chap, isn't he? It's clear he doesn't like me sniffing around." Charles frowned suddenly. "He doesn't have any interest in you other than as his widowed sister-in-law, does he? I mean, you're not blood relatives, and—"

"Charles! What a thing to suggest!" Anna interrupted, managing to sound scandalized even as she blushed bright red. If anyone were to suspect exactly what kind of interest Julian did have in her, or how tenuous their relationship really was, there would be a dreadful scandal. Being branded a scarlet woman before her friends and neighbors was a horror she did not like even to think about.

"I didn't mean it quite that way," Charles said, shamefaced. "Of course, as your brother-in-law, he's interested in guarding your good name. It's only natural. And you have Mrs. Fisher in the house—not that you need her, of course. It's just for the look of the thing. Still, it's not as if he's your blood brother. But I can see I'm upsetting you, so I'll say no more. Only, Anna—if you should need, uh, protecting, and Chase, for whatever reason, is not, uh, available, please be assured that you can turn to me."

"Thank you, Charles, but I hardly think—"

"No, of course not," he said hastily. "Well, I'll take my leave of you. Although I'll call again next week, if I may."

"Of course," Anna answered. He kissed her hand and left the room. Anna stared after him in some dismay. Julian might not want her himself, but he didn't want anyone else to have her either. His attitude might be more dog-in-the-manger than anything else, but Charles had noticed it. And if Charles noticed, someone else might, too. A little gossip spread here and there could give rise to a nasty scandal, and Anna quailed at the prospect.

She should ask Julian to leave now, before it happened. But she had already asked him to leave— several times, in fact—and he had refused to go.

And if she were honest with herself, she didn't want him to.

Her eyes fell on the box at the foot of the bed, and

she reached to pull it toward her. Had Julian really brought her a present? True, he'd been unprecedentedly kind to her in the week since her accident—but a present! Julian didn't seem the kind of man to bring tokens of his regard to any female, much less herself.

Anna's fingers trembled slightly with anticipation as she undid the string and lifted the lid on the box. There, beneath layers of tissue paper, was the gleam of soft green silk.

A dress! And not just any dress, Anna saw as she pulled it out, but a lovely confection of shimmering Indian silk, lavished with lace and cut in the latest style. It was a dream of a dress, a dress such as she had never possessed, and she didn't waste any time. Swinging her feet out of bed, clutching the garment to her bosom, she made haste to try it on.

# XXXVII

The dress became her as nothing ever had in her life. Anna stood before the cheval glass marveling at her own reflection. The unusual silvery green shade of the silk showed off her alabaster skin and darkened her eyes to emerald. It intensified the silvery tones in her hair, which she quickly twisted behind her head to get the full effect of how she would look with her hair properly dressed. Turning this way and that, she admired her reflection. The low-cut, lace-lavished bodice with its tiny puff sleeves left her shoulders and arms and a considerable expanse of milky bosom on view; the nipped-in waist was wrapped in a wide sash that made her own waist look impossibly slender; the belled skirt with its lace flounces was trimmed cunningly with silvery green bows that echoed the bow that tied the sash in the rear. The dress was both breathtakingly gorgeous and impossibly elegant. In it she looked beautiful. Anna thought of Julian choosing such a thing for her, gifting her with it, and felt a flutter deep in her stomach.

Why had he done it? The possibilities made her heart speed up.

Cautioning herself not to read too much into a gesture that might have been prompted simply because he disliked the color black, Anna nevertheless felt a tiny smile curl her lips. Julian was impossible, a rogue in many ways, unfeeling and high-handed and maddening to the point of making her want to murder him at least half the time, but still . . . She refused to finish the thought. He had bruised her heart, not once but twice. She would be a fool to leave it unguarded again.

Yet she could not help the glow that pinkened her cheeks and sparkled in her eyes when she examined her reflection in the glass. If the very idea was not ridiculous, she would think that she looked like a woman in love. With Julian? The thought frightened her.

To allow herself to fall in love with him would be to open herself up to heartbreak.

With that sobering thought, her hands moved to the hooks at the back of the dress. It was time to put the lovely gown aside and return to the reality of her mourning clothes. She could not let what was no more than an intense physical attraction to a handsome man blind her to what was real and what was not real in life.

The silvery waves of hair that fell in a rippling cascade to the small of her back obscured her vision as she struggled with the hooks. She had managed to work first one, then another, and a third free when she became aware that someone was watching her. Hands falling to her sides, she whirled with a gasp.

"You look beautiful. Like a mermaid," Julian said.

"Don't you ever knock?" Anna demanded, nettled, shaking her hair from her face as she stared pointedly at the door to her bedroom, which she had carefully shut before removing her nightdress.

"When the occasion warrants it." His odd, lopsided smile lent his dark face devastating charm. Just looking at him made Anna's heart beat faster. He was so tall, so handsome, so very much a man. . . .

But he was not for her, she reminded herself sternly. Her frown deepened into a scowl.

"I thought you were going to show Charles some tea plants."

A shark's smile curled Julian's lips. "I lied," he said, coming toward her with that lithe tread that was already branded on her memory for all time. Anna, suddenly shy of him, turned back to her reflection in the mirror. He came to a stop behind her, his height and wide shoulders making her seem tiny as their reflections merged, his eyes meeting hers in the glass. "When he got downstairs, I suddenly remembered a pressing appointment. Which, now that I think about it, wasn't a lie after all. I wanted to see how the dress looked on you."

Anna regarded herself in the glass, then raised her eyes to his reflection. "It's beautiful. Thank you. I love it, although I've no place to wear it."

"Wear it anywhere you like. To a dinner party. Out to visit your friends." His hands rose to rest lightly on her bare shoulders. Anna tried not to react to his touch.

"You've forgotten that I'm in mourning."

His mouth twisted. An ugly gleam sprang to life in his eyes. "I've forgotten nothing. But it's been a year, and more. Don't you think you're carrying this a bit too far?"

"I loved Paul."

"Past tense. Or are you telling me that you love him still?"

"I'll always love him."

That quiet avowal had the effect of making his mouth turn down. His hands tightened on her shoulders, and then he was turning her around, his fingers biting into her soft skin until she cried out.

"You little fool," he muttered harshly, and lowered his mouth to hers.

Anna didn't try to evade his kiss. One part of her craved the touch of his mouth even as another part of her screamed danger. But she was weak where he was concerned, too weak to resist. She loved him. . . .

Dear God, did she? The thought was apalling. She couldn't, surely she couldn't, love a blackmailing, thieving rogue who had a way with the ladies! It was folly, and worse than folly. But the feel of his mouth on hers was exquisite, warm and rough and oh, so right. Her hands slid up his shirtsleeves to rest against the solid muscles that bunched in his upper arms. She rose on tiptoe to fit her mouth to his.

He made a deep, harsh sound under his breath. His arms went around her, and he pulled her hard against the unyielding length of him. Anna melted in his embrace. Her arms stole up to wrap around his neck. Her fingers burrowed into the thick black hair at the nape of his neck. She kissed him back as if she had been starving for the taste of his mouth, kissed him with all the passionate abandon that her body could no longer deny. Did she love him? She shied from the thought. But did she want him?

More than anything in life.

It was a shock when he suddenly thrust her away from him, holding her at arm's length as he scowled at her so ferociously that she was taken aback.

"Julian . . ." she began, then faltered at the black expression on his face.

"Julian," he mimicked in a ruthless falsetto. "At least this time you've got the name right."

With that he thrust her away from him and turned to stalk to her wardrobe. While Anna watched, dumbstruck, he jerked open the doors and, after a quick survey of the contents, began to yank the dresses one by one from their hangers, tossing them carelessly over his arm.

"What on earth do you think you're doing?" Anna gasped when she had regained the use of her voice.

"This farce has gone on too long. You've mourned him for a year, and that's enough."

He was emptying her wardrobe of every single black dress she possessed! Anna hurried to stop him, catching his arm only to find herself ruthlessly shaken off.

"You can't just take my clothes!"

"Can't I? Just watch me, you little hypocrite." He slanted her a glittering look over his shoulder.

"Hypocrite!"

Her indignant echo earned her another fierce look. "What else would you call it? You lie with me, let me love you, love me back hotter than any lightskirt I've ever had, yet you go around claiming that you love your dead husband and wearing the mourning to prove it!"

"I do love—" Anna began, protesting, only to break off as he turned on her, rage twisting his face.

"If you say his name one more time, I swear I'll throttle you." The threat was forced out between his teeth.

His mouth was twisted into a snarl, and he looked so savage that Anna, alarmed, took a step backwards.

His lip curled with jeering satisfaction. "Afraid of me? I don't blame you. You've got cause."

"Julian—"

His eyes flamed at her like twin coals fished up from some pit in hell. Anna, eyes widening, broke off.

Without another word, he turned to strip the rest of her mourning gowns from her wardrobe. Then, with a last smoldering glare, he stalked from her bedchamber.

Anna, speechless, stared helplessly after him. It took her several minutes to register that he had really, truly, made off with every decent dress she possessed. What was left was a hodgepodge of gowns that dated from before Paul's death—and the shimmering green dress she still wore. Angry as she was, Anna knew a sudden urge to rip the fragile silk into shreds just to spite Julian. She actually had her fingers in the garment's neckline before the sheer beauty of the gown stopped her. Seething, she got out of the dress as quickly as she could and into the lavender one she had donned once before because of Julian. The memory made her angrier than ever, and there was a decided spark in her eyes as she went in pursuit of her clothes and the man who had dared to make off with them.

"Why, Anna, it's good to see you in colors!"

Ruby emerged from the house's nether regions in time to make this comment—and be rewarded by a glare and a fierce mutter as Anna stormed past. The other woman was left gaping, but not for long. She hurried to catch Anna.

"My goodness, lovey, where're you off to in such a snit?"

"He took my clothes!"

"What?"

"You heard me: the swine took my clothes!"

"You mean Julian?" Ruby, having fallen in beside Anna as she stalked out the door onto the rear veranda and then down into the garden, sounded intrigued.

"Of course I mean Julian!"

"But why . . . ?" As she absorbed this information, Ruby suddenly sounded hugely entertained. Anna cast her a fierce look.

"Why? Why? Because he says—never mind what he says!"

"Tired o' your blacks, is 'e?" Ruby nodded sagely. "I can't say I'm surprised. 'E's been in a rare taking over you since you got 'urt. If you was to ask me, I'd say 'e's smitten."

"What do you mean?" Anna turned on Ruby so fiercely that the other woman blinked.

"Why, just that it's as plain as the nose on your face that 'e's daft about you. Why else would 'e make off with your blacks? I'd say 'e's bloody jealous."

"Jealous!"

"Of Paul."

"Paul's dead."

"That don't make no matter if 'e's still alive to you."

"That's the most ridiculous notion I ever heard in my life!"

Ruby shrugged.

"Julian and I—he dislikes me most of the time. How could he possibly be jealous of Paul? It's absurd!"

Ruby shrugged again.

"I—" Anna broke off abruptly, recollecting the events that had led to Ruby's amazing suggestion, and looked furiously around her as her momentary distraction gave way again to pure temper. The garden, the stable yard, and the surrounding areas were apparently deserted. "Whyever he did it, the fact remains that the swine stole my clothes. If I don't find him before he does something to them, I won't have a stitch to my name!"

"Look there," Ruby said suddenly, pointing beyond the stables.

Anna saw a rising plume of smoke and felt her anger shoot to red hot.

"If he dared . . . !" She gritted her teeth, hurrying toward the smoke.

Following, Ruby said nothing, but her face was alive with amusement, which she was careful not to let Anna see.

"I do like a forceful gent," she murmured, almost to herself.

"What?" Anna glanced back over her shoulder as she rounded the corner of the stable.

"Never mind, lovey, it weren't important. Will you look at that!"

The sight that provoked Ruby's comment caused Anna to stop dead. Then she picked up her skirts and ran, straight for the pile of flaming brush and wood on the top of which smoldered—her clothes!

"You low-life, arrogant bastard!" she hissed at Julian, who had turned from raking up the flames to watch her headlong rush. Anna repeated the epithet, relishing the sheer badness of the forbidden word. She snatched up the rake he had dropped and tried desperately to fish at least a few of her dresses from atop the pile.

"Now, is that any way for a vicar's daughter to talk?" Julian grabbed her around the waist, swinging her away from the task that she already saw, to her despair, was useless. Her clothes were ablaze. Flames ate hungrily at the fine silk and muslin and taffeta.

"Just look what you've done!" Anna wailed in despair as the garments smoked and curled, already crumbling into ashes. His arms around her waist held her back from the fire, and she struggled furiously against them. When it was clear there was no hope of salvaging anything, he let her go.

Anna promptly turned on him with the rake, swinging with such fury that if the blow had connected it would have taken off his head. Julian ducked.

" 'Old, there!" Jim, whose smirking presence had just registered on her consciousness, grabbed her from behind before she could let fly with a second swing. Julian, grinning, wrested the rake from her grasp.

"Let her go, Jim," he directed once the rake was safe in his hands.

"If you say so." Jim sounded dubious. He set Anna free, then took a hasty step out of the way.

But he was in no danger. Anna was barely aware of his presence, much less that of Jama, who stood watching from the safety of the stable door, or of Jama's wide-eyed assistant, who had emerged from the stable holding two saddled horses.

Her attention was all for Julian.

"I'll just order more," she hissed, her fists clenched at her sides. The knowledge of her own inability to injure him enraged her.

He smiled with great charm. Taking a step closer, he caught her chin and turned her face up to his.

"You do that, sweetheart, and I'll burn them, too. In fact, if I see you in one more black dress, I'll strip it off you where you stand. In company or not. I give you my word." The threat was soft, too soft for anyone but Anna to hear.

Furiously she knocked away his hand.

"Touch me again and I'll—I'll . . ."

"You'll what, sweetheart?"

When she merely glared at him, at a loss for a threat that would bother him in the least, he chuckled. Exploding rage rendered her momentarily speechless.

"That's a good, sensible girl," Julian said carelessly, his voice a little louder so that their audience could hear. Anna, fury making her cheeks flame, was still struggling with words bad enough to call him when he turned away, strode to where the boy held the two horses, and swung into the larger one's saddle. Jim followed like a faithful shadow.

"See you at supper," Julian called to her, gathering the reins. Then, with a last mocking grin in her direction, he put his heels to the horse's sides and rode away, Jim trotting behind him.

"That—that . . ." Anna spluttered furiously to Ruby, who had come up to stand beside her.

Ruby took a deep breath. "Lovey, if you ever get tired of him, give him to me," she said. Then, as Anna turned blazing eyes on her, Ruby hastily began to recant.

# XXXVIII

Deprived of almost her entire wardrobe, Anna spent the next few days sulking in her chamber. Ruby, sympathetic but oddly amused, visited her, as did Chelsea and Kirti. Of Julian she saw not so much as a whisker.

Which was just as well. Every time she thought of the mocking devil, her ire rose. She wanted to slap his swarthy face, kick his powerful shins, bite his well-muscled shoulders—and that was just for starters. What she really wanted was to kill him.

How dare he put her in such a position? She had the hideous feeling that she was the laughingstock of the household, if not of the community at large.

If she could not appear in her customary mourning, then she would not appear at all. And so she told Ruby when, on the morning of the second day, the other woman came to inform her that a seamstress was belowstairs to start work on her new wardrobe. Courtesy, of course, of Julian.

"I have no intention of ordering new clothes," Anna snapped. "And so you can tell that—" She broke off, thinking, then smiled. "On second thought, you may send her up. I will order something, after all."

Ruby regarded her thoughtfully, but if she had some inkling as to what was in Anna's mind she didn't argue. "I'd have a care what I was about were I you, lovey," was all she said.

Anna, defiant, ordered half a dozen new dresses made to her measurements—every single one in widow's black.

She would soon teach Julian Chase not to threaten her!

Until the dresses were delivered—the woman promised them for five days hence—she would keep to her room. Then she would appear as before, and if Julian dared to lay so much as a finger on her, she would claw out his eyes.

In the meantime, visitors descended upon Srinagar in such numbers that Anna was glad to be keeping to her room. The only fly in her ointment of satisfaction lay in imagining how pleased some of the female callers—she couldn't call them ladies—must be to have a chance to have Julian to themselves. Of course, he was probably away from the house a great deal of the time, but she had no doubt that his particular favorites—such as Antoinette Noack—would manage to track him down. Doubtless they would pretend a great interest in the cultivation of tea for just that purpose!

Along with the callers came invitations to dinner parties, musicals, literary evenings, and various other entertainments, addressed not only to Anna but to Julian as well. Although the plantations were spread out, they were not so far-flung as to make socializing impossible, and Anna's neighbors were a sociable group. Before Paul had taken ill, they had attended parties several times a month. She had been to a few small gatherings since her return to Ceylon.

But Anna declined all of the invitations. Her excuse was that she did not feel recovered enough to attend. The reality was far more complex: she was too confused about how she really felt toward Julian to want to be forced into interacting with him in a public setting, especially if everyone was whispering

about his disposal of her mourning! And for the time
being, of course, she had nothing suitable to wear.

Then Julian, the high-handed swine, took it upon
himself to accept an invitation for both of them.

"What do you mean, he sent a note around to
Antoinette Noack telling her that *we* would love to
attend her supper party? He can speak for himself,
of course, but I have no intention of going, and so
you may tell him!"

"Not me, lovey," Ruby said. "You tell him."

"Well, I will."

Anna fetched writing paper and ink from the table
by her bed and proceeded to scribble a note to Julian. Summoning Raja Singha, she asked him to
please see that Julian received it as soon as he entered the house. Then, with a satisfied smile, she got
into her nightdress and climbed into bed.

She was feeling far too poorly to attend a party.

Two hours later, Anna was propped comfortably
on a mound of pillows in her bed, although it was
still only mid-afternoon. She had a pile of scrap material beside her and was engaged in sewing a doll
wardrobe as a surprise birthday gift for Chelsea, who
would soon be six. Anna was working on a cunning
little lace dress, and Ruby, who had drawn up a slipper chair to her bedside, was putting the hem in the
matching cloak, when an all too familiar step echoed
along the hall.

"Uh-oh. Here comes trouble," Ruby murmured
to Anna.

"Not at all," Anna replied haughtily, and bent
her head to her sewing again. A not unpleasant thrill
of anticipation coursed through her as she waited
for Julian's advent. She had not expected him to take
that note at face value. Of course he would come to
see for himself if her lungs were troubling her too
much to permit her to leave her bed.

"What's this?" Julian, her note crumpled in one
hand, entered her room without ceremony. He was
coatless, of course, which was only sensible in the

heat, although many of the Englishmen thereabouts wore coats whether it was sensible or not. His shirt and breeches were grimy and damp with sweat, and his hair had been tied in a little tail at the nape of his neck. Perspiration gleamed on his face, making him look swarthier than ever. Clearly he had just come in from the fields—and clearly he was not happy.

"Did no one ever teach you to knock?" Anna lifted her eyebrows haughtily, her needle freezing above the miniscule frock as she gave him a look that she hoped would make clear her feelings about his uninvited intrusion.

"No," he answered, his eyes narrowing as they met hers. Anna frowned at having the wind taken so neatly out of her sails and jabbed the needle into the cloth with enough force so that it went clear through into the thumb of her opposite hand. Stifling a yelp, she put the injured member to her mouth and surveyed him crossly.

He stood at the foot of her bed, tall and handsome despite his dirt, and overpoweringly masculine, looking her up and down as if he had every right to do so. Anna had pulled the bed coverings up to her armpits, and wore a demure bedjacket over her nightdress, so she was far from inadequately covered. But something about that look made her feel naked. Drat the man, for being able to make her uncomfortable with no more than a twitch of his eyebrows! She lifted her chin at him.

"Did you want to see me about something?"

"You know damned well what I want to see you about. You're going to this party tonight."

"If you had read my note, you would know that I can't: I don't feel well."

Julian said a word that more than adequately expressed his opinion of that excuse. The tips of Anna's ears reddened at the profanity, but she didn't flinch.

"There's no need to swear."

"I'll swear any time I bloody want to. I've had enough of your sulking in here. You're coming with me to that party if I have to drag you by your hair."

Anna's lips compressed. "I tell you I'm ill."

"The hell you are."

"Since you took it upon yourself to destroy my wardrobe, I have nothing to wear."

"That green dress looks beautiful on you."

"I have no intention of appearing in public tricked out in that. At the very least I must wear half-mourning. Lavender or gray."

Julian's eyes went suddenly black. His voice grated. "My dear, if, when it is time to leave for Mrs. Noack's, you appear in anything but that green dress, I will personally march you back up here and dress you myself. You have my word on it."

"Don't you dare threaten me!" Like Julian, Anna abandoned all pretense of civility. She sat bolt upright in bed, her eyes flashing at him.

"Oh, I'll dare a lot more than a mere threat. Put me to the test and see."

"I'm not afraid of you!"

"Then you've got the sense of a peahen." His hands clenched for a moment over the footrail of the bed, then, as if he had just become aware of the gesture, were forcibly relaxed. "The carriage will be ready at six. And so shall I expect you to be."

"Expect all you like. I won't be," Anna threw after him as he turned and headed toward the door.

"On your own head be it, then," he said, and walked on out the door.

# XXXIX

Downstairs the clock chimed six. Anna, stubbornly ensconced in her bedchamber, heard the faint reverberations that marked the hour with nervous anticipation. At any moment she expected to hear Julian stomping along the corridor to fetch her, although she had absolutely no intention of permitting herself to be fetched.

She was not disappointed.

His booted footsteps were quick, decisive, and impossible to mistake. Anna tensed as they paused outside her door, then smiled grimly as she watched the knob turn beneath his hand. What kind of fool did he think she was? Of course the door was securely locked.

Ruby, the coward, had refused to support her when, as Ruby put it, "all 'ell breaks loose," so Anna was alone. Her back was very straight, her palms damp as she stared at the door. She'd been too nervous to remain in bed—and really, what was the point as Julian would not be able to get in to see her?—so she stood with her back to the window, her hands clasped in an unconsciously prayerful attitude between her breasts. Earlier she had exchanged her bedjacket for a sprigged cotton wrapper, which was caught beneath her breasts by a wide blue sash. Her hair was tied back at the nape with a simple blue ribbon. Satin slippers protected her feet. It was the attire of a lady who meant to spend the evening in her bedchamber, which was precisely what Anna meant to do.

The knob turned once more, futilely, and was followed by an imperative knock.

"Anna?"

"Go away!" She was proud of her voice. It was firm and cool.

"If you don't open this door, right now, I'll kick it down."

"You wouldn't dare!"

"Try me."

Anna frowned. The door was of stout oak, the lock solid and strong. Surely he couldn't knock it down—could he?

Before she could consider the matter further, the panel shivered as something crashed against it. The noise made Anna cringe. It would bring everyone in the house running.

She wanted no more witnesses to the war between herself and Julian!

"All right, I'm coming!" she cried as the panel shivered beneath his weight again. Quickly she crossed to the door, turned the key in the lock, and swung the door wide. Julian stood on the opposite side, dazzlingly handsome in the stark black and white of conventional evening wear, a scowl on his face.

Anna scowled right back at him.

"Memsahib?" Raja Singha materialized in the hallway, his eyes sliding from Anna to Julian and back again without any readable expression. "Have you need of me, memsahib?"

For no more than a single moment Anna was tempted. But she did not wish to cause trouble for Raja Singha, and if he challenged Julian, trouble there would certainly be.

"No, I'm fine, Raja Singha," she answered as pleasantly as she could. "Thank you."

Under Raja Singha's watchful gaze, she could not quarrel with Julian in the hall. Biting her tongue, Anna stood back to let him in. Julian brushed by her without a word, and she shut the door behind him.

The enemy had successfully stormed the castle; this particular battle was as good as lost. The idea of Julian triumphant put a militant spark in Anna's eye. It intensified to a full-scale martial gleam when she turned back to him to discover that he was already at her wardrobe, withdrawing the green dress.

"I told you I'm not going!" The words were forceful, but she was careful to keep her voice down.

"Oh, yes, you are. Come here."

When she still remained stubbornly by the door, her arms crossed defiantly over her breasts, he strode across the room to catch her by the arm. To her horror, he reached for the bow-tied sash to her wrapper, evidently meaning to strip her where she stood!

"Don't you dare!" Panicked, she slapped at his hands, which were tugging at the ends of her sash. He paused, his fingers tangled in the loosened bow, and looked up to meet her eyes.

"You had your chance." His voice was implacable. "Now get undressed. We'll be late as it is."

"I can't—with you here."

"You can and will. Or I'll do it for you." He tugged at the bow again, which finally came free. Her wrapper gaped, revealing her thin nightdress, and Anna quickly pulled it shut again.

"No!" She stepped quickly out of his reach, both hands holding her wrapper together over her bosom. The prospect of being forcibly stripped by him was worse than humiliating. Better to dress herself as he wished and preserve some dignity than to have him force her to his will. The swine!

"You win, all right? I'll come with you. If you'll leave, I'll get dressed." Her words were icy.

He actually laughed, but the sound was devoid of mirth. "Oh, no, my fine lady. You had your chance.

I don't trust you not to do something like climb out the window. You'll get dressed with me in here—or I'll dress you myself.''

''I hate you!''

''Very likely. Well?''

Anna knew when she was beaten. Fuming, she retreated behind the screen in the corner. As she removed her wrapper and nightdress, he tossed garments at her: a filmy white chemise landed on top of the screen, to be followed in rapid succession by two petticoats, stockings, and garters. It was demeaning to think of him pawing through her underwear, but he seemed to know just what a lady wore beneath her dress. Of course he would, the womanizing rogue!

Anna pulled the chemise over her head, then hastily stepped into first one petticoat and then the other. She didn't trust him not to come barreling around the corner of the screen at any moment.

When her stockings were on, and she had tied her garters, she stood for a moment, biting her lip in indecision. Then she reached for her wrapper, slipped it on, and stepped from behind the screen.

Julian was lounging in the slipper chair that ordinarily sat before her dressing table. His booted feet were crossed at the ankles, his heels propped on her unmade bed. His black evening jacket had fallen open to reveal a black-and-gray striped waistcoat; his legs looked long and powerful, stretched out in their black breeches and shiny black boots. Above snowy linen and an impeccably tied cravat—really, she had never seen him so nattily turned out, although she would bite her tongue before she would tell him so!—his bronzed face with its expression of sardonic amusement was maddeningly handsome. As he surveyed her, brows lifted, Anna haughtily tilted her chin at him and proceeded to her wardrobe to extract what she needed from one of the small drawers in its bottom. Then she turned back

to glare at him, the necessary addition to her attire
wadded in her hands.

"If you'll leave, and send Ruby or one of the
maids to me, I'll be ready in five minutes. I give you
my word."

He made a derisive sound, dropped his feet to the
floor, and stood up.

"I didn't know you wore a corset." His eyes were
on the garment bundled in her hand. "You never
have before."

Really, the man knew too much about the intimate
details of female attire for common decency! Cheeks
burning, Anna snatched up the green gown and
marched back behind the screen.

"Would you please call Ruby?"

"And leave you to skulk in here for hours? Oh,
no. If you need help, I'll do it. I think you'll find
that I'm quite competent at acting the lady's maid."

"I don't want your help!"

"I've even assisted more than one—uh—lady into
her corset."

"Well, you won't assist me!"

But she might as well have been talking to herself.
As Anna had feared, Julian came around the screen
as casually as he might have strolled into the parlor.
She had already removed her wrapper, and for a
moment he merely studied her as she stood there in
her flimsy undergarments, the unmentionable corset
pressed to her bosom serving as a most ineffective
shield from his gaze. Something flickered in his eyes,
and for a moment Anna feared she was about to be
the recipient of some coarse comment that would be
branded in her mind for life.

"Turn around," was all he said. When she was
slow to obey, he pulled the corset from her hands
and turned her about himself, his hands on her
shoulders. To her humiliation, he fitted it around
her middle with an ease that could have been born
of nothing short of experience, nestling the whale-
boned edge up under her breasts with surprising

deftness for so masculine a man. Or perhaps his very masculinity should have made his skill less surprising. No doubt he had performed much the same service for a legion of lovers before now!

"So why the corset?" he asked conversationally as he adjusted the strings.

"Because the dress needs it! I noticed when I tried it on before."

"Too snug in the waist, eh? I had it cut to the measurements of one of your crow's dresses—must be all the curry you've been eating at supper. Better watch it, sweetheart, or you'll get fat."

He was grinning, Anna could tell by the amusement lacing his voice. Her teeth gritted, but before she could respond he gave such a jerk on the strings that she gasped.

"Grab something and hang on."

Humiliated, she barely had time to obey, gripping the windowsill tightly with both hands as he yanked at the lacings. Anna caught her breath, the circumference of the corset contracted violently—and then he was tying the ends into a firm knot before stepping back, mission completed.

Anna could barely breathe. She rarely wore a corset anyway, and certainly she had never worn one tied so tightly. Blackly she suspected the grinning devil of cinching her in as hard as he could on purpose—but she would suffocate before she would plead with him to make it looser.

"Is anything the matter?" he asked blandly, his eyes sweeping her from head to foot.

He *had* done it on purpose!

"What could be the matter?" she asked with forced sweetness, when what she really wanted to do was kick him in his leather-booted shin. "As you say, you're an accomplished lady's maid. Would you please hand me my dress?"

His brows rose, but he obligingly tossed her the green dress. Anna pulled it over her head, then presented her back to him.

"Do me up," she said. She had herself well under control by this time, and it had occurred to her that she might be able to turn the tables on Mr. Julian Chase with a vengeance. So he would force her to attend the Noack woman's party, would he? He'd see who would live to regret that!

As Julian deftly fastened the hooks at the back of her dress, Anna began to smile.

"Is something funny?" He gave her a narrow-eyed look as he followed her from behind the screen. Silk skirts rustling, Anna stopped before the dressing table to brush and pin up her hair. She looked lovely, she had to admit: the green dress lent her a shimmering beauty that made her resemble something out of a fairy tale. Looming behind her, Julian's dark-visaged handsomeness was a startling contrast: rather than Prince Charming, he reminded her of a brooding Hades, come to claim the virginal Persephone as his bride. The allusion sent a shiver through her, and for a moment the brush she was wielding faltered in mid-stroke. Then she recovered, consciously untangling her hair with slow, sensual strokes. Through the mirror, she could see the gradual darkening of his eyes as she at last twisted the silvery mass into a soft coil and pinned it atop her head. His arms were crossed over his chest, his expression almost brooding, as he watched her screw a pair of dangling opalescent earbobs into her ears.

"You look beautiful," he said, taking a step forward to rest his hands on her milky bare shoulders. His eyes met hers in the mirror. Anna felt a momentary rush of heat at the hard warmth of his hands on her skin—and immediately forced it back.

If he thought he could order her about, manhandle her, bend her to his will, and then have her melt into his arms, he was sadly wrong.

Tonight she meant to teach him a sorely needed lesson. In fact, she could hardly wait to begin!

"Shall we go?" she said coolly, slipping out from under his hands and turning toward the door.

With a spurt of satisfaction, she saw that he was frowning as he followed her.

If she had anything to say about it, he would have far more to frown about before they concluded this night!

# XL

Antoinette Noack lived in an English-style stone plantation house some forty-five minutes by buggy from Srinagar. Her much-older husband had made a fortune in cinnamon before obligingly dying and leaving his wife everything he owned. Everyone had expected her to sell up and return to England, but so far she hadn't. It was whispered that she stayed because in England she was naught but a barmaid's daughter, while in Ceylon she was accorded the respect due a lady.

Whatever the reason, her plantation, Spice Hill, was the best producer of cinnamon on the island. She was rich as a nabob, pleasing of appearance with her smooth, dark brown hair, plump bosom, and corseted waist, and well-mannered enough to pass as well-bred.

In fact, the lady was quite a catch for any gentleman hopeful of improving his lot in life by combining his worldly goods with those of a wife. That fact should not have lessened the warmth of Anna's smile as Antoinette hurried to greet her, but it did. Or maybe it was the warmth of Julian's smile at his hostess that chilled her own.

"My dear Anna, I'm so pleased that you could join us! I certainly would have understood if you had not quite recovered from your dreadful ordeal—

but I see you have, and in splendid looks, too! That's a gorgeous dress!''

''Thank you.''

Antoinette was already turning to Julian, who greeted her with a slow smile guaranteed to raise the temperature of any female over ten and under ninety. It certainly raised Anna's temperature, although certainly not in the way he had intended. Her back stiffened, and the smile she summoned for Antoinette froze.

''Hello, Antoinette,'' Julian said.

So they were on a first-name basis, were they? How very charming!

''Julian, you are quite the best brother I've ever seen. My brothers would no more squire me around to parties than they would sail to Africa.''

''They are sadly lacking in judgment, then.''

''He is not,'' Anna muttered under her breath, ''my brother.''

But her companions were too wrapped up in themselves to hear, which was just as well. Anna had nothing to do but stand there, smiling fixedly, while they flirted. It was obvious that the merry widow had set her cap for Julian, while Julian's smoothness in the face of such fulsome attention led Anna to wonder, not for the first time, precisely where and how he had acquired such elegant manners. But elegant manners or no, the rogue was not above casting his eyes down the front of their hostess's lavishly flounced dress as they talked. On the other hand, with so much of that abundant white bosom on view, how could a mere man be blamed for ogling?

Anna bethought herself of her own small bosom, displayed to advantage in her beautiful dress but still no match for the voluptuousness confronting her, and instinctively straightened her shoulders to make the most of what was there. Then, ashamed of herself, she deliberately let them relax. She was not—repeat, not—going to compete for Julian's attention.

It was clear that the man was a rake, and she had already succumbed far too easily to his blatant attraction. She was not about to add to her folly by hanging on to his sleeve and casting evil eyes at every other woman who made up to him. Her morals might have vanished with his advent, but she still had her pride!

"Do come into the parlor. We're having drinks before dinner. Everyone is here except Major Dumesne and the Carrolls." Placing her hand on Julian's elbow, Antointette led them toward the parlor. Anna, doing her best not to appear as disgruntled as she felt, was left to trail a pace or so behind.

The Carrolls, Grace and Edward, were a middle-aged couple who, with their daughters and son, were a fixture at the larger gatherings. The Carroll girls, Lucinda and Lucasta, were about Anna's own age, but as they were both very plain and had never been married they were considered comfirmed spinsters. Both were well-liked and seemed content to pass their lives with their parents. Anna, following their hostess into the parlor, was pleased to hear that they would be in attendance.

Thom Carroll, on the other hand, was something else again. He'd been educated in England and had returned only shortly before Anna had left Ceylon. He was a slender young man, perhaps twenty-two or three, and very vocal about his discontent with the planters' way of life. "Demmed flat" was how he described it, which made Anna wonder if his parents truly thought he was cut out for taking over the reins of the family plantation, as they intended.

Everyone's gaze turned casually toward the door as Anna entered with Julian and Antoinette. Anna just happened to be looking at Thom Carroll as he saw her. To her surprise, he abruptly stopped talking and stared.

"Oh, I say," he said enthusiastically to no one in particular, and hurried to her side. "Do I know you?'' he asked, rudely ignoring both Antoinette and Julian as his spaniel brown eyes fixed on Anna.

"I believe so,'' Anna answered, taken aback to find herself the object of such attention.

"This is Mrs. Traverne, Thom,'' Antoinette supplied, amusement coloring her voice. "Surely you remember her?''

"Oh, you're married.'' He was clearly disappointed, and started to turn away.

"She's widowed,'' Antoinette informed him, openly amused now. "But not unprotected. This is her brother, Julian Chase. Julian, Thom Carroll.''

"Mr. Carroll.'' Julian inclined his head. His jawline was hard as he looked Thom Carroll over, but after he subjected the young man to a thorough scrutiny, the tension in his face dissipated. Apparently he saw little threat in the slight figure with the pomaded hair and dandified clothes.

"Can I fetch you a glass of sherry, Mrs. Traverne?'' Thom asked. Even as Anna, slightly bewildered that he should want to, nodded her assent, Michael and Jonathan Harris joined their little group. Like Thom Carroll, they were in their early twenties, and Anna knew their parents well. She and Paul had entertained George and Elizabeth Harris numerous times at Srinagar, and been entertained in return at The Fannings, the Harrises' tea plantation. But never before had the boys, as Anna thought of them although they were her age or close to it, paid her more than perfunctory attention. Suddenly, like Thom Carroll, they were eyeing her with an interest that took her aback.

"You look smashing, Mrs. Traverne,'' said Jonathan, the elder of the two, as he bowed over her hand.

"Simply smashing,'' Michael agreed, taking her hand in turn. Instead of merely bowing, he pressed a kiss to the back of it. Eyes wide, Anna hastily withdrew her fingers.

"I thought you were in the process of fetching

Mrs. Traverne some sherry?'' Julian, soto voce, reminded Thom Carroll when he showed an inclination to hover jealously around the newly enlarged group. Like Antoinette, Julian was amused. Anna could hear it in his voice, see it in his eyes. She cast him a pleading glance even as Antoinette introduced him to the others, and Thom Carroll, looking back every few feet, took himself off to bring her a drink.

''Darling, you'll be married again before you know it,'' Antoinette whispered in her ear. Before Anna could deny any such ambition, Antoinette took Julian's arm and prettily requested him to come help her sample the appetizers.

''You can't just leave me!'' Anna protested beneath her breath, clinging to his other arm just as doggedly. The sight of two—no, three now, because Thom Carroll was back with the sherry, which he handed to her—eager young men eyeing her with as much avidity as dogs might a bone was unsettling in the extreme. With a shock, Anna realized that, except for Paul, she had never had any dealings to speak of with males. She didn't know what to do, what to say. . . . It was disconcerting to discover that she was now considered available for masculine pursuit. She wasn't sure she liked the idea. It was certainly something that she needed time to get used to.

''You'll be fine,'' Julian murmured in response, giving her hand a reassuring squeeze before firmly removing it from his arm. Then, with Antoinette in triumphant possession, he walked away. Anna was left to deal with her would-be swains as best she could.

Fortunately for Anna's equilibrium, Mary Childers, a comfortable, middle-aged matron, chose that moment to join the group. Anna turned to her with relief. Then Lucinda and Lucasta Carroll came up to them, along with Eleanor Chasen. Fortunately for Anna's peace of mind, Eleanor seemed determined to attract the young men's attention, which left her

free to chat with the older women. She considered
herself to have far more in common with them than
with a young, unmarried girl like Eleanor, whose
primary interest was attracting a potential husband.

"Oh, my dears, did you hear about the dreadful
thing that happened to that family near Jaffna?"
Helen Chasen, resplendent in mauve silk, joined
them, standing beside her daughter. "The Evanses—
they had that big rubber plantation, Calypso I believe they called it. They were found slaughtered in
their beds just last week, all six of them! David"—
David was her husband—"David says it's the work
of some dreadful cult!"

"How hideous!" Anna said.

"I know—knew—their sons. Good God, don't say
Richard and Marcus were killed?" Jonathan Harris
was frowning.

"All of them, my dear. The parents and all four
children," Helen Chasen confirmed. "It's simply
awful."

"A cult, did you say? What kind of cult?" Lucasta
Carroll sounded horrified. Her sister shuddered and
clung to her arm.

"Some sort of native religious cult, I believe. They
call themselves the Thugs, or Thuggees, or something like that, David said. My dear, they believe in
a goddess—I can't remember what they call her—
who wants them to kill. Oh, let David tell you about
it. You know him. He knows all about every odd
thing there is. Sometimes I wonder how I put up
with him."

She summoned her husband to her side. Before
she could tell him why she wanted him, Eleanor
spoke.

"Daddy, Mama was telling us that a family of
planters was murdered by some cult. Is it true?"
She sounded scared.

David Chasen frowned at his wife, then put a reassuring hand on his daughter's arm. "It's true, but
I saw no reason to tell you. Indeed, it's nothing for

you to worry about. Jaffna is far away. It won't happen here.''

"But what kind of cult is it?'' Michael Harris interrupted impatiently.

With a reproving look at his wife, David Chasen explained. "They're called Thuggees, although they're really the Hindustani Thaga. Their religion is murder. They must shed blood constantly to appease their goddess, whom they swear to serve. They consider killing to be an honorable thing, and those they kill to be honored. It's true—the murder of the Evans family is said to be the work of the Thuggees.

"There have been rumors that a few members of the sect have been trying to bring their barbarous religion to our island. But it could just as easily be the work of a turned-off servant, or some such, craftily carried out so that the Thuggees would be blamed. I, for one, am inclined to believe that the Thuggees have nothing to do with it. They wouldn't dare slaughter a whole family of British nationals, take my word for it.''

"No, of course not.'' Eleanor sounded much relieved. Her mother cast her husband an apologetic glance.

Jonathan Harris was still frowning. "What do they look like, these Thuggees? How would one recognize them?''

David Chasen laughed dryly. "That's the trouble—they look just like any of the other natives, unless they've been sent out to kill. Then they pierce their skin with tiny spears and wear a kind of body armor. Or so I hear.''

All of a sudden Anna felt a chill shoot along her spine. When she had been trapped in the fire, she had seen through the smoke—*thought* she had seen— a turbaned man wearing a breastplate and something shiny on his legs. Body armor? No, of course not. She was allowing herself to be frightened by what was nothing more than idle gossip. It had likely been no more than a figment of her imagination—or perhaps a native, running like herself to get out of the fire.

Although . . .

"Good evening, everyone." Charles, having arrived at last, walked up beside her and nodded at his assembled neighbors. He was greeted with a chorus of hellos, and the attention of the group was effectively distracted. Talk became general, and after a few moments Charles turned to smile down at Anna. As his eyes swept over her, they narrowed appreciatively.

"Why, Anna, you look lovely!" he said. "It's good to see that you've put your mourning behind you at last." His voice lowered. "Perhaps—but we'll talk of that later, shall we?"

"Dinner, everyone!" Antoinette called out. Thom Carroll and the Harrises immediately asked to take Anna in to eat, but she was thankfully able to say that she had promised Charles, and went in on his arm.

The meal was lovely, a true English dinner of roast beef and potatoes and pudding such as one rarely got in Ceylon. Cows were sacred amongst many of the islanders, after all, and were treated more as pets than as beasts to be slaughtered for their meat. However Antoinette had managed it, the food was delicious. Julian especially tucked in with relish. Seated at their hostess's right hand, he laughed and chatted and ate with an enjoyment that irked Anna more than a little. It was not his pleasure in the meal she minded; rather it was his enjoyment of his hostess!

Afterwards, the ladies conversed about fashions and children until the gentlemen finished their brandy and cigars and rejoined them. To Anna's embarrassment, Jonathan Harris and Thom Carroll both made a beeline for her chair. Michael Harris, summoned by a crook of his mother's finger and a beaming smile from Eleanor Chasen, seemed to recall himself enough to remember that always before he had paid court to Eleanor. He went to her side, and the pair of them were soon laughing at some quip he made. Charles, who also headed directly for Anna, seemed surprised to find her already possessed of two swains.

Julian, on the other hand, threw her no more than a careless glance before allowing himself to be monopolized by his hostess again. Nettled, Anna set herself to be charming to her small court, and surprised herself by how very well she succeeded.

"What shall we do for entertainment?" With a sparkling smile at Julian, Antoinette seemed to recall her duties as a hostess at last. Getting to her feet some ten minutes after the gentlemen joined them, she addressed the question to the company at large, but it was Julian at whom she looked appealingly. "There's the pianoforte. We could sing, or dance, or the gentlemen could play cards. . . ."

"Oh, let's dance," Eleanor squealed, clasping her hands beneath her chin in an attitude of childlike delight that Anna suspected she had practiced before a mirror. "Please, Mrs. Noack, may we?"

"Certainly, my dear, if it's agreeable to everyone else." Antoinette looked around. There were a few affable groans from the older gentlemen, who expressed a preference for playing cards, but they were voted down as their wives sided with the younger guests and scolded them good-naturedly for being old fogeys.

Grace Carroll was recruited to play the pianoforte, and in a few minutes the furniture had been pushed to the wall. Then Grace struck up a tune, and Anna found herself under seige. Thom Carroll won by the simple expedient of pulling her onto the floor. Anna, laughing, found that she remembered the steps of the lively country dance very well. As she skipped around the room, cheeks flushed, she realized that she was enjoying herself.

She sought out Julian. He was dancing with Antoinette Noack, but over the lady's head he was watching her. He had been right, drat him, although she'd be boiled in oil before she'd ever admit it. But then, she didn't have to admit to a thing. From the slow smile with which he favored her, he read her thoughts in her eyes.

# XLI

"Anna, will you dance?"

After partnering each of her new admirers in turn, Anna had managed a stealthy retreat to the chairs placed at the side of the room for the matrons who wished to gossip. It was there that Charles found her. It had been years since she had danced with a man other than Paul, and at first to do so had felt vaguely disloyal. But Paul was dead, and now that Julian had dragged her kicking and screaming out of her mourning, there was no reason why she shouldn't thoroughly enjoy herself. At the thought she felt suddenly, impossibly young and carefree.

"I'd love to." She smiled gaily up at Charles and allowed him to take her hand. Beside her, her companions glanced up long enough to beam their approval as Charles pulled her to her feet.

Grace Carroll struck up another lively country dance, and Anna skipped through it effortlessly. She was having fun! It felt so good to laugh and dance and yes, even flirt innocently with a variety of men. It felt good to wear a beautiful dress and to know that it became her and made her attractive. It felt good to see the admiration in the eyes of her partners.

Julian, drat him, had been right to pry her out of her mourning, and right to make her come.

Her eyes sought him. He was dancing with Eleanor Chasen, looking impossibly handsome in his evening clothes. His coat and breeches were black, his waistcoat striped and his linen a blinding white. With his black hair brushed severely back from his forehead and tied with a simple black ribbon at his nape, and his eyes sparkling with devilment as he teased his petite partner, he was a sight to steal Anna's breath.

A pang of jealousy smote her as she watched him. His enslavement of females seemed effortless, and as natural to him as breathing. Had he set out to attract her simply because he could not help himself? Was it a part of his personality that he must charm every women he met?

The idea was unsettling. But Anna had no more time to dwell on it as the tune ended with a flourish. Grace rose to her feet for what was apparently to be a short break.

George Harris and David Chasen had pulled two chairs to a table in one corner where they were engaged in a quiet hand of whist, while their wives seemed content to gossip on the other side of the room. Mary Childers fanned herself and chatted with her husband. Next to them, Antoinette held both Harris boys in effortless thrall while the Carroll girls looked on helplessly. Anna felt a quick stab of sympathy for Lucasta and Lucinda. With their dull brown hair and plain faces, to say nothing of their thin figures in their unflattering too-youthful gowns of frilly yellow and ribbon-bedecked peach, they were no match for Antoinette's blatant attraction. Anna wouldn't have been surprised to learn that the woman had painted her face for the occasion. Her cheeks and lips were nearly as bright as the cherry-red stripes in her gown, and her cleavage spilling out of that eye-popping bodice was a feast for male eyes. All that soft white flesh had certainly been enhanced by a thick coating of rice powder, but of course, gentlemen being what they were, not one of them would realize that. The Carroll girls were out-classed by her, and it was clear from the nearly identical looks on the faces of the Harris brothers that they were completely dazzled.

It was amazing what advantages accrued to an overample bosom! Anna thought with disgust.

Charles escorted Anna to the edge of the floor and procured for both of them cups of punch. Anna was sipping the deliciously cool liquid and smiling at him over the rim of her cup when the voice she had been wanting to hear all evening spoke behind her.

"Enjoying yourselves?" If there was an edge to Julian's greeting, which betrayed that he did not quite like to see her so cozy with Charles, only Anna seemed to perceive it. For a minute their eyes met, and it was as if, suddenly, there was no one else in the room.

"Immensely. And you?"

"Of course. Miss Chasen here is a most delightful partner."

Eleanor, on his arm, giggled and cast her eyes modestly to the ground. It was all Anna could do not to roll her own eyes in response. Really, what could Julian possibly see in such a young and obvious chit? Besides the fact that she was really quite pretty and would one day be rich to boot, of course.

Anna's smile dimmed a little at the thought.

Eleanor's eyes lifted then, and she gave Julian a shy smile. Anna would have wagered her earbobs that the chit had practiced that smile in front of a mirror, too. She'd known Eleanor casually since she was a child of thirteen, and one thing the minx had never been was shy.

Perhaps her mother had impressed upon her that boldness was no way to win a husband. At the thought that Eleanor might be husband-hunting with Julian in mind, Anna frowned. She was still frowning when Grace Carroll, having apparently used the short break to fortify herself with a cup of tea, sat

down again on the piano bench with her husband
perched cozily beside her.

"What shall I play this time?" Grace called over
her shoulder to the company, her fingers poised
above the keys ready to strike up another air.

"A waltz! Oh, a waltz!" Eleanor trilled. Immediately she blushed and cast her eyes down again.
Anna bit the inside of her lip. Surely Julian wasn't
fool enough to be taken in by such false innocence?
A quick glance at his face left her disappointed; all
she could read there was polite interest in his partner. But Charles clearly found Eleanor charming. He
was smiling quite paternally at her.

Across the room, Antoinette abandoned the Harrises to move toward the group that contained Julian. Anna, watching her approach with the same
enthusiasm with which she might have viewed an
oncoming spider, watched also as Lucasta and Lucinda lost no time in reclaiming their men. With Antoinette out of the picture, the Harris boys were
quickly subjugated. Lucasta was paired now with
Michael Harris while Lucinda was partnered by Jonathan. Grace, looking on from the piano bench,
smiled triumphantly. It was common knowledge that
Grace had high hopes for a match between her
younger daughter and the Harrises' older son, so it
was no surprise when she nodded in gracious acquiescence to Eleanor's request and struck the opening chords of a waltz.

"Anna . . ." Charles began, turning to her. She
smiled tightly up at him, all too aware of Antoinette,
who was rapidly closing the distance between herself and her prey, and Thom Carroll, who was hurrying toward her. She should dance with Charles;
after all, Julian, who was the only gentleman present with whom she really cared to dance, had not
even asked.

But she couldn't; she absolutely could not abandon Julian to the predatory clutches of either the

merry widow or the wide-eyed innocent. Not when she wanted him for herself.

"I believe I've promised this dance to my brother-in-law," she said, smiling a sweet apology at the other two even as she placed her hand on Julian's coat sleeve. "Is that not right, Julian?"

For a moment, just a moment, he merely regarded her without saying a word. Anna began to fear that he would, most humiliatingly, deny that any such promise had ever been made. But then he smiled at her and drew her hand into the crook of his arm.

"What a wonderful memory you have, Anna my dear. If you'll excuse us, Miss Chasen? Dumesne?"

Eleanor clearly pouted as Julian turned to lead Anna onto the floor. Antoinette, too late by mere seconds, had the presence of mind to smile. Charles was left with the dilemma of entertaining two lovely women, neither of whom particularly wanted to be with him, while on the dance floor Julian pulled Anna into his arms.

The most unnerving part for Anna was realizing that in his arms was precisely where she most wanted to be.

"To what do I owe the honor of this very flattering desire for my company? Earlier I had the distinct impression that you weren't overly pleased with me."

"I'm not."

"So you haven't forgiven me for—ah—persuading you to come."

"No, I have not."

"Liar."

That was all he said, but he smiled slowly down into her eyes. There was a world of knowledge in that smile, as if he knew exactly why she had dragooned him into dancing with her. Trying to subdue a guilty flush, Anna dropped her eyes, Eleanor Chasen style. He was impossible, the rogue. She had the most lowering feeling that he knew precisely the effect he had on her. She was forced to suffer his arm around her waist, forced to endure the feel of his warm, strong hand gripping hers, forced not to react to the sensation of his thighs brushing hers, and all with no more than a polite smile for the benefit of nosy onlookers. Her skirt swished around his boots, the sight and sound disturbingly intimate. Her hand rested on his shoulder; with a quick thrill she registered the breadth of it in comparison to her palm. Her eyes were on a level with his jaw, and she could not help but be tinglingly conscious of the blue-black stubble of close-shaven whiskers that shadowed his skin. His mouth—she tried not to look at his mouth. But it was either look at his mouth, his eyes, or the moving scene over his shoulder. The scene over his shoulder made her dizzy as it whirled by, and his eyes—she did not like to meet his eyes. The smile in them made her dizzy, too, in a different though equally disturbing way. So she looked at his mouth, and wished she hadn't.

Just looking at that long, firm-lipped mouth, parted now as he smiled to reveal dazzlingly white teeth, made her remember what it felt like when he kissed her.

Suddenly, fiercely, she wanted him to kiss her.

"If you don't quit staring at me like that, I'm going to scandalize all your friends by making love to you here on the dance floor."

Scarlet color flooded Anna's cheeks. Shocked, she shot her eyes up to meet his. He could not possibly have guessed what she was thinking—could he?

"Your face is very easy to read," he told her, as if she had put the question into words.

"I don't know what you're talking about!"

His eyes mocked her. "I thought you weren't a coward, Anna."

"I'm not!"

"Oh yes, you are. You want me, and I know it. And I—I want you."

The last words were a husky murmur. Anna felt the texture of his voice like a physical caress.

"Stop it! Someone will hear!" she hissed at him, casting a quick look around to make sure no one had. Other couples danced past, oblivious to the hot blood stirring in her veins, to the tremors that snaked along her nerve endings. Dear Lord, the man could reduce her to mindlessness with nothing more than words!

"Do you like being the belle of the ball?" He was smiling down at her, his expression indulgent.

"Very much." Anna stiffened her spine and lifted her chin defiantly. She would not allow him—or anyone else!—to guess the effect he had on her!

"I thought you would. You married Paul too young. You've never had a chance to have fun."

"I wish you'd quit harping on Paul." Her words were tart. She was having so much difficulty keeping the required twelve inches of space between them that it was making her cross. What she really wanted to do was slide her arms around his neck.

"I will—when you forget him." Though he was smiling, the words were spoken through his teeth.

Then, suddenly, it hit her. With an awful flash of clarity she knew precisely why he was pursuing her so determinedly.

"Dear God, that's it, isn't it?" she asked, appalled. Her eyes fastened on his as she spoke scarcely above a whisper. "You want me because I first belonged to Paul. I'm just another spoil in your stupid private war with your brothers!"

He said nothing, merely stared down at her for a moment in a silence as shocked as if she'd slapped him. Just then the tempo of the music changed, quickened, and Julian was whirling her about the dance floor, faster and faster with his arm hard around her and his hand gripping hers as if he meant to crush it. A hard smile twisted his mouth. Anna forced herself to smile, too, and straightened her shoulders. To the other twirling dancers and the gossiping onlookers she guessed they looked no different than they had moments before: he so tall and dark, rakishly handsome with his chiseled features and knowing smile; she small and fragile-looking with her silvery green dress floating out around her like fairies' wings as they danced, her skin pale as milk and her upswept hair the color of moonbeams. As that picture lodged in her mind, Anna was once again reminded of Hades and Persephone, and wondered if the love-hate that Persephone had felt for her captor had been anything as strong as what she felt for Julian.

She wanted to hurt him, to make him suffer, to pay him back for the way she was hurting at that moment—and yet she also wanted to curl up in his arms and have him hold her as if he'd never let her go.

From his reaction, she knew she'd been right. The thought made her want to weep.

"It's true, isn't it?" she asked quietly when the tempo of the dance had moderated so that she could speak again.

"You know me so well," he sneered, and pulled her insultingly tight against his body.

"Let me go! You're holding me too closely!" It was an outraged hiss. The buttons of his waistcoat were pressing into her breasts. His hips ground into hers, and every movement of his legs thrust them against her thighs. To struggle would have been un-dignified, and would serve no purpose other than to call the attention of the assembly to their sud-denly scandalous posture. Anna thought for a min-ute, then deliberately trod hard on his toe with her tiny sharp heel.

"Ouch!"

To her relief, his grip loosened enough so that she could pull herself from his arms. The other couples pirouetted around them, their eyes on the intriguing scene being played out in their midst. Anna could feel interested stares from all sides.

"I have a headache," she said clearly, for the benefit of whoever might be listening. ''I believe I'd better sit down.''

''If you have a headache, then I'll take you home,'' Julian answered, his voice stony, and took her arm.

Anna was left with nothing to say as he escorted her off the floor.

# XLII

He was drunk. Or, if not completely cast away, then certainly extremely well-to-live. Julian, sprawled at his ease in the book-lined office at Srinagar, minus his elegant evening coat and waistcoat and with his cravat twisted wildly to one side, pondered the ramifications. After a moment he took another swig from the nearly empty bottle in his hand—the glass had long since been abandoned—and swirled the potent liquid thoughtfully around his mouth before swallowing it. The irony of it was that he was not ordinarily a drinking man. He'd tried this method of drowning his sorrows as a youth, only to discover that the only thing that he gained from such excesses was a blinding headache and a mouth like a washboard the next day. So why was he abandoning such hard-earned knowledge in favor of what he knew was pure folly?

The answer was embodied in a single word: Anna. Had there been any truth in the accusation she'd hurled at him tonight? Did the fierce attraction she held for him have anything to do with the fact that she had once been his golden half brother's wife?

Julian probed the thought as carefully as if it were a sore tooth. Did it matter that she had once been Paul's?

Damn the green-eyed little witch. Here he sat

drinking himself senseless when what he really wanted to do was storm her bedroom and take her, over and over again, until she was reduced to a quivering mass of need in his arms.

And even that wouldn't serve to douse the hunger that raged inside him. He wanted her surrender to be total: not just her body, which he knew he could have pretty much at will, but her heart and her mind as well.

He wanted all of her for himself alone.

The idea that she'd once belonged to Paul made him want to break things. But not because he'd always wanted what Paul had; he would have felt that way no matter who her husband had been. In Anuradhapura, when he had recovered the emeralds only to discover that they were no longer central to his happiness, he'd faced the dismal truth: he loved the chit. Loved her to the point of madness or folly. Loved her above and beyond any depth of feeling of which he had ever thought himself capable. Loved her with a hard-edged hunger that possession of her body failed to appease. What he wanted was to possess her soul.

He wanted her to love him, not Paul.

Jim called him crazy, and Julian supposed Jim might not be far wrong. To hesitate even for a second to claim the prize he had longed for all his life when he had the means of doing so within his grasp was folly, and worse than folly.

But instead he waited. Waited for Anna. Hadn't some poet once opined that the world was well lost for love? That was exactly how he felt. Nothing—not the emeralds, not his dazzling new birthright, not all his once-grand plans for revenge—meant anything to him in comparison with his craving for Anna's love.

At first he had felt a fierce glow of elation as he'd contemplated returning in triumph to Gordon Hall, ousting his despised half brother from the ancestral acres, and reigning there himself as lord.

Then the thought of Anna had brought him thudding back to earth. The expression "cream-pot love" took up residence in his mind. If he returned to her, announced that he was Lord Ridley, and asked her to be his bride, she would very likely agree. Certainly she would be a fool if she didn't. She would be gaining a rich husband, a title, a stepfather for Chelsea of whom the child was already more than fond, and a bed partner who was obviously to her taste, all in one fell swoop.

But he would spend the rest of his life wondering: did she truly love him? Or, underneath her kisses and sighs, was she secretly mourning the thrice-damned Paul?

Julian knew he wouldn't be able to stand the torture of imagining that. One night he'd end up wrapping his hands around her throat and choking the breath from her body, just to assure himself that his golden half brother was truly driven from her thoughts for good.

So he had said nothing of his discovery to anyone but Jim. He'd resolved to make Anna love him and then tell her the truth. If, then, she wanted the two of them to return to England and claim their rightful place as lord and lady of Gordon Hall, he would be only too happy to oblige her. But if she chose to stay in Ceylon, that decision would please him well, too.

He didn't care where he was, as long as Anna, loving him, was by his side.

The fire in which she'd nearly been trapped had brought the depth of his feeling for her home to him. If she had died . . . it didn't bear thinking of. He would spend the rest of his life like a wild beast, howling at the moon.

He wanted her; he meant to have her. Countless females from all walks of life had fallen like dominoes before him since the days of his gangling youth. Why should this one whom he desired beyond all reason be any different? She might not be easy to win—her dogged clinging to the bonds that still tied her to his brother precluded that—but she was worth the fight. He would teach her to love him, however long it took.

The first step, of course, was to get her over Paul. Julian's teeth clenched, as they did whenever his younger half brother's image intruded on his consciousness. All his life he had considered Lord Ridley's two acknowledged sons as his bitter rivals, but never had he thought to feel the extent of the jealousy that consumed him at the idea of Anna loving Paul. The golden boy had won again, staking a preemptive claim to what Julian would have given his right arm to call his own. Where he had had to fight for everything of value he possessed, Paul had been handed it effortlessly. Even Anna. Had he appreciated her? Had he loved her?

Not as he, Julian, loved her. Not with this burning need to possess and protect and cherish her for all the days of his life.

Paul had not been capable of a love like that. Julian knew it in his bones.

Why could Anna not see?

Julian propped his feet up on the huge teakwood desk, leaned back in the leather chair, and took another swallow of whiskey.

Folly or no, he meant to get good and drunk. Drunk enough so that he would pass out. Drunk enough so that, for one night at least, he could get Anna out of his head.

Blessed oblivion sounded pretty good at the moment.

# XLIII

It was very late, or, rather, very early, since the clock had chimed midnight some two hours before. Anna, pacing her chamber, had given up any attempt at sleeping. The beautiful green dress was hung neatly in her wardrobe. Her shoes and underclothes had been stored away too. There was not one visible reminder of the evening just past, but still she couldn't get it out of her mind.

Julian had been like a bear with a sore paw as he had driven her home. To do him justice, the few necessary remarks she had addressed to him had been icy. Perhaps she had deserved to have her head snapped off in return. But the last half hour of the drive had passed without so much as a single word being exchanged between them. Then, when they had reached the house, he had said something under his breath that had made her eyes widen, and had dragged her into his arms.

The kiss had been long and shatteringly intimate. He'd held her twisted across his lap, his arms tight around her, his hands bold as they moved over her. Anna had begun by resisting and ended by twining her arms around his neck.

Then he had practically pushed her from the carriage and driven toward the stable in the rear.

Since then she'd been listening for his step on the

stairs. But he hadn't come to bed. She wasn't even entirely certain he was in the house.

And until she was certain, she couldn't sleep.

She had tried a hot bath, soaking in scented water until her skin was rosy pink. She'd washed her hair, drying it with long brush strokes, an activity that had never failed to soothe her—until tonight. In despair, she had even managed to drink a glass of warm milk, although she hated the stuff.

But here she was, at quarter past two, still wide awake.

Because of Julian. Everything wrong in her life could be laid squarely at his door.

Where was he, the devil?

Anna paced from door to window, and then, for variety, from dressing table to wardrobe. The plank floor felt cool beneath her bare feet. The long windows were open to the night, the mosquito netting that swathed them billowing in the breeze. The ends of her nightdress fluttered, too, as a welcome draft swept the floor. The garment was prim but sleeveless, in deference to the tropical heat. It ended at the throat in a tiny, upstanding ruffle, and more ruffles adorned the hem and edged the armholes. The thin muslin was elaborately pin-tucked in front, affording her some modesty where she needed it most. The single layer that made up the back was translucent.

It was a garment strictly designed for sleeping alone—or with a lover. At the thought of Julian seeing her in it, Anna shivered. She forced the erotic image away.

Julian was a problem that, for the sake of her own peace of mind, had to be dealt with. Did she love him?

Her heart shied away from that question.

Did he love her? Or did he merely want her flat on her back in his bed?

She shied away from that question, too. But that was the issue that had to be addressed. If he loved her . . . Her heart pounded at the thought. If he loved her, then perhaps she might loosen the iron grip she had tried to keep on her emotions and allow herself to love him, too.

Maybe, just maybe, the girl who had loved Paul had gone away with him. Maybe it was the woman who'd taken her place who longed for Julian.

There was a faint crash from somewhere downstairs. Anna's head came up, and she stared intently at the door. Then she made up her mind. Snatching up her wrapper, she shrugged into it and tied the sash even as she made her way out the door.

If Julian was up and about, then she would have it out with him. The time had come to ask him point-blank what his intentions toward her were.

And if she didn't like the answer, why, then, at least she would know.

So late at night, the house was deserted except for Moti, who darted along the upstairs passage at Anna's heels. The stairs, barely lit by the fairy light at the top, were dark and shadowy and drafty. Below, all was silent. Reaching the downstairs hall, Anna strained to listen. She had heard nothing more, but a light shone faintly around the bend in the hallway. Heading toward it, she turned the corner that led to the rear veranda and found that the light was spilling from beneath the office door.

It took her only a moment to turn the knob and walk in.

The sight that met her eyes caused her to pause inside the threshold, her hand still on the knob, her eyes widening. Julian lounged at his ease in the chair in which she usually did the household accounts, his booted feet on the desk, his evening clothes wildly askew. The smell of whiskey was almost overpowering. A large, yellowish stain on one whitewashed wall trickled tiny golden rivers toward the floor, where lay the shattered remains of a bottle in a puddle of liquid.

"Well, well, if it isn't milady Green Eyes herself."

There was the faintest slurring to the words. He smiled, a nasty mockery of amusement, and his booted feet hit the floor. He stood, slightly unsteady on his feet, and executed a travesty of a bow. "Do join me, milady."

"You're drunk."

His eyes narrowed at her, and he sank abruptly back into the chair.

"Damned right I'm drunk. And why not, pray? You're enough to drive any sane man to drink, you may take my word."

It was not much more than a mutter, and seemed to be directed as much to himself as at her. Fearing that their voices might carry and awaken the household, Anna eased the door shut behind her and stepped farther into the room to eye him with some exasperation. Clearly there would be no getting any sense out of him on this night!

"You should go to bed," she said in the scolding tone that mothers habitually use toward wayward children. Skirting where he sprawled in the chair with some caution, she crouched beside the mess on the floor and began to carefully pick up the shards of glass.

"Now there's a suggestion." Julian watched her progress broodingly. Then in a much sharper voice he snapped, "Leave it! The maids can get it in the morning."

Anna glanced up at him. "I don't want them—"

"I said leave it!" It was a snarl. "Go back to bed and leave me the hell alone, will you please?"

Carefully cradling pieces of broken bottle in one hand, Anna rocked back on her heels to study him.

"I should do just that, but I'll not abandon you in this state. You're liable to break your neck on the stairs." Her brows twitched together thoughtfully. "Shall I send Jim to you?"

"To bloody hell with Jim!"

Anna's lips tightened with impatience. Standing up, she moved to drop the broken glass in the wastebasket by the desk, then stood leaning against the far corner, frowning at him. He met her eyes with an insolent stare, then slowly dropped his gaze over her. The suggestion in that bold look was unmistakable. He was doing it merely to antagonize her, Anna knew. She frowned at him.

"That's something I must say for Paul: never, in all the years that I knew him, did I ever see him . . ."

Julian's head rose with the awful menace of a cobra's. His mouth twisted in a furious slant.

". . . drunk," Anna finished lamely, her eyes widening at the rush of blood that rose to darken Julian's face.

"Don't you ever, ever again compare me to bloody Paul!" he said through clenched teeth, his knuckles white as his hands gripped the arms of the chair. "May the bugger burn forever in hell!"

His body was tensed as if he would shoot from the chair at any moment. The muscles in his shoulders and arms, the outlines of which she could clearly see through the thin linen shirt, were bunched. He looked like a man on the brink of extreme violence.

"Why, you're jealous!" she said in surprise. "Ruby said you were, but—"

He shot up from the chair as if it had catapulted him forth and was around the side of the desk to stand looming over her before Anna could do more than shrink back.

"You're damned right I'm jealous," he said through his teeth. He was so close that she was forced to half sit on the edge of the desk, leaning away from him; so close that the whiskey on his breath hit her in a sickening wave. His hands came up to rest on either side of her face, tilting it up toward his. Then they slid upwards, his fingers threading beneath her hair to massage her scalp. His eyes bore down into hers. His lips parted to show the faintest gleam of white teeth in a predatory smile.

Anna felt the steely caress of those large hands on the delicate bones of her skull, and for a moment, just a moment, she was afraid.

"Let me go," she said clearly.

He laughed, the sound brutal, and his hands slid down to curl around her neck.

"Do you know what you called me, that first night after I made love to you? You were smiling in your sleep—for me, I thought—and then you called me Paul. I wanted to strangle you. It was all I could do to keep my hands from wringing your pretty little neck." His thumbs caressed the delicate tracery of bones that marched up the front of her throat, while the rest of his fingers spread out, sure and strong, along the back of her neck. "It would be so easy—I could snap your neck with a flick of my wrists. Then you wouldn't be able to think of Paul anymore. . . ."

"You're drunk, Julian. You don't know what you're doing," Anna said in as reasonable a tone as she could muster, given that his thumbs were now pushing up under her chin, forcing her head back. She was not afraid of him, not really, and yet—this Julian was a stranger. She had never seen him in such a state, never guessed that he could turn such savagery on her, for such a cause. He must be wildly, madly jealous to threaten her with violence. Insane as it was, her heart speeded up at the ramifications. Then what he'd said registered: he had left after that first night because she had called him Paul!

His thumbs now rested against the base of her chin, forcing her head to tip so far back that her hair, left loose to finish drying, spilled in a silvery cascade across the desk.

Her lashes lifted so that she was looking him full in the eyes. Her eyes blazed green as emeralds in the white oval of her face, cutting through the fog of whiskey that befuddled him to bring a sudden frown to his face.

"You have no reason to be jealous, Julian," she said softly. "It's you I love, not Paul."

His fingers stilled, tensed. His eyes narrowed on her face.

"Lying bitch," he said.

Anna shook her head. "I'm not lying."

Julian stared at her a moment longer, then all at once his face contorted. "God help you if you are," he said hoarsely, and then his mouth was on hers, kissing her fiercely, while his hands slid from her throat to cradle the back of her head.

Anna parted her lips on a little sob, her hands moving to clutch his arms, his shoulders. His tongue thrust into her mouth, urgent, demanding, and she met that urgency with a hunger of her own.

He leaned over her, pressing her backwards, one hand slashing violently sideways as he sent all the items atop the desk crashing to the floor. Then she was lying on her back on the polished surface, and he was coming down on top of her, kissing her greedily, his hands pulling at her clothes.

# XLIV

"Anna. Oh, God, Anna." It was a broken whisper. He pressed stinging kisses over her face and throat, nuzzling the soft underside of her neck, tracing the outline of an ear. Uncaring of his drink-fueled roughness, Anna wrapped her arms around his neck, murmuring soft endearments, stroking his rough black hair. The smell of whiskey, at first so overpowering, was forgotten in the blinding heat of passion. She loved him. How she loved him!

His voice was unsteady as he murmured her name, over and over, like a litany. His hands were unsteady too as he jerked her nightdress and wrapper out of his way, leaving her naked from the waist down while he tore at the buttons on his breeches. One popped, flying across the room to land with a clatter on the floor. Then he was free, coming into her where she lay ready for him, his need too hard and urgent to permit him to wait a second longer.

As he pushed himself inside her, Anna gasped, then moaned. He was huge, hot, filling her to the point of bursting—and she trembled at the sheer wonder of it. His mouth was on her neck, his hand on her breast, squeezing and kneading and caressing her through the thin muslin, while he thrust, hard and fast, in and out. Anna arched her back to meet him, barely aware of the unfamiliar feel of the

hard polished wood beneath her bottom. He
groaned, his lips turning to burn against her neck,
his hand closing hard over her breast.

And then with another deep thrust and a cry he
lay still.

Anna, on the brink of ecstasy, trembled in anticipation as he lay unmoving atop her. It took a moment for her to realize that he, at least, was sated.
For a little while more she lay there, her hands automatically caressing his rough black head, willing
back her disappointment. But her body, unrepen-
tant, continued to throb and ache.

When he lifted himself off her, he looked as unsteady as she felt.

"See what happens when you tell me you love
me?" he asked with a rueful smile as he adjusted
his breeches.

Anna, still lying on the desk top as he had left
her, suddenly recollected how indecent her posture
was and sat up, pulling her clothes down to cover
her nakedness. She drew her knees close to her chest
and wrapped her arms around them.

His eyes were both hooded and faintly wary as
they regarded her, from the top of her tousled head
to the small pink toes protruding from beneath the
hem of her crumpled nightdress.

"You did mean it? I didn't just scare you into saying it, did I?" He took a deep breath, faint color
rising to his cheekbones. "I wouldn't really hurt
you, you know."

"I know." For a moment she had an urge to tease
him, but he was so still, so very still, despite the
casualness with which he had tried to infuse his
voice, that Anna realized her answer was important
to him. Why, he's as vulnerable as I am, she thought
with amazement, and suddenly all the tenderness
for him that she'd fought for so long to keep hidden
rushed to the surface.

She rose to her knees and moved the short distance to where he stood, tense and waiting by the

edge of the desk. For just a moment she looked at him, drinking in the height and breadth of him; the hard, dark, handsome features; the glittering eyes; the disordered hair black as a starling's wing. Then she slid her arms around his neck and pressed a quick, almost shy kiss against lips that were as rigid as if they'd been carved from stone.

"I meant it," she whispered, watching him. At first he didn't move, didn't so much as blink. Then his eyes widened, lightened, until they were more blue than she had ever seen them, blue as rich velvet. His muscles relaxed, and his mouth curved into the faintest of smiles.

"Oh, Anna." He turned his head, pressed a soft kiss to the silky skin on the underside of her arm. "My Anna."

There was a slight emphasis on the possessive that told her what he wanted.

"All yours," she agreed tenderly, her fingers threading into his thick dark hair.

"And Paul?" There was a steely undertone to that.

"He was only a boy and I only a girl when I loved him. Now I'm a woman grown, and the man I love is—a man." Even as she said it, she knew it was true.

"I'll not have you moping after him."

"I won't mope."

"Nor sighing his name in the middle of the night."

"I won't sigh."

Julian eyed her. "And no more of Dumesne, either."

"Charles is just a friend."

"Still, I won't have him hanging about."

"Dictatorial, aren't you?"

"What's mine is mine."

"I'm far from faithless, Julian."

That earned her a wry smile. "That I have reason to know very well."

"I expect you to remember that."

"I'll try my best."

"And, Julian. . . ."

"Yes?"

"What's mine is mine, as well."

"Are you admitting to a jealous streak? For shame!"

"Don't laugh. I mean it."

"I think I'd enjoy making you jealous."

"You wouldn't, I promise you. I've discovered that I can be quite fierce where you are concerned."

He grinned, clearly delighted. "Can you indeed? The thought makes me shake in my boots."

The look she gave him was severe. "It should."

She still knelt at the edge of the desk, her arms looped around his neck. His hands had risen to grip her waist, and he gave her a quick hard squeeze.

"You'll never have cause to question my faithfulness, I give you my word."

"That's better." She smiled at him and slid her hand around to tweak an ear. "Is there nothing else you have to say to me?"

He lifted his eyebrows questioningly.

"You drunken dolt." The words were half affectionate, half exasperated. "Will you leave me no pride at all? Must I spell it out for you?"

Still he looked all at sea.

"Do you love me?" It was an exasperated demand.

"Oh, that."

"Yes, that."

"I suppose I must." His eyes glinted teasingly down at her. Anna, her arms sliding from his neck to cross over her breasts, subsided onto her heels with an affronted "Hmmph!"

He smiled then, broadly, and scooped her up off the desk into his arms. Holding her close against his chest, he moved toward the door.

"Where are we going?" she asked, her arms curling around his neck. In truth, she was content to let

him take her where he would. The very ease with
which he carried her sent a tingle coursing along her
spine. He was so effortlessly strong!

"To bed."

Anna raised her head from its comfortable spot on
his shoulder. "Oh, yes?" Her voice was a trifle cool.
His "I suppose I must" still rankled.

He had managed to open the door without letting
her drop or banging her head against the jamb,
which in his less than sober state was, she supposed, something to be thankful for. He headed toward the stairs. "I'm a man of action, not words.
You'll get precious few pretty speeches out of me."

"I don't want pretty speeches."

He reached the foot of the stairs and began to
climb. Again her weight seemed not to bother him
in the least. She put down the fact that he stumbled
on the first stair to the effects of strong drink.

"I can walk, you know."

He stopped in the middle of the staircase to look
down at her. In the shifting shadows, all she could
see clearly was the proprietary gleam in his eyes.

"Not on your life. You're mine now, my girl, and
I don't mean to ever let you go."

"Oh." Anna's response was meek, but her arms
curled tighter around his neck. In truth, she could
stay in his arms forever.

"Oh." He mimicked her, tone and all, and then
his mouth came down on hers, claiming her lips,
kissing her so thoroughly that she feared for their
safety—while she could still think at all. When at last
he broke off the kiss to climb swiftly on, she was so
dazzled by the aftereffects that she didn't even worry
about the state of his balance.

He took her to his room, not hers. Anna registered that fact with a small part of her mind even as
he shouldered the door shut behind them. Inside,
the darkness was eased by bright moonlight flooding through the windows. They had been left partly

open, but fortunately the mosquito netting had been drawn over them, and it was this that billowed in the cool night air, lending an otherworldly atmosphere to the silent room.

The silk hangings on the half-tester bed rustled faintly as he placed her on the coverlet. Anna lay there for a moment, shrouded in shadows, her head turning on the pillow as she watched him tug, first carelessly and finally with clear fury, at his twisted cravat.

The knot would not come loose. Anna smiled with rueful fondness at her love and clambered to the edge of the bed.

"Let me do it for you," she told him, catching his arm and drawing him toward the bed, where she knelt at the edge.

"Damned thing," Julian muttered, but he stayed obediently still as her slim fingers worked what magic they could on the recalcitrant knot.

"I hope you don't get in this state often," she said in a scolding tone as she at last freed the tight knot and pulled the cravat from around his neck.

Julian's hands came up to rest on her waist. "The last time I drank too much was when I was seventeen, and for the same cause, too."

"And what cause was that?" Her fingers moved on to unfasten the buttons on his shirt. Being able to take such liberties with him was intoxicating, and as the final button left its hole she was emboldened to run her fingertips down the front of his chest.

"A minx of a woman was driving me mad." He captured her wrists, stilling her hands against him. Anna felt the soft prickle of his chest hairs beneath her palm, the solid heat of his chest, and suddenly the ache deep inside her that she had almost succeeded in willing away sprang back to full, throbbing life.

"And what woman was that?" Scarcely aware of what she was saying, she pressed her hands more closely against him. Beneath her right palm she could feel the strong, steady beat of his heart.

"I've forgotten. See? You've driven every other female but yourself clear out of my mind."

"See that it stays that way." She twined her finger in a curl of chest hair and yanked it threateningly. He yelped, laughed, and released her hands to sit down on the edge of the bed.

Arms looped around his neck, Anna leaned against his broad back and watched as he tugged off his boots. When he stood up again, he was barefoot. When he stripped off his shirt to reveal his wide muscled shoulders and broad chest, Anna watched admiringly. When he stepped out of his breeches to reveal his narrow hips and long, strong-looking legs, she felt her blood quicken in her veins. Then, when he turned fully toward her, her breath stopped altogether. That part of him that was most fully a man was huge, stiff as a tree limb, and ready.

The reawakened ache in her loins pulsed in almost painful response.

"Come here, sweetheart."

He drew her off the bed onto her feet. Anna went, unresisting. Her heart was thudding so loudly that she could scarcely think above the pulsing of her own blood as he lifted first her wrapper and then her nightgown. When she was as naked as he, he pulled her against him. The friction between his hot, hair-roughened flesh and her own soft silkiness made her dizzy. Her arms rose to link behind his neck even as his head descended. Their mouths met in a hard, explosive kiss. His hands slid down her spine to close around her bare bottom, lifting her clear off her feet. He pressed her against him so that she felt the hard urgency of him probing at the nest between her thighs. Then he lifted her higher, and instinctively her legs twined around his waist.

Even as he entered her they were falling, tumbling together back into the bed.

This time when he loved her, she went wild. Her

hands and lips and body made demands of him that she never knew how to make before. But she wanted all of him, wanted him to fill her, to take her, to give her the ecstasy that he had taught her to crave.

And he did.

At the end he gave her even more. He thrust himself deep, holding her close while she cried out his name in glorious abandon, then sought his own release.

"I love you, love you, love you," he groaned into her neck as he quaked and shuddered inside her.

Anna was smiling as he shuddered one final time and went limp.

# XLV

Five minutes later he was snoring. Lying against his side, her head pillowed on his shoulder, her hand resting against his black-furred chest, Anna was dreamily contemplating the unexpected turn her life had taken. Who would have imagined that she would one day fall crazily in love with the terrifying housebreaker she had surprised all those months ago at Gordon Hall?

Then came the first of a series of furniture-rattling snores. No mere hard breathing were these. They were loud, full-throated, and almost funny. At least, they would have been funny if they hadn't come from the adoring throat of the man who had just promised to love her forever.

Sitting up, Anna looked down at her insensible beloved and shook her head. Of course he would have to choose this of all nights to drink himself into a near stupor. They should have been cuddled up together, exchanging tender endearments, then making love until dawn. But clearly those things would have to wait for another night. Tonight, she was privileged to witness her lover in his natural state: sprawled flat on his back, whiskers darkening his cheeks and chin, naked as a babe—and rattling off snores loud enough to wake the dead.

So much for romance. Anna sighed, mentally castigated her lover as a castaway idiot, and clambered off the bed. She could not leave him this way for the rest of the night, and however far into the morning he meant to sleep. She tugged the bed coverings from the side of the bed he was not sprawled across, then set herself to rolling him onto the clean sheet thus revealed. It was not an easy task. He was a big man, and heavy. Pausing once or twice to admire the sheer magnificence of him, Anna pushed and pulled and prodded without noticeable result. Finally she had to stand on the far side of the bed and give a hard yank to the arm opposite to where she stood. Still, when he moved, she didn't flatter herself that any effort of hers was more than marginally responsible. He simply decided to roll over, incidentally landed in the spot she wished him to occupy, and, reaching up to loop both arms around it, buried his face in the pillow. For a moment more Anna watched him, admiring the strong back and the firm round curves of his bottom. Then, almost regretfully, she pulled the bed coverings over him and left him to sleep in peace.

Really, she reflected as she slipped into her nightgown and wrapper and left his room, it was just as well that he had sunk fathoms deep into unconsciousness. If he had not, she would almost certainly have spent the night in his bed. And it would never do for her to be found there in the morning. Such scandalous behavior had no place in the life of a respectable widow with a young child.

She was smiling faintly as she moved along the corridor to her own room. It was near dawn, and the darkness outside was just beginning to lighten to a thick charcoal gray. Soon stray sunbeams would pierce the gloom, and the sun would peep over the horizon before at last rising to brighten and warm the day. Rather like her own emergence from grief, Anna realized with some surprise. When the night of her loss had fallen upon her, she had never expected to wake up, smiling, to face a brand-new day.

But she had, and suddenly her life sparkled with previously unimagined possibilities. Happiness washed over her in a huge warm wave as she reached her bedchamber, turned the knob, and entered her room.

The first thing she noticed was Moti's tiny eyes glowing at her from the floor near the bed. If she hadn't recognized the creature almost at once, she would have been frightened to death. Under the circumstances, she was mostly puzzled. How had Moti gotten into her room? She was sure—almost sure—that he had followed her down the hallway when she had gone to confront Julian what seemed like centuries ago.

All at once a memory of the cobra that had found its way into the east wing on the day of Julian's arrival popped into her head. Conscious of a sudden rush of fear, Anna stepped with extreme caution toward the bedside table, where she quickly lit a candle.

As she lifted the candle high and turned to peer into the corners, the spreading golden glow revealed Moti's furry brown body but nothing else. Marginally reassured, she turned toward the bed—and got her second shock in as many minutes. Someone, or something, was curled up beneath the covers in the middle of her bed!

Biting back a scream, Anna set the candle down and leaned over to twitch the covers back to reveal the intruder.

Chelsea! Curled into a little ball, her golden hair tangled all around her face, her knees drawn up to her chest and hugged so that not even her toes were visible beneath the hem of the dainty white nightdress, Chelsea was fast asleep.

In the days immediately after Paul's death, Chelsea had come to her mother's room in the middle of the night and climbed into bed with some regularity. Anna, grief-stricken herself but hurting even more for Chelsea, had welcomed her daughter, and the two had slept snuggled as close as spoons, comforting each other. But Chelsea had seemed past the need for such reassurances for months now, and Anna frowned as she tried to imagine what could have brought Chelsea to her bed on this of all nights.

It occurred to Anna then to thank a watchful Providence that Julian had chosen to carry her off to his room rather than her own.

"Chicken." Anna sat down on the edge of the bed and lightly shook her daughter's thin shoulder. "Wake up."

On the second shake Chelsea stirred, then suddenly sat up. As she shook the hair from her face, the child's eyes were wide with fright. Then, spying her mother, Chelsea gave a little gasp and scooted close to throw herself into Anna's arms.

"Mama, where were you?"

"Did you have a bad dream?" Anna, prudently ignoring the question, stroked the silky blond head that burrowed into her bosom.

Violently Chelsea shook her head, her arms tightening around Anna's waist.

"It wasn't a dream, Mama, it wasn't! At first I thought it was, but I wasn't screaming and my eyes were open, and you don't dream like that, do you?"

"I wouldn't think so. Unless you were dreaming that your eyes were open, of course."

"Well, I wasn't! There was a coolie in my room. He had spears through his cheeks, Mama, little tiny ones, and he looked so strange! He just looked at me for a few minutes, and then he shook something at me and dropped it on the end of my bed, and I was so scared I shut my eyes, and when I opened them again he was gone! I wanted to scream but I couldn't, and Kirti wouldn't wake up so I came to find you, but you weren't here!"

"I'm so sorry, chicken." Anna held her trembling daughter for a few seconds, then pushed her a little away and smoothed the hair from her face with both hands. "It must have been scary. But it was only a dream, you know."

"It wasn't! I know it wasn't! Truly, Mama!"

Chelsea was so upset that Anna could do nothing but wrap her daughter in her arms and rock her back and forth, crooning wordless comfort. It was some little while before she ventured to say, "Would you like to sleep with me for the rest of the night?"

"Oh, yes, Mama, please!"

Anna dropped a quick kiss on the child's forehead, settled her down, tucked her up, blew out the candle, and climbed in beside her. Chelsea cuddled against her like a frightened animal. Holding her daughter close, Anna listened until she heard the soft, even breathing that told her that Chelsea had fallen asleep.

Then, moving carefully so as not to awaken the child, Anna slid out of bed and pulled on her wrapper once more. More than likely what Chelsea had seen was no more than a spectre out of a dream. Still, that Kirti couldn't be awakened seemed odd. If nothing else, she could check and make certain that the old ayah was all right.

It was dawn now, and creeping tendrils of light were curling along the corridor as she walked toward the nursery. Moti, liberated from the bed chamber where he had apparently fled in Chelsea's wake, padded at her heels. Anna was glad of the animal's presence. In the uncertain quiet of dawn, it was comforting to know that there was some other creature besides herself awake in the house.

The nursery door stood wide. Anna glanced in, saw Chelsea's bed with the covers thrown back where the child had apparently abandoned it, and let her gaze slide over the rest of the room, which was apparently undisturbed. The door that led to the schoolroom was open, too. Since Kirti's bedchamber opened off that, Anna assumed that Chelsea had run through there to awaken Kirti. Before moving on to check on the ayah, Anna walked over to Chelsea's bed. Of course the child had merely suffered another nightmare. . . .

But something was lying on the foot of her bed, half buried by the disheveled bedclothes. Anna's eyes widened as she stared at it for a long moment before daring to touch it with a single probing finger. It was a large, trumpet-shaped flower, brilliantly colored, waxy to the touch. Harmless, surely.

But how had it gotten on Chelsea's bed?

Perhaps the child hadn't been dreaming after all.

The thought was frightening. A coolie, with tiny spears through his cheeks, shaking this blossom over Chelsea's bed? The very idea was bizarre—but there lay the flower.

Biting her lower lip, Anna gingerly picked up the blossom, holding it between her thumb and forefinger as she went to awaken Kirti. It was only a flower, and she knew that her reaction to it was largely the product of an overactive imagination, but still it seemed evil. Almost threatening. . . .

Kirti was fast asleep in her small chamber off the schoolroom, snoring almost as loudly as Julian had been. Brusquely Anna shook her awake. She refused to admit even to herself how relieved she was when Kirti opened her eyes almost at once.

Had she really feared that the ayah was drugged?

"Memsahib?" Kirti sounded groggy, which was only to be expected, as she blinked up at Anna before sitting bolt upright, her eyes huge with consternation. With her hair flowing around her face and her sari replaced by a simple linen sleeping shift, Kirti looked a very different person from Chelsea's devoted ayah. "Is something wrong with the little missy?"

"She's had another bad dream, and she's come to sleep with me. I wanted to tell you. Kirti, do you have any idea how this might have gotten on Chelsea's bed?"

Anna lifted her hand so that the flower dangled before Kirti's face. If the ayah had been wide-eyed before, it was nothing to what she was when she looked at the brightly veined bloom. The color seemed to drain from her face, and then she began to rock back and forth, muttering something that sounded like an incantation or a prayer in what must have been her native Tamil dialect.

"What is it, Kirti? You must tell me at once!" Fright sharpened Anna's voice. Kirti, still swaying, looked gray and ill.

"It is the blossom of the thorn apple, memsahib. On missy's bed, did you say? Oh—ay, oh—ay, great trouble comes to us who . . ."

Kirti was slipping back into her singsong keening. Anna had to restrain the urge to shake her.

"What does it mean, Kirti?" she demanded in an urgent tone.

"The thorn apple—it has much power. Kali—the worshippers of the goddess Kali use it in their rituals."

"Why would anyone want to put it on Chelsea's bed?"

"To warn her—to warn us to watch her—to warn all of us. Oh—ay, great trouble comes to us who—"

Anna turned abruptly on her heel and left the room. Whether he was sleeping off a drunk or not made no difference: she had to show this to Julian.

# XLVI

He was still sprawled on his stomach, his black head buried in the pillow, snoring lustily. He didn't look as if he'd moved so much as a hair since she'd left him.

"Julian, wake up!"

Leaving the bedroom door half open behind her in her haste, Anna carefully placed the flower on the bedside table for safekeeping. Then she plopped on the edge of the bed and vigorously shook the muscled bare arm closest to her. The only response she got was another enormous snore. Anna shook him again.

"Julian! I said wake up! It's important!"

"Mmmm?"

"Julian, I have to talk to you!"

"Come 'ere, sweetheart." The words were groggy, the action that accompanied them surprisingly deft. To her annoyance, Anna found herself captured by one long arm and dragged onto the bed beside him.

"Julian, stop it! I . . ."

But before she could say anything more he was rolling atop her and stopping her mouth with his kiss. Annoyed, Anna beat at his back with her fists even while her body thrilled to the heated plundering of her mouth.

After a moment, her protest apparently sinking in, Julian broke off the kiss and lifted his head to peer into her face.

"Are you always such a little ray of sunshine in the mornings, or is this an exception?"

Anna scowled up at him. "Are you sober yet? You're no good to me if you're still three parts drunk."

"Sober as a judge, my love. Shall I prove it?" The wicked glint and suggestive movement of his body caused her to push impatiently at his shoulders.

"This is important, Julian!"

"I'm all ears, of course." He accompanied this statement by lazily cupping and squeezing a breast. Anna felt the intimacy of the casual gesture all through her body. He was treating her as if she was his to do with as he pleased—and she, shameless hussy that she was, loved it.

"Get off me!" she ordered, fighting her own inclination to surrender to the hard warmth of his body—which was, from the physical evidence pressing against her thigh, far more awake than he was. His thumb flicked over her nipple through the twin layers of her nightdress and wrapper, momentarily distracting her.

"Are you sure you don't want to . . ." He trailed off to press a suggestive kiss to the nipple he tormented.

Anna shivered, then gritted her teeth, doubled up her fist, and punched him smartly on one hard shoulder. "I said get off me! Julian, something's happened!"

The blow probably hurt her more than it did him, Anna reflected ruefully, shaking her hand, but it did serve its intended purpose: with a regretful grimace he rolled off her and hitched himself up on a pillow that he propped against the headboard. At the last minute, for modesty's sake, he dragged the coverlet across his lap.

"So tell me." At last he sounded more than mar-

~~ginally alert.~~ Thankfully Anna sat up, drawing her
legs beneath her and leaning toward him as she re-
counted the events of the past hour.

"Let me see it."

He was frowning. Anna reached to retrieve the
flower from the bedside table and passed it to him.
Turning it over, he examined it closely, then looked
at her again, handing the flower back. Anna, hardly
able to touch it without shuddering, replaced the
hateful thing on the table as quickly as she could.

"It's just a flower."

"I know, but whoever brought it has no business
in Chelsea's room, much less while she's in there
herself, sleeping. And Kirti says it's a warning."

"Chelsea says that some coolie—with spears in his
cheeks—shook this over her bed, then dropped it?"
He sounded faintly skeptical.

"I know it sounds incredible, but yes."

Julian's lips compressed. He studied the flower
again, his expression thoughtful.

"What about the ayah?"

"Kirti was sleeping. Chelsea says she couldn't
wake her up."

"I meant do you trust her. Would she be a party
to a stunt like this? Perhaps to scare the child into
behaving, or something?"

"Oh, no, I'm sure she wouldn't. Kirti loves Chelsea, and she was so horrified—I'm sure she
wouldn't."

"All right, then." He swung his legs off the bed
and got to his feet, clearly not one whit concerned
by his nakedness in her presence. Anna permitted
herself a moment's silent admiration as he stood
there without moving, one hand pressed against the
wall to aid his balance. A stray sunray glittered
through the open curtains to strike his eyes, and he
grimaced. Wincing, he lifted a hand to shield his
face.

"Christ, I've got the mother and father of a headache."

"Serves you right. You shouldn't drink so much."

"That makes me feel better."

"It's nothing but the truth."

Julian grunted. Then, taking a few toddling steps to where the washstand stood in the near corner, he bent over the bowl and poured the entire contents of the pitcher over his head. Anna gaped to see him dunk his head in the filled bowl, then shake it as if he were a wet dog. Water droplets went flying everywhere, but when, moments later, he emerged from behind the linen towel he did look marginally better. At least the grimace was gone.

This time, Anna got the impression that he was really seeing her. She colored a little at the sheer intimacy of her position, sitting in the middle of his bed while he stood, casually naked, rubbing his head with a towel as he eyed her. It would take a little time to get over the newness of Julian as her lover, she supposed.

"What are you going to do?" She hurried into speech to cover her sudden embarrassment.

"Have a talk with Raja Singha. He knows everything that goes on, in the house and out of it. I want to find out what he has to say about this."

"Kirti said we should watch Chelsea." Fear tinged Anna's voice.

"Don't worry, nothing is going to happen to Chelsea. If necessary, Jim and I will take turns watching over her twenty-four hours a day. But first let's find out what Raja Singha has to say."

He emerged from his dressing room scant moments after entering it, breeches in place, tugging on a shirt, which he proceeded to button as she watched.

"Why don't you go back and stay with Chelsea? If she wakes, she's bound to be frightened not to have you there. As soon as I find out anything I'll come tell you."

"All right." This course of action made sense, although Anna was conscious of a sudden intense re-

luctance to part from him. But Chelsea's well-being
had to come before her own intoxication with Julian.
Reluctantly she clambered off the bed and headed
toward the door even as he was stamping his feet
into his boots.

"Anna."

She had nearly reached the door when his voice
stopped her. Turning inquiringly, she saw that he
had his boots on now and was coming toward her.

When he reached her side one hand came up to
cup her chin and turn her face up for his kiss.

"You're beautiful in the morning," he told her
softly when he lifted his head at last. When Anna,
dreamy-eyed, would have swayed against him,
wanting more, he put her away from him and sent
her on about her business with a smart smack on
her behind.

"Go along with you now. There'll be plenty of
time for that later," he told her with a glinting half-
smile.

Anna, rosy, returned to her room as he headed
purposefully toward the stairs. She would stand
guard over her daughter—and pass the time dreaming of Julian.

As it happened, she no sooner walked into her
bedroom than Chelsea woke up, yawning.

"Mama?"

"I'm right here, chicken."

"Did I have another bad dream?"

"Sort of." Unwilling to tell her more until she
knew more herself, Anna resorted to the age-old de-
vice of distracting her daughter. First she told how
she had stepped on Moti's tail in the middle of the
night and been nearly pitched down the stairs as the
mongoose had leapt forward, pulling his tail from
beneath her feet. Then she told of getting locked in
the privy the day before and having to stay there
until she was rescued by Ruby. Both stories were
totally false, but they made Chelsea giggle, and
Chelsea's delight infected Anna. Mother and daugh-

ter were seated in the middle of the bed, snickering
helplessly together, when a quick knock sounded at
the door.

"Anna?" It was Julian.

"Come in," she called, relieved. For some reason
the knock had made her nervous. Her imagination
working overtime again, she supposed.

Julian stepped inside the room, where he stopped,
surveying them with a smile. Chelsea, beaming,
bounced up and down in excitement.

"Good morning, Uncle Julie!"

"Good morning, sprite. I hear you had quite an
experience last night."

Immediately Chelsea stopped bouncing and
looked apprehensive. "Did Mama tell you?"

Julian nodded. Anna, frowning, shook her head
at him behind Chelsea's back. She didn't think it
was good to discuss the topic any further before the
child. Least said, soonest forgotten, she had always
believed.

But Julian apparently felt differently. Ignoring
Anna's silent attempts to shush him, he walked to
the bed and sat down on the edge of it, close to
Chelsea, who regarded him gravely.

"Your mama was worried, so she went to your
room this morning and checked to see whether what
you saw was a dream or not. She found a flower on
the foot of your bed, a big, beautiful flower, but she
didn't like the idea of how it might have gotten
there. So she asked me to find out for her. I've been
talking to Raja Singha, and he talked to all the other
servants, and we've gotten to the bottom of it. You
know Oya, the cook?"

Chelsea nodded, her eyes big and solemn. Anna
had to admit that, while she wouldn't have addressed the issue so directly, such an approach did
not seem to be having any adverse effects on Chelsea. Julian spoke to her as to an equal, and Chelsea,
with the dignity of her nearly six years, listened in
a surprisingly adult fashion. Maybe, Anna thought,

~~she had~~ a tendency to baby her daughter. Julian clearly had a care for the child, and would do her no harm. She must stay out of the way and allow them to forge their own relationship, independent of her interference.

"Oya has a son who lives in a village near Badulla. He is traveling to Kandy for the Festival of the Tooth, and two nights ago he stopped off to see his mother. He is something of a medicine man in his village, apparently, and when Oya told him about the nightmares you sometimes have he decided to help you get rid of them. According to Oya and Raja Singha, what you saw last night was Oya's son casting a spell over you to ward off nightmares."

"I told you it wasn't a dream!" Chelsea crowed to her mother.

"You were right, darling." The relief that should have flooded Anna at this perfectly obvious—for Ceylon—explanation for Chelsea's midnight visitor failed to materialize. The Festival of the Tooth celebrated a most important holiday to the island's Buddhists. In August of every year all those who could journeyed to Kandy, where the Buddha's tooth was enshrined in a magnificent temple. The relic was paraded through the streets with much fanfare, and the celebration lasted for days.

It was kind of Oya and her son to be concerned about Chelsea's nightmares. Still, whatever Oya's son's motivation, Anna did not like the idea of a stranger, any stranger, wandering about the house at night, much less entering her little girl's room and scaring her half to death.

"If the medicine man's spell works, I guess I won't have any more nightmares," Chelsea said thoughtfully.

Anna hugged her daughter. "I guess not." She looked over the silky blond head at Julian. "I hope you told Raja Singha and Oya that, while we appreciate the thought, such an occurrence is not to be repeated?"

"Don't worry." Julian smiled blandly. "I told them. In future, at night the doors and windows are to be kept locked, and none of the servants—or their relatives—is to enter without permission." He gave Anna a significant look. "Jim and I will see to it. You don't have anything to worry about."

"No." Anna smiled, the relief she'd been missing filling her at last. It was so good to have someone else to depend on. And Julian, she knew, could be depended upon utterly. Without the slightest hesitation she would trust him with her own and Chelsea's lives. "Thank you."

"Surely you can do better than that." His answering grin was wide and wicked. Then his gaze flickered down to Chelsea, who was attending to this exchange with wide-eyed interest. "Later," he added, and stood up.

"Where are you going, Uncle Julie?"

"To shave, sprite. I'll see you in the garden later, all right?"

"All right."

He grinned rather ruefully at Anna, tousled Chelsea's hair to the child's loudly expressed indignation, and took himself off. Anna had only a minute to stare longingly after him before Chelsea demanded her attention again.

It took all her willpower to persuade herself that the truly shameful things she was imagining would have to wait for the coming night.

Julian, on the other hand, was thinking about something other than sex. He had not wanted to worry his ladies—that expression, with all its possessive implications, was not lost on him—but something was definitely wrong at Srinagar.

For all their sakes he meant to find out what it was.

# XLVII

The next three days were Anna's idea of heaven on earth. She was happier than she had ever dreamed she could be. In the mornings she caught herself singing foolish songs about the house. In the afternoons she rode out with Julian, ostensibly to check on the progress the workers were making in clearing the fields but really to sneak away alone with him for a few precious hours. And at night, after supper, when the rest of the household was abed—suffice it to say that Anna got very little sleep. Not that she minded the lack.

During this time Julian was everything she had ever dreamed a man could be, and more. He was charming, funny, solicitous of her well-being—and so exciting a lover that a mere look from his midnight-blue eyes was enough to make her heart go pitty-pat. Under his tutelage, Anna became more fully a woman. And she fell ever deeper under his spell.

To please him, she even agreed to try to learn to swim. He insisted that everyone should know how, for his or her own safety, and vowed to teach Chelsea next. The swimming lessons weren't spectacularly successful, but the lovemaking sessions that inevitably followed them were. For that reason, and to humor Julian, Anna was willing to tolerate being half-drowned once a day.

"It's a mystery to me how a female as tiny as you are can sink to the bottom like a stone time after time," Julian remarked in some exasperation in the midst of their fourth swimming lesson. They were halfway to the middle of the pool (from bitter experience, Anna refused to go out past her depth), and he, soaking wet and naked, looked like a pagan water god. The water came only halfway up his chest. The muscles of his shoulders rippled enticingly as he supported her with a hand wound in the back of her shift. His wet black hair shone like a seal's in the filtered light, and his bronzed skin glistened with moisture. All in all, he was a picture to stop a woman's breath—if swallowing half a pool of water hadn't already done so. Next to him, Anna guessed that she looked like a drowned rat. She certainly felt like one.

"If the good Lord had wanted us to swim, he would have given us fins," Anna responded, sweeping the soaking strands of hair from her eyes with one hand. It was already clear to Anna that she was not meant to be a water nymph, but Julian doggedly refused to give up on her. To humor him, she had vowed to try this one last time. But she already knew that she and deep water did not, and never would, mix.

"There is absolutely no reason why you cannot learn to swim." If there was a trace of exasperation in his voice, it was not surprising. He was really being most patient with her, Anna knew, but she just could not seem to get the knack of staying afloat. Clad only in her soaking shift, she was doggedly kicking her feet and waving her hands back and forth as he had shown her. The object being, of course, to keep her head above the water. But she knew as well as he did that the minute he let go of her shift she would flounder and sink.

No mermaid, she.

Without warning Julian removed his hand from her shift. He did it stealthily, as if he hoped she wouldn't notice. But of course she did. Her eyes widened, her muscles tensed—and she concentrated as hard as she could on moving her feet and hands in the proscribed rhythm. But it was no use. No matter how hard and fast she flailed, she went under. She barely had time to draw a quick breath before she sank.

Already her toes were scrabbling against the bottom as Julian's hand in her shift hauled her up.

"Good God," he said, disgusted, as she surfaced, spitting out what seemed to be oceans of water.

"Can't we take a break?" Her voice, and her eyes, were unconsciously pleading. Julian looked at her, grimaced, and relented.

"All right. A short one. Come on."

Catching her hand, he towed her from the water in his wake. Anna was too exhausted to do more than barely register how magnificent he looked, rising from the pool as nature had made him. Water streamed from them both as he dragged her ashore. Anna stumbled as far as the carpet of glossy leaves near the rock where they had left their clothes, and promptly collapsed, silently thanking God for the blessing of solid ground. Julian, grinning, dried off with one of the towels they had brought, wrapped it around his waist, and, carrying the other one, hunkered down beside her.

"You can't be that tired."

"Drowning is hard work."

Julian ran the towel over her face and body, drying her as best he could. Since her chemise was soaked, her hair, too, the results were less than thorough, but at least, when he was finished, she no longer felt as if she was oozing water from every pore. The afternoon was hot and steamy, and her hair and chemise would remain damp for hours. Which was just one more pleasant thing about her swimming lessons to look forward to.

"Ready to try again?"

Anna shuddered. "No! Talk to me, why don't you? Tell me about—about your granny. She sounds fascinating."

"She was fascinating—and I'm tired of talking about her. When are you going to marry me?"

The throwaway question was so unexpected that Anna blinked. Had she really heard him right?

"What?"

"I said, when are you going to marry me?" There was patient humor behind the words. Without waiting for her reply, Julian stretched out full-length beside her on the leaves, his arms raised so that his hands pillowed his head, his shoulder and thigh brushing hers. Taken aback by the sudden turn the conversation had taken, Anna abruptly sat up and swiveled to stare down at him. All the doubts she had once harbored about his motives for pursuing her came flooding back.

"Why do you want to marry me?" The words were carefully enunciated. Her face felt stiff; she guessed her expression was wary. It would be the perfect revenge, under the circumstances. He could not change the facts of his birth, or wrest love and respect from his father or brothers, but he could marry the widow of the brother he had envied almost to the point of obsession.

Anna couldn't bear it if he meant to wed her for that.

His eyes narrowed on her face.

"I thought marriage was the logical culmination of what we have together. Obviously you don't."

"No—I mean, no, it isn't that." Anna took a deep breath. "I mean—Julian, it's not that I don't want to marry you, but I have to wonder if you just want to marry me to get back at Paul."

"What you're saying is that you're refusing me because you don't trust me." His voice was as hard and cold as granite. Sitting up, he levered himself to his feet and stood glaring down at her, fists on his linen-swathed hips. Tall, wide-chested, black-haired, and muscular, he was a glorious sight—had she been in any mind to appreciate him. But Anna was too miserable to appreciate anything except her own clumsiness in handling a situation that anyone but an idiot would have foreseen.

Kneeling almost at his feet, she looked up at him beseechingly. "Julian, I didn't mean—"

He didn't let her finish. "Would you be less distrustful if I were a rich nobleman—say, Lord Ridley? Would a title and a few estates and all the money you could spend tone down your distrust a little? I just bet it would." He sounded as furious as he looked.

"You know that's not true! Julian!" But it was too late. He dropped the towel, grabbed his breeches, and pulled them on even as she scrambled to her feet.

"Julian, you're being ridiculous!" She laid a pleading hand on his arm, only to be shaken off. "I'm not refusing you, I just—"

He was slamming his feet into his boots. "Don't trust me enough to accept me when I don't have enough to offer to sweeten the pot. I quite understand. And you, my damnable lady Green Eyes, can go straight to hell."

"Julian!"

But already he had snatched up his shirt and was storming off. Anna stared after him, feeling sick to her stomach. She had made a terrible mistake, and she knew it. Why, oh why, hadn't she been quick-witted enough to just say yes, and let his motives go hang? Even if his reasons for wanting to marry her were mixed, did it really matter? Julian was the man she loved, in a far stronger, more mature fashion than she had ever loved Paul. Whatever had prompted his love for her—and she wasn't sure whether or not he even knew if revenge against his brother figured into his feelings—he was the love of her life.

And he was furious with her. With a sigh, Anna wondered how long it would take her to make amends.

By the time she dressed and made her way back to the house, she had decided that she would grovel, if necessary, that very night. She loved him, she would marry him if he wished, and if it took some persuading to convince him that only an idiotic brainstorm had caused her to question the reasons behind his proposal, why, then she would persuade him very thoroughly. In fact, it would almost be fun.

She had a very specific kind of persuasion in mind. One that she doubted very much Julian would be able to resist.

The path from the pool led past the stable to the back of the house. She spent a few minutes visiting the stable, where she and Chelsea had made a great pet of Baliclava. The little donkey had singed three of his legs and lost most of his tail in the fire, but he was nearly healed now. The treats and lavish attention bestowed on him by his new friends had apparently made up for a great deal: he was growing quite spoiled. As had become his habit, he greeted Anna with a great hee-hawing bray and permitted her to rub his nose and ears. Wishing that she had an apple or some other treat to feed him, she left him at last with a final pat and made her way up to the house.

Chelsea was in the garden with Kirti and Ruby, while Jim hung about on the outskirts of their game, looking sour. Anna suspected that Jim had his eye on Ruby. Certainly he seemed to appear with suspicious regularity wherever she happened to be. Not that it was any of Anna's business, of course, but she wished Ruby joy of the gloomy little man if that was what she wanted. She waved at the quartet but did not stop.

None of the servants were in sight as she went up to her room to tidy herself and change her dress. When the knock on her door came, she was engaged

in vigorously brushing her hair to remove the last
traces of dampness from the long tresses.

"Yes?" she called.

"Memsahib, there is a visitor. From England."

"From England? Who?" Frowning, Anna put
down the brush and moved to open the door. Raja
Singha stood in the hallway. In response to her
question, he spread his hands.

"A gentleman. He asked for you but would not
give his name."

"I'll be right down."

Frowning, Anna dismissed Raja Singha with a nod
and turned back into her room to pin up her hair. A
visitor from England who would not give his name:
the prospect smacked of trouble.

A Bow Street runner looking for Julian? Or
worse . . . ?

"Graham!" Anna gasped on a note of loathing as
she entered the parlor some few minutes later. Her
brother-in-law rose to greet her. In that first lightning glance, Anna saw that, physically, he hadn't
changed a bit.

"Did you think to outwit me forever, Anna? I'm
not quite a fool, you know."

Then, before she could prevent him, he caught
her shoulders with both hands and bestowed a
smacking kiss on her lips. Even as Anna stepped
back, wiping instinctively at her mouth with the back
of her hand, he gave her an ominously smirking
smile.

# XLVIII

"Really, I must say I was surprised when I figured out who had really made off with my emeralds. And you a vicar's daughter! For shame, Anna." Graham was clearly enjoying himself.

"What are you doing here?" She spoke through horror-stiffened lips.

"I see you don't deny it. Very wise of you. I would hardly have traveled all this way had I not proof of your infamy. I have only to contact the nearest authority to have an order issued for your arrest."

"Anna?" The voice belonged to Ruby, followed seconds later by her entrance. She saw Graham, frowned, then stopped dead, her eyes widening.

"Lord Ridley!" she gasped.

"Mrs. Fisher. Of course, I remember you from our church." Graham bowed, grinning at them with a well-satisfied air that made Anna long to slap him. "I had heard that you were traveling with my dear sister-in-law as a sort of companion cum partner-in-crime. But the game is over for you both, I'm afraid. Do they hang females for merely being accessories after the fact of a theft, I wonder? If I were you, Mrs. Fisher, I'd make it my business to find out."

"You're being ridiculous, Graham. We neither of us know what you're talking about." Anna had to

337

force the words out. Her mouth was suddenly so dry that she could not even swallow.

Graham's lips curled derisively. "Oh, don't you? Then how, pray, did you come by the funds to purchase this place? Really, it was most ill-advised of you, Anna. Did you think I wouldn't learn who the purchaser was? That, on top of the incredible coincidence of the timing of when you fled my house and board, made me suspicious. And once I was suspicious, it required very little effort on the part of the men I hired to unravel the whole thing. Tell me, Anna, don't you ever feel the smallest twinge of conscience that a man was hanged for a crime you committed? No? Well, I'm not surprised. I always thought you were more than ordinarily resilient."

"Graham. . . ." But there was nothing left to say. She did not doubt he had the proof of her guilt that he claimed. He would not have traveled all the way from England to confront her without it. But it was equally clear that he believed Julian had died—she had to get Graham away before he set eyes on Julian. Saving herself might be impossible, but perhaps she could still save the man she loved.

"Very well, Graham, you're quite right in your suppositions, as you must know. I did steal the emeralds, and sold them for enough to get us to Ceylon and buy back Srinagar. I cannot believe you mean to have me arrested and hanged, so what do you want of me?"

"Anna!" Both of them ignored Ruby's gasp.

Graham's grin widened. "Why, you must know that."

"I suppose I have an idea, but why don't you make it clear."

An admiring glint showed briefly in Graham's eyes as they met hers. "I would have thought you would prefer to conduct our business in private, but—"

"There is nothing you can say to me that Ruby can't hear."

"Very well. You will return to England with me and live with me as my mistress for as long as I desire. In return, I am prepared to be generous: I will support my brother's brat during her sojourn in an unexceptional boarding school for young ladies, I'll provide for you, and I'll forget that I ever owned jewels called the Queen's emeralds."

Anna lifted her chin. The prospect he outlined made her sick to her stomach, but there was no time to give in to emotional megrims. If it was possible, she had to get Graham away before Julian put in an appearance. "Since I have no choice, I agree to your terms. But if I must go, then I would go at once. Ruby can oversee our packing and follow with Chelsea. Perhaps we can wait for them in Colombo."

" 'Ave you lost your mind?" Ruby gaped at her.

"No, I have not," Anna returned fiercely. "If it must be done, 'tis best done quickly. Well, Graham?"

Even he looked surprised. "I must say, I had not expected you to be so reasonable. Certainly we may leave at once, if you wish it."

"Anna. . . ." Ruby sounded horrified. " 'Ave you thought?"

"Yes. I must get my hat, and we'll go. I'll leave it to you to tell Chelsea what you must. I'll explain the rest to her when she joins us in Colombo." Anna's voice faltered, and she continued in a lower tone, "Have a care to her, Ruby."

"You know I will. But what about—?"

"No one else need concern us," Anna interrupted firmly, and practically pushed Ruby toward the door. Her gaze slid to Graham, who looked to be almost as confused as he was gratified. "I'll be right back. Pray wait for me here."

"Certainly. In fact, take your time. I could use a spot of tea—"

"If I must wait, I will likely lose the courage to go," Anna told him fiercely. "We will leave as soon as I fetch my hat."

"But . . ."

The sound of booted feet stalking across the veranda brought Anna's heart to her throat. Her eyes, wide with horror, flew to the front door, which opened even as she willed it not to. Julian entered, his eyes narrowed as he passed from the bright sunlight to the relative gloom of the hallway. At first he seemed unaware of the two pairs of eyes fixed on him from just inside the parlor door. Graham, who was farther back, was out of his line of vision.

Then Julian saw Anna. His lips parted as if he would say something, but his eyes moved to Ruby and he stopped. Unless severely provoked, he would not quarrel with her in public, for which Anna was suddenly thankful. Graham would surely recognize his voice.

Not that there seemed much hope of keeping him away from Graham. Still, Anna tried. She hurried to him, caught his arm, and tugged him urgently back toward the veranda while Ruby watched with dawning comprehension mixed with horror.

"What the devil ails you?" Julian growled, and when Anna desperately shook her head at him he stopped dead, frowning down at her, refusing to move another step.

"Julian, please," she whispered frantically, but it was already too late. Graham stood in the doorway beside Ruby, his face paling as he saw his half brother. Although Julian was no more than a large, dark shape silhouetted by the sunlight streaming through the open door, Graham seemed to have no trouble recognizing him.

"Good God! I thought you were dead!" Graham's voice was a croak.

Julian's gaze shot to Graham. After a moment in which midnight eyes clashed with sky blue, Julian began to smile. It was not a pleasant smile, and it fell far short of reaching his eyes. Anna, shivering, was glad to see that it was directed at Graham instead of herself.

"Now I begin to see," he remarked obscurely, glancing down at Anna, who still clung to his arm, before looking back at Graham. "Well met, brother."

"Well met? Well met!" Like Julian's just seconds before, Graham's eyes shifted to Anna and widened before returning to his half brother. "Hell and the devil, you're in league! You were working together, the two of you, to rob me! I don't believe it! But now you'll pay. I don't know how you escaped the hangman the first time, you gypsy bastard, but you won't be so lucky twice! I'll—"

"You, little brother, won't do a bloody damned thing." The quiet conviction in Julian's voice dammed Graham's furious sputters. Anna looked up at Julian in disbelief. That was not the tone to take with a man who held your life in his hands, a man who hated you. But Julian seemed unmoved by any thought of danger to himself. It was almost as if he did not recognize the threat that Graham represented. Very calmly he shut the door and leaned against it. Anna, glancing apprehensively from one man to the other as they stared measuringly at each other, saw that an expression very like triumph lurked in Julian's eyes, while sheer hatred twisted Graham's face.

"The hell I won't! I—"

"I have the emeralds," Julian said quietly. Anna stiffened, flicked a lightning glance up at him. It must be some kind of bluff. . . .

"You think you can return them, and I'll forget the whole thing? Not bloody likely! I'll see you hang if it's the last thing I ever do! You—"

"And something else. Something that was secreted behind the lining of the pouch they were in. My mother's marriage lines—to our father."

It took a moment for the full import to sink into Julian's listeners. When it did, Anna gasped in disbelief, Ruby looked bewildered, and Graham came away from the parlor door, fists clenched, face bellicose with rage.

"You lying scum! My father would never have wed your slut of a mother! She was a whore, and a—"

Julian moved so swiftly that Anna never even saw the blow that felled Graham. One minute Graham was ranting in the middle of the hall, and the next he had measured his length on the floor while Julian stood over him, his eyes as black and angry as a storm-tossed sea.

"I have endured all that I mean to of your insults. I won't put up with another one of them." It was a quiet warning. Anna, shivering as she looked from the victor to the vanquished, thought that Graham would do well to heed it. There was something in Julian's eyes that spoke of a man pushed to the wall once too often.

"You're lying. D'you think I'm such a flat as to take your word for such a thing? If it's true, then show me those marriage lines. I have a right to see them—if they exist."

Julian looked no less dangerous, but he stepped a pace or so back from Graham. Then his gaze shifted, moving farther along the hall. Raja Singha stood there, his expression impassive. So involved was she in the drama of what was happening that Anna had not even noticed him before that moment.

"Fetch me the leather case at the bottom of my wardrobe," Julian said shortly to Raja Singha, who bowed his turbaned head in acquiescence and moved swiftly up the stairs. Julian's gaze moved back to Graham.

"Get up," he said brusquely. "You look like the ass you are, lying there."

Graham, his face contorted with anger, said nothing as he scrambled to his feet.

"I'll never accept you as my brother. Never!"

Julian shrugged. "Only a stupid man won't accept the truth."

Graham's eyes narrowed at the implied insult, but before he could reply Raja Singha returned with the leather case.

Until she set eyes on it, Anna had not been absolutely sure that Julian was telling the truth. When, and how, had he regained possession of the emeralds? He had said nothing about it. . . .

Raja Singha brought the case to Julian, who took it from him, flipped it open, and slid his hand behind the silk lining. He pulled out a yellowed square of paper, which he held up so that Graham could see it.

"Behold the marriage lines of one Nina Rachminov, spinster, to Thomas Harlington Traverne of Gordon Hall, dated January 2, 1797." As Graham made as if to take the paper, Julian pulled it back and shook his head. "Oh, no, brother. Look but don't touch."

Graham did, and his face suddenly went pasty white. "It's a forgery. It must be!"

"It isn't." Julian folded the paper and slid it back inside the case that had held its secret for thirty-five years. "I was born in November of 1797, and my mother died soon afterwards. Our father wed your mother some two years after that. You were born in 1801, and Paul was born in 1807. You do understand what that means? I am our father's legitimate issue, and I am four years your elder. That makes me—*me*, Graham, not you—Lord Ridley, with all that that implies."

As he delivered the blow Julian smiled almost sweetly at his brother.

"It's not true," Graham muttered, but from the stricken look on his face Anna knew he was beginning to believe. "It can't be true! You're nothing but a bloody gypsy!"

Julian looked dangerous again. "I'd watch my mouth if I were you."

"I'll fight it in every court in England!"

"That's up to you." Julian shrugged. "There's

something else you should realize. Since I am the rightful Lord Ridley, the Queen's emeralds were and are mine. Therefore nothing was stolen from you, by myself or Anna or anyone else. So you may as well slink back to England with your tail between your legs and pray that I allow you to keep some part of what you no longer legally possess. Perhaps, when I come to claim my inheritance, I'll be generous. Who knows? But not if I have to put up with you for a moment longer.''

Graham stared at his brother without speaking. Looking from one to the other, Anna was shocked to observe for the first time some small familial resemblance between them. There was something in their expressions, in the jut of their jaws and the taut set of their shoulders, that was alike. Shocked, Anna realized that what she was seeing was old Lord Ridley alive again in both of them.

Then it hit her: they truly were brothers. And she realized that, despite the fact that Julian had lived at Srinagar and claimed her as a relative, Anna had never quite believed his claim of kinship to Paul.

She'd thought him a charming rogue of a liar and had fallen in love with him anyway.

When what he truly was was Paul's older brother—and the rightful Lord Ridley.

Dear God, what was this going to mean to her—to them?

Julian must have felt her eyes upon him because he glanced down at her, where she still stood by his side. His expression was not reassuring. It held anger and a touch of bitterness and some cynicism besides. But perhaps those emotions were there for Graham, and were not meant for her at all. Before she could decide, he had shifted his attention back to Graham.

''It's time you left,'' he said softly.

Graham regarded him for a moment, his mouth twitching. His hands were clenched by his sides, but Anna did not really fear violence: unless he was some kind of fool he would not physically attack Julian. Then Graham's gaze moved to Anna.

"Are you going to allow yourself to be taken in by this—this charlatan?" he demanded, his voice harsh. "Since you are my sister-in-law, and your daughter my niece, I will give you this one chance to walk away from him and come with me. If not, if you choose to stay, then I warn you I will wash my hands of the both of you henceforth."

"Good-bye, Graham," Anna said from the shelter of Julian's side. Graham stared at her furiously. But with nothing to threaten her with, and Julian clearly prepared to protect her physically, there was nothing he could do. Graham stared balefully from one to the other. Then, without a word, he finally stomped past Julian and out the door.

Anna held her breath as she listened to his footsteps retreating across the veranda. Moments later the sound of carriage wheels crunching down the drive caused her to breathe again. Incredible as it seemed, Graham had gone, and he had not succeeded in causing them harm.

Julian was frowning down at her. "Don't worry, my offer still stands," he said bitterly, then before she could reply he headed toward the stairs, which he took two at a time.

Anna, shaken by what she had seen in his eyes, was left alone with Ruby, who was staring after Julian with an expression of awe.

"Blimey," the other woman breathed, casting Anna a sideways look. "A man like that, and 'im Lord Ridley to boot. Lovey, the day you met 'im must 'ave been the luckiest day of your life!"

# XLIX

Now he would never know the truth. With a certain bitterness Julian faced that fact as he stashed the case holding the emeralds in one of the narrow drawers at the bottom of his wardrobe. Or, rather, he would suspect that he did know the truth, and the suspicion would drive him wild.

Of course, now Anna would be willing to marry him. Certainly she would. He was, after all, Lord Ridley, and a great deal of wealth came with the title. She could hardly do better for herself and Chelsea.

The pitiful thing was that, despite his knowledge of her motives, he was still willing to wed her. More than willing, in fact. Even if he was second-best to her, no more than a substitute for the husband who was forever lost to her, he was too besotted to let the knowledge stop him.

When had he turned into such a maudlin fool?

Disgusted with himself, he shut the wardrobe door with a snap and turned away, meaning to head downstairs. From there he would go outside and seek out some hard, physical work. Anything to distract himself from his thoughts.

Then he saw her.

She was standing in the doorway, one hand resting gracefully against the jamb, watching him. Clad

in a simple lavender gown that he didn't remember
having seen before, her silvery hair pinned primly
atop her head and her green eyes wide and troubled
as they met his, she was so beautiful that he wanted
to curse. A furious scowl darkened his face. She had
made him love her, damn it, to the point of madness. But she refused to love him back in the way
he wanted, and he could almost hate her for that.

Almost.

"Come to throw yourself at my feet?" Because he
was hurting, he lashed out at her. The sneer in his
voice pleased him.

"Yes."

She was nothing if not surprising, his Anna. He
had not expected her to admit it.

"You don't have to worry. As I told you downstairs, my offer still stands."

Those damnable green eyes were wide and grave
as they met his. "I would have accepted by the pool
if you'd stayed around a little longer."

"I'm sure you would have."

"I love you, Julian." The soft words stabbed him
like a spear through the heart. "I'll be pleased and
proud to marry you."

"Don't you mean Lord Ridley?" There was a satisfying bite to his voice that covered the pain in his
heart. Lying bitch, he wanted to rage but didn't. He
was afraid to reveal too much of how he felt about
her. If she ever realized how truly head over heels
he was, she'd have the power to make his life a
bloody hell.

"I mean *you*, whatever your name is. I love you."

"Stop saying that!"

"Why should I? It's the truth." She came away
from the door, walking determinedly toward him.
When she was no more than a hand's breadth away,
she stopped and tilted her head back so that she
could look him full in the eyes. "Julian, if you think
I only want to marry you because I've discovered

you have a title, and all the wealth and privilege that goes with it, then I have a suggestion for you.''

''What's that?'' It was all he could do not to grab her and throw her down on the bed and make love to her until they were both exhausted. Maybe then he'd manage to find some ease for his bruised pride and aching heart. They were good in bed together. Fantastic, in fact. Maybe he was a fool to want anything more. What could be sweeter than that hot explosion of passion that wiped away the world and everything in it? Her breath-stopping body was his for the taking. What the hell ailed him that he must continually hanker after her heart?

''Let Graham keep it.''

''What?'' Either his mind was as befuddled as his emotions or she wasn't making any sense.

''Why don't we just stay here and forget about England and titles and family estates? Do you really want to be Lord Ridley and live in baronial splendor at Gordon Hall? The place is huge, and freezing cold in the winter, and the roof leaks. There's the responsibility of the land, and the tenants, and the lord and his family must set a good example. Think how wearing! While here—here we can do as we please, you and me and Chelsea. There's money enough, not as much as comes with being Lord Ridley, but if the new tea fields work out there should be substantially more some day. Besides, I've never been rich, and I don't care about it. So if you want to be sure I'm marrying Julian Chase, and not Lord Ridley, then leave Lord Ridley to Graham, and you be my own dear Julian. Please.''

She had managed to surprise him yet again. Julian, frowning, stared down at the delicate face turned so pleadingly up to his. To just forget about being Lord Ridley—the notion was mind-boggling. All his life he had yearned for the title, with its connotations of legitimacy and worthiness and being somebody at last. As a despised gypsy boy, he had been so ashamed of the Rachminov family name that he had plucked Chase out of the air to please himself. The Traverne family name had seemed so far above him that he had not even considered using that. Now the name was his, rightfully his, and the title too—and Anna was suggesting that he just turn his back on it?

And on Gordon Hall, with its vast acres and wealth and respect? In favor of his despised half brother Graham, with whom he had had a lifelong, bitter rivalry?

A rivalry in which he had now triumphed, hands down?

But he had to admit, the long-anticipated triumph had left a bitter taste in his mouth. This afternoon, when he had confronted Graham with the truth, had been the culmination of every daydream of revenge he'd ever had. But now that he had what he wanted, he suddenly found that it wasn't enough.

His legitimacy, the title, and all that went with it meant little to him if Anna didn't come with it. And not just her body. What he wanted from Anna was uncontested possession of her heart and mind and soul as well. He wanted her to love him, Julian Rachminov or Julian Chase or even Julian Traverne, Lord Ridley. But him. No one else. And without reservations.

"Well?" She was watching him intently.

Julian stared down at her for a moment longer.

"You must be joking," he said at last, pulling her into his arms and grinning ruefully at his own avariciousness over the top of her head. But after all, why should he give up anything when he could have it all, and Anna too, if only he could drive the demon of jealousy from his heart? Which for both their sakes he meant to make a Herculean effort to do.

As she had said, Paul was dead, while he himself was alive, with a lifetime to win out over his rival. And as he had learned today, victory after a protracted battle tasted doubly sweet.

He'd drive Paul from her mind and heart if it took

the rest of his life. And make her trust in his love for her, too.

"You mean you won't give it up?" Anna pulled back from his embrace. Her eyes were wide as they searched his face, and there was disappointment in her voice.

"I'm many things, my love, but not, I hope, a fool. Only a fool would give up that kind of inheritance. But I appreciate the fact that you were willing for me to do so, and I apologize for my behavior by the pool. I seem to be of a somewhat hasty bent where you're concerned."

"You've no need to doubt me, Julian. It's you I love, rich or poor, lord or gypsy, and no one else."

"Yes, well. . . ." He took a deep breath, let her go, moved around her to close the bedroom door, then came back to her and caught her hand. Anna, puzzled, was frowning at him as he led her to the giltwood chair on which she had perched once before, and pushed her down upon it.

"What . . . ?" she began blankly even as he sank to one knee before her and took one of her hands in both of his.

"I behaved so badly earlier that I feel I owe you amends. Behold me, on my knees, most properly beseeching you for your hand and heart."

Torn between surprise and laughter, Anna could only stare at him. He was smiling, his expression whimsical. His attitude, as he pressed her hand theatrically over his heart, was ridiculous in the extreme. But the gesture touched her, too. Julian was not a man to humble himself easily.

"In other words, my love, I am asking you to marry me."

For brief seconds she made him wait, while her eyes ran over him, affixing this moment forever in her memory. She had a feeling that she would not often see Julian on his knees asking for anything. What he wanted from life—and from her—he was far more likely to take.

"Well?" His brows had twitched together as he waited. Anna smiled at him. The hand that he had not imprisoned came out to touch his cheek.

"Of course I'll marry you," she answered softly. Then, leaning forward, she pressed a tender kiss to his hard mouth.

"My Anna." If there was a certain huskiness to his tone, there was fierce possession too. He rose to his feet, drawing her up with him, into his embrace. Anna melted against him, her arms going up to link behind his head, her lips coming up for his kiss. When he lifted her to carry her to bed, she made no objection, although it was still the middle of the day with servants roaming all over the house and Chelsea liable to come searching for her mama at any moment. But what did any of that matter against the necessity of convincing Julian that she loved him with all her heart? Because she knew, as surely as if he had spoken the words aloud, that he still doubted.

It was possible that he would always doubt. But she meant to love him long and well and always, and perhaps that would be enough to ease the pangs of insecurity that ate at his soul.

As it happened, they were not interrupted. They loved each other passionately, cuddled, murmured soft words of endearment, then loved each other again. Finally, exhausted, they slept. When they awoke it was, from the look of the moon floating high outside the uncurtained windows, near midnight.

Julian stretched luxuriously, wrapped her in his arms, and rolled over with her to kiss her. Instead of responding in kind, Anna wriggled restively in his embrace.

"Julian."

He loosened his arms, frowning down at her. "What?"

"I'm hungry." It was a plaintive moan. He chuckled and rolled off her, sitting up and flexing his bare shoulders. Anna, no longer self-conscious about being naked in his presence, sat up too.

"You mean you prefer food to me? For shame!" But he was grinning at her. "Ah, well, I confess I'm hungry, too. Why don't you wait here while I go foraging?"

"I'll come with you." She swung her legs over the side of the bed and stood up. Julian eyed her backside appreciatively as she bent over, gathering up her clothes.

Then, all of a sudden, she straightened and sniffed.

"Do you smell something?" she asked in a very different tone than she had used before.

Julian sniffed the air too. Then he shot up off the bed and grabbed for his breeches.

"What is it?" Anna asked, alarmed at the abruptness of his response.

Julian didn't even stop to look at her as he yanked on his breeches.

"Smoke."

# L

The house was on fire. Even as Anna, having dressed almost as hastily as Julian, followed him into the hall she saw thin gray wisps of smoke feathering up the stairs. Below, the air looked hazy. The smell of burning was much stronger here, and she thought she could hear a distant crackle.

"Chelsea!"

"Get her, and I'll rouse the others." Julian headed in the opposite direction from the one Anna took, throwing open the doors and shouting "Fire!"

Flying along the corridor, Anna threw open the door to the nursery and was relieved to find her daughter snugly asleep in her bed.

"Wake up, chicken!" Anna said urgently, wrapping the child in a quilt and scooping her up in her arms without waiting to see if her words had penetrated. Thank goodness Chelsea was a featherweight! Although Anna was not very large herself, she could still carry the child with scarcely any difficulty.

"Mama?" Chelsea blinked owlishly at her mother even as Anna hurried with her to arouse Kirti.

"It's all right, sweetheart. I've got you safe." Even as Anna uttered the reassurance, she was bent over Kirti, shaking her shoulder. The ayah started up with a gasp. Her eyes widened.

"The house is on fire. We've got to get out. Hurry!" Anna barely waited to see the old woman swing her legs out of bed before hurrying from the room with Chelsea. There was Ruby to rouse, and Jim, although she supposed Julian had taken care of awakening one or both of them. The smell of burning was stronger now. There wasn't much time.

"Anna!" Julian was shouting from the hallway.

"Here!" She emerged to find Julian barreling toward her, Ruby in his wake.

"Thank God!" he said as he saw her, and scooped Chelsea from her arms. Grabbing Anna's hand, he hauled her toward the stairs, which were now oozing smoke.

"Where's Jim?" She panted as she half ran in Julian's wake. Ruby was right behind her in a surprisingly prim nightdress, while Kirti, still in her sleeping shift, had emerged from the nursery and was running toward them.

"He's not in the house. I set him to keep an eye on Graham, just in case." At the head of the stairs, he turned back to bark directions. "Anna, take Ruby's hand. Ruby, hold on to Kirti. Don't let go. The smoke's liable to be thick until we can make it out the door."

"Uncle Julie, I'm scared!"

"Nothing to be scared of. Just shut your eyes, press your face against my shoulder, and we'll all be out of here in a few minutes. That's a good girl." Chelsea, her arms wrapped tightly around his neck, did as Julian said. Then he looked back at the others, who were lined up behind him, tightened his grip on Anna's hand, said "Come on!" and headed down the stairs.

Toward the back of the house, the fire was already roaring. Smoke billowed through the downstairs hall, to be drawn up the stairs as if it were a chimney. As they reached the bottom of the stairs the air grew increasingly more difficult to breathe. Anna coughed, choking. The others were coughing, too,

and Chelsea was clinging to Julian for dear life. Her
eyes were watering, making it difficult to see, but
Julian was leading them surely toward the front
door. From the corner of her eye Anna noticed as
they passed the front parlor. Just a few more feet to
go. . . . He had his hand on the knob but drew it
quickly back, swearing as the metal burned his palm.
Then, using the tail of Chelsea's nightgown to protect his hand, he tried again, this time pulling the
door open. Smoke billowed through this new opening even as Anna, gasping for fresh air, crowded
behind Julian, who seemed, inexplicably, to have
stopped dead no more than one step onto the veranda.

"God in heaven!"

He sounded so horrified that Anna, eyes streaming, forced herself to focus on whatever it was that
had drawn such a reaction from him.

"Would you look at that!"

"Oh—ay!"

Behind Anna, Ruby and Kirti also saw the menacing figures moving toward them through the
smoke-filled night, even before Anna was sure that
what she was seeing was real.

An army of islanders was spread out across the
lawn in single file, shoulder to shoulder, chanting as
they marched toward the house: islanders in horrific
costumes consisting of conical hats, metal breast-
plates and belts, and multilayered sarongs in shades
of saffron and gold. Dozens of silver bracelets and
anklets caught and reflected the moonlight as they
moved. Their very skin seemed to bristle threateningly. As they drew closer, the moonlight suddenly
brightened enough for Anna to see that all of them
had pierced their cheeks, arms, and even their thighs
with tiny spears. Each carried a huge, razor-tipped
spear, which they shook menacingly in time to their
chants.

"Dear God!" Anna breathed. Chelsea, staring
fascinated at the approaching mob from the safety

of Julian's arms, peered back at her mother over his shoulder.

"That's what the coolie looked like who did the nightmare spell!"

"Is Thuggees! Oh—ay, great trouble comes. . . ."

Kirti, moaning, was silenced as Julian suddenly turned on her.

"Thuggees?" he demanded sharply. "What the hell are they?"

"I told the memsahib—the flower was a warning. Quick, quick, we must go back in the house. They will kill us all! For the sake of the little missy, we must hurry!"

"We can't go back in—the 'ouse is burning!" Ruby sounded terrified, and Anna didn't blame her. The chant of the approaching islanders was drowning out the roaring of the fire. Smoke poured around them; Anna wasn't sure if the islanders had seen them or not, but suddenly the thought of being seen by them made her shiver.

Kirti had said they would be killed. . . .

"There is a way—a passage. Come, sahib, memsahib! Hurry!"

Kirti turned and darted back into the burning house. Julian stared after her for a split second's uncertainty, then appeared to come to a decision. His hand tightening on Anna's, he thrust Chelsea's head down on his shoulder and plunged back inside the house, pulling Anna and Ruby with him. The smoke was so thick now that Anna's eyes watered instantly. She stumbled blindly in Julian's wake as he almost ran down the hall. Behind her, Ruby coughed and choked, but hung on.

It was getting harder and harder to breathe. The air was thick and so hot that Anna feared it would singe their skin as they plunged toward what seemed to be the very heart of the fire. Ahead, sparks shot toward them, at the forefront of what seemed to be an oncoming orange glow. Of course, the fire was spreading toward them. The crackling roar was so loud now that the noise in itself was terrifying. Anna picked up her skirt to shield her mouth and nose from the worst of the smoke, but it didn't seem to help.

It occurred to her that she, and the rest of them, might die after all.

Please God, protect us. Please God, look after Chelsea. Those two phrases ran over and over through Anna's mind, to the exclusion of almost everything else. Except for the thought that burning to death would be an awful way to die.

In front of her Julian stopped, bent, and seemed to wrench something out of the floor. Through streaming eyes Anna saw that he was holding what seemed to be part of the floor aloft, while Kirti disappeared into it. Then Julian was handing a sobbing Chelsea beneath the floor. Either smoke or terror must have affected Anna's brain, because it was only after Julian dragged her forward that she saw that there was a hole in the floor leading to some sort of passageway beneath. Gaping at it, she barely had time to register that they were in the keeping room before Julian was lowering her.

The space where she found herself was less than three feet tall, with an earth floor beneath and the floor of the house above for a ceiling. It was not smoke-free, but the air here was fresher—enough so that she could at least breathe as she followed Kirti and Chelsea, who were crawling single-file ahead of her. Chelsea looked back once at Anna, whimpering, but Kirti, with a hand in the child's nightdress, dragged her on. Behind Anna came Ruby, with Julian, who had stayed to replace the trapdoor, in the rear. Judging from the direction of the smoke and the roar, they seemed to be crawling parallel to the fire above them. But it was gaining ground with ominous speed.

At any moment the floor above them might collapse.

Kirti reached a mud wall that marked the eastern

boundary of the house's foundation, crawled quickly to the left, and then, without warning, simply disappeared. It took Anna an instant to realize that she had dropped through a jagged black hole in the floor.

"Mama, I can't!" Chelsea hesitated on the brink of the hole, staring down into what seemed to be limitless blackness below.

"Yes, you can, chicken. Kirti's there," Anna told her daughter, and then as the floor above them gave an ominous creak she put her arms around the child's waist, dropped her legs into the hole, and, closing her eyes, prayed.

The two of them slithered feetfirst along a midnight-black, lichen-slick, plunging passageway that seemed to go straight down.

Chelsea screamed and clung tightly to her mother's neck. Anna held on to her child for dear life and braced herself for what would come.

What came was jarring contact with a flat patch of ground. Anna hit it feetfirst, and, with Chelsea's weight added to hers, crumpled. Then, quickly, remembering Ruby and Julian behind her, she scrambled out of the way. Chelsea still clung to her neck like a monkey, but Anna felt some of her fear subside as she realized that they were in what appeared to be a tunnel, perhaps five feet tall and a little more than half as wide, lined with bricks. The bricks were ancient, and covered with slime, but still they were bricks, and therefore man-made. And they could not be very far below the surface. Chinks in the bricks that made up the roof allowed tiny slanting beams of moonlight through, enough to enable them to see their surroundings and each other. Kirti was there, standing a little way down the tunnel, waiting. As Anna shot into view with Chelsea, Kirti put her finger to her lips, signaling for silence as she pointed overhead. Chelsea eased her grip on her mother's neck, and Anna thankfully put the child down. Then she was distracted by the wooshing appearance of Ruby, followed by Julian.

When she glanced around again Kirti was disappearing along the tunnel, Chelsea with her. The ayah had the child firmly by the hand.

"Come, quick!" Kirti whispered over her shoulder. With Chelsea's eyes looking fearfully back at her, Anna hurried after them. At a little distance behind her came the others.

Anna was no judge of distances, but they ran along the tunnel, stooped over, for what she calculated was a good ten minutes. Then the passageway ended abruptly. Kirti and Chelsea waited by what appeared to be half-rotted wooden rungs set into the brick wall. There seemed nowhere left to go, and Anna felt a fresh stirring of alarm.

"We must go up," Kirti whispered when they were all together. "The passage ends here. But we are not safe. The Thuggees are everywhere tonight. They want to kill you—and me too, now, for helping you. But I could not let them hurt the little missy, or you, memsahib, her mother. We must be very careful."

"Why do they want to kill us?" Julian caught Anna's hand and held it tightly. She felt a tad comforted as her fingers twined with his.

Kirti shrugged. "It is their religion. They kill to please the goddess Kali. I told you, memsahib, the flower was a warning."

"But I thought it was a spell to keep me from having nightmares," Chelsea piped up.

Kirti shook her head. "All that they told you was a lie. I was afraid to say more. Always I feared they would kill me, as they will if we are caught. We must move very quickly and quietly if we are to get away. This tunnel, it is known to only a few, but who knows if those few are friend or foe? Not far from here is a cave. In the cave is another tunnel, which leads to my village. We will be safe there until daylight. They will not kill in daylight. Then, when

the sun comes, you must go, back across the great
sea in your ship. It is the only way you will be safe.''

"We owe you a great debt, Kirti," Anna said quietly.

Kirti looked at her with her liquid dark eyes. ''I
love the little missy as my own. There is no debt
owed.'' She turned to Julian. ''Sahib, if you will
push against the roof, a door will open.''

Julian straightened to his full height and did as
she said. For a minute, more, nothing happened.
Then, with a groan, the bricks overhead shifted
sideways, and Anna was staring up at the night sky.

"Remember, very quick and very quiet," Kirti
whispered, while Julian, making scant use of the
ladder, thrust his head and then his whole body into
the night.

Ruby followed as Kirti turned to Anna.

"Memsahib, trust me with the little one. If they
come, they will more surely seek harm to you than
me.''

Anna looked from Kirti to Chelsea, whose face was
white with fright.

"Mama," the little girl whimpered.

"You go with Kirti. I'll be right behind you,"
Anna told her, then followed Kirti and her daughter
up into the danger-filled night.

# LI

The tunnel had at least taken them behind the chanting, prancing lines of the murderous islanders who, Anna saw, ringed the house. Kirti, Chelsea clutched tightly in her arms, was already running through the jungle, her footsteps as soundless as a big cat's. Ruby was following her, while Julian had waited for Anna. As soon as she emerged, he caught her hand and pulled her after the others. Anna's feet barely touched the ground. Once she stumbled, to be caught up by Julian's arm around her waist. They could not afford to lose sight of Kirti; only she knew the way to safety.

Behind them, the Big House was ablaze. The stench of burning lay everywhere. Flames had engulfed the rear and most of the front, lending a brilliant orange glow to the night. The heat from the fire could be felt even at such a distance; the crackle and roar of the burning combined with the chanting of the islanders in a terrifying cacophony of sound that Anna knew would be etched in her memory forever.

But at least they were alive. Anna knew that she should be forever thankful for that. If she and Julian had not awakened when they had, would they all have been incinerated in the burning house? Or would the Thuggees have gotten to them first, to drag them screaming from their beds to their deaths?

From somewhere not too far to their left came the sudden, shattering sound of a man's terrified scream. The sound so startled Anna that she nearly screamed herself. Only the knowledge that to do so would bring the Thuggees down upon them intruded at the last minute to save her. Still, her head swiveled in the direction from whence the sound had come. What was happening?

"No! Oh, God, no! I'm on your side, you bloody beggars!"

After that came another scream, pain-filled rather than terrified as the first had been. Julian, who had been running with the silent speed of a native, suddenly stopped dead and turned toward the sound.

"That's Graham," he said, his eyes straining to peer through the darkness. Anna, halting beside him, felt a sudden burst of nausea as she realized that the sobbing voice did indeed belong to her brother-in-law. Somehow he had fallen into the hands of the Thuggees. Dear God, were they to be forced to listen to the sounds of his murder?

"Go on. Go with Chelsea and Ruby," Julian said, releasing her hand and giving her a little push toward where Ruby's nightgown was a flash of white disappearing down the path.

"What about you?" Terror lent shrillness to Anna's words.

"The bloody bastard's my thrice-damned brother. I can't just let them slaughter him, no matter how much I might like to see him rot in hell," Julian said. "Go on, get out of here. Now."

"Julian, no!"

"I must. Go!"

He gave her another shove. Then, as Anna obediently began to move away, he turned and ran swiftly toward the piteous cries. Anna slowed, then stopped as she watched him go. She was in a terrible quandary. She needed to go to Chelsea—but she could not abandon Julian.

He was headed into terrible danger.

Looking swiftly around her, Anna realized that she was alone. She could no longer see Ruby, or Kirti and Chelsea. If she continued down the path, would she discover them? Or would she run into something—or somebody—else?

Anna shuddered. Then, her decision made, she turned her back on the path and flew, as silently and invisibly as she could, after Julian.

Before she could catch up with him, she saw him hesitate on the edge of the jungle. He went utterly still, staring at the clearing that served as the Big House's rear lawn. Looking past him, Anna saw with horror what had stopped him in his tracks.

Graham, screaming, was being carved to pieces by a circle of machete-wielding Thuggees.

It was a hideous sight. Blood covered him from head to toe. He was trying, futilely, to ward off the slashing thrusts that were apparently meant to torture, not kill. He was screaming, keening really, like an animal in mortal pain and fear. Anna, watching, wanted to keen herself. She wanted to turn and run from the horror and block it from her mind forever. . . .

But there was Julian. Dear God, surely he realized there was nothing he could do?

He was not even armed, had not so much as a knife about his person. How could he possibly think to help Graham? And why should he, when Graham was all that he despised?

Before Anna could reach him, Julian was moving again. With a great shout he burst from the jungle to sprint catty-corner across the lawn, no doubt intending to disappear into the jungle opposite as suddenly as he had appeared. The machete wielders froze for a moment, their heads swiveling in Julian's direction. Then some of them—some, but not all—gave a hallooing cry and took off in pursuit.

The ones who were left surrounded Graham, herding him, weeping, away. As a distraction, Julian's ruse had proved effective. As an intelligent move on his own behalf, it was a disaster. Anna watched, horrified, as another band of Thuggees sprang from the jungle toward which Julian darted. He was sandwiched between the two bands, and, although he swerved and tried to run in another direction, there was no time.

The Thuggees surrounded him. Anna saw the flash of metal as machetes were lifted high. Then Julian, her brave, strong Julian, cried out and fell to the ground.

Anna forgot about herself, forgot the danger she was in, forgot everything in that moment but Julian. Her hands rising to her throat, she screamed, and screamed, and screamed.

Then something struck her in the cheek. The pain of it shocked her into silence. Her hand rose to slap instinctively at the hurt. Her first thought was that she had been stung by a particularly vicious insect. Then her fingers touched something small and hard protruding from her skin. Pulling it out, Anna stared in disbelief at a tiny, dark-tipped dart.

She looked up, her eyes moving to where Julian had disappeared beneath the mob of machete-wielding natives. The fate from which he had tried to save Graham was now his. Anna felt her heart swell to bursting. Tears rushed to her eyes. Her every instinct urged her to run to him, to try to save him, but she knew she could not. All such an action would accomplish would be her own death.

Oh, dear God, why did the men she loved have to die?

Suddenly, the jungle and everything in it began to swim around her. She blinked once, twice, then sank to her knees. The jungle rustled, and she felt a sudden stab of pure terror. But she was too dizzy and weak even to cry out. Much as she wanted to look around her, to see what and who it was that threatened her, her neck would no longer support the weight of her head. She was falling. . . .

Her head had not even touched the ground when the night went totally dark.

# LII

When Anna awoke, she was being lifted from what she saw, groggily, was a papyrus canoe. Her head swam as she was carried away from the water, but she regained enough awareness to know that it was closer to dawn than midnight, although the sun had not yet risen. The sky was now charcoal gray, not black, and a few precipitous birds were beginning to stir in the treetops overhead. A curious smell assaulted her nostrils, and she realized that it belonged to the oil that anointed her captors. There was a small band of them, perhaps a dozen, one of whom was carrying her in his arms. She looked up into the fearsome, spear-riddled face. Dear God, the man even had spears piercing his nose and tongue! Then her eyes closed again, blocking out the hideous sight, and she concentrated on staying limp in the monster's hold.

They hadn't killed her yet. Maybe they were waiting until she was awake.

It was all she could do not to shudder with fright.

She was nauseated, weak, and freezing cold despite the island's heat. It had something to do, she knew, with whatever had tipped the dart that had struck her. A poison—terror rose like bile in her throat.

366

She sensed that whatever death they had in mind for her would be hideous.

Her captor stooped, and Anna's lids opened enough to permit her to see that he had carried her inside a hut. She had barely registered that when he dumped her unceremoniously on the hard-packed dirt floor. It was all she could do not to cry out as she landed on her arm, certainly bruising it and possibly worse. Then he was leaning over her, dragging her to a pole in the middle of the hut. Dragging her hands above her head—how the bruised arm ached at such treatment!—and binding her wrists with rough efficiency, he tied her to the pole.

Then he was gone. Left alone, Anna let out the breath she had been holding and allowed her eyes to open. She was in a mud-and-wattle hut with a hole in the conical top that allowed smoke from a presently nonexistent fire to escape. The walls were low; only in the center was the hut tall enough to permit a person to stand upright. A single door covered with a rush mat opened outward. There was no other means of escape.

Not that she could escape in any case, with her hands tied securely to the pole.

Then there was a great commotion outside, and Anna shut her eyes again. Seconds later the hut seemed to be full of people. She did not dare to so much as flutter an eyelash as more apparent prisoners were dumped beside her and tied to the same pole.

This time she could hardly wait until the Thuggees were gone to open her eyes. Would one of them be . . . ?

Julian! Anna thanked God with a silent, heartfelt prayer. Not dead, then, but injured, a great dark gash on his forehead where some kind of club had apparently been used on him, and hundreds of tiny cuts about his person that sluggishly leaked a small amount of blood. He had suffered the same fate as Graham, those slashing, tormenting slices from a dozen machetes that were meant to cause pain rather than death. His clothes were in bloody ribbons; even his boots were sliced. But he lived! Thank God he lived!

Only then did Anna's eyes shift to the other prisoner: Graham. He was curled in a fetal ball, his breathing labored, and he looked to be in far worse shape even than Julian. Blood covered him from head to toe, so much blood that it seemed to ooze from his pores.

With only her hands tied to the post, it was not difficult for Anna to wriggle around until she could nudge Julian's face with hers. His cheek was bloody but, she was thankful to discover, still warm. His breathing was regular, not the shallow pants that came from Graham. Below his ear, she could see the beating of his pulse: slow and steady and regular.

"Julian!" She whispered it in his ear. "Julian, can you hear me?"

To her joy, his lashes fluttered once, and his face twitched. Had her words penetrated, or . . .

"Julian!" She tried again. This time he grimaced, and then his eyes opened.

"Anna?" His voice was weak.

"Shh, darling, be very quiet. They mustn't hear us."

"Who?"

"The Thuggees. They brought us here—oh, Julian, I thought they had killed you."

"They probably will give it a damned good try before this is over." Julian gritted his teeth and closed his eyes, only to open them again seconds later. Anna watched him anxiously. "Why the hell didn't you follow Kirti?"

"I couldn't just leave you," Anna answered simply. "I told you I love you, you dolt. But you wouldn't believe me, so I had to prove it. This was the only way I could think of."

This attempt at humor brought a quirk to his lips, but it was gone almost as soon as it appeared.

"Christ! I'd sooner cut out my heart than let them—" His eyes met Anna's, and he abruptly broke off. Clearly he didn't want to frighten her by referring to what he thought their ultimate fate would be. "Are you hurt? Did they hurt you?"

"Not really. Not like they did you—and Graham. They knocked me out with a drugged dart, and when I woke up they were carrying me in here."

"Thank God for small mercies, then." His head swiveled around. "How's Graham?"

Anna followed the path of Julian's eyes.

"I think he's in bad shape."

Julian grimaced. "They cut him up pretty good, didn't they? Hell, I should have left them to it. I don't know what got into me."

Anna regarded him solemnly. "I think that what you did was the bravest thing I ever saw."

Julian grunted. "The bloody thing about it is, when I heard him screaming all I could think about was that he was my brother. I hate him down to his toes, but—"

Graham grunted, whimpered, and opened his eyes. Looking around, he made a noise deep in his throat, then started to thrash frantically, his legs making useless kicking motions against the dirt floor, his arms jerking as he yanked against his bonds.

"Graham! Stop it!" Julian's voice was low but harsh. "Damn it, man, do you understand me?"

Julian's words must have registered, because Graham stopped thrashing and lay still. His eyes closed, then opened.

"I'm hurt. Oh, I'm hurt," he moaned. Anna, her heart filling with pity for him, scooted around so that he could see her.

"We're here with you, Graham. Julian and I. You're not alone."

"B-bloody gypsy bastard," Graham muttered. Anna wasn't sure that the rest of her words even registered. Graham's speech was barely coherent; his eyes had a glazed look to them.

"He saved your life, Graham." After what Julian had sacrificed, Anna could not stand to hear his brother revile him.

"Leave it, Anna. It doesn't matter." This came from Julian. He was lying on his side, his head turned so that he could see them, his expression hard beneath the blood and gore that streaked his face.

"It does matter!" Anna said fiercely. Graham's eyes opened again. He looked at Anna for a moment without even seeming to see her. Then his eyes moved past her to rest on Julian. Suddenly they sharpened, the glazed look disappearing. For that single moment it was clear that he was totally awake and aware.

"God, I hate you," he said to Julian in a tone of abject loathing. "You should never have been born."

With that his eyes closed. Instants later, his chest heaved violently and a rattling sound came from his throat. His mouth twitched once, and then he was still. Anna looked at him in silent shock. Surely he couldn't be . . . ?

"He's dead," Julian said bluntly, and shut his own eyes.

# LIII

It seemed like hours later, but in reality could not have been more than twenty or so minutes, when the flap opened and a white-turbaned head atop a magnificently cloaked body ducked inside the hut. It was not until the islander straightened in the center of the hut that Anna recognized him.

"Raja Singha!" she gasped, and felt relief flutter in her heart.

But he regarded her unsmilingly. Any hope that he had come to rescue them died aborning.

"Memsahib," he said, his tone remote. "I am sorry you have to die."

"Oh, no! Raja Singha, no! Please. . . ."

"She's done you no harm. Let her go."

"I cannot do that, sahib. For either of you. For some time now it has been ordained that she should die. The goddess calls her. You did not have to die, had you not been with her. Your fate is merely unfortunate. But she—she has been chosen."

"But why?" Anna's voice was no more than a whisper, her eyes huge and piteous as they fixed on her former servant's face.

"The goddess loves emeralds. Her eyes—they are emeralds. Like yours, memsahib. You will make a most pleasing sacrifice to the goddess because of your green eyes."

"Oh, no! Please. . . ."

"You need have no fear, memsahib. You will not be alone in death. The sahib Paul is there, and we will send the little missy after you. You will have your family."

"Not Chelsea!" Anna cried, terror-stricken.

"She was trapped in the house. In all likelihood she is already dead." Julian's voice was hard.

Raja Singha merely looked at him, clearly disbelieving. "You should not have come to Ceylon, sahib. In doing so, you chose the path that leads to your death," he said, and turned away as if to leave them.

"Wait!" Julian's voice was sharp. "You have tried to kill the memsahib and the little missy for some time, haven't you? Did you also bring the cobra into the house and set fire to the field?"

"Alas, nothing succeeded," Raja Singha said regretfully.

"So you thought to kill us all by burning down the house."

Raja Singha looked pained. "We had no hand in that. The sahib here"—he pointed to Graham disdainfully—"did that on his own. Had he not, we could have sent the memsahib and the little missy to the goddess together. As it is . . ."

He shrugged. Then, despite Julian's attempt to delay him further, he exited the hut. Seconds later four hideously costumed Thuggees entered. Without a word for their captives, they produced machetes and sliced through the prisoners' bonds.

"Anna, I love you," Julian said clearly as he was half dragged, half carried away.

Immediately Anna understood what he was telling her: that they were being sent forth to meet their deaths.

"I love you too," she cried after him, despairingly. Then they were pulling her, too, from the hut.

Outside, Anna saw that the sun was peeping over the horizon. Great orange-and-scarlet pinwheels swirled through the purple sky. Birds called, monkeys chattered, a breeze rustled the treetops.

It was beautiful, this day on which she would die.

Anna trembled at the thought. What would they do to her? Would it hurt? Her thoughts flew to Chelsea. Please God protect her child. Kirti would hide her until Ruby could get her away. And Jim—Jim was not taken. Surely, between them, they could keep the child safe, get her on a ship bound for England.

The thought of her little girl orphaned brought tears to Anna's eyes.

Up ahead Julian was being dragged down a sloping path. His hands tied behind his back now, he hung limply from his captors' hands. Was he unconscious, or was he waiting to fight for his life, and hers, when he thought it would do the most good?

Looking at the chanting Thuggees around them, Anna despaired. One man was useless against so many, and Julian was weak and hurt.

They were yanking her along, one man on either side. Anna saw blue water in the distance and realized that they were near the ocean. The canoe must have carried them down the Kumbukkan River during the night. If her calculations were correct, the bit of shoreline they now faced was located in one of the remotest regions of Ceylon.

There would be no rescue by her fellow Englishmen. Anna doubted if anyone was even yet aware of the horror that had befallen Srinagar during the night.

Perhaps two dozen Thuggees waited on the beach. Raja Singha, in a magnificent robe, stood slightly apart from the others. At his feet was a canoe equipped with a sail and an outrigger, which was designed to prevent the fragile craft from turning over even in the heaviest of seas.

It was to this vessel that Julian was taken, and it was there that he tried to make a stand. Straightening with a roar, he managed to throw off one of the natives holding him—only to be swarmed by the others. He went down fighting, but he went down, to the accompaniment of Anna's screams. Which were abruptly silenced as an oily, hideous-tasting gag was forced between her teeth.

It took only seconds for them to beat Julian unconscious. As far as she could tell they didn't cut him again with their machetes, for which small mercy she was thankful. Instead they stripped him naked and placed him on his side in the canoe, his hands bound behind him and a gag in his mouth. Then, to Anna's horror, they stripped her too, as methodically and disinterestedly as if she had been an object. Naked, struggling, she was carried to the canoe and forced to lie back to back with Julian. They were bound together, the ropes passing tightly around their throats and chests and thighs and ankles. Then great lashings of seawater were thrown over them, leaving Anna shivering despite the growing warmth of the day as the ropes were tightened yet again.

Raja Singha stepped up to the canoe at the last. Anna didn't even bother to plead for mercy. It would be useless, she knew.

He reached beneath his robe and withdrew a flat velvet pouch, which he opened. Anna's eyes widened as she realized what the pouch contained.

The emeralds! Raja Singha had stolen Julian's emeralds! He must have taken them the previous night, before he slipped out to bring the Thuggees down upon them.

"You will take these with you as a gift to the goddess," Raja Singha said. Leaning over Anna, he carefully fastened the gleaming green stones around her throat and waist. Anna felt them, cool and heavy against her bare skin, and she felt Raja Singha's warm fingers as he worked the clasps. The remaining pieces he placed beside her in the velvet pouch. Only then did the notion that she was to be sacrificed in accordance with some pagan religious ritual really sink in. What a hideously foolish way to die!

Coughing violently, Anna managed to spit out her gag. "Raja Singha, you know better than this!" she said, desperation lending urgency to her voice. "There is no goddess! She does not exist! You—"

"You will not speak so of the goddess!" Roaring, Raja Singha slapped Anna's face so hard that her ears rang and roughly shoved the rag back in her mouth. Tears sprang to her eyes as he stepped away with a curt signal to the others.

Amidst much shouting, the canoe was thrust into the surf, propelled by four islanders running and then swimming on either side until the craft was well beyond the pull of the tide, well beyond the headland even. Then the sail was set, and the natives turned as if one and headed back to shore.

Anna and Julian, naked and bound, were left alone to face the uncertain temper of the sea.

But they were alive. Anna, not knowing the full extent of the horrors that faced them, was inordinately grateful for that.

# LIV

The sun came up, and the ropes dried and tight-ened, making it difficult to move or even breathe. The salt water dried on Anna's skin, making it sting and itch unbearably. As the sun progressed over the sky, its rays burned her tender flesh until she was brick red and hurting all over. Even the emeralds grew warm in the heat and chafed her salt-roughened skin. She couldn't even writhe in agony; the bonds were simply too tight.

A half inch or so of water in the bottom of the canoe added to her misery. It made the skin of her right side soggy and raw, while the skin on the rest of her body cooked. Her bruised arm ached; her mouth was parched, from the gag and lack of water, and her limbs had long since gone numb. Julian, whom she could feel breathing against her back, must be in the same miserable shape. They couldn't even talk; the gags prevented that. She wasn't even sure he was conscious.

If she had known the misery that the canoe rep-resented, instead of thanking God for being set adrift in it she would have prayed instead for a quick death.

By early afternoon Julian was stirring. He had been unconscious, Anna realized, because it was so ob-vious from the movements of his body just when he came back to himself. Not that he could move much; because of the tightness of the ropes the least shift in his position caused her unbearable agony. The muffled whimpers emerging from behind her gag as he struggled to somehow free himself of his bonds made him go rigidly still. After that he was careful, although she could feel his hands moving between them as he worked to free himself. Which was hopeless, as Anna could have told him. The Thuggees had set them adrift in the pitiless sea to die, and die was precisely what they were going to do.

The sun went down at last, giving Anna a small amount of temporary ease as its burning rays could no longer roast her skin. But the cool wind that blew up as the night moved on soon caused her to shiver uncontrollably, while the skudding of the light-weight craft up and down over the waves made her so nauseous that she didn't much care if she did die, as long as it was soon. Fatalistically she tried to sleep, dreading the morning and the reappearance of the sun. How long did it take one to die of thirst? she wondered as her tongue swelled in her mouth. Two days? Three?

So miserable had she become, and so resigned to her misery, that, when Julian's hands, which had been writhing ceaselessly for hours, at last came free, she could not believe it. Even with his hands free, it took some time for him to maneuver his bound arms enough to permit him to pull his gag loose. But he did it, and Anna felt a quiver of renewed hope rise within her as for the first time in nearly twenty-four hours she heard his voice.

"Anna." Her name was a dry rasp. "My poor Anna."

Then he wriggled some more, and finally his fingers found the knot at the back of her head. It took a long time, his movements hampered by the ropes that cut ever deeper into her skin and his fingers working blindly, but he finally got it free. As the stinking cloth was pulled from her mouth, Anna took in deep, shuddering breaths. Her tongue ran over her parched lips but was so dry that it did little good.

"Julian," she croaked when she could speak. "Oh, Julian, I don't want to die."

"I know, my love. I don't, either. And we might not. If we can just get untied. . . ."

"The ropes are too tight," she told him, despairing. "They poured seawater over the ropes to get them wet, and then, when the sun dried them, they tightened."

Julian said nothing for a long moment. Then, when she called his name with sudden sharp anxiety, he spoke.

"Even with my hands free, there's no way I can reach the knots. We have to throw ourselves over the side."

Anna had already thought that to allow herself to drown in the small amount of water that had accumulated in the bottom of the canoe might be preferable to dying of thirst and exposure in the open air, but the idea of deliberately going over the side with him made her shudder.

"If we must," she whispered. Anything was better than facing another blistering day.

Julian said nothing for a moment. Then, as her meaning penetrated, he stiffened.

"Good God, no," he told her, sounding angry. "I don't mean that we should give up and throw ourselves over the side to die. I mean that we should somehow get into the water, hold on to the outrigger, and let the water loosen the ropes. It might take some time, but there's a chance it could work."

Only a slight chance. Anna knew that as well as if he had said the words. Still, any chance was better than no chance at all.

"Wait—the emeralds!" she said, as the memory of the precious stones he had risked so much for surfaced. "The Queen's emeralds! I'm wearing the necklace and stomacher, and the rest of them are in their pouch in the bottom of the canoe. Oh, Julian, your parents' marriage lines must be in there, too. They'll be soaked—ruined!''

''To hell with the bloody marriage lines—and the emeralds too! Do you think I care about them now? What I care about is you.'' Julian's voice was fierce. Despite their situation, Anna felt a little glow of happiness at his words. ''How on earth did you come to be wearing them? I thought they burned with the house.''

''Raja Singha had them. He put them on me so that I could take them with me as a gift to the goddess when I died.'' Despair reduced her last words to no more than a husky whisper.

''Damn the bloody animal to hell, you're not going to die! We're not going to die! You're not to give up, do you hear? I told you, we'll tip the canoe and let the water loosen the ropes. It will work, Anna.'' There was grim determination in his voice.

''What do we need to do?'' she asked, feeling another tiny flicker of hope. Julian sounded so sure. . . .

''With the outrigger, the canoe won't tip. So what we're going to have to do is somehow tip ourselves over the side. I'll try to catch hold of the pontoon as we fall. Then all we have to do is wait until the water loosens the knots.''

If it ever did. Anna finished the sentence silently.

Julian said nothing more for a moment. Then, ''I'm going to turn over so that I'm lying on my stomach. It's probably going to hurt you when I move, and for that I'm sorry. But . . .''

''It doesn't matter,'' Anna said. Unspoken between them was the thought that, if he was unable to catch hold of some part of the pontoon as they fell, they would sink beneath the surface. Bound as they were, if that happened, they would almost certainly drown.

''All right. I'm going to try to get my hands beneath me and push up. When I go up, you throw

your weight as hard as you can to the right. I will,
too. Maybe it will be enough to pitch us out of the
canoe." He hesitated, then, to her amazement, Anna
thought she detected the tiniest touch of humor in
his voice. "And, Anna, be sure to take a deep
breath, hear?"

"I hear."

"Let's go, then."

As Julian had warned her, the ropes cut unbearably into her sunburned skin as he twisted and
squirmed onto his stomach. But she bit her lip, refusing to make so much as a single sound. He was
hurting too, she knew. Like herself, he must be sunburned, and the ropes must be sawing into his skin
like knives. And he had been terribly cut. How the
seawater in the bottom of the canoe must burn in
those cuts!

"Ready?"

"Yes."

"Throw yourself to the right!" With that as a
warning, he heaved himself violently up. Anna felt
him buck beneath her and threw herself to the right
as hard as she could. Her body scraped painfully
against the side of the canoe—and then, miracle of
miracles, they were going over the side.

Only to sink just as abruptly under the surface.
Just as Anna was sure they would sink forever, and
end by drowning, their downward progress halted
with a jerk. She felt the emeralds around her waist
loosen, watched with a curious detachment as the
stomacher floated in lazy spirals downward to join
the velvet pouch, and then she was being pulled up
again, toward the surface, until at last her head
broke through the water and she was gasping for
air.

"Anna, we did it!" He was jubilant. Anna, hanging like a papoose from his back, smiled, only to
wince as the movement caused her parched lips to
stretch painfully.

"We did, didn't we?" She rested against him, trying not to notice that, with her weight against them, the ropes were cutting more painfully than ever into her tender skin. She must be bleeding. . . .

But at least now they had a chance.

As the sun climbed the sky Anna's optimism faded. The ropes felt no tighter, but, although Julian doggedly tried to work his arms free, he seemed no closer to succeeding. Anna's thirst was like a living thing inside her, eating her up. It was all she could do to resist the temptation to gulp seawater. That, she knew, was the worst thing she could do. The salt in it would literally dry her up.

With her body safe beneath the water, only her face caught the sun. She supposed she should be thankful for that, but as her eyes swelled shut and her lips puffed and split she could not summon much gratitude.

As hour upon blistering hour crawled by, she again found herself almost wishing to die.

And then, as she squirmed about in an effort to ease the cutting pressure of the ropes, she felt something so unexpected that she had to squirm again to make sure.

"Julian," she said in the hoarse croak that was all she could manage now. "The ropes—I think they're slipping! My leg is free!"

She felt him kick, felt him make the same discovery—and then one of his legs was free, too. With the resultant loosening of the ropes, it was not long before Julian managed to free them both entirely. Gasping, Anna turned toward him, no longer able to smile but catching his hand and giving it a happy squeeze. With her broiled skin, even a hug would have been too painful.

For the first time in two days he got a good look at her.

"Your poor face," he breathed, his eyes darkening as he took in the evidence of what she had suffered. Then his hand came up to gently touch her cheek. "I love you, Anna."

"I love you too," she managed painfully.

His eyes shifted to the emerald necklace, which was all that remained of the stones that had haunted him all his life.

"Let's get these bloody things off you," he said, his fingers gentle against her damaged skin as he worked the clasp. When the necklace fell free, he caught it in one hand and tossed it into the canoe as if it were no more than a handful of pebbles.

"We're going to be all right," he told her with fierce determination. "You'll see."

And then he helped her back into the boat, where she tried to sit up but ended by lying shivering on the bottom, while he protected her from the rising sun as best he could with his own body, and used the sail to bring the little craft about, heading for land.

The question was, would they make it in time? They had drifted with the current for nigh on two days. Without fresh water, they had another forty-eight hours at best. Anna especially was already showing signs of becoming delirious from dehydration.

Julian gritted his teeth and grimly battled the delirium that threatened him as well. If he succumbed, they would both die. Her life depended upon his strength. And he could not, would not, let her die.

Toward late afternoon the wind began to pick up. Dark clouds blew up on the horizon, and the canoe, under sail, fairly skimmed over the waves. Julian, watching, prayed as he had never prayed in his life.

His prayers were answered. Even as he tilted his face to the sky he felt a spattering of rain.

"Anna! Anna, wake up!" Holding the sail with one hand, he leaned down to shake her, wincing at the necessity of taking hold of her sun-broiled skin. As fair as she was, she had burned much more severely than he had. After a moment she roused, looking at him as if she did not quite know who he was.

She had been without water for two and a half days.

"It's raining!" he told her urgently even as the heavens opened and an icy deluge descended upon them. "Sweetheart, it's raining!"

When she still didn't seem to comprehend, he lashed the sail, cupped his hands, and ladled fresh water into and over her until at last he was satisfied that she had had enough for the moment.

Then he freed the sail, and, making use of the wind and the rushing current and every bit of sea lore he had ever learned, he headed their craft for land.

When at last he heard the roar of breakers and saw the white foam of waves crashing against the shore, he felt tears fill his eyes.

They had made it! He gave thanks to the God that he had not really, until now, believed in.

Then he lowered the sail and allowed the canoe to catch the waves. Riding on the crest of one, the craft traveled swiftly until its bottom gently skidded against sand. Then Julian, with his last bit of strength, scooped Anna up from the bottom of the canoe and gently carried her ashore.

The emeralds lay forgotten in the bottom of the canoe as tears of thanksgiving mingled with raindrops to wet his face.

# Epilogue

A little more than a year later, Lord and Lady Ridley stood arm in arm on the terrace at Gordon Hall. It was early March, but the weather had continued unseasonably warm for the past few days. On the manicured path below them a little blond girl skipped and sang with her new playmate, the gatekeeper's son. The child was dressed warmly in a velvet pelisse and bonnet, but the late-afternoon sun made the garments almost unnecessary. The temperature was far closer to spring than winter.

Anna watched her daughter's antics with a smile. Really, it was good to see Chelsea so happy and well-adjusted at last. When they had found her after their nightmare experience, she had been dressed as a coolie child and her hair had been crudely dyed a muddy brown. Hidden away with Ruby in the heart of Kirti's village with the ayah and her entire clan standing guard, the little girl had been almost catatonic with fright. Seeing her mother, Chelsea had burst into noisy tears and clung as if she would never let go. Despite the pain of her injuries, Anna had clung to Chelsea, too. Each had feared never to see the other again.

Jim had been equally overjoyed to see Julian. He had spat and declared that he had known his Julie was too tough to kill, even as he had turned away

to wipe what he called "those bloody cinders" from
his eyes. It seemed that he had been, as Julian had
instructed, keeping an eye on Graham, when Graham had suddenly turned back halfway along the
road to Colombo. Jim, caught by surprise, had lost
his quarry, only to discover him again hours later
when he had given up the search and headed home
to Srinagar. Graham had been in the act of dousing
the rear veranda with fuel—and had, when surprised in the act, dealt Jim such a ferocious blow
with a shovel that Jim had been unconscious for
most of the night. When he had recovered his senses
and made his way back to the house from the jungle
where he had been dragged and left, it had been to
find nothing left but a burned-out, still-smoking
shell.

What had become of Julian and the rest, he could
only imagine. And what he had imagined had not
been pretty.

Julian had whisked them all out of Ceylon so
quickly that there had barely been time for Anna to
say good-bye to anyone. She did manage a word for
Charles, who was shocked by the news of what had
happened to them. He was not, however, altogether
surprised when Anna told him of her intention to
marry Julian. He said he had seen it coming for some
time, and was resigned to her loss. He managed to
wish her happy before Julian pulled her to the waiting carriage by main force, but there was no time for
anything more. Julian was determined to get them
to Colombo, and from there aboard a ship to England, with the smallest possible delay. Almost
losing Anna had frightened him, and he was
determined not to risk such a thing again.

That she was even permitted to take leave of
Charles was only because Julian felt they should
warn the English community of the killers in their
midst and apprise Charles of what had befallen Srinagar. Charles, suitably horrified, had promised to
do what he could to round up those responsible and

to alert the other colonists to the danger. In the last communication that they had had from him, he had reported that Raja Singha had vanished. They continued to look for him, but Anna, who was thoroughly familiar with both Sinhalese justice and Raja Singha, doubted he would ever be found.

Graham had been buried in the plot beside Paul. Anna took some comfort from the notion of the two brothers facing eternity together.

Julian, having recovered somewhat from his ordeal, had determined not to relinquish his birthright if there was any chance he might be able to claim it. After several weeks of racking his brain, he had at last remembered the name of the vicar who had signed his parents' marriage lines. After that, the task had been easy. The vicar was retired, but his name was still on church records, and the marriage itself was still recorded on the parish registry. With the help of Graham's erstwhile solicitor, Julian was duly confirmed as Lord Ridley.

The visit to the solicitor had another consequence as well: Julian at last discovered who had sent the note about the proof being in the emeralds. It seemed that the solicitor's father had been old Lord Ridley's solicitor. It was this gentleman whom Anna and Paul had seen arguing with the old lord in the library all those years ago. The disagreement had been over Lord Ridley's wanting to set aside an early, secret marriage that had produced a son; a son who, if allowed to remain legitimate, would be his heir instead of his dearly beloved Graham. The solicitor, disapproving, had refused to cooperate. It was he who, having seen where Lord Ridley kept the proof of his first son's legitimacy, sent the note to Julian. He said that he couldn't keep quiet any longer after the old lord's death. His conscience would not let him rest. Julian had thanked the man and offered him monetary recompense for his trouble. The old gentleman had told him that it was reward enough merely to see justice done.

With Anna and Chelsea, Julian had traveled down to Gordon Hall to take his place as the true, rightful Lord Ridley. Ruby took up residence in the dower house, while Jim continued to come and go as he pleased. Graham's wife, Barbara, was generously provided for by Julian and took up residence in London, where it was assumed she hoped to assuage the grief of her widowhood by speedily taking a second husband.

Anna's injuries had been minor and, except for her skin, had healed in a matter of a week or so. Her skin, severely burned, had swollen and blistered, then flaked and peeled, until she had despaired of ever looking like herself again. But finally, about halfway through the voyage home to England, her skin had regained enough of its normal appearance to make her feel able to appear in public without self-consciousness.

It was then that she had wed Julian, in a shipboard ceremony conducted by the captain. Jim had given her away, and Ruby and Chelsea had been her attendants. The wedding had been attended by nearly every passenger and crew member on the ship.

"Miss Anna—I mean, my lady—here's someone who wants to see you."

Anna turned and smiled at Mrs. Mullins, who emerged through the French windows behind them with a blanket-wrapped bundle in her arms. The newly hired nursemaid trailed jealously behind, but Mrs. Mullins had claimed little Christopher Scott Traverne as her own when the infant was not in his mother's arms. In consequence, the nursemaid had little to do, and resented the housekeeper accordingly.

"Thank you, Mrs. Mullins. Hello, sweetheart." Anna held out her arms for her son, but Julian took the baby, holding him gingerly as befitted the new father of a child less than a month old. His grin was warm as he looked down at the tiny form, with a

shock of black hair and deep blue eyes so much like
his own. As the baby stared boldly back, Julian
reached down to tickle his chin. Little Christopher
promptly grasped his father's finger and attempted
to put it in his mouth.

"I think he's hungry." Julian quickly handed the
baby over. Anna was smiling as she took her son
into her arms. Julian as a father was absurd—and
absurdly lovable.

When she had told Julian that he was going to be
a father, he had been delighted. Then, when the realization that she was actually going to give birth, in
pain and suffering, had burst upon him, he had been
terrified. But he had held up surprisingly well, although to get him through the night of the delivery
Jim had had to pour pints of whiskey into him. Still,
by the following morning, both father and son had
been doing well.

"If you'll excuse me, I'll go feed him."

As Anna took the baby back into the house, Julian
ran down the steps to play with Chelsea and her
friend. Anna, smiling, was content to let him go.
Chelsea had come to adore Julian, and she was fascinated with her tiny brother. She had ceased to
grieve for Paul at last and even spoke of him sometimes, as someone she fondly remembered.

Anna's world, like Chelsea's, was whole again.
Her heart was full of Julian and her children. Her
life pleased her well, and she was happier as Julian's
wife than she had ever dreamed she could be.

When the baby had finished eating—he was a
greedy little thing, nursing quickly and eagerly—she
passed him over to the nursemaid to be put down
for his nap. The girl bore him off with a triumphant
sniff at Mrs. Mullins, who harrumphed in her turn.
Anna, ignoring these signs of incipient warfare, but-
toned up her bodice and went back outside in search
of Julian.

She found him down by the lily pond, engaged
with Chelsea in an earnest attempt to catch a bull-

frog. As Anna appeared, Chelsea's friend proposed building a frog trap, although exactly what he envisioned Anna was afraid to inquire. Still, Chelsea was enthused about the idea, and Julian was grinning as he climbed the bank to join his wife.

"They'll probably both fall in and get soaked to the gills," Julian predicted comfortably as the children ran off in search of the necessary materials.

"Or else they'll catch the hideous thing, and Chelsea will beg to keep it as a pet." The nursery at Gordon Hall was already home to an odd assortment of such creatures.

"How's my son?" There was such pride in Julian's voice that Anna had to smile at him.

"Your son is just fine, although Mrs. Mullins and Lisette may come to blows."

"Do you think that girl is experienced enough? We could get someone else. . . ."

"She's fine," Anna said firmly, having learned already that Julian was subject to a new father's anxiety more than most. He worried about everything from the length of the baby's naps (should he be sleeping this much?) to the amount of spitting up little Christopher did (he'll starve to death at this rate!). Anna, though she occasionally rolled her eyes, did what she could to soothe his concerns, and hoped fervently that the terrors of fatherhood would soon wear off.

"You're looking beautiful, as usual." Julian, distracted from his concern for Christopher, leaned forward to give his wife a kiss. Anna settled against him, letting her arms slip around his neck as her lips parted in response. It had been so long since they'd made love that his slightest touch could arouse her to a fever pitch. There'd been that whole month before the baby's birth, and then the four weeks after. Julian was afraid of hurting her, she knew, but she was healed now, and her body throbbed for him whenever he was near. Perhaps this afternoon. . . .

Julian put her away from him and was regarding her strangely.

"What is it?" Anna asked, perplexed by his expression.

"It just came back to me," he answered, which told her nothing at all, "when the sunlight hit your hair."

"What just came back to you?"

"When I first met you, I thought that I had seen you before. I suddenly remembered where."

"Well, where?"

"Right here, by the pond. You must have been about six years old. It was when I came down here to confront my father, and he had me thrown out and beaten. I finally picked myself up from the road and started walking. I ended up in that copse of trees over there." He pointed to a nearby orchard. "I was lying there—I wasn't up to walking any farther—and you ran into the trees after your ball. You saw me and came up to me and asked me if I was all right. I looked up at you, and the sun was glinting off your hair. I can remember those big green eyes staring at me so gravely. . . . Then Paul ran up and took your hand. I hated Paul, who had everything I ever dreamed of having, including a little fairy girl for a playmate. I felt like a beggar child with his nose pressed to the window of a candy shop, always on the outside looking in. And I told you two to get the hell away from me, and you did."

The story touched her to the heart. Catching his hand, Anna rose on tiptoe to press a kiss to the hard lips that at the moment wore a rueful, self-mocking smile.

"You're not on the outside any more, my darling," she told him softly as her fingers entwined with his. "And you never will be again."

And then, his misgivings be damned, she half coaxed and half led him back to the house.

# America Loves Lindsey!

## The Timeless Romances
## of #1 Bestselling Author

| | |
|---|---|
| KEEPER OF THE HEART | 77493-3/$6.99 US/$8.99 Can |
| THE MAGIC OF YOU | 75629-3/$5.99 US/$6.99 Can |
| ANGEL | 75628-5/$6.99 US/$8.99 Can |
| PRISONER OF MY DESIRE | 75627-7/$6.99 US/$8.99 Can |
| ONCE A PRINCESS | 75625-0/$6.99 US/$8.99 Can |
| WARRIOR'S WOMAN | 75301-4/$6.99 US/$8.99 Can |
| MAN OF MY DREAMS | 75626-9/$6.99 US/$8.99 Can |
| SURRENDER MY LOVE | 76256-0/$6.50 US/$7.50 Can |
| YOU BELONG TO ME | 76258-7/$6.99 US/$8.99 Can |
| UNTIL FOREVER | 76259-5/$6.50 US/$8.50 Can |
| LOVE ME FOREVER | 72570-3/$6.99 US/$8.99 Can |

*And in Hardcover*
SAY YOU LOVE ME